37988
4-14-95

4137

BURN, KILLER, BURN!

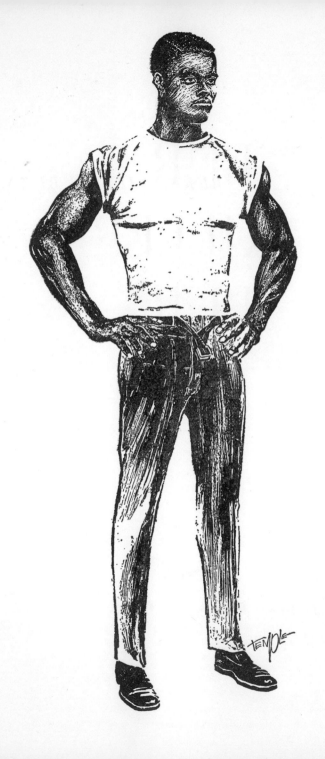

BURN, KILLER, BURN!

Paul Crump

Johnson Publishing Company, Inc.
Chicago

Appreciation is due the following publishers for permission to quote passages from the following songs: Irving Berlin Music Co., *Gone With The Wind*, © 1937. E. B. Marks Music Corp., *God Bless the Child*, © 1941. Joy Music Inc., *Sweet Leilani*, © 1937. Chappell & Co., *Gloomy Sunday*, © 1936. We are grateful to Mr. Allen Ginsberg for permission to use an inexact version of a portion of *Howl* © 1956.

L. C. Catalog Card Number 62–21088

*For Mama, who gave so much
and got so little*

Which of us has known his brother?
Which of us has looked into his father's heart?
Which of us has not remained forever prison-pent?
Which of us is not forever a stranger and alone?
                              —Thomas Wolfe

Chapter 1

Luzon!

My mind shouted her name with the positive certainty that held not the slightest need for additional confirmation, even though I sat with my eyes closed and my back to the door. Her presence permeated the musty atmosphere in the courtroom of jam-packed, sweat-oozing, ghoulish spectators with a fresh, cool fragrance. Turning slowly, in deference to the pain of my unhealed wounds, I faced her.

She stood in the towering polished frame of the wide, thick, oak-paneled doorway. The smooth ivory of her skin held a subdued radiance whose glow perforated the gray, late afternoon light in the hall behind her, creating an illusion of white on white, punctuated by the black of her dress and her smoldering eyes. I had to blink, for the sight of her was like the sudden explosive ignition of a silver acetylene flame on a darkness I had taken to be eternal.

She stepped inside the massive doors held open by the two uniformed bailiffs, whose drooping shoulders shrugged into respectful stiffness. Inside the door, she paused, her icy, sea-green eyes surveying the room with chilled curiosity. The sophisticated hauteur of her chin held a queenly disdain for the tremendous silent applause her entrance was receiving. Even the hot, vehement words of the state's attorney's damning denunciation of me to the twelve good and true lily-white jurors was momentarily congealed.

"The man sitting there on the defense side of the table is an inhuman, bloody wanton, who has stalked the streets of *our*

1

fair city, and committed foul murder on *our* policemen beneath the black cloak of night. He . . . he . . ."

The inflaming words of the prosecutor faded into silence as did everything else—the judge, the jury, the spectators, the courtroom, the whole world. All of my senses were completely concentrated upon Luzon. Our eyes met, locked; we were the only two people on earth. Her red lips shaped my name and though they emitted no sound, I heard an enchanting music.

I watched her slow approach. Each step that she took towards me brought an increased contentment. Her movement possessed a jungle felineness which the slanted, oriental cast of her eyes heightened. The low neckline of the plain black dress sheathing her willowy body like a second skin extended past the point of daring, but the tiny gold cross around her ivory neck restored whatever virtue the dress' design threatened to destroy.

Each step she took held a primitive rhythm, and offered a flattering, sleek display of exquisitely shaped legs through the slit of one side of the dress. Her raven hair was piled high upon her head, giving added height to her normal statuesqueness.

She stopped at the front row seat. My eyes complimented each slight indentation of her body, every supine line and sensual curve. I devoured her hungrily, recalling with gall-bitter regret the lost opportunities to indulge the crowning splendor of the love I had always held for her, and had foolishly tossed aside with blind, youthful ingratitude.

Now, as I stared at her, although we were only a few feet apart, we were separated by an uncrossable sea of trouble.

". . . And there he sits, ladies and gentlemen, enthroned on a mountain of fabrication, crowned with defiance . . ." the attorney for the state droned on.

Luzon sat, crossing her legs. Slowly, she began swinging them back and forth, the movement flapping the hem of her

2

dress, scenting the air with the perfume of the cologne she wore. Her wide, sensuous lips formed words; her eyes told me they were of love.

I frowned with the effort to read her lips, to interpret the passion of the prodding red tongue. I shook my head uncomprehendingly at her look of inquiry. She dropped her head for a moment, deep in thought. When she looked up, her eyes glinted impishly. Slumping slightly in her seat, she wiggled the fingers of her left hand until she caught my eye, then began to write in the deaf-mute language she had taught me when we were kids. Her fingers moved with blurring rapidity.

I shook my head and wrote haltingly: *"Too fast. Slower."*

She nodded enthusiastically, wiggling with a childish impatience. *"Do you remember?"* she wrote.

"Yes, but slow," I replied.

"How have you been?" she asked.

"Fine."

Out of the corner of my eye, I caught a glimpse of the prosecutor. He was kneeling before the jury box, his hand reaching up imploringly. Tears glistened on his cheeks.

". . . If you let this man go, if you don't find him guilty, if you come back with a verdict other than guilty, all I ask of you, all I ask of you, my people, is that you give me warning so that I will have enough time to move my family out of the city, out of this country. For if you come back with a verdict other than guilty, you might as well burn down the courtroom and give them back their spears and clubs . . ."

His voice faded from my mind.

"Do you love me?" Luzon wrote.

"Yes, too much," I replied.

"How is that?" she asked.

"Too late," I answered.

"Never too late, never," she said.

". . . Think of it, ladies and gentlemen." The prosecutor cut back in. "Think of it. Picture it in your mind. Concentrate

3

deeply upon it. The red blood oozing down the heroic face, staining the blue uniform, speckling the silver star . . ."

"I object, your honor, I object to the highly improper, prejudicial remarks of the prosecutor—the over-zealous prosecutor, I might add—" my defense attorney cut in.

"Objection overruled," the judge declared, rapping with his gavel. "Proceed, Mr. State's Attorney."

My lawyer sat down, shaking his head in disgust.

"Some joke," Luzon wrote.

"That's life," I said.

"Will comedy end today?" she asked.

"Yes," I replied.

"Not guilty?" she inquired.

"Not a chance," I said.

"Guy, Guy," she wrote.

"I love you," I said.

"Are they crazy?" she asked.

"No, just white."

". . . The gaping red hole, the spattered, gallant brain. My God, what can I say to you? Can't you people see it? Are you blind? Doesn't the sight of it make you want to come out of the box and do something to Morgan? . . ."

The prosecutor's face was contorted with hate. Tears and sweat dripped from his chin.

"All he needs is sheet, tree stump and hounds," she wrote.

"I object, your honor," my attorney interrupted. "This line of argument by the state's attorney is maliciously calculated and viciously designed to—"

"To take the life of a mad dog in exchange for that of a brave human," the prosecutor interjected.

"Now wait a minute," my attorney shot back. "We're still in a court of law, and I have made an objection. At least I started—"

"Objection overruled," the judge rapped. "Proceed, Mr. Prosecutor."

4

"But your honor, I—"

"I have overruled your objection, Mr. Public Defender. Now sit down and let us proceed. The hour is late."

"Exception, Judge," my lawyer said wearily, slumping into his seat. He cursed bitterly beneath his breath.

"You're lovelier than yesterday, a moment ago," I wrote.

She smiled and looked down, veiling her eyes for a moment behind long, thick lashes. When she looked up again, her eyes were pools of tears.

"Guy, they can't, they just can't. You're too young. We haven't begun to live yet. What of our love?"

"They can. They will. I am as old as the first slave freed from chains. Our love doesn't mean a damn."

"I wish they had called me for jury duty," she wrote. *"For first time in life would have enjoyed being able to pass for white."*

"Wishful thinking," I said. *"Had you been called, you're only one vote. Need twelve."*

"I'm hip. Would get twelve, too."

"How?"

I thought of the eleven men who made up my jury.

"The bed is mightier than the pen, the sword or the atomic bomb," she replied, her eyes glinting with angry determination.

"I'd rather die," I wrote, looking at the jury. The eyes of the eleven men darted furtively to Luzon, holding a mixture of hate and naked, passionate desire. I turned back to her.

"You die now. They are having me. What difference?" A sardonic smile pulled down the corners of her mouth.

"Pull down dress and uncross legs, damn you!" I flashed, letting the anger show in my face.

She obeyed, crossing her trim ankles sedately, then wrote: *"Sorry. Bitch in me. How's this?"*

I didn't reply. I couldn't. I was in the grip of a jealous rage.

". . . They have come in here and tried to throw sand in

5

your eyes, tried to insult your intelligence with a play of words about self-defense that is so illogical," the prosecutor's voice yelled.

"Say something. Smile a little, please, for me; for the love I've always bore so sadly, so painfully," she wrote, her eyes pleading.

I smiled and closed my eyes, blowing her a kiss.

"My man, my man, my man," she wrote, over and over again, an intense, burning, hungry look in her eyes.

"My woman, my woman," I answered, matching her look of hunger.

"If you're going to continue this little romantic by-play with that broad, Guy," my attorney leaned over and whispered to me, "you'd better tell her to paint a sign saying 'I'm colored' and hang it around her neck, otherwise she's getting you beat in the face with a shovel with every movement of her fingers. Can't you see the jury looking at her, you fool?"

"Guy, Guy, what will I do without you?" she asked.

"Live!" I said, *"Live deep, tall, wide, full. Gorge yourself with it, choke yourself on it. Live, Luzon, live!"*

"I can't. How, without you? All shallow, shrunken, empty without you. Oh, Guy, where is God?" She ended, letting her hands fall to her lap.

". . . You said that you would be willing to bring back a verdict calling for the death penalty if this man were proven guilty of murder beyond a reasonable doubt. Well, we have done that, ladies and gentlemen. We have done that and more. We have shown him to be guilty beyond the scintilla of a doubt. And the law provides that he should be put to death— the law of the land and law of the Bible," the prosecutor screamed.

"God is dead, buried in the pages of the Old Testament," I wrote Luzon.

"No, no, don't say that. Don't. It frightens me. He must be —He's got to be real—real," she said.

6

"Well, if He is, He's not in this room. He's never been with me. He wasn't with Mama, He wasn't with Crow, He wasn't with Kay. He's never been with me. We—God and me—are strangers."

"I feel like I'm going to cry," she said.

"Don't you dare," I flashed back. *"Don't you dare let them see you cry now!"* I was almost up out of my seat.

"Say you love me then. Say it, over and over."

I began to write: *"I love you, I love you, I love you, I love you, I love you, I love you—"*

". . . Look at it, ladies and gentlemen. Look at *him*. They ask mercy. Look at him. Is he deserving of mercy? Is he deserving of any human consideration? Why he sits there even now, insulting the dignity of law and justice with finger play. Is this the kind of man deserving of mercy, a man who has no respect for the black robe of the court, for the history of law and civilization? I tell you if you show him any mercy, you will be laughing in the face of God, and you would do the progress of civilization a far greater justice by taking to the jungles and teaching apes how to speak."

My lawyer got wearily to his feet.

"Although I know it would be senseless for me to object to this line of argument by the prosecutor," he began, "I nevertheless feel duty-bound to my client, and for the purpose of the record, I would like to at this time register my objection."

"Objection overruled. Sit down, Mr. Public Defender," the judge hammered.

My lawyer slumped into his seat. Toying with his pencil with one hand, he bit the fingernails of the other.

"Maybe you get life," Luzon said.

"That will be the day," I answered.

"Guy, where did our lives, our youth go?" she asked.

"Down the drain," I said. *"Down the drains and the sewers in the gutters of the slums."*

7

Chapter **2**

I closed my eyes to the courtroom and let my mind drift back through space to another time, another place. I had closed my eyes then, too, back there at that other time, that other place—

High on the dirt hill, I closed my eyes and savored the illusion of being miles in the air. The tiredness that pulled at my leg muscles and caused them to quiver spasmodically was a pleasurable feeling. Spreading my legs, I dug my bare toes into the cool dirt: *King of The Hill.*

My chest heaved with the labored breathing from my mock battle with an army of boys, all named Jackie. It had started when, home from work on my lunch hour, I had stood in my back door and gazed at the hill and imagined it swarming with invaders. I kissed Mom and dashed out to return to the pool room and my shine stand, but as I crossed the vacant lot, I had stopped, taken off my shoes and socks and charged my invisible enemies.

Each step of my ascent to the summit had been hard-fought and bitterly contested, but I'd finally vanquished the trespassers at the cost of a torn shirt and a small cut over the right eye. This seemed a small price for the satisfaction swelling within me, even over this sham encounter.

Suddenly something struck me behind the knees and I went tumbling down the hill. At the bottom, I sat up, dazed.

"What the hell?" I shouted, looking up.

There at the top was a grimy, ragged boy, about eleven or twelve, standing where I had been. He was pounding his chest and yelling: "I'm the king o' thah hill! Aaahooooooh-aaah! I'm the king o' thah hill!"

I got to my feet, keeping my eyes on him. It was like looking at a part of myself.

"Hey, dirt-dobber!" I called out. "Who are you? And what do you mean by knocking me off my hill?"

He fixed me with a belligerent stare as I slipped on my socks and shoes.

"Mah name's Archibald, and I konked ya off my hill cause I'm the king o' dis hill! It's mine! So you better keep de hellie off if yas don't wanna get konked off again!" he shouted.

Still staring at him I thought: *Yeah, it's your hill, little smut doll. You're king now—for a while—'till another Archibald knocks you off.*

I shouted back at him, "Yeah?"

"Yeah!" he replied.

"I could come up there and take my hill back if I wanted to," I threatened him.

"Oh yeah?" he scoffed, taking a more defensive stance.

"Yeah," I answered him, getting up.

"Th' hellie ya say," the kid defied, spitting on his fist and then touching it to his lips, eyes and nose threateningly.

"Yeah, the hellie I say," I yelled back. "I ought to beat your tail for being on my hill, but I'll let ya slide. You can have it. The air on top of it stinks anyway."

I gave him a disdainful wave of my hand and headed for the sidewalk. Turning, I looked back. He stood with legs spread wide, wrists resting on his hips. His head was thrust forward and an expression of disbelief spread over his impish face.

"Thah hellie ya say!" he shouted hotly.

Silently mourning the death of my childhood and my lost kingdom, I headed for 111th Street—Morgan Park.

Chapter 3

Morgan Park: the abrupt end to the beginning of civilization, and the start of the countless inhumanities of the white man against his kidnapped black brother.

Morgan Park: the other side of the tracks of human dignity, and a greasy, dirty gag to the hysterical scream of the nobility of Christ and man's likeness to God.

Morgan Park: ink blot of black poverty, walled about by frosty white indifference, compounded group denial breeding an ever greater criminality into the filthy cradle of the tear-spattered gutter.

Morgan Park: Darkytown, the dingy, tattered side of life, where strife-ridden and woe-begone little pickaninnies with big, button, rag doll eyes gawk with reverent awe across the line which divides Niggerville from Beverly Hills, where supercilious whites look down from their Merion blue grass-surrounded patios on their ebony brothers and hold their noses and shut their ears to the blues crying up and down the middle of the one-way street of misery that is 111th Street between the tracks and Vincennes.

Morgan Park is one of many slums hugging the fringe of windy, racket town Chicago. It is a gutter-dirty, thumb-sucking, bastard urchin, clutching the unlaundered skirt of its cosmetic-plastered, prostitute mother.

On nearly every corner a cluster of churches glare righteous reproach at gin mills, dope dens, bookie joints and sex pads.

Through the window above my shoeshine shop in Hank's Recreation Room, I contemplated the activity of Black Babylon, the name the ebony Apostles had branded the neighborhood during the heat of an all-out crusade to drive out the Devil and his imps.

Tomorrow, I mused, the hell-fire and brimstone preachers —my father, the Rev. Guy Morgan Sr., included—will mount their pulpits. Windows will vibrate from the thunder of their voices as they beseech God to rain down his wrath on this miniature Sodom. Tears and sweat will combine in the damp entreaty to the brothers and sisters to turn away from the wickedness that flourisheth on every hand and flaunts its scarlet pomp with every drawn breath, before the ever-dreaded men of the Apocalypse come riding.

"Why, God?" I whispered, voicing aloud for the first time in my life the question which had plagued me since I had come to feel that there existed a difference between light and dark, a breast and a chest, a slap and a kiss. The softly-breathed question crescendoed above the blaring juke box and crackled with the loudness of a quake.

Looking fearfully toward the Greater Hope Church where my father ministered, I searched for his sin-discerning stare. "Please Father, forgive me," I said softly, without really knowing whether it was God or my father I was addressing. "I didn't mean it, honest."

A stream of raucous laughter from behind me halted my "cross-my-heart" gesture. I turned and saw a shapely, thinly-dressed girl stop before the fountain in front of the church. With practiced sensuality she bent to drink. Then she moistened a lacy handkerchief and wiped perspiration from between the swelling ovals of her breasts.

Miss Rachel Ann Brown, organist and nurse, stepped from the dark interior of the church and, pausing before the fountain, cast the girl a cold glance which was ignored with stoic, professional grace. With a contemptuous toss of her head, Miss Brown pranced haughtily away.

"Poor Rachel" I sympathized aloud with words I had heard

11

Mom use in talking of the old maid nurse. "You've cradled hundreds of babies to your flat breast, but none of them were your own. Poor Rachel."

A teen-aged white boy slammed his souped-up Ford to a screeching stop before the fountain. A few seconds later, with a roar and a swirl of black exhaust, the car and the boy and the girl were gone. Jezebel was in business; the early bird had copped the worm.

After a glance at the poolroom clock, I closed the polish drawer of my three-chair shine stand and hurried outside. It was 4:29 P.M. as I hunched down in racing position. When the minute hand ticked off the half-hour, I dashed down the street.

I can get in a half-hour with the gang before supper time, I told myself. *No, twenty minutes,* I corrected as the coins jingling in my pocket reminded me of the reason I had defied my father and worked in the stick hall for the past three days. Today was Mom's birthday, and for the first time I was going to buy her a present—thirty-four roses—with money I had earned myself.

Reaching the corner of 111th and Throop Streets, I glanced at the big clock in the window of Cohen's All Produce Grocery. Disgusted with the time I was making, I strained for more speed. *Slower than yesterday. You'll never win a scholarship that way,* I told myself.

Too late, I saw the boy wheeling a large basket-delivery bicycle through the store doorway. I slammed into him and we both went down.

He came up rubbing his shin and yelling. "Jeezus! So who shoved a jet up your pratt, Buck Rogers?"

"Practicing," I said, climbing to my feet and beginning to kick at the patched tires of his bike.

"Hey! Lay off that crap! What are ya tryin' to do, put me on the hoof with a ton of groceries on my back? Cut it, man, cut it!"

12

We stared at each other, still breathless from the collision. The boy was Vance Cohen, and he and his father and mother were the only white residents of Morgan Park. Vance, who we all called "Dipper" because of the way he scooped up hot liners down the third base line, was a member of the Gaylord Athletic Club, of which I was captain.

"Where's the gang?" I asked him, helping to pick up his bike.

"Crow and the rest headed toward the battleground half hour ago," he said.

"Let's go," I said, climbing into the big delivery basket.

As Dipper pedaled toward the vacant lot on 110th Place, he suddenly piped up: "You been hanging out with that little Marion doll for a long time, ain't ya?"

"So?" I asked with forced indifference.

"So, have you ever got any of her—?"

"Dammit, Dipper, zip your lip or I'll—"

"Okay, okay, so don't bust a gut," he apologized. "I was just wondering."

"Well don't!" I snapped. "And come on, pump this junk. I ain't got all day."

"Jeezus, don't ya ever get tired of running and jumping and all that stuff?" Dipper asked.

"Naw, that's why I'm going to be a physical ed instructor," I told him. "Now, will ya pump faster?"

"Okay, okay. Ya work a guy to death," he complained, then added: "Say, I nearly forgot, them damn Gabriels are probably at the battleground, too. I saw Jackie with Big Al and the rest headed that way. So why do we let those punks come into our territory and—"

"Why do ya have to leak? Because it's a free country," I told him. "And why do you have to talk so much?"

Reaching the empty lot called the battleground, we parked the bike beside the dozen or more on the sidewalk. At the far corner of the lot, a bunch of boys noisily struggled for pos-

13

session of the large dirt hill, and as Dipper and I approached it, one of them broke free and scrambled to the top.

I started running toward the hill, yelling back to Dipper: "Come on! That punk Jackie is up there!"

I fought my way into the confusion and then clawed through it and faced Jackie. He was pounding his chest and shouting victoriously: "I'm the king of The Hill! I'm the king of The Hill!"

"You were," I challenged, springing onto him.

We struggled around in a circle, trying to throw each other. He gripped my shirt; it tore. Then I got one leg behind him and flipped him over my hip. He tumbled down the hill, sprawling on his face at the bottom.

"Aaahoooowaah!" I shouted. "I'm the king of The Hill."

"You're a goddamn sissy!" Jackie shouted angrily, getting to his feet and slapping the dirt from his clothes. "A goddamn earring-wearing sissy freak. And if ya take that and don't fight, you'll eat crap!"

Jackie's words snatched all the joy out of my hilltop victory. I slid down the hill in a flurry of dust and faced him.

"Why do ya have to be a damn kill-joy all the time, Jackie?" I demanded.

"You're a sissy freak!" Jackie repeated, picking up a small stick. He placed it on his shoulder. "Slap that chip off, sissy, and I'll knock ya block off, ya freak! Slap it off! I dare ya! I double-dog dare ya!"

Members of my gang jumped at the bait, egging the fight on with yells of: "Slap it off, Guy!"

"We can't let him call no Gaylord a sissy and get away with it!"

"Let me lam de loon!"

The last voice was that of Crow, the dark-skinned, bow-legged runt of the crowd, who, grinning broadly, spit into his palms and tried to push by me. I shoved him aside, then slipped the chip from Jackie's shoulder.

14

We squared off, cautiously at first. This was an old story, Jackie and I trying to beat each other's brains out.

As we shuffled around watching for an opening, his foot suddenly hit a rock and for a moment he was off balance. My left shoulder twitched but I didn't throw the punch. Jackie got back on his toes and danced toward me. I pretended to stumble on that same rock and he stabbed a left at my head, just as I had expected. I side-stepped and sank a right in his stomach and the battle was on. As we punished each other with vicious blows, the chorus rose up from the crowd:

"Butt 'em, Jackie!"

"Boot 'em in the balls, Guy!"

We clinched and swayed together, momentarily stalemated. Then Jackie threw back his head. I tried to duck—too late. His skull slammed into my mouth.

Dazed and bleary-eyed from the shock, I fell back. Instantly he was raining blows on my face. Maddened with pain and blood spilling from my mouth, I leaped through his guard and threw my arms around his shoulder. My teeth ground into his ear. He screamed. We hit the ground with a jolt and thrashed around in the dust. Then I saw a rock in his hand. It came down against the side of my head, again and again.

"Here, here! Cut that out!" a gruff voice demanded.

Half conscious, I looked up at the bulky form of Patrolman Harris looming above. He was holding Jackie by the seat of his pants.

"Let me go! I'll kill 'em, I'll kill 'em!" Jackie shouted, flinging the rock at me.

I struggled to my knees, and then everything faded—

I woke to the smell of alcohol and the murmur of low voices. My eyes focused on the white walls, then the big clock on top of a glass cabinet. I tried to sit up, but, groaning with pain, I fell back, reaching for my head.

"Just keep those dirty paws off it, mister."

15

I recognized the voice of Nurse Ann.

Then I heard Patrolman Harris: "You would have had to see it to believe it, Doc. They were trying to kill each other."

I lay quiet, my head pounding. Dr. Bruce was giving instructions to the nurse at the other side of the room. After a moment they bent over another table and I heard Jackie whimpering.

"You almost lost half that ear, young man," the doctor said.

Turning to me, he went on: "Shame on you both, fighting like alley cats. What will your father think, Guy?"

"He never thinks about me," I said bitterly, wishing that he did. "Besides, I didn't start it. He did, the clown."

"I didn't start it; no such thing, doctor. *He* did—the sissy!" Jackie shouted hotly.

"You're a liar!" I hollered back. "You're always starting something, ever since I beat you at stump-the-leader in kindergarten. You start something and then you won't play fair or fight fair. You're a stupid clown, a show-off!"

"You're just saying that because somebody's here to keep you from getting a boot in the snoot, ya sissy, earring-wearing freak!"

For a moment Jackie and I struggled to get at each other, but the nurse and doctor held us back. Then the room fell silent, and after a while Nurse Ann walked over to the window and stood there, tears slipping quietly down her cheeks.

Jackie and I watched her until Dr. Bruce's voice cut sharply through the room.

"Will you two young men kindly come over here?" he said.

We shuffled in the direction of the desk behind which he had taken a seat. This was the doctor who had brought us both into the world, helped us through sickness and treated many of the injuries we had inflicted on each other.

"Now it is obvious," he started, "that you two have failed

16

to learn something that both your families and I have tried to impress upon you for years: God hates a brutish man. And, civilized man in modern society will not tolerate street brawling. I've been treating your injuries for years, and today, four stitches in your head, Guy, and six in your ear, Jackie. If Officer Harris hadn't been there, by the grace of God, to stop you, you might have—well, I'll tell you this: if you don't learn to control yourselves, you're going to find out what real trouble is."

Dr. Bruce removed a small Bible from his desk, placed it in front of us and continued: "You two are going to take an oath to the God who spared you today, never to lay violent hands on each other again."

The sounds of the clock ticking and Nurse Ann's sniffling filled the room as my eyes met Jackie's.

"Well, is it agreed, young gentlemen?" Dr. Bruce demanded.

I nodded, hesitated a moment, then placed a hand on the Bible. Jackie put his hand on mine.

"Nurse Ann, Officer Harris," called the doctor, "will you step over here and witness this." Then to Jackie and me: "Raise your right hand and repeat after me: I do solemnly swear, before God and these witnesses, never to raise violent hands against each other again, so help me God."

We repeated the oath, and there was silence again.

"Considering your family backgrounds," said Dr. Bruce, "I'm sure you both understand the sacredness of such an oath. Now you may leave after you've apologized to Nurse Ann for your disrespectful behavior."

Turning to the nurse, Jackie and I stammered out shame-faced apologies. She took us by the hands and led us to the door and, with a kiss on our heads and a slap on our behinds, she shooed us out.

On the sidewalk, Jackie straddled his brand new bike and looked at me contemptuously. I tried to match it.

Fingering his bandaged ear, he hissed: "You freak sissy son-of-a-bitch!"

"You clowning, pampered bishop's bastard!" I answered.

He rode off, the bike winging silver mockery at my envy.

Turning, I muttered a stream of bitter curses and started to run.

Three minutes later I came to a panting halt before Hollis' Florist Shop. Old man Hollis was pulling the black window shades for the night. The 6 P.M. whistle blew while I rapped on the glass. He shook his head and pointed a shaky finger at the shop hours painted on the door: "Open 9–6."

"But I made it in time, Mr. Hollis!" I cried out, on the point of tears. "Please, please! It's my Mom's birthday. I want to get her some flowers—roses. This is the first time I ever had my own money to buy her a present. Please!"

Then the scowling face was gone from the window. I stared at the glass door with its forbidding "9–6." Tears blurred my eyes. For a full minute I considered putting a rock through the glass, but then I turned and ran toward home.

At 111th Street I staggered into Byrd's Novelty Shop. Crow sat yogi-style on one of the glass showcases, polishing his roller skates. He didn't look up at the tinkling of the little bell on the door, but instead sang out:

"Good evenin', ladies an' gen'amen! Nice night, ain't it. Just help you'sef t' what evah yo' wants. De price is marked on de items an' de cash regista' an' wrappin's is by de doah. Jes' remembah dat honesty's de best Christian virtue, or so me ol' man sez."

Going over to the counter, I snatched a handful of artificial red roses and returned to where he sat. "How much?" I asked.

"Huh? Why didn't ya heah me say—" he started, and then looked up. "Hey, Deacon, momma! Ah didn't know it was you! Say, wusn't dat de damnest humbug today? Man, you should'a seen me lammin' de hell outta dat loonly Big Al!—"

"How much?" I repeated, holding the flowers out to him.

18

"Why, nothin' to you, Guy. You know we's ace-boon-coons, momma."

I tossed a handful of change on the counter and dashed out of the door for home. The air was crisp and smelled of snow about to fall.

Chapter **4**

The family car wasn't parked by the church or the neatly-curtained, brick parsonage where we lived when I got there. I let the screen door close quietly behind me and tip-toed in the direction of the softly-hummed spiritual coming from the kitchen. My stomach growled involuntarily as I inhaled the smell of fresh rolls and roasted meat.

Mom was perched on a stool at the sideboard, putting chocolate icing on a large cake. I watched her for a moment, fascinated as always by her smallness. It was a constant wonder to me how she could be considered a grown woman.

Aping a gesture of my father, I crept up behind her and slipped my arms around her waist, burying my face in her midnight hair.

"Oh, Guy! You're home!" she sang out, leaning her head back against my chest. But, as she looked up into my face, the laughter faded from her eyes.

"Oh, it's you, Clucky," she said, freeing herself from my arms and turning back to her cake.

Her use of the hated pet name set my teeth on edge. It was bad enough that she so quickly showed her disappointment at finding me, instead of my father, with my arms around her. Did she have to call me that nickname I despised so, too? I decided to return the compliment.

"Happy birthday, Fluff," I said cheerlessly, placing the flowers in her lap.

She glanced at the wall clock as she turned to face me. "Clucky," she said, "how many times must I tell you not to call me that name. I know you mean well, baby, but it sounds —well, kind of cheap, don't you think?"

She toyed with the stems of the phony flowers. The flowers looked cheap enough, all right, beside the dusky bloom of her skin. I felt ashamed at having tried to strike back at her. She smiled and seemed to flutter from the stool as she stepped down. "Give me a kiss and go wash up," she said, flinging her arms around me.

I nibbled at her button nose, and all was well again. I placed one of the flowers in her hair, just above the right ear, and the sickly-looking imitation seemed to bloom radiantly in the rich ebony loam.

"We shouldn't let your father know where we earned the money, should we?" she asked with a look of sly conspiracy as she admired the reflection of the flower on the highly-polished surface of one of her skillets. "And you must never work at that place again," she added.

"But Mom, how else can I get the money for a bike?" I protested.

"I thought we agreed that we wouldn't talk of that anymore, Clucky," she said. "You know how your father feels about placing such importance on material things. Now please don't be rebellious. It's evil. Besides, you're as fleet as a deer, and there's really little difference between running and pedaling a bike, is there? And you know your father says it doesn't look right for a minister's family to be surrounded by rich worldly goods."

I looked at the faded neatness of Mom's much-laundered housedress, and thought of the people I knew in Morgan Park who were surrounded by "worldly goods," many of them families of the ministry. I puzzled over the contrast between Mom's clothes—a couple of housedresses and two or three others for church and special occasions—and my father's extensive wardrobe. I thought of her scuffed shoes, which I polished every Friday, and his big, new car which sped him "conventioneering into the world to preach the gospel to every creature," as he so often proclaimed. Why, I wondered, when according to what Mom read to me out of the Bible each night, Christ had instructed his Apostles in their journeying "to put on sandals" and "not to put on two tunics."

I stood there, lost in the confusion of my questioning thoughts. Finally, all the "whys" piling up inside me started to spill out as I said softly, but with irritation: "But big cars are more worldly than bikes, and—"

"That's enough now," Mom warned. "Let's get upstairs and clean up before your father gets here." She slapped me on the seat of the pants and sent me towards the door. She had not even looked at me.

Upstairs in the bathroom, I sprinkled water on my face and rubbed the dirt off onto a towel. Then I went into the bedroom and slipped into a pair of clean jeans and a shirt, picked up my conga drum and went back downstairs.

The living room held the only modern piece of furniture in the house, a combination record player, radio and television. There was a lone record on the turntable, and without looking I knew what it was.

Seven years ago Mom and my father had made a trip to his home in the West Indies, and she had brought me the drum back from the islands. Soon after, she had purchased the record, which I now turned on. The soft, lulling words of the song went swirling through the house: *Sweet Leilani, heavenly flower, nature fashioned roses after you . . ."*

The first few bars lured Mom from the kitchen, as they had many times before. Eagerly I joined in the music with my drum.

Mom listened for a moment, then ran to the door, locked it, pulled down the shades and hurried into the bedroom.

A faint whispering of cloth announced her return. My heart skipped a beat as she stepped into view, wrapped in a

22

bright-hued native costume: her souvenir of the islands. With a wide smile and her eyes sparkling, she began to dance.

She swayed in the dim light, her movements like those of a delicate plant in a soft breeze. Gliding across the room with her hands weaving a rhythmic pattern in accompaniment of her graceful body, she paused before the large photograph of my father, which commanded the room from its regal position atop the false fireplace. With tender love in every look and gesture, she danced.

For the second time that day, burning envy pricked my heart.

The record came to an end, and I switched it off before it could repeat. Mom stood gazing at the photograph in worshipful silence.

"Mom, when can we eat?" I asked, trying to end the scene of devotion.

She did not answer.

"Mom!" I repeated.

She turned toward me, hypnotized. The yellow death's head, white scorpions and black snakes which patterned her garment seemed to intensify my apprehension at her fixed stare.

"Mom!" I called again, "Are you all right?"

A slow smile wiped the deathly immobility from her face. "Of course I am, silly," she said suddenly.

"Mom, do we have to wait supper for Poppa? I'm hungry."

"Don't you want to wait for your father?" she asked.

"No," I said.

"Well," she sighed, frowning reproach at my impatience, "I suppose you must be hungry. It is late."

She headed for the bedroom. "Go on to the table, Clucky," she called back. "I'll be with you in a jiffy."

A half hour later we sat quietly at the table, our food barely touched. Mom's obvious listening for sounds outside the door and frequent sighs had filled me with emptiness. Finally, for the third time since we'd come to the table, she got up and hurried to the window at the sound of a car door slamming.

This time, I left the table too, picking up my drum and going up to my room. I put the drum in its regular place next to my pillow, undressed, said a quick prayer that began and ended with Mom's name, and crawled with tired nudity between fragrant sheets. One arm automatically embraced the smooth contour of my drum.

Why did it only happen when *he* was away, I wondered.

Drawing the drum closer to me, I thumped its ancient bald head and thought of Mom's dance. Then I remembered my father and told myself, as I had done many times before, that he was a great and righteous man who preached the word of God and had great power over people. I shouldn't find fault with him so much. But why, if he were so righteous, should things be as they were in our house? Mom needed things, and he had so much. And why shouldn't I have a bike? But Poppa was a man of God, and I shouldn't question his actions. Why didn't I understand? Over and over the thoughts pounded in my head: *Why? Why? Why?*

Then I seemed to hear my father's voice thunder: "Because the day of the Lord is upon you!"

I remembered standing in the aisle of Greater Hope Church. All around me were faces: brown, copper, gold, black; old and wrinkled; young and wide-eyed. All held a look of deathly fear, and fear gripped me, too, as I looked up at my father. He stood as if giving battle to a horde of demons, his dark, sweaty face holding the wrathful look of a Moses shattering the stone tablets. With arms raised and fists clenched he towered over the congregation.

They swayed and cowered and cried out: "Have mercy! Lord, have mercy! Sweet Saviour help us!"

Babies wailed in panic. A richly-dressed, high-yellow woman pressed her forehead against her knees and screamed.

24

A huge, black stevedore flayed the air with futile hands and begged: "No, Lord! I couldn't help it!"

"Howl, ye!" my father commanded. "Come down and sit in the dust, O daughters and sons of Babylon, for the day of the Lord is upon you. Thou shalt not covet thy neighbor's wife, and if ye look upon her with lustful eyes and desire in thy hearts, ye commit adultery! As man has the electric chair to punish evil-doers, God has hell! Fire! Fire! Pouring down from the sky like boiling rain. Hell fire on the heads of sinners! Scorching! Burning!"

I turned and ran screaming out of the church.

On the sidewalk, people milled around wildly and the sky was blood-red. The ground rocked, the air roared, the world shook and exploded.

Gasping and wide-eyed I sat up in bed with body rigid, trembling. *"That was six or seven years ago,"* I whispered when reason had disentangled itself from the nightmare.

I sank back on the bed, remembering what had really happened that night when I ran from my father's preaching in terror. I had dashed wildly from the church and down the street, stumbling blindly into an open door. I found myself in another church, where people were rolling and tumbling on the floor, kicking and jerking under the lash of an unseen whip while a woman preacher yelled shrilly.

"Come up to the mourner's bench and repent your sins!" she commanded them. "For the wages of sin is death! Death!"

Turning in fright, I had resumed my mad dash, with the cries of fire and death loud in my ears. All the swaying and wailing people and the fearful voices of the preachers had filled me with a longing for peace and quiet. I tried to outrun the insane screams and soon found myself heading for the cave at the base of the hill on the empty lot. It was there that I took refuge.

Lying in the darkness, trembling, expecting some horror to descend on me from the sky, I saw flash before my eyes the naked picture of Marion the day before. For it had been then, while she and I were playing in the basement of my house and I still had Jackie's first taunts about my being a sissy freak ringing in my ears, that I had asked her about the difference between boys and girls. Marion had casually removed her clothes and shown me.

As I lay cowering there in the cave I had pleaded: "Honest, God, I didn't mean to commit a sin. Honest, I didn't. I just wanted to see something, to see if I was a freak, different from other boys; a sissy, like Jackie said. That's all, God, honest."

Soon I had quieted down and fallen asleep.

Now, in my bed, I was almost asleep after recalling that fearful night.

"Guy, are you awake?" Mom called from my door.

"Yes," I answered.

She came in and perched on the side of my bed and switched on the lamp. A Bible was in her hand. She had come in for the ritual of nightly scripture reading that my father had begun as soon as I had shown signs of understanding.

Closing her eyes, she flipped open the book and pointed at a line. This method of blind selection was her idea. Then, opening her eyes, she prepared to read the passage and elaborate on it. She glanced up at me, but before she could quote the biblical lines her eyes fell on the bandage near the back of my head.

"Why, Clucky!" she exclaimed. "What have you done to your head? Has that bandage been there all evening? I didn't notice it before."

No, I thought bitterly, *you didn't notice it. You don't notice anything when you're dancing for his picture or sitting at the table with your thoughts on him and your ears out on the street waiting for the sound of him.*

Then, aloud, I stammered out a detailed and truthful account of my fight with Jackie.

"Oh, Clucky, God hates a brutish man," she reproached,

26

peeking beneath the bandage. "A man that does violence flees to the pit," she continued, trying to capture my father's quality of sternness.

I lay quiet, shamed before her displeasure.

Then she said: "What must the bishop think of me?"

That was always the problem of fighting Jackie. It wasn't just the fighting, it was also the fact that his father was bishop in the church, and as such was my father's boss. But even that didn't give the bishop any right to think anything wrong about Mom.

"He will think what everybody else thinks—that you're an angel," I told her.

"Why, you little flatterer!" she said, rewarding me with a kiss. "No wonder Marion tags after you so. By the way, did you tell her that she could go with us tomorrow?"

"Ah, Mom," I protested, "I get tired of having a girl follow me around."

"Oh, you do, do you?" she said smiling. "But what about tomorrow—"

"I don't know what you're talking about, Mom," I interrupted.

"No, well, we'll talk about that later. It's past your bedtime, now go to sleep."

She smoothed down a loosened end of my bandage and said: "I wonder what your father is going to say about—"

The sudden slamming of a car door sent her running from the room.

Angered at her abrupt departure, I stood up in bed and pointed a condemning finger at my nude image in the mirror.

"Howl, ye!" I shouted, then stood horror-struck as the room suddenly went pitch black. The lamp bulb had blown out. I ducked beneath the sheets and after a few moments fell asleep.

Sometime later I awoke to the sound of sobbing. Slipping on my pajama bottoms, I went to Mom's room.

"What's wrong?" I asked, looking down at her averted face.

"Nothing, Clucky. Go back to bed," she answered softly, burying her face in the damp pillow.

I tried to lift her head, but she pulled free of my grasp.

"No, let me be. Please leave, please," she begged.

"But, Mom, why cry for—"

"Oh, Clucky, you wouldn't understand. I—I—oh, it's too deep for you. Please now, go back to bed," she sobbed.

Yeah, I thought, *too deep. Much too deep. But that doesn't make my misery any less.*

Filled with renewed rage against my father, I hurried out of the room. But before I could close the door, Mom called out: "Clucky, come back! Don't go!"

I turned around quickly and the movement flung tears from my eyes. She held the covers back for me, and I crawled in beside her and pressed my face against her soft, warm breast. Her flowery scent performed its special magic of blotting out the rest of the world.

"You're growing so fast," she whispered, toying with the gold ring in my ear. "How pretty your sister, Greta, would be now if only—"

She sighed with the memory of my twin, who had died a few hours after our birth. It was then that Nurse Ann had put the ring in my ear.

Lulled by Mom's voice and the warmth of her bed, I began to slip into sleep. From the street came the sound of three shots. A woman screamed, and a man laughed and called out drunkenly. An alley cat answered mournfully the distant howl of sirens. Another violent Saturday night had begun in Black Babylon.

But with Mom so near, it all seemed far away. As if in a dream I heard a whispered call of: "Guy, Guy!" as her hot tears fell onto my face.

Chapter **5**

The big car stalked down the highway in pursuit of the fleeting December sunset. Poppa handled the three hundred-odd horsepower engine with ease and nonchalance.

Leaning over the back of the front seat, I looked down at Mom. She lay with her feet curled beneath her and her head pillowed on my father's lap, humming softly to herself.

Contented, I thought.

My father's right hand rested gently upon Mom's head, his fingers rooted in the silken root of her hair. I reached over and brushed her lips with my fingertips. Her eyelashes fluttered slightly and the smile on her lips broadened. She blew me a kiss, her feathery breath upon my hand heating the slight chill in the car.

"Little Jack Frost certainly did a bang-up job for you white Christmas lovers," my father said, brushing the light mist fogging the windshield with the back of his hand. It was still snowing big, fluffy flakes that looked like goose down.

"Are the cherubs still pillow-fighting?" Mom asked.

My father grunted.

The flashing landscape was a giant, white blanket, and from doors, windows and lawns of the houses lining the highway, the bright red and green and silver of Christmas glowed merrily.

"Honey, do you think there'll be a goodly crowd at the convention?" Mom asked.

"Tolerable, tolerable," my father replied.

"Good," she said, and started into song:

29

"I went to the well to wash my toe;
And when I got back my black-eyed rooster was gone,
Shoo, ol' witch, what time—"

My father's rich bass joined Mom's lilting soprano in the old folksy jingle of their childhood. Mom sat up suddenly, clapping her hands, her black eyes sparkling. "Come on, Clucky, join in," she entreated. I did.

> "Limba, limba, lumba lock,
>   Six geese makes a flock;
>   One flew east, and one flew west,
>   And one flew over the coo-coo's nest.
> Shoo, ol' witch, what time!"

Mom threw her arms around my neck and kissed me. "Come on, Clucky, sit up here with us," she invited, making room between them.

I climbed over the seat. It was warm and snug there, like when I was just a little kid and slept between them. Mom put her arm around my shoulders, her fingers caressing the back of my father's neck. I inhaled deeply of their scent: my father's strong, burnt-almond tobacco one, and Mom's fresh, forever midsummer flower smell.

"Are you happy, boy," my father asked, dropping his hand to my knee.

I nodded my head. I was happy, but not completely so, for I knew that after the church convention and the Christmas holidays, my father would be off again down the asphalt path of some unknown highway, spreading "the word" in one of the steel jungles speckling the earth with scarlet. He would be gone, and so would the light from Mom's eyes.

Minutes later, we pulled into the parking lot of Temple Star, a gigantic auditorium in Phoenix, Illinois, where the United Evangelist Ministers' Association of America was holding its Christmas Jubilee.

The next few hours were filled with back-slapping, introductions, speeches and singing, and by the time we finally adjourned to the basement dining room I felt starved.

The dining room was filled with mouth-watering smells of corn bread, meats and wines. The food was being served on gigantic steaming platters: whole pigs with big, red apples clamped between their teeth, golden brown birds and oozing rich buttery gravy in nests of creamy, mashed potatoes greeted my eyes. It was like a scene out of a Robin Hood movie I had once seen. My stomach growled hungrily.

"Clucky, put your tongue back in your head," Mom said gently. "A person would think that you are underfed."

My father laughed and beckoned for a waitress.

A woman detached herself from the scurrying mass of females darting from table to table with food and wine. As she moved toward us, male eyes glued themselves to the hydraulic swing of her hips. The knit suit that she wore gloved her body. Her slightly parted lips were scarlet silk ribbons, and her smile a string of pearls. She was all thrust and bulge: swelling breasts, flat belly, curving hips and taunting buttocks. She walked with the boneless undulation of a snake. The whiteness of her skin looked foamy and soft as bubbling fresh milk. Her beauty was hypnotizing, like a magnetic beacon of sin.

My father's Adam's apple struggled in the clamp of a collar suddenly grown too tight for comfort.

The woman stood between his chair and mine, her body radiating an odd heat that prickled my skin with goose pimples. I drew back from her touch. Her bright smile held a chill. "May I serve you?" she asked, glancing first at Mom and then at my father.

He stared at her, speechless for a long moment that for some unknown reason held great embarrassment for me because of the odd expression on Mom's face.

"Guy," Mom said with what sounded like suppressed hurt.

The laughter that we had shared earlier was now completely gone from both their eyes.

My father asked the woman for food and wine in a mumbling voice, his eyes never leaving her. He watched her, entranced, as she left and when she returned.

As she sat the food on the table, her hips brushed against my father's shoulders slightly. He gave a startled jump at their touch as if burnt, knocking the water glass to the floor. The sound of the shattering glass was like an explosion.

The woman spilled out apologies as she rubbed at the dampness on his lap with a napkin she'd snatched from the table. "Oh, how clumsy of me," she gushed. "I'm so very, very sorry, Reverend Morgan. I'm afraid I'm not very good at waiting tables!"

My father sat transfixed, his eyes glassy. The veins stood out on the back of his hands, which were gripping the table tightly. His shoulders hunched slowly beneath the caress of the napkin; his eyes began to close. A tremor shook his body for a brief, violent moment, then his chin dropped to his chest in slow jerks, until his head was completely bowed.

I turned to Mom. Naked pain glinted from behind the tears pooling her eyes as she stared at my father. "Thank you, that will be all," she said to the woman. They stared at each other for a fleeting half-moment, then Mom's gaze returned to my father.

The woman turned to go. I saw the large name-button pinned between her breasts: "Miss Zola Campbell."

My father reached out blindly for the tall glass of wine before him and drank it down in one long gulp.

"Guy, Guy," Mom whispered, "what have you done to me?"

I dropped my eyes from the anguish distorting her face and looked into my plate. The hunger I'd felt only a moment before was completely gone. In its stead, a freezing, heavy loathsomeness filled me with a strangling disgust.

Midway through my father's second bottle of wine, Mom's touch on my shoulder startled me from my trance. She held my coat, scarf and cap. The food on her plate was barely touched, as was mine.

"Come on, Guy, I think we had better go," she said, more to my father than to me.

I had been ready to go instantly after the incident with Zola, and sensed that Mom had too. But a chattering, laughing crowd of preachers and their wives had descended upon our table, and Mom, as wife of the vice-president of the association, could not have withdrawn without having seemed rude. So, she had been forced to sit through two hours of smiling and talking with her long lashes veiling the hurt in her eyes.

My father and the other wine-filled delegates were laughing and telling jokes, and he protested my mother's efforts to leave.

"But Clucky is tired, he can hardly keep his eyes open," she argued. "Besides, we have a long drive ahead of us," she added, eyeing his half-filled glass meaningfully.

"Well, you two sleepy-heads go on out and get in the car. I'll be with you in a minute," he said.

Outside, we hunched in the chill of the car for half an hour before my father reeled out, laughing gaily. The snow was falling thickly as he got inside.

"Don't ever ask me to take you to another convention," he growled to Mom as he inserted the key in the ignition.

"I won't, Guy, I won't," she promised softly. She sat as if made of stone in a corner.

The car leaped forward in a sudden burst of speed, then jerked to a stop, the motor dead.

"Goddamn!" my father exploded.

I sat bolt upright, surprised and shocked. I heard the hiss of Mom's indrawn breath, but she remained still, deathlike.

The car started again and roared out onto the icy highway,

skidding wildly from side to side. My father fought the wheel, his skill of some hours ago gone.

The snow was falling in blinding sheets. The glaring headlights stabbed at it unpenetratingly. My father mumbled grimly under his breath and pressed the gas pedal further to the floor.

I sat clutching the back of the front seat. My fingers ached and my head throbbed with pain. A cold sweat ran in icy rivulets down my spine, making my underclothes sticky, and I sucked in my breath and fought to keep back the rush of urine that welled up in my kidneys. The needle of the speedometer rose steadily . . . forty-five, fifty, fifty-five—

My father switched on the radio, turning the volume up to ear-shattering loudness. A swinging gospel choir on the midnight church hour shouted forth. My father joined in:

". . . I'm a-working on de building . . ." from the choir.

"Yes, I'm working on the building," from my father.

"It's truly a foundation . . ." from the choir.

"Yes, it's truly a foundation!" from my father.

"Ah'm holding up de blood-stained bannah fo' mah Lawd . . ."

"Blood-stained banner for my Loooord, yeeeeeeeeh!"

"Guy, you're going much too fast!" Mom cautioned.

My father laughed wildly.

I stared at the luminous hand . . . sixty-five . . . seventy . . . The boiling urine slowly began freezing to ice inside my bladder. I felt its gut-tearing formulation and set my teeth, transfixed with fear.

The speedometer needle leaped . . . eighty . . . eighty-five . . .

"Guy! You're scaring us to death! Please—" Mom pleaded.

". . . Th' mothah's by th' bed a-cryin' . . ." from the choir.

"Hal-le-lu-jah! I said hal-le-lu-lah!" from my father.

"Ooh, yes, th' mothah's by th' bed a-cryin' . . ." from the choir.

"Hal-le-lu-jah! Good God, hal-le-lu-jah!"

"Guy!" Mom cried.

. . . Th' mothah's by th' bed a-cryin' . . ."

"Guy! Guy! Guy!"

". . . Laaawd, Gaaawd A-mighty, mah child is dyin'! . . ."

"Guy! Guy!"

The car careened sickeningly, in wild uncontrollability. For a moment I caught a glimpse of massive black steel and gray mortar looming suddenly in the ghostly glare of the headlights, and felt the rake of Mom's fingernails as she reached for me with desperate hands.

"Oh! Guy!" she screamed as the whole world burst into flames with a thunderous roar, jarring the ice in my bladder into instant, boiling liquid that cascaded a scorching lava path down my leg.

". . . Laawd, Gaaawd A-mighty, mah child is dyin' . . ." the radio choir shrilled insanely.

"Guy! Guy! Oh, mercy, Jesus. My baaaaaaby!" Mom screamed.

Glass and steel sliced into my flesh and axed jaggedly into the bone. I tried to run from the pain; it reached out and noosed me in a flaming knot. I tried to wiggle free. Each movement seemed to snap a bone, the shock vibrating a searing agony throughout my being.

I opened my eyes. I was in the bosom of hell. Blue and red flames were everywhere, leaping out of the ground, boiling the white snow and bubbling the black asphalt. My body felt lifeless, although each tissue quivered and jerked with a multiplicity of bleeding, raw hurts. I moved my eyes, my brain struggling. A big, black mass of gleaming, hissing steel lay across my hips and legs, pinning me to the shoulder of the highway. Over it, I saw Mom. She was in a circle of red, white and blue flames whose blinding reflection sparkled the blackness of her terror-stricken eyes and highlighted every line of the pain-twisted face. She crawled on her hands, sliding on her stomach, pulling her twisted, lifeless legs like some broken, animal-human thing.

I felt the bitter, sour sickness gushing between my clenched teeth. I strangled on it as I tried to call to her.

"Guy! Guy! Guy! Oh God, where is my baby?" she cried.

My father staggered through the fiery wall and stood reeling, his hands covering his face.

Mom inched her way blindly toward him, reaching out with bleeding, clawing fingers.

"God! God! Oh Guy, please! Please find my baby. Please, Guy! Bring me my baby. Please, Guy, bring—"

* * *

". . . Bring the torch, Jeanetta, Isabella, bring the torch to the cradle run . . . This is Jesus, good folks of the village . . . Christ is born and Mary is calling . . . Ah, ah, beautiful is the mother . . . Ah, ah, beautiful is her son . . . Bring the torch, Jeanetta, Isabella, bring the torch to the cradle run . . ."

I listened to the Christmas carolers through the heavy fog of pain which blanketed my body. *Yes, bring your torch, Jeanetta, Isabella, and you bring yours, father Rev. Guy Morgan Sr., sir; bring your goddamn torch and see if I care.* Bring them to the cradle—my bed—and throw them on with the rest of the flames you've lit under me and Mom. See if I care. I'll laugh, you hear, laugh! As long as I know she's over there on the other side of that screen, hurting inside and out like me, with me. Yeah, we'll laugh at your pain, for we have something in common. We'll enjoy our hurt like a present.

The throbbing pains that I had been feeling began to subside. I intentionally jerked my body against the weights and pulleys which elevated my arms and legs. Instantly the pain, which had always been near, leaped up like a furnace fire.

Flames of it licked me from head to toe. I closed my eyes tightly.

You want me to cry out, don't you, Mr. Pain, Daddy Pain, Rev. Guy Morgan Pain. Just because I'm a fourteen-year-old kid and all, you think I'm a baby, but I ain't. I am—I am— what was that poem Miss McGill taught us in the seventh grade at school, how did it go?—"Master of human destiny as I?"— No, no, that's not it. That one has got something to do with opportunity.

I thought about school, and wondered what Marion was doing. Poor little Miss Muffet. My being in the hospital was sure messing up our chances to go to high school and college together like we planned. I wondered if Jackie and the rest of the boys were messing with her, now that I wasn't there to knock their blocks off. I bet they were pulling her pigtails and hitting her with snowballs and stuff.

I made the pain-bringing movement again.

Could people plan their opportunities, make them be all by themselves? What was that other poem and that thing about luck that Miss McGill had told us?

Luck means "laboring under correct knowledge," that's it, that's where luck got its name, from the first four letters of the four words. So I guess you can plan your opportunities just like Miss Muffet and I planned ours. Yeah, and I ain't gonna let no broken bones keep me from doing what we planned. Yeah, despite what that old horse-faced nurse said about me not being able to run anymore. A guy can do almost anything if he wants to. What was that poem?

". . . Bring the torch, Jeanetta, Isabella, bring the torch to the cradle, run . . ."

Yeah, bring your torches. Come on, come on, I can take it. I can take anything without crying out loud. Crying aloud! That's it, that's part of the poem:

"Out of the night that covers me, black as a pit from pole to pole, I thank whatever Gods may be . . ."

37

"Why, who is this young fellow?" a jolly voice asked.

I opened my eyes, looking out of the peepholes the doctor had left in the bandages that swathed me from head to foot. Blue eyes filled with friendliness stared down at me with a happy twinkle.

"I've brought you a present, a music box that plays funny tunes that will make you laugh," jolly-face said. He held up an object shaped like a circus wagon and painted several bright colors. Animals were drawn on it. His hand pushed a button and the tune *The Animal Fair*, which had always made me laugh, chimed out merrily. My bandaged lips started to smile when suddenly I remembered that I didn't want to smile. At the same time, I saw the white clerical collar as he leaned over me.

"Get away from me! Get away!" I shouted. "I don't want to laugh! I don't want your old music box! Get away from me or I'll kill you!"

I screamed, struggling to free myself from the ropes and pulleys.

"Now son, now, now. You mustn't get yourself excited. I only want to make you happy," he said, patting my shoulder.

"I don't want your kind of happiness, and I ain't your son, so keep your hands off me!" I shouted angrily.

The horse-faced nurse appeared above me.

"Now, Guy, you lie still," she directed.

"Get him away from me! Get him away!"

"All right, all right, but you hush now," she said, then turned to the priest. "I'm sorry, Reverend, but I must ask you to leave," she told him.

"Yes, yes, by all means. I didn't know that I would upset him so," he apologized.

"Well, he's rather an excitable young man," she explained as they moved away. "But then he's been through a great deal. He's been trussed up like that for weeks."

"Poor little fellow. Will he walk again? . . ."

38

". . . Bring the torch, Jeanetta, Isabella . . . " sang the carolers.

Will I walk? Determination welled up inside me, drowning the pain. *Yes, I will walk. Not only walk, I'll run . . .*

". . . Bring the torch to the cradle, run . . ."

I'll run, run with the Olympic torch, like Jim Thorpe and Jesse Owens . . . I will, I will. . . The words of the poem came back to me:

I thank whatever gods may be for my unconquerable soul . . . In the fell clutch of circumstance I have not winced nor cried aloud . . .

". . . This is Jesus, good folks of the village . . ."

Under the bludgeonings of chance my head is bloody, but unbowed . . . Beyond this place of wrath and tears looms but the horror of the shade . . .

". . . Christ is born and Mary is calling . . ."

And yet the menace of the years finds, and shall find me, unafraid . . . It matters not how strait the gate, how charged with punishments the scroll . . . I am the master of my fate: I am the captain of my soul . . .

The bandages about my eyes were wet.

". . . Ah, ah, beautiful is the mother . . . Ah, ah, beautiful is her child . . ."

"Mom, I will, I will! I'll make it all up to you," I whispered. "We don't need him!"

Chapter **6**

In the age-fogged mirror of the antiquated chest of drawers, the scar running through the bristle of my crew-cut to the outer edge of my eyebrow reflected with a ghostly whiteness. With fingers shaking in fury, I traced the hairless path of the burn. The hateful whiteness of the scar was heightened by the dark mahogany of my complexion.

Branded for life, I thought.

I glanced at my reflection and that of Crow who was sprawled out amid a litter of magazines on the big four-poster bed behind me.

"Branded, and still I look like—like him! Why couldn't I have taken after her side of the family? Or better still, why couldn't Greta have lived instead of me? Why, Crow? Why? Why do I have to grow up and turn into the double of the person I hate most?"

I stared at the mirror, the bitter questions racing through my mind; the bitter questions that had hounded me since the night following Mom's thirty-fourth birthday.

"Why? Why?" I asked aloud. "In truth, 'tis better to be dead than alive! Yea, better still to have never been born. Why died I not in the womb? Oh, let the day perish wherein I was born, and the night in which it was said. 'There is a manchild conceived!'"

"Jeezus!" Crow cried. "La sound just like ya old man."

"That's a damn lie! You'd better take it back or—"

"Okay, okay, so it's took back. Now will ya sit down and shut up? Ya 'bout t' make me blow my stack with all ya walkin' and moanin'. And that ain't inta nothin'. A cat can't allow hisself to lose his cool in dis day 'n' age. An if—"

"Now who needs to shut up?" I cut in, returning to the mirror.

"Look at me," I said, after a moment of eyeing the network of surgical scars on my fever-wasted body.

Crow grunted, but didn't look up from his magazine.

"A fine ace-boon-coon you are," I flared, at his indifference to my mutilation. "I might as well have a hog for a friend. Will you look at my back. How many scars on it?"

"Not many, momma—and ya wouldn' even see 'em if ya put on some clothes."

"Clothes wouldn't stop me from knowing they're there, or how, when and why they got there, or who put them there," I replied, hotly. "They wouldn't stop me from being a part of him, like him, I mean—"

"I mean, I mean!" Crow mocked irritably. "What do ya mean, d'ya know y'self? Will ya stop singing de same ole song for cry-yi? So you're a part of 'im. So be wha'cha is! 'Cause wha'cha ain' ya can't be anyhow!"

"But it's what I am that—"

"So Cain was a part of Adam. Did de ole man go around bumpin' off people wid bricks? Your situation is jes reversed."

"Listen, you don't understand—"

"I unn'erstan' dat de monk', de ape, de chimp, de baboon, and de gorilla is all de same clan, but ah bet dey don' all swing de same."

Finding no answer to Crow's argument, I strolled to the window. The scene of boyish rough and tumble in the street filled me with a fierce desire to fly from the house that had been my prison during a six-month convalescence following a two-year jaunt to the hospital. Dr. Bruce's departure an hour before, after removing the last plaster cast from my body, had marked the end of my confinement.

41

The banging Fourth of July noises as a prelude to the coming evening's celebration intensified my desire to go outside.

"Jeezus, ain't she ever gonna come?" I said flinging myself across the bed. My reference was to Marion's daily attendance to Mom.

"She'll come when she comes," Crow answered, then exclaimed: "Wow! Will ya dig de bootie on dis beauty!"

He held up a magazine with a picture of the current female pole-vaulting champion, and then placing a smacking kiss on her rear end as she soared gracefully over the cross bar.

"Christ! Is that all you can think of?"

"D'ya mean dere's somethin' else t' think about?" he questioned. "Me ole man sez dat 'das de black man's big contribushin t' de avancement o' society, his reason fer livin' an' his cons'latshun fer bein' poor. Also de pillow what soaks up all de tears o' his frusterashun. An' . . .'"

"Is that all you got to think about?" I repeated.

"Hell," he answered, "if'n ah wanted ta, ah could think o' mo' things than a seven months gone nun in a mount'n top nun'ry in de middle ob de sea. But who wan'sta think. Ah digs de beauty heah! See de woman climb de pole," he cried like a carnival barker. "De higher she gets de mo' ya see her ho—ld yo' tickets pa—lease!"

"See Crow! Crow, the lover-boy. He eats, sleeps, walks, talks like a man, but'll crawl on his belly fer a broad!" I chided.

"Amen, Deacon," he said solemnly, using a nickname I hated. "Amen, Deacon Scars," he ended.

"Don't call me no scars, ya little runt!"

"Don't ya call me no runt, Deacon Scars," he cried back. We sprang at each other.

"Guy! Crow!" Mom called from the next room, as our scuffling knocked a chair noisily against the wall. "Must you two ride rough-shod over my furniture?"

We broke apart panting, and I dropped back onto the bed and lay staring at the soot-grimed ceiling of the old house we'd been forced to move into since the accident and my father's desertion.

"Yhat'cha thinkin' 'bout momma?" Crow asked after a long silence.

"Now that I'm well, I gotta clean this lousy dump."

I got up and walked to the dresser and looked down at my school books. Fingering them, I said, "Crow, I need a job."

"Yeah," he said, sitting up, "an' what 'bout school?"

"What about it?" I snapped.

"My question, remember? But be'en as how y'ask, and see'n as how y' can't be President anyway, o' so m' ole man sez, ah repeats—how 'bout school?"

"Yer old man talks too much," I switched.

We were silent. Then he informed me. "De shine stan' at Hank's is out a boot-black agin!"

He got up and slung his skates over his shoulder.

I thought of my dreams of being a physical ed instructor, in the fresh air and sunshine or in a clean gym. Then I pictured the pool room; air thick with tobacco smoke, the stinking feet and sweat as I worked over an endless parade of shoes to be shined.

Shine, suh? Shine 'em up Cap'n? Yawk, yawk, yawk! I mentally aped in disgust of the occupation which was looked upon by the teens in the Park as a slap in the face of the Emancipation Proclamation.

"Sure y' won't change y' mind 'bout going skatin' wi' me?" Crow asked, heading for the door.

I shook my head.

"Well, later momma," he saluted.

"Later," I returned.

He banged out of the house.

As soon as he was gone, I realized that I did want to go

skating. Yeah, there were a whole lot of things I'd like to do. After a guy is laid up and out of circulation for a couple of years, he—

I grabbed my thoughts and broke them off. *Freeze that action,* I forced myself to think. *Forget it—skating, girls, the gang, sports, right now, forget it all. You got things to do, money to earn, starting now.*

I was suddenly weary. Dropping to the bed, I lay on my back and tried to relax. The clock ticking on the table beside me sounded like a village blacksmith. I slapped it to the floor and then lay staring at the photograph which had been hidden by the ticking monstrosity. I picked it up for a closer look. A young, dark-skinned woman smiled gaily at me. With her brightly-colored island costume and tip-toed stance she seemed like a tropical bird poised for flight. The wind tore jealously at her long, black hair and the sea strove to kiss her feet. One hand waved a white flower and the other, hanging at her side, held a palm leaf. The lower right corner of the picture bore the happy observation: "Oh! it's beautiful—Mom"

As I stared, I thought of the hands that had held the camera when this picture was taken, the hands of my father—the ex-Reverend Guy Morgan. My hatred for him was so great as to be frightening. A violent consuming desire to smash him, destroy him, gripped me; I lashed out at the pillow, then at the wall, and finally sank my teeth in the frame of the picture I still clutched in my left hand.

Then, fury somewhat spent, I relaxed and placed the photograph back on the table.

Chapter **7**

The tempestuous furies of a Chicago spring seemed to be boiling inside me that morning as I walked toward Gale's Drug Store. March winds and April showers had attacked the city, sweeping it clean and washing it down. Now, the winds and rains were gone, but the storms inside me continued to blow. Crippled for life, Mom still baptized herself in the pool of admiration and lost love for my father, even though his complete abandonment of us had taken place during our long hospital confinement. If it had not been for Mom's two well-off sisters, Agnes and Emma, there would never have been enough money to pay all of the bills or move into the small frame cottage we had. They still sent Mom a little money from time to time, a fact which only increased my resentment of them when I fancied myself as our sole support, even though the money I had earned the past year hustling at Hank's poolroom would hardly have stretched to cover meat and bread.

But there was more than Mom's devotion to my hated father or the unwanted charity of my aunts bothering me this morning: there was the old feud with Jackie, sharpened now by the competitive influences of high school athletics. And the basketball game and locker room rumble with Jackie afterwards had not served to sweeten my disposition any. My mind was dwelling on this as I walked, swinging my zipper bag containing my uniform and practice shoes.

At Gale's Drug Store, I stopped and looked in through the open door. Four kids were grouped about the huge, multi-colored juke box which spewed hot jazz in brassy crescendos upon the warm spring air. The kids wore the teen-age uniform: blue jeans. The girls had theirs rolled up to the knees and the boys had ten-inch deep cuffs, which they used as pockets. Three-inch belts with heavy, sharp-edged metal buckles, worn unclasped, were standard equipment for the boys. The tight-fitting jeans needed no support, so the belts were carried as weapons.

My fingers ran over my own belt hanging low on my hips. There were ten notches in the smooth leather, each representing a wound inflicted on a member of a rival gang. Only one other belt in the community had almost as many notches as mine—Jackie's had seven.

I glanced at the drug store clock and saw that it was five minutes to one. *Should have been back to work twenty-five minutes ago,* I reproached myself.

I brushed my hand over my close-cropped hair, tugged my jeans down a little lower on my hips, and walked toward the kids at the juke box. They were rocking their heads and popping their fingers in time to the music as they talked.

"Dig this passage, baby. Miles always kills me with this riff."

"Yeah, but what he's blowing ain't nothin', to the puffin' he put down when he was at the Opera House last month."

"Oh, Jim, but didn't that cat wail."

The tall, six-footer in the group, Treetop Williams, who was captain of the park district basketball team, spotted me walking up. "Hi ya, Guy," he called. Then, pointing to the small bandage over my eye, he said: "Don't tell me you ran into a doorknob."

"So how about concentrating on putting balls in the basket and leave curiosity for the cats, or have you got nine lives you want to lose?" I said disagreebly.

"Well for cripe's sake! I only asked you a friggin' question," Treetop protested.

"And I gave you a friggin' answer," I shot back.

"Now ain't you smart though."

46

"Uh-huh," I said, "and I'm getting smarter by the day, which is exactly to my liking because the best things in life are got by being that way, and second best ain't my go. You cop?"

"Yeah, I really dig you the most when you talk like that," sneered Treetop, "especially behind that game last night. Why, don't you and Pretty Jackie know that the—"

"Oh, for Christ's sake," I cut in heatedly. "Don't tell me you're on the kick too!"

"What kick?" he demanded.

"That 'Pretty Jackie' kick," I told him. "Pretty Jackie! Don't make me puke!"

"Oh, but he *is* pretty," a girl's voice sighed from behind me.

I turned and looked at Millie Clay standing with her right hand pressed to her heart, making a sensual offering of the breast which bulged beneath her white shirt, the tail of which was tied about her waist to expose her bronze belly.

"Why, everytime I see Jackie my little old heart just pounds something awful. Butterflies begin to flutter down here." She put her left hand below her navel and with widespread fingers began to caress the area.

"On these occasions you speak of," I said haughtily, "can you remember what you ate earlier?"

"What has that got to do with it?" Millie asked.

"Oh, maybe nothing," I answered, "but that heart-pounding, butterfly stuff reminds me of the way I feel after eating sauerkraut—real gassy, you know."

Treetop, a yellow-complexioned boy named Dale, and a bug-eyed, thick-lipped girl named Helen all laughed.

Millie dropped her sexy pose and her eyes blazed at me angrily.

"You're just jealous of Jackie," she taunted. "Anybody that isn't blind can see it. That's why you low-rate him every chance you get. We all know you hate him because you have to work and he doesn't, and because he wears nice clothes and has money to take girls out and have a good time while you have to stay home and nurse a cripple——"

I reached out and grabbed for her wrist, wild with anger. Millie tried to duck behind Helen, but I caught her and yanked her to me, my eyes spitting sparks. She cringed, wild-eyed with fright.

"Listen, you lousy little bitch," I exploded, "I don't care what you think or say about me! But if you ever again mention my mother, I'll put a permanent lid on that slop jar you call a mouth! Understand?"

She opened her mouth wider to answer, but fright kept the words from coming, so she simply nodded her head. I threw an arm around her neck, pulled her head down and began to wipe the mascara from around her eyes with the tail of my shirt. She cried out and tried to wriggle free as I rubbed at her face. When I finally released her, she backed away and glared at me through tears of rage.

"Now you look civilized," I appraised.

"You beast! You bully! I hate you! I hate you!" She screamed and ran from the store.

"What the hell did you go and do that for," Dale demanded belligerently.

"Keep out of it, lame," Treetop warned, shoving him against the juke box.

"But she was going to fix me up as soon as it got dark. Now he's gone and run her away," Dale mourned, flopping into a booth. "Jesus crap! I've never seen it fail—everytime I get a lay on the line, something messes it up."

"Oh, for cryin' out loud," Treetop said. "Come on, Guy, I'll pop you to a cherry Coke."

We turned and walked toward the fountain, leaving Dale and Helen at the juke box.

At the fountain, Treetop rapped on the marble top with a

48

pop bottle as we sat down on the stools. "Hey! Give me some service before I get nervous! Hey, Marion!"

Marion Gale, the druggist's doll-faced, four-foot-ten, daughter, came toward us from a little room off behind the fountain. She was ninety pounds of curves and walked—completely unintentionally—as if the whole world were watching.

"All right, Mr. Treetop," she said sweetly, "and what would you like to have today?" She smoothed her dress about her hips with caressing palms as Treetop gazed at her and stroked his chin.

"Well, now, pretty thing," he started, "I think I'd like to have a little—"

"Anything behind this counter that moves is not for sale," Marion cut in, "with the exception of the laxative, which is probably what you need."

"Well, now why don't you just walk yourself around from behind that counter and we can settle that little problem, honey child," Treetop said.

"Don't you get tired of the same old routine?" I cut in impatiently. "Are you going to pop me to that cherry Coke or not?"

"Say, man, why are you so touchy today?" Treetop asked. "Give us two cherry Cokes, Marion."

"Coming up," she said.

"Look, man," Treetop said, turning to me, "getting back to what I was going to say before you and Millie tangled all over the place, and I might add that she was right about your being jealous, not only of Jackie but of anyone who tries to get near you or threatens to equal you in something. It's hard to find the right words, I guess you might call it self centered. But that's your business. If it kicks you off to go around warring with people, it's all right with Treetop. But when your war causes the team to lose, as it did last night, then as captain of the team I think it's time for me to put in my two cents worth. Don't you know that there are four other guys playing on our side with you?"

He paused for an answer, but I remained silent.

"Well, I'm here to remind you that there are," he went on. "It takes five men, all pulling together, to play a winning basketball game, pops. We can't have you trying to be a one-man team, playing the game your way, not even in an exhibition like last night. Guy, you've either got to cooperate or turn in your uniform."

I reached down and took the uniform out of my bag.

"Of course," he went on nervously, "we'd hate like hell to lose you. After all, you are the star when you pull with us. But damn it, Guy, you said that second best wasn't your go, and it so happens that it's not mine, either."

He picked up one of the Cokes that Marion had sat before us and drank deeply. Then he fumbled matches from his pocket, lit up a cigarette, and, after blowing out the flame, sat staring at the charred match.

"That was a damned long speech for a guy who usually never says more than ten words at a time," I told him slowly.

He kept staring at the burnt match as my anger mounted.

"Okay," I snapped, "you've delivered old man Brown's message, but all you did was bring the weakest stuff to the strongest people. So here's my message to him, to you and to all the rest of the bootlicking lames on 119th Street: All that 'Rah! Rah! Yea' team!' jazz leaves me cold. It fails to impress me because I know what the real lowdown is. You say I'm jealous of Jackie. Well, that's a goddamn lie and you know it. Sure, he's got nice clothes and stuff, just like Millie said. But they don't cover up his lack of guts. He hasn't got it; I have. You know it and he knows it. And I don't need sharp clothes to spotlight it. He pops you punks to a bottle of wine once a week and rides you around in his ol' man's Caddy and boom! That makes him an all-American boy, that and his

50

father's influence. Have you ever noticed how often you hear: 'your father, the bishop,' when Jackie is around? The clown pimps his old man's rep. Yeah! All-American boy, but not to me. He never won anything on his own or according to the rules. He fights dirty, plays dirty and when he wins, he wins dirty.

"You punks talk about me being jealous of him when you know damn well it's the other way around. I can beat him fair and square; anywhere, anytime, at anything. You talk about pulling with the team; when I went into that game last night those blond boys were kicking us around, 32–20, in the third quarter. After I got my eye, that basket began to look as big as a window. I couldn't miss. So what happens? Ol' man Brown lets me shoot us to a coasting lead and then snatches me out to cool off. Don't he know that a monkey's not in the swing unless his brow is wet? He sends in 'Pretty Jackie,' the bishop's son, to make with the star action on my lead, a lead I built up by sinking shots from every trick position on the court because those gray boys were playing us so damned tight we nearly had to ask their permission to breathe. But did ol' brown-nosing Brown let me play without that pressure after I took it off? I fight a losing team to a winning position and get benched. Great! Rah! Rah! Rah! Yea' team!

"You're gassing off about pulling with the team and right now you're breaking training by smoking. And before the game last night, Jackie was making out with Millie in the locker room, so full of wine he looked like a grape. I've been at practice every day, even when I should have been working. Where were you and Jackie on some of those days? Why wasn't I allowed a chance to show my stuff last night? Because I didn't have a bishop father in the audience? Now you just unwind your long ass from that stool and go tell ol' man Brown that I'm through creating thunder for some other clown to steal."

I tossed my uniform to Treetop.

"I'm through," I said, "so you also-rans have a clear field. Tell Brown to take his uniform and wipe the crap from his nose after he sticks it up the most reverend bishop's fanny!"

I thought of the day nearly three years ago when Patrolman Harris had dragged Jackie and me apart and of the oath taken in Dr. Bruce's office. A year after my release from the hospital found us warring as fiercely as before in sports. And, as always when we had fought or played by the rules, I'd continued to triumph over Jackie.

Yeah, I'll go on beating 'em, I told myself grimly, *'cause they play the games for flattery, for red lips and bouncing tits; for tight-fitting levi's and thighs and skirts and I play 'cause I have to.*

I had always played and ran and boxed because I had to, and now that my injured body had mended after the accident, it seemed to demand greater effort of me as a reward for not letting me down.

A month after going back to work at Hank's pool hall I had launched what I had hoped would be a career in sports. Beginning with a first in the 50-yard dash in the annual high school track and field meet, I had gone on to pile up wins in several types of events offered by the schools and the park district. My bedroom was decked with trophies and medals, but the thought of them left me as indifferent now as I had been when they were first presented to me. I had given Marion some of them and once, while returning from a meet, I had dropped two medals in her pocket. She had tried to give them back.

"Now, Guy, don't be foolish," she had said. "They're yours. You won them."

"You're the foolish one if you think I get a kick out of copping these," I answered.

"Well, what do you get a kick out of? The fact that you win? The cheers and—"

"I get my kicks from feeling my legs run, my toes kick and fists strike," I interrupted. "Every movement is a bang. Why, today in the 220 I felt like a resurrected, reshafted arrowhead, zooming with only one fear: the loss of thrust power, the return to earth to be buried in worries, monotony and hate—yes, and love."

"You really love sports, don't you Guy?" Marion had said.

"No," I answered. "But it's the only way I can be myself. Besides, I never was much with books, and since the accident, I'm worse. I'll never be able to build a bridge or write a book, but I can run and swim, and then I'm beyond the 'thou shalts' and 'thou shalt nots' that Poppa used to scream at me. I really hate to have an event end, even though I win, 'cause it's not the winning that counts, it's the—well, the feeling I used to get when I was a kid at Christmas, under the tree unwrapping packages, the excitement of tearing off the string and paper with hardly a thought of the present inside, just the frantic action. Like I said, the thrill of doing it, you understand? I always looked for more wrappings to tear off. I even wrapped them over, like now in sports, I'm always looking for another finishing line, another whistle or bell or starting gun. Do you see?"

I really wanted her to understand, but I knew that she didn't. I had expressed myself poorly—again.

"Uh-huh, here," she answered, putting her hand over her heart. "But not here," added, pointing to her head.

That was the problem; nobody understood. Nobody truly understood. And maybe the only time I really understood myself was when I was on top of The Hill—

There was complete silence in the drug store. Treetop let his eyes meet mine in the fountain mirror, where I had been staring ever since I started talking. His lips twitched as though he were going to say something, but he picked up his drink instead, took a sip, and then seemed to stare into the glass for words. Finally he cleared his throat and said:

"Look, baby, you got it all wrong."

"You still here?" I snarled, turning from the mirror to look at him. My hands fell to my belt. "The reason I asked is because if you're here one minute from now, I'm going to cut you down to midget size. Compared to you, I'm a small axe, but you know that I chop big!"

His eyes dropped to my belt buckle, then he slowly got up and walked toward the door.

"One more thing," I called.

He stopped.

"Tell those apes over in the jungle that they're barred from 111th Street, cop?"

"Yeah, I cop. Do you?" Treetop said.

"Yeah, it's war."

He walked out.

I stared back into the large mirror, a wild excitement spreading over me. Never since I had been leader of the Gaylords had I declared war on another gang. We had fought only when attacked, and confined our rivalries mostly to sports. Although the "A.C." had long been dropped from the name of the club, I never let the guys forget that athletics was the reason for our banding together. But all that was over now. My words to Treetop had erased the "A.C." for good. No longer a club, we were now *really* a gang; a gang which was going to do battle, and I was its leader: a warlord. I sat still, enjoying the strange feeling of power.

"Guy," Marion called, and the feeling vanished.

I took my Coke over to the booth where she sat before a pile of textbooks.

"You ought to be ashamed of yourself," she reprimanded, "starting a gang war with Treetop. I know you've got growing pains but—"

"Yeah, I'm growing up, a mile a minute," I said, "and I'm getting sick of this old "hooray-for-me, to-hell-with-you" attitude, sick of being the one sent to hell. That beanpole fat-

54

mouthing to me about trying to star. I don't think about that when I'm playing. I just play, play hard. If that makes me a star, what am I supposed to do, cramp my style?"

"What have you done, developed a super-man complex?" Marion asked. "Oh, why do men always have to go around fighting things? First you against the team, now a gang war. Why is it, Guy? Why?"

"I guess we're funny that way," I answered.

"Well, fighting isn't my idea of being funny. Wars and killing don't impress me as comedy. Isn't there enough of it around here already without adding more? You could get into trouble, hurt or killed. Stick to sports, Guy. Pull with the team. You're a good athlete."

She placed a hand on my wrist. "Besides, what will your mother think about—

"She's not going to think anything about what I do in the streets because she's not going to know about it. Understand? I don't want you telling her about anything I do out here, ever!" I imprisoned her hand in mine, and for a moment we just looked at each other.

"What's wrong, Guy?" Marion pleaded. "You're changing on me."

I shrugged.

"Can't you tell me?" she asked.

I didn't answer.

"I waited nearly two hours after the game was over for you to walk me home. Where were you?"

"I went for a walk, Muffet," I said. "I was plenty hot under the collar so I took a long walk to cool off. Sorry I stood you up, but after I started walking I discovered I had a whole lot of thinking to do. Lucky there was no school today, 'cause I didn't go home 'til one-thirty this morning."

"You must have had an awful lot of thinking to do if it kept you out that late," Marion said. "I hope you were able to solve all your problems."

"Yeah. I'm finished with sports. That's one of the things I've been giving so much thought."

"Oh, no! You can't be! Why? What about the scholarship? Our plans? Why are you tossing everything away?"

I didn't answer.

"I'll bet it's because Coach Brown pulled you in the game last night. He was right, you know. And when he told you to go back in, you should have gone. When you didn't you helped lose the game."

I leaned toward her. "Look, Muffet," I said. "If anyone lost that game, it was Jackie; drunken, clowning Jackie!"

"All I know is that you let the team down when they needed you," Marion said, "all because of this rivalry between you and Pretty Jackie—"

I smashed my glass on the table and felt the sharp fragments cut my hand.

"Pretty! Pretty! Pretty!" I shouted. "Everywhere I turn it's 'Pretty Jackie this' and 'Pretty Jackie that.' Even my own girl thinks that damn punk's pretty. Well, let me tell you something: I'm fed up with being part of the glorifying of your pretty pampered punk! I'm tired of playing to rules that limit me to being a springboard. I didn't let the team down, Miss Know-It-All, the damn team let me down. I'm always being let down. Everything in this goddamn world lets me down. And now my own girl lets me down and that's the end."

I slammed my bleeding fist down on the table.

"You talk about a scholarship," I went on. "Well, Mr. Watts, the locker room man, told me before the game that there were two pro basketball scouts in the house. Old man Brown must have known it, but did he tell me? No, but I bet he told Jackie. Bishop Lindy was in the house too. Why, hell, I don't have to be a fourth grade student to figure what went down. For the first time I really wanted to impress somebody and Coach spiked my chances. Well, not anymore. From now on I'm going to play the game like everybody else, without any regard for the rules. I'm sick of being cramped. As for your 'Pretty Jackie,' when my girl sides with my enemy then the situation looks pretty messy to me. So, Miss Marion, you can really begin to sing praises to that phony's beauty now, because we're through. Quits; done; kaput. Dig?"

Snatching up my bag, I raced out the door.

Chapter 8

As I ran the two blocks between Gale's Drug Store and the pool hall, the street lights began to flicker on. Stepping into the open door of the poolroom, I flipped on the light switch by the door. The large neon sign which hung outside shimmered and blinked into a red glare. I looked to see if all the letters were lighted up. It read "Hank's Recreation Room" and in small letters at the bottom: "Ladies Invited." Not only were ladies invited, they were welcomed with open-armed enthusiasm which wasn't limited to making use of the eight highly-polished pool tables lined in two rows at the back of the first floor, but included the five bedrooms on the second floor also. Thinking of these upstairs rooms, I headed for the closet next to the shoe shine stand that stood along the west wall. Opening the door, I got out the broom, pail and mop and headed for the upstairs entrance.

"Hey, kid, what the hell happened to you?"

Looking over to the two men who stood leaning against the display case, I met Hank's eye. He gave the deck of cards which he held in his dark hands a lightning shuffle and set them down on the counter. The short, dapperly-dressed, light-skinned man across from him cut the deck. Hank dealt off five cards swiftly without taking his one eye off me.

"Come here a minute," he said.

I set the cleaning equipment down. He took a card from the deck and spread his hand. The short man grunted and pushed a five dollar bill over to Hank.

"What's the bandage over your eye?" Hank asked.

"Had a little accident," I replied.

"Fight, huh?"

I didn't answer.

"Hell, it doesn't matter, only you had better get Shelley to fix up that hand before you bleed to death." He nodded to my left hand.

It was dripping blood. I looked at the tiny scarlet pool on the floor in surprise, then remembered the glass I had smashed. I marveled anew at how action had a way of lifting me above pain and worry. Taking a handkerchief from my pocket, I wrapped it about my hand. Hank spread his cards again.

"Of all the friggin' luck," the short man said despairingly.

"All in knowing how, Smitty. You can only take down what your hand calls for," Hank stated nonchalantly, gathering the cards.

"You lucky bastard," Smitty said hotly.

"The word is, some of us are lucky at cards and others at love. I should have told you, Smitty, that my love life ain't worth a damn these days." Hank was the type of guy women referred to as being tall, dark and handsome. The white patch covering his left eye made his appearance even more striking. Hank was a fair gambler, a pimp and a dope peddler. Rumor had it that he had killed two men in gambling disputes. I'd more than once seen him slap Velma and Ofelia, the two prostitutes who worked for his old lady, Shelley, into unconsciousness because of their failure to hustle up a certain amount of trade.

I had been working for Hank for a year as bootblack and odd job man. He paid me thirty-five dollars a week for work which actually was worth only ten. He knew that I was being overpaid, and also that I was ashamed of the fact. He spared me the embarrassment of accepting unearned pay from his hand by leaving the money on the dresser of his bedroom, which I cleaned every Friday.

"I had better get going on those rooms if I'm going to get

them done before the game starts," I said, picking up the cleaning equipment.

"Tell Shelley to make the girls clean up their own rooms. You just do the game room and my room. There's a box on the dresser for you."

Upstairs, I set the equipment down in the middle of a long hall running the length of the building. Going to the big, comfortable furnished front room, I went over the combination radio, record player and television and picked out a record from his large collection and placed it on the turntable. The sultry voice of "The Lady" filled the room.

"*. . . Them that's got shall get, them that's not, shall lose. So the Bible said and it still is true. Momma may have, Poppa may have, but God bless the child that's got his own . . .*"

"Sing 'Lady,'" I whispered.

"Guy? That you?"

I turned at the sound of Shelley's voice. I hadn't seen her lying on the couch when I came in.

"Yes, Shelley," I said, walking over to the couch. Taking the cloth from my hand, I looked at the cut palm. "Can you fix this for me, Shelley? Hank says to have Ofelia and Velma clean their own rooms. I'm to do only his and the game room."

Shelley sat up, slipping her feet into a pair of men's house shoes. She stood up and stretched.

"Oh, ho," she yawned, looking at the expensive man's watch on her arm. "I guess it's time for my two lazy broads to be getting up. Another night's work to begin. Oh, well, the way of the transgressor is hard." She strutted over to the combination with long masculine strides.

"Yeah, I guess you're right," I said following her. She stood with hands clasped behind her, legs spread wide apart. Her head was tilted to one side in a listening attitude.

"*. . . Money you've got lots of friends hanging around your door. But when it's gone, and spending ends, they won't come back no more . . .*"

Reaching into the pocket of the satin man's bathrobe, Shelley took out a gold cigarette case, withdrew a cigarette and lit up. Expelling smoke toward the ceiling, she asked: "Why do you play this one singer all the time?"

"Because she sings of truth and reality," I explained.

"She does at that," Shelley said in a reflective tone. "Which is why I hate to hear it. There was a time when I too used to love the real and the truth. But not anymore. There's too much pain in them. Now, all that I want out of life is to get real high and make love. That's the only pleasure I can see in truth."

Dropping the cigarette into the ash tray, she left the room. Shelley was a "jasper."

"*. . . Rich relations give crusts of bread and such; you can help yourself, but don't take too much . . .*"

When the last soft beat of the rhythm died away, I turned off the record player and headed for the bathroom at the end of the hall. As I passed one of the bedrooms, I saw Shelley sitting on the edge of the bed. Ofelia was reclining with only a sheer nightgown covering her shapely yellow body. She was protesting in a voice heavy with sleep:

"Oh, but Shelley, I'm so tired. Can't I lay here just a little longer, please, momma-dad?"

Shelley's hand was cupping the bulge of Ofelia's full, round breast with gently plying fingers. Bending her head, Shelley pressed her lips to Ofelia's in a long kiss. Ofelia removed Shelley's hand from her breast and placed it on the lower part of her body, where she coached it into short, stroking caresses. There was a sound of moaning as I continued on to the bathroom.

There, I ran water over my hands in the face bowl, I took gauze, tape, cotton and alcohol from the medicine cabinet and, after cleaning the cut, attempted to bandage it.

"Here let me do that for you, Guy."

"Hi! Velma!" I greeted the dark-skinned girl who had entered the bathroom. "I didn't know that you were up."

"I've been up all day and all night. I just can't seem to be able to sleep although I'm just about dead on my feet."

I noted the smoothness of her face as she leaned to bandage the hand. Velma was a whore who never wore lipstick or other facial cosmetics. She was tall, willowy and built like a brick outhouse. Her sexy, man-attracting walk was a pleasure to see.

"What is a stallion?" she asked, surveying her racy body in the glass.

"It's a horse, why?"

"No, no, I don't mean that kind. I mean, when a guy calls a girl a stallion, what does he mean?"

"Oh, that stallion. It's a compliment really. When a woman is stacked up, I mean, built like, well say like you, then the guys call them stallions, especially if they're tall."

Cupping her firm breast in her hands, she raised upon her toes and cocked her head in self-appraisal. "Stallion, stallion, hmmmm. You know I think I like that description. There is a close similarity in the work I do and that which a stallion does, isn't there?"

I walked away without replying.

"Velma is a stallion, a stallion, a stallion. Riding her is so much fun . . . ," she sang over the sound of running water.

I retrieved the cleaning tools and entered the large back room used for gambling. I cleaned up the previous night's litter, left by thirty or more people who thought they had had a winning hand. They hadn't.

In Hank's bedroom I repeated the process of sweeping, mopping, dusting and waxing. Then, stepping over to the large dresser, I picked up a five and three ten-dollar bills. Next to the money was a shoe box. Opening it, I removed the tissue paper from around an expensive pair of track shoes. The words, "Alpha and Omega" were stamped in gold letters on the outside of each shoe. Mom had given me the motto in a wild burst of sentimentality when I'd participated in my first sports event after the accident. As I fingered the soft leather of the shoes, a card fell from them. I picked it up. Shelley's scrawled writing met my eyes. "Happy Graduation. Run a good race from beginning to end—Shelley, Velma, Ofelia and Hank."

I swallowed the lump which had lodged in my throat as I stared at the name of a "jasper," two whores and an all-around bad man.

Replacing the card and shoes, I tucked them beneath my arm and headed for the door. The sight of my bandaged hand reaching for the knob made me stop, reminded me of my decision of last night. Anytime somebody gave you an expensive pair of track shoes, they meant them to be used for serious running. I returned the box to the dresser and left the room.

Passing the door of the front room, I saw Velma, Shelley and Ofelia sitting on the couch.

". . . *You walked by and made my old world new. You walked by and all my dreams came true. Gone were all the tears I used to know . . ."* sang a new male singer.

"Oh, momma-dad, isn't that pretty?" Ofelia asked.

"No," Shelley said as I went down the stairs.

Hank met me middle way down. He was counting a large roll of bills. A newspaper was under his arm.

"Watch it." He stepped close to the wall. "Come on past."

I reached the bottom of the stairs.

"Hey, kid, didn't you forget something?"

"What?" I asked, knowing that his reference was to the shoes.

"Why, your present on the dresser. Didn't you see it?"

"Yeah, but I couldn't take it," I replied, wishing that I didn't have to tell him why.

"Oh, you had too much junk to carry, huh? Wait, I'll toss them down to you." He turned to the door.

"I can't take them Hank. I'm not gonna run anymore."

"What?" He wheeled about to stare down at me in surprise.

"What kinda damn fool talk is that, what the hell ya mean you're not gonna run anymore?" he demanded, his forehead wrinkled angrily.

"Wait a minute, Hank," I said, resenting both his tone and having to explain to him. "All I said was that I wasn't gonna run anymore, I'm through with sports. Why all the furnace action?"

He tramped down the stairs, taking them two at a time and came to a clattering halt amid the bucket and wringer I'd set down. The hard glint of anger in his eyes surprised me.

"Listen, kid, you ain't quittin' nothin' until after next month's meet. Get me?" he shouted hotly.

I stepped back from him, my heels struck the wall.

"Hey, what the hell goes on here?" I said, matching his tone. "Who do ya think you're shouting at and telling what to do? You ain't my friggin' daddy you know, and what I do outside of this building is my business, cop?"

He grabbed me by the shirt front.

"Now don't you go getting smart with me kid, or I'll smack ya teeth out. I've been damned good to you and I'll continue to be as long as you don't give me no hard time. I don't know where you got this stupid idea about quittin' sports, and I don't care 'cause you're gonna drop it right now. Do ya hear? Right the goddamned now! After the meet, you can pick it up again, but right now you'll run, and you'll run like hell, ya understand? You'll run like hell, 'cause if ya don't, I'm breaking your back. You ain't leaving Hank Johnson in no lurch!"

His grip on my shirt tightened, the grinding teeth and blazing eye filled me with fear.

"Hank, what in God's name are you talking about? Why I never left you in no lurch. I've always tried to do my work well and all. What are you talking about?" I was completely shaken up. Chills of fear shook my body.

Finally he loosened his grip on me and went to sit on the

64

stairs. Removing a cigar from his vest pocket, he bit off the end and lit up. "Go put your tools up and come back here," he said, staring at the glowing tip.

I did as I was told, snatching my bag from the shine stand as I returned. Hank was sitting as I had left him, only the shoe box was on the step beside him.

"Shut the door and come here," he commanded.

I shut the door and went to him.

"Read this."

I took the newspaper he held out to me and read the indicated column.

"Police are investigating an assault by three unidentified men upon Allan Brown, an athletic instructor who was found beaten unconscious in an alley near his W. 112th Street residence last night.

"Although Brown had been carrying a considerable amount of money, none was taken."

Hurriedly I scanned the rest of the story and handed it back to Hank.

"I still don't get it," I told Hank. "Do you think I had something to do with beating up old man Brown? Look, Hank, I hated that old fart, but cracking gray heads ain't my speed, especially with two other guys. I was nowhere near—"

"I'm not trying to pin that rap on you," Hank said. "I know what happened."

"Well, why don't you hip the man then, if you're so concerned?"

"Because I had the job done," he said matter-of-factly.

I stared at him in astonishment, realizing the ominous meaning of his casually spoken words.

"But why have old man Brown smashed up?" I asked incredulously.

"Because he left me and my people in the lurch with his straight coaching tactics last night. Look kid, me and my people had about five grand tied up in that little exhibition last night. Five grand which said you kids was gonna win despite the fact that those blond boys were an eight-point favorite. The game was in the bag until that stupid ass snatched you out. Do you know what that loss cost us?"

"No."

"Well, I'll tell you; roughly about eight grand, eight big iron men all shot to hell and gone, 'cause an old dingy bastard wanted to impress a mother-feeling bishop. Mister, nobody is gonna mess me out of that much money and get away with it." He ground the cigar viciously beneath his heel.

"Buddy!" I said wonderingly, "I didn't know all of that was going on. Ha! Just think, I was salty because I wasn't permitted to impress a couple of scouts."

"Walt told you about that didn't he, about the scouts, I mean?"

I looked at the smug smile on his face. "Yeah, just before the game, why?"

"Nothing, only you can stop worrying about the scouts. There weren't any." He sighed, "I wish that I could get rid of my worries as easy as that."

"What do you mean there weren't any scouts?" Flames of anger began to heat my brow.

"Just that, there weren't any there. I had Walt and a few more of the boys plant that rumor just before the game."

"But I played my goddamn heart out because of that!" I shouted, completely enraged. "Why of all the dirty, rotten, filthy tricks! Why you one-eyed son-of-a-bitch, if I had twenty pounds I'd bounce you—"

His fist exploded multi-colored lights before my eyes and rammed a hot brand of pain into my brain, slamming me flat against the wall. His knee sank into my stomach. I flopped up in a ball waiting the contemptuous, rib-breaking impact of stamping heels, which usually followed as a matter of course when a guy lost his feet. But they didn't come.

"Get up!" Hank hissed.

66

I staggered to my feet in obedience to the soft-spoken command. Hank was on the steps as before.

"Next time wait until you get those pounds before you start fat-mouthing. Now you listen to me. I planted that tale about the scouts because I knew that you kids would play your goddamned hearts out, especially you, with your scholarship dreams. That's the kind of playing I wanted and that's the kind of running I want out of you in that meet next month. You say it's low and dirty? How? Because I was smart enough to turn your greed, your ambition, to an advantage? Hell, I didn't try to corrupt you by bribes and the likes did I? So what's your beef?"

I remained silent, sagging against the wall.

"If there were scouts in that crowd their eyes wouldn't have been on black skin anyway, not unless there was a sensational player on your team. You're good, but you ain't no whiz, so don't flatter yourself. Don't you know that you black boys would merely be mirrors to reflect those grays? I knew that you were no book worm, but I thought you had copped a few of the facts of life. I see that you haven't. If you had, then you'd realize that this is the blond people's world. A darky can't cop nothing but caskets and tombstones. And you gotta be a dead nigger t' get that. That's your winning hand, kid, money! You and your scouts! Ha! So scouts were there, let's say. So you impress two or three of them. So goddamnit what? Your name goes in a little black book, right on top, along with a little check which will indicate that you're black. There's always a little check for black. They write it in many colors, but it always means the same: black, nigger, coon, second best. In cases of extreme emergency, call. Okay, so we get you top billing in the black book. Bear in mind tho', that a year has gotta pass before they can refer to the page you're on. In that year a couple of hundred more names get jotted down in that book. Blond names, names with no checks behind them. So now what? So now we start from the bottom

67

of the page and work up. You get what I mean? Don't be a sap, kid. You've got a crippled mother. Constant treatment takes bread, money. Why not make life pay as you play it? It's too short to depend upon contenting yourself with second best futurity. There's a lot of good stuff in you. I like the way you shouldered the responsibilities of your mother's care, and I think I showed some of that admiration during the time you've worked for me. And I'll continue to do so as long as you program with me. Now you're going to run next week, right?"

I'd finally got my breathing under control. "That was a real pretty speech, Hank, I didn't know that you were a race man," I said with as much sarcasm as I could muster.

"I ain't, kid, naw, I'm not that humble, tho' I am able to recognize the fact that this is the white boss' plantation, the whole goddamned hunk of dirt called the world. I can't help from recognizing it, despite the equality crap which the politicians fling around at election time, and the big headline reminders in the newspaper once a year, informing the white people to love their black brothers for a week. Not ten blocks from here is a hospital that wouldn't admit a colored person if he was dying. And not five blocks from here is a new skating rink that won't allow you kids in for love nor money. Hell, if—"

"Oh, can that crap, you're breaking my heart," I cut in.

"I'm gonna break your back if you ain't in that meet next month," he threatened.

"Well start breaking, 'cause I promised myself last night that I wasn't going to let myself be used by nobody no more. Like you say, I ain't so smart, but from what you say you've been using me."

I had set my body in muscle sagging readiness for his lunge. He leaped. I pistoned a one-two in his direction. He caught both punches expertly on his forearms. I side-stepped swiftly but my foot struck my bag. Hank's large hand clamped in a vice hold on my neck.

"You're not only gonna run, you're gonna win, understand?"

Frig you! Frig you! Frig you! My brain shouted as my tongue began to slowly exit from my mouth.

"Understand?"

I nodded. The vice released me. I sprawled to the floor.

"Before you leave, pick up them damn shoes, ya hear?"

I nodded.

The fire in my throat began to cool. I staggered to my feet. Picking up the shoes and the bag, I lurched through the private entrance into the warm night. I drank the air in gulps as I leaned against the building. A car backfired. I ran.

I'm a bullet, a burning hot bullet aimed at Hank's heart.

Within a yard of Gale's Drug Store, I crossed to the opposite side of the street, to avoid having Marion see me. She was sitting on a high stool behind the counter, with a book in her lap. She stared out the window, her elbows on her knees and her fist on her cheek.

Look, Marion, I'm a bullet, I'm a bullet. Bang! Bang! Bang! Hank, you're dead!

I ran, terrified with fear and anger, through the night.

Chapter 9

When I reached our house, I let myself in the back door and went straight to my room and kicked off my shoes. Then I stripped off my dirty T-shirt, rolled my socks into it, and tossed them on the floor of my closet, and walked out.

At the door of the living room, I stopped. Except for the glare from the television, the room was in darkness.

"Clucky?" came the soft voice of my mother. She was lying on the couch with her back propped against three pillows.

"Hello, Mom," I greeted, walking over to kneel by the couch. She reached out and cupped my face between her small hands and kissed me on the nose.

"You know, for a moment, I thought you were your father, standing there in the doorway."

I wrenched at being compared to the man I hated with all my heart.

"You've grown so very tall until I'm always surprised at having to look up to you instead of down," she sighed and lay back on the pillows. "I wish your father could see you, for you are so very much like him. Wide shoulders and small hips."

Fighting down the hate which every mention of my father's name was causing to boil up in me, I attempted to distract her thoughts from him.

"Why, I do believe that you are sorry I'm not a crawling baby anymore," I teased, turning my head to nibble at the small hand which had remained on my bare shoulders, toying with the earring in my ear.

"Nooo, I'm not sorry," she said reflectively. "Because no matter how tall you get or how old you become, you will always be my baby. I think that is one of the main reasons why women have babies so that they can watch them grow up, I mean, grow from little boy and girl babies into big men and women. But that's the fun of being a mother. It's almost like playing house all your life. But, of course you wouldn't know what I'm talking about. That's what I mean, you need your father here to give you a man's explanation of these things."

Oh, God, don't let her mention him again, I prayed inwardly.

Sighing deeply, she added, "If your father were here then it would be exactly like playing house. You know, Guy, your voice is going to be as deep as your father's. When your father used to sing to me in that deep bass voice of his, I would go all soft inside."

"I can just bet," I said in a dry tone which she missed.

"Guy, how is Marion? Are you going to take her to the prom?"

"She's okay," I replied, flexing my cut hand. "I don't know if I'm going to the prom. I'm finding it hard now to get along with the crowd."

"But you must go, baby. There is so little good, clean, wholesome recreation for you kids around here to enjoy, and dancing is so much fun, Guy, especially at proms. You've got to go."

Turning her face from me, she sighed: "When I was your age I simply adored dancing. Your father danced so divinely. Yes, your father was marvelous."

I cringed and begged her inwardly: *Oh, please don't mention him again, Mom, he's gone. Can't you see me, I'm here with you. Can't you feel my warmth?*

Plucking at a spot on my blue jeans, she inquired: "Do kids still give those turnabout dances?"

"Uh-huh," I said.

"Well, Marion had better look out or she might lose her future husband. You're so much like your daddy, the girls would no doubt mob you, too."

Denial roared through every part of my being, screaming the lie to the description. *I'm not like him, I'm not!* I inwardly denied, remembering a shapely jezebel named Zola.

"Clucky, am I a burden, I mean my condition and all—?"

"Mom, why don't you ask me if my heart is burdensome?"

"Oh, Guy, you do speak so nicely. No wonder Marion loves you so. You must never give her any cause to regret that love. 'Let the fountain be blessed and rejoice with the wife of thy youth.' That's the way I want you and her to be. You have to anyway, for as your father says, a promise made is a debt unpaid."

"Oooh," I groaned.

"How come you go around in those old jeans all of the time?" she reproached mildly. "You're a big boy now, with a steady girl. I'm sure Marion would prefer seeing you in a suit or sports clothes sometimes. I know I would. When your father and I were courting, he was the sharpest dresser in our town. Why, he wouldn't be seen dead in overalls and the likes on Saturday nights. This is Saturday, isn't it?"

An anger more intense than I had ever experienced before prevented me from answering her. I clenched my hands in a struggle to keep from trembling with the insane hate that strained out of me. *Forget him! Forget him!* My heart begged her with every beat.

"Yes, it is Saturday night and a very nice night out," she continued in a faraway voice. Her eyes held deep longing. "Don't you wish that he were here to take us for a nice drive? I do. You know, Guy, your father—"

Before she could finish, I was up on my feet. Hot hate bubbled from every pore of my skin. Rage made me insensible to the small gasp she uttered.

72

"Your father! Your father!" I shouted wildly. "That's all I've heard since I stepped in here. That's all I've heard since I dropped from you. I've heard it and endured it until I'm sick! Sick! Sick! 'Your father this,' 'your father that'— father, father, father! What father are you talking about? That grinning gigolo who drove us racing through the snow storm at ninety-five miles an hour—who crashed us into a steel viaduct and smashed you into the cripple that you are now? Is that the man you're sitting there mooning about?— huh? Is that the kind of father you're so fond of referring to, flinging in my teeth? That rotten, whore-hopping baboon who ran off with that nymph, Zola, while you and I laid half dead in the hospital where he put us? Is that who you're sighing to feel all over you? Is that who you're talking about? That chippie-chaser! That mad hunk of ebony! Do I wish that he was here? Ha! Wish! Yea, merciful God, how I wish it! Not only do I wish it, I've prayed minutely for it—for him to be here flat on his spineless back, so I could kick his filthy guts out and feed them to the mongrels in the alley! Don't ever compare me to that chunk of dung again, 'cause before I would permit myself to be as low as he, I'd curse God and blow out my brains. So now you know what I think about my father. I hate his bloody guts and you'd be far better off doing like-wise. Look at what he's done to you! Look! Look! My God, Mom, the monster has crippled you for life, and where is he? Does he care how you get in or out of bed at night? Does he care that day after day you sit there with lifeless legs that he has murdered and sigh flames over this?"

I snatched the large photograph from beneath her pillows and continued in a voice wrought with hate of long suppression. "You didn't think I knew you had this, did you?" I hissed, completely carried away in the rage. I shook the glass-framed photo in her face. "You don't think that I know you sit here day in and day out, eating your heart out and bestowing love upon the image of a person who neither God

73

nor Satan would dare to love. You should smash this, Mom! Smash it like he did—you—like this!"

Raising the picture above my head with both hands I prepared to smash it against the back of her wheel chair, "And may God damn him to hell and—"

"Oh stop it!" Mom screamed. She had somehow managed to pull herself upon her knees. " 'Whosoever curseth his father his lamp shall be put out in obscure darkness.' Stop it! Stop it! Give me—"

I stood transfixed as she tumbled onto the floor, tearing the picture from my hands as she fell. Her head struck the protruding foot rest of the chair. The sound of it instantly erased my anger, replacing it with cold fear. I dropped to my knees and raised her still head to my lap. I tried to wipe away the blood on her face with a portion of her gown, but more welled up from the gash on her forehead. Panic seized my heart with icy fingers. *Oh, God; Oh, God!*

"Mom," I whispered, "Mom, don't die, please! Please! Please!" I kept repeating it as I lifted her into my arms and staggered to the phone. Sitting on the floor, I snatched the phone from the stand. It thudded to the floor. I pulled it to my side and began dialing Dr. Bruce's office. The receiver admitted the faint ringing noise on the other end. "Be there, be there, please, Dr. Bruce," I whispered fervently. Sweat was popping out all over my head, but I felt frozen. After a minute's ringing I knew that the phone would not be answered. Nurse Ann never permitted it to ring over four times.

I dialed again with clawing fingers, then waited. After an eternity a familiar voice said sleepily, "Hello, this is Gales—"

"Marion, Marion, thank God—come quickly—I've killed my mother," I sobbed.

"Guy—Guy—what are you saying? What happened? Where are you?" Marion wanted to know.

"I'm at home—please come over as soon as you can—help

me, Marion, I think she's dying. I've got to get her to a hospital."

"I'll be right there, Guy. You just stay put, I'll be right there," the voice faded away.

I remained on the floor with Mom in my arms. As I waited, I tried to stop the bleeding but couldn't. Finally, automobile tires scattered the gravel on the driveway. Then Marion was beside me, feeling for Mom's pulse. "We've got to get her to a hospital quickly," she said.

I struggled to my feet with Mom in my arms. Marion opened the front door and I hurried toward the car.

"Come on, Marion let's hurry!" I said.

"You'd better get on some clothes," she said.

"To hell with clothes!" I shouted, getting in the back seat of the car. Marion ran from the house carrying something in a blanket. She tossed it on the seat beside me and slid beneath the wheel. "I locked the house up," she said, backing the car out of the driveway and accelerating it forward with screaming tires.

Turning south on Throop Street, she drove to 111th Street and turned east. As the street lights flickered on Mom's still face, my fears increased. "Go faster, Marion, we've got to hurry!" I said, raising my head. As I did, the black and white sign caught my eye: "Quiet Hospital Zone." As we neared a wide half-moon driveway, I shouted, "Hold it—turn here, Muffet!" Marion eased the car into the driveway. Looking over her shoulder, she said, "But Guy, this—"

"Watch where you're going!" I cautioned as we neared the brown brick building. Over the door of the receiving room was a sign that read "Moreland Hospital." As soon as the car stopped, I jumped out, gathered Mom in my arms and hurried into the sparkling receiving room. Going to the man sitting at the desk writing, "Excuse me, Mister," I said, "my mother here is real sick. She needs help quick."

"What-what?" the man said quizzically.

75

"My mother here—she's crippled, paralyzed, and she's had a nasty fall. She's hardly breathing," I repeated. The man moved from behind the desk. Placing an arm around my shoulders, he pressed me with gentle firmness toward Marion, who stood quietly in the doorway.

"Sorry, fellah," he said. "Sorry, but we can't take your mother in unless a staff doctor orders it."

"Where is one of the staff doctors? Get one down here, will you? My Mom's badly hurt!"

"Look, fellah, there's no staff doctor, or any kind of doctor for that matter, here right now."

"Well, who is here?" I asked, leaning against the pressure on my shoulder. "There must be someone in charge—"

"I'm in charge of this department, if that's what you mean," he said. Removing the thick glasses, he held them up to the light and began to polish them with a large white handkerchief. I looked into his watery eyes.

"Well, if you're in charge, will you please examine my Mom?" I pleaded.

He replaced the glasses carefully. "Sorry, fellah, ah—as you may have noticed when you came in, I'm pretty busy filling out some important papers right—"

"But man, Mom may be dying. For Christ's sake, if you're a doctor do something; if you aren't call one. There must be one around a hospital as big as this!" I shouted in fear and anger over the man's casualness.

He looked into Mom's face, then turned to me. "Why don't you try one of the colored hospitals?"

"What?" I asked perplexed. The man cleared his throat, "I said why don't you—"

"Come on, Guy," Marion cut in, "We are wasting valuable time. They won't admit us here." The words were like a blow in the stomach.

I stumbled to the car as Hank's voice came back to haunt me.

Why, there's a hospital not ten blocks from here that wouldn't admit a colored person if he was dying—

Marion had arranged a pillow in the back seat. I laid Mom upon it and covered her with the blanket. Marion was behind the wheel. As I started to slam the door, the man came hurrying out of the hospital.

"Hey, there!" he called, "Wait a minute!"

I got out of the car, my heart racing with renewed hope. *Hank, you're wrong,* I thought.

"Where is she?" the man asked, peering near-sightedly into the car. "I'll fix that cut on her head."

I stared at the band aid he held.

Hate again flooded my mind and body in flaming waves. He stooped to enter the car.

"Put a finger on my mother, you bastard, you, and I'll drink your filthy heart's blood," I vowed hoarsely.

"Huh—what?" he said, stepping back from the car. "Oh, well, that's all right with me, fellah, if that's how you want—"

I struck him, putting all the hate I felt into the blow. He staggered backwards, then crashed to the pavement.

I stood staring down at him. *Naw, kid, I'm not that humble—* Hank had said.

I leaped into the car. Marion gunned it down the driveway and into the busy thoroughfare. We traveled fast on 111th Street to South Park. Turning north, we drove a few blocks in silence, Then:

"Guy?"

"Yeah."

"He—he had on glasses and you hit him."

"Uh-huh, with all my might, and I hope that he will have to make out those important reports in Braille from now on," I said, slipping into the chukka boots and T-shirt she had brought to the car in the blanket.

Bending to Mom's ear, I whispered: "Mom? Mom? Oh, Mom, please say something. I'm sorry, baby, I didn't know what I was doing, what I was saying. I'm sorry. I didn't mean it, Mom—I didn't mean it. You know I wouldn't try to hurt you, Mom. I love you. I was trying to hurt him, not you. Him! Him!"

Her face held the look of death. My fear increased. "Say something, please, Mom—say—"

"Stop it, Guy! Stop it!" Marion yelled. "She'll be all right, she'll be all right."

"But, Marion, she's—she's so still—she's lying so still. Oh, my God, have mercy—I've killed my mother!"

Chapter **10**

Provident Hospital, white-cloaked angel of mercy to Chicago's black South Side; where the Hippocratic Oath is not predicated upon the color of a man's skin.

Muffet turned into the emergency entrance and I was out of the door almost before the car came to a halt. Gathering Mom's still figure in my arms, I carried her into the emergency waiting room . . . Muffet at my heels. Almost immediately two interns had taken her from me and, placing her on a stretcher, had wheeled her into one of the examining rooms. I attempted to follow, but the large, dark, and quiet young doctor, shooed me away as he pulled the white curtain in the cubicle where they had placed Mom, assuring me all the while, "She's in good hands."

I went back to the nurse at the desk where Marion stood waiting. "Do you have a family physician?" she asked.

"Yes, Dr. Jack Bruce, but he's not in. I tried to get him before we left home," I replied, my heart cold with fear.

"Dr. Bruce is a staff physician so he'll routinely check with us before too long. Why don't you and your sister go into the waiting room? We'll let you know when the doctor finishes his examination."

Neither Muffet nor I bothered to correct the nurse's assumption that she was my sister.

We walked into the tiny waiting room off the main lobby of the hospital. A man who had smoked countless cigarettes, as evidenced by those he had ground out on the floor, stared out the window into the dark night. Two ancient women sat wordlessly on one of the leather couches lining the wall. Marion and I went over and sat on the other.

"What time is it?" I asked.

"12:45" Muffet replied as the fairer of the two interns looked in the waiting room.

"Oh, there you are. Dr. Bruce just called in. We told him of your mother's illness and he is on his way. You might as well relax. You may have a little wait on your hands."

Hours passed.

I sprang up at the sound of footsteps in the corridor outside the door. It was Dr. Bruce, accompanied by another physician.

"How is she, Dr. Bruce, how is she?" The question leaped from my throat.

"She's resting comfortably at the moment," he said quickly. "Guy, precisely what happened?"

A sick lump came into my throat and my voice turned to a hoarse whisper as I tried to explain about my rage at Mom's constant chattering about my father. My explanation sounded weak, too weak. How could I try to tell them about all the other things that had happened? About the basketball game, Jackie, my arguments with Treetop and Marion, the fight with Hank. Weren't these all part of it? I didn't just blow my top at my mother.

But somehow I couldn't get all the words together, all the thoughts. I just told Dr. Bruce of my anger and Mom's fall.

"That explains it all, then," Dr. Bruce said when I had finished. "I'll give it to you straight, young man. That cut on your mother's forehead is no more than a flesh wound. She lost a little blood, which isn't good for a woman in her condition, but it isn't anything serious. The reason she fell, however, is that she suffered a stroke, which is serious. And, I'm afraid, sir, you will have to accept the blame for that."

"Oh, God, no!" I whispered.

"She's going to need the care of a neurologist, who we'll

have to bring in from one of the other hospitals, and she's going to have a long stay here," Dr. Bruce went on briskly. "This is going to cost money, a good deal of it."

"I'll get it," I said quickly. "I'll work and scrape and borrow and—"

"It will take more than that," Dr. Bruce interrupted. "This may run into two or three thousand dollars."

My heart froze.

"Does your mother have any hospitalization insurance?" Dr. Bruce asked.

"No," I said, the old hatred of my father stealing over me. "Before the car accident—well, you know, my mother always left things like that up to my father and he had funny ideas about your time to die and all. We never had any serious illness in the family before. After the accident, we found out he had never taken out any insurance on us. And then, after the smashup and Mom was an invalid, no company would give her a policy."

"How about your aunts—your mother's two sisters— didn't they help out with your medical bills when you had the accident?" Dr. Bruce asked.

"They paid them," I said.

"Yes," Dr. Bruce said slowly. "I believe I remember now. You have them get in touch with me as soon as possible."

"Yes sir," I said.

"You might as well go on home now. Your mother is asleep. Perhaps you can see her tomorrow."

Dr. Bruce and his companion left the room.

Marion and I walked out of the hospital into the cool, black, early morning air.

"Where in the world am I going to get that kind of money?" I asked hopelessly, breaking the silence.

"Don't you think that your Aunt Emma and Aunt Agnes will help this time?" Marion asked.

"They've got to," I answered. "They've just got to."

We got into Marion's car and fell silent again as she drove south.

We had gone ten or twelve blocks when I asked: "Marion, do you really think Mom will pull through this time?"

"Oh Clucky, yes. The doctors will do all they can and then, well, we just have to pray."

"Yeah," I murmured darkly, "pray." I fought back the tears that tried to come into my eyes. "Do you think God will listen to any prayer of mine behind what I've done? I know if I were Him I wouldn't."

"Guy, what's wrong with you? Of course He will listen to your prayers. Yes, and answer them, too, if you are sincere. So stop talking like a child."

Marion's voice was a sharp reprimand, causing anger to swell up and join the hurt inside me. "Let me tell you about this child deal," I said evenly. "Some people think that little kids are just a bunch of dirty little grubs who toddle around looking cute with nothing on their minds except how to cop a bellyful of milk. But that's not so. A person doesn't have to be grown before he can feel sincerity. I know because when I was little I used to pray and pray for things, and you can't tell me I wasn't sincere because I was. But did my sincerity ever cop a reward? No sir, not a damn one. I used to pray—sincerely—that my father would stay home more. But did he? No. I used to pray—sincerely—that the next knock on the door would be his so that the smile would stay on Mom's face when she jumped to answer it. Oh I prayed for a lot of things, loads of them, and my little heart was bellowing with sincerity. After the accident, I used to pray—sincerely —every night for Mom to be walking when I awoke the next morning, that she'd be laughing and dancing to *Sweet Leilani* in that island rig of hers. Yeah, I even prayed—sincerely— that my father would come back if it would make her happy. But d'ya know what I found when I awakened? I found Mom sitting in the front room in that damned wheel chair, the native

82

dress in her lap, looking at his picture. Ha! Sincerity! I was
so full of sincerity that I wet the bed until I was 12 years
old. I even stopped praying for bikes and baseball gloves
just so I could concentrate all my sincerity upon the one
prayer of, 'Lord, just make my mother well.' And what happens? What happens? Well, you've just seen some of what
happens tonight. Don't talk to me about sincerity. Yeah, and
don't talk to me about prayer, either."

We did not speak the rest of the way to my house, and I
got out of the car and slammed the door with a simple: "Good
night." I did not hear Marion drive away until after I was in
the house.

I turned off the flickering, pictureless TV set, got Mom's decanter of holiday wine from the cabinet and flopped on the
couch, my mind swirling with thoughts of money, lots of it,
more than I had ever seen of it, three thousand dollars worth
of it. I thought of my aunts, Agnes and Emma, and looked
at the clock on the mantel. It was 3:30, Sunday morning,
They would be in church today, I could catch them there. I
drank the wine straight from the decanter. It burned and it
warmed and it was sweet.

Aunt Agnes and Aunt Emma had the money, there was no
doubt of that. Both were married to men who drove Cadillacs;
they wore expensive furs and jewelry and made large con-
tributions to church and charity. They had been prepared, too,
to lavish their generosity upon Mom, their kid sister, until
her marriage to my father, whom they never liked or trusted.
For a while, the family gap was so big that Mom and her
sisters did not speak, but all that had changed with the auto
accident. My aunts still weren't too fond of me, however,
seeing as how I was the child of a man they disliked. I gulped
more wine.

Well, anyway I would be in church with bells on come
eleven o'clock.

Where else could I get money? Hank? Things were bad

enough between us. If he loaned me money, he would really own me. Everything had to add up to dollars and cents for him. But what about the money he had lost on the basketball game? That meant he was gambling on me and, except for that one time, making money on it. Why couldn't I gamble on myself? That was it! Bet on myself! Why play like hell for nothing while somebody else reaped the reward?

Fingering the thirty-five dollars I had in my pocket, I added up my coming pay for the next five weeks. One hundred and seventy-five dollars wasn't a lot of money to bet unless the odds were great, but if I were able to find enough odds on the track meet next month—

Yeah, I was turning into a great guy: threatening a gang war, giving my mother a stroke, planning to gamble on the one thing I had hoped to keep clean and decent: my athletic talent. All because of *him*. My gaze fixed on the photograph of a man. It lay on the floor where Mom had dropped it. The man peering out of the ornate frame was about six feet tall and athletically built. He was nattily dressed in sports attire, the pants a darker color than the jacket. He wore two-toned shoes and carried a Panama hat in his hand. The narrow face bore high cheeks, below which was a wide, full-lipped mouth, split in a sardonic smile. The eyes above it were slightly slanted with half-closed lids. Thick eyebrows met in an inverted "V," giving his face a satanic appearance which the deeply waved, processed hair heightened. Emptying the wine jug, I got up and reached for the photograph, taking it over to the large, blue-tinted mirror that hung over the imitation fireplace. I gazed intently into the mirror, and the image it reflected was an exact replica of the one in the picture. I closed my eyes as tightly as I could, then opened them again: the likeness remained. The words of Mom's favorite song filtered through my brain:

Jealous of my sweetheart, jealous because you're mine.

Cursing, I struck the hated image. It disappeared in a shower of glass. I looked around for it, and found it looking up from the frame in my left hand. I smashed my fist into the smiling face again and again.

"I've got you now!" I cried aloud.

"Guy! Guy! Stop it!"

I looked up dazedly. It was Marion, she had come in the unlocked door and, tossing the pillow and a blanket onto the couch, she ran to me.

"Oh, Guy, Guy! What's wrong, baby? What are you doing? Oooh, your hand is all bloody. I knew I shouldn't have left you here alone in the mood you were in! It's a good thing I discovered the blanket and pillow in the car before I got home." She led me into the bathroom and I sat on the edge of the tub while she cleaned my hand and bandaged it—the same hand I had used to smash the glass in her drug store.

"Clucky, you've got to snap out of it baby," she scolded softly. "Why, you were like an insane person in there. Smashing mirrors and punching pictures isn't going to eliminate the fact that you are your father's son."

"Yeah, I don't just *look* like him, I *act* like him," I spat disgustedly. "Like father, like son."

"So what do you intend doing about it?" Marion asked. "Go through life smashing everything that reflects the fact? Well, you might as well start stomping your shadow, too, because in your mind it looks like your father's too." Then eyeing the empty decanter, "Clucky, you're drunk." I walked over to the couch and fell upon it, my head whirling. I closed my eyes to make it stop. I could hear the sound of glass tinkling as Marion cleaned up the broken mirror and picture frame.

Minutes passed, and then I felt the weight of her body jar the couch on which I lay. I spoke to her with my eyes still closed, telling her of what had happened, my fight with Hank and the betting on neighborhood sports. Then I told her how I hoped to raise money for Mom's hospital bills by gambling on myself.

She was quiet for a long time and then she said: "Guy, I've got about three hundred dollars saved. I'd like you to bet it for me."

I frowned and shook my head.

"But I really don't need the money now," she said hastily, "and, well, I want your mother well, too, you know."

I looked up at her and she smiled, tapping a tiny finger to her head. "If she doesn't, my steady is going to be unsteady in the noggin, I'm afraid," she said.

I continued to stare in silence, the sweet wine making me feel almost lightheaded. "Besides, it's not as if I were going to lose. Why, Clucky, you can outrun anybody in that meet next month. Say you'll take the money, Clucky, please."

I pulled her into my arms. Her lips were warm and soft, like the small breast beneath my pressing fingers. I probed with my tongue; the closed teeth parted and I drank warm, sweet breath in long draughts. She trembled under my caress, then began to whimper. I turned to raise up on the couch and pull her down to me when suddenly my foot struck the wheel chair.

"Mom!" I cried aloud and stood up.

"What?" Marion asked, peering through moist eyes.

I stared at her. Her skirt was twisted above her knees and she had kicked off one tiny shoe. A sea roared deafeningly in my head. Marion was on her knees, reaching for me.

"Clucky, Clucky!"

Darkness began to engulf my mind. A heavy weight was dragging me to my knees.

. . . *Sweet Leilani* . . .

"Oh, Mom, Mom," I cried.

Chapter **11**

I opened my eyes, instantly conscious of the sour taste in my mouth and the pain in my right hand. The room, bathed in sunlight, made my head hurt. I reclosed my eyes. The pain continued to throb in my head. Easing my eyes open, I saw that my head was pillowed on Marion's lap. We were on the floor, her back against the couch.

I sat up, tossing aside the blanket that covered me. Looking at her sleeping face, I thought: *Buddy, what a clown she must think I am.* Reaching out, I applied button-pushing action to one of her breasts protruding jauntily beneath the skin-tight blouse. Long lashed lids fluttered, then looked at me sleepily.

"Hi! Sexy boon," I greeted.

"Hi, yourself." She stretched languishly.

I tried to pull her into my arms. Placing a hand over my mouth, she twisted her face. "Nothing doing, Clucky. Last night was close enough for a single lifetime, you know. Besides, if you are going to church, you had better make it into the shower. It's almost that time."

Lurching to my feet, I glanced over to the clock beneath the blank mirror frame. It was 9:15.

Marion extended her hand to be helped up. "I'll fix you some breakfast as soon as I clean up a bit," she offered.

In the bathroom, I watched her wash and dry her face and hands. "Why be scrimpy?" I asked, nodding toward the bathtub.

"No thank you, sir, I'll take one later at home."

As she attempted to pass me, I wedged her against the door. Struggling free, she backed toward the kitchen. "Your kindness is only exceeded by the lust in your eyes." She stuck out her tongue at me.

Stripping hurriedly I stepped into the tub. For fifteen minutes I alternately tingled and chilled to the sprays of hot and cold water. Stepping from the shower, I awkwardly dried myself with my left hand. Twisting the towel around me sarong fashion, I entered the bedroom. Suit, shirt, tie and underwear were neatly arranged on the bed. Marion was leafing through a pile of socks in one of the dresser drawers. Hearing me enter, she looked up. A frown wrinkled her forehead.

"Why, they're all of a solid color," she puzzled. "And why haven't you got a sports outfit in that whole closet?"

"I'm simply the conservative type."

"But who ever heard of a seventeen-year-old boy who—"

"Listen, why is it that all you broads go for some punk dressed to look like a stripe-assed ape or monkey wrapped in a rainbow? One gaudy dresser in the family is enough."

"Excuse me, Mr. Buttermilk, I didn't know you would clabber," she apologized.

"Sorry," I said.

"Oh! Let's forget him!" she said, poutishly, bouncing up and down on the bed. The movement exposed the flesh above her knee. "You know, you've got a darn nice physique," she observed critically.

Keeping my eyes on her legs I walked over to her.

"I think you have a nice one too, Jane."

"Jane?" she puzzled, looking around searchingly.

Expanding my chest, I thumped it with my thumb and said, "Me Tarzan, you Jane." Then looking about, I asked, "Where's boy?"

Aping me, she said, "Boy, him not born yet."

"Me fix that damn quick." Springing onto the bed among the neatly-arranged clothes, I gathered her squirming into my arms.

88

"Mrs. Morgan! Make Guy quit!" she called gaily.

The cry converted my flaming desire into icy frigidity. I stared down into the smoky depth of her sparkling eyes. The laughter flowing from her lips ceased its bubbling at my look.

Rolling free of her, I flung the suit coat over me and gazed at the ceiling.

"What's wrong?" Marion asked, sitting up.

"She didn't answer," I replied. Remembering how quickly Mom always responded to Marion's cry for help whenever I became too rough in our play.

She stroked the scar on my forehead with tender fingertips. After a long silence, she said, "Do you love me?"

"Sure," I replied automatically, as I had on the day she first asked me the question. "Why?"

"Oh, nothing, really, only last night you—you—"

"I forgot about your—our dream chapel in the sunlight," I murmured, letting mockery enter my voice as I pulled the congo drum from beneath the bed. I tapped it lightly. "For one split-second I wanted to hold something in my palms and know for sure it was mine to possess instead of hope for; to experience and not merely dream of. But, of course, I was wrong. Vanity, yes! Vanity of vanities, all is vanity! I'm sorry, Marion, I'm just a brutish bastard. I've cursed my father, hospitalized my mother—"

"What—what do you want, Guy? Can I help you? Do I possess this—this whatever it is that's making you sick? Does anyone? Is it my body you want? If so, then take me now— please." She fell across my chest. "You could have had me last night, tho' I—I would have felt used, just another sport to indulge in. A timely punch or a well put shot. I—" she broke off sobbing softly.

"Oh, come off it, for crying out loud," I said in the grip of an unknown savagery. "You'll have your chapel in the sunlight, with flower-strung aisles and people throwing rice at us as if we were a couple of starved Chinese, and an organ playing, *Oh, Promise Me,* while I—"

"While you lay in the darkness of your jungle of self-imposed loneliness, pounding your drum of invented frustration and bewailing a non-existing woe," she flared between sobs.

At 12 o'clock we pulled up at the drug store on the corner by the church. The street was thronged with well-dressed people coming from the morning service. We sat silently for a moment, then with a reluctant sigh she opened the door and slid from beneath the wheel. I got out and waited for her to come around the car. We stood facing each other.

"See, now you've missed your aunt," she said.

There was a tap on the store window. We turned. Her father peered out at us from behind the counter. He pointed with a long mixing spoon toward a group of teen-agers lining the opposite side of the fountain and clamped a hand over his eyes and forehead despairingly. We walked to the entrance of the store.

"Oh, Clucky! Clucky!" a voice rang out. Surprised at being called aloud in public by the pet name, I halted in the doorway.

"It's your Aunt Emma," Marion said looking back. "Good, now you can talk to her after all."

"Marion, for God's sake, stay and give me a hand, will you?"

Her father called in a frantic voice.

"Okay, Dad, okay," she said, hurrying toward the store. "I'll see you later," she tossed over her shoulder to me. "I'll have to tell Dad we spent the night at the hospital," she winked and was gone.

I turned and walked to the Cadillac double-parked in front of the store. A well-dressed woman sat beneath the steering wheel while a mousy, light-skinned man, sat pressed in the corner of the seat opposite her, attempting to look incon-

90

spicuous. The woman was my Aunt Emma. Her dark face was thickly overlaid with make-up and wore a look of vexation.

"Hello, Aunt Emma, Uncle Milton. How have you been?"

"For an athlete you certainly are slow in responding," she said. "We are fine, thank you." She spoke for my uncle as always. "But your Aunt Agnes is sick with a mean headache. It prevented her from attending service this morning. She missed a splendid sermon, poor dear. Reverend Kelly delivered a wonderful message on the virtue of charity, which I might add, is not practiced widely enough. This afternoon we're going to attend a charity dinner which the A.B.S.— Animal Benevolence Society—is giving. A very worthy organization. How is your mother, poor dear? Oh, yes, I promised your Aunt Agnes I would pick up some aspirin for her. Will you be a good boy and run into the drug store for them?"

She extended a half a dollar toward me, I took the coin, went in, made the purchase and returned.

"Thank you, Clucky," she said, pressing a dime into my hand. "You're really a good boy, Clucky, only you should attend church more often."

"Aunt Emma, Mom is sick. It's serious. She's in the hospital."

"What, Lonnie sick? In the hospital? Oh! No!"

The coin was biting into my tightly clenched hand.

"Yes," I said, "she's in the hospital again. Provident. I took her there last night. Dr. Bruce said she needs a specialist and that it's going to cost a lot of money. I need help in raising it and I would appreciate it if you and Aunt Agnes would—"

"Well, I do declare, if it's not one thing, it's another. A relapse from the accident, no doubt. Your father needs to be taken out and horse-whipped. We tried to tell her that marrying him would be her undoing, but would she take heed? No!"

91

"I don't see where that's got anything to do with your helping me," I said, unable to conceal my anger any longer.

"Oh, you wouldn't, you're still a child. But you had better learn to control that temper of yours or you'll end up like him, bad." She put the car in gear. "Well, I'm in a hurry right now, but I'll talk to your Aunt Agnes and we'll contact Dr. Bruce and the hospital to make some financial arrangements."

The big car eased into the traffic. I stood watching it for a moment, my body shaking with wrath.

"You mean, domineering, sanctimonious, old bitch," I muttered. Turning, I entered the store. The juke box was playing a racy be-bop number. Syncopated drumming thundered forth. Halting before the phonograph, I inserted the dime, then walked on to the first booth. I saw it was occupied by a boy and girl. They stared at each other with dull, half-closed eyes. The boy's name was Raymond Miller. He lived across the street from Hank's pool room, next to Crow's dad's novelty shop. He pushed dope for Hank and was an addict. He made enough from his sales to keep his habit up.

Scratching the side of his face with languid movements, he drawled to his companion in a drugged voice: "Dig my man Roach kicking them weird sounds, momma."

"I'm digging him, daddy," replied the girl, scratching somewhere beneath the table.

I had always disliked Raymond. He was a petty thief who stayed out of jail by informing on other thieves and dope peddlers. Tapping him on the shoulder, I said, "Okay, dad, you and your horse-riding momma find another place to nod."

"What's that, man?"

"You heard me, I said for you to stoke up and steam off to another spot. Scram! Cop?"

"Look, Jim, we were here first. I don't see no reserve sign on this booth, so I really don't dig what you're beefing about." He turned back toward the scratching girl.

Reaching down, I grabbed his necktie and jerked him to his feet. "Look, hypo, I said move, now do you move or do I have to fatten your drooling lip?" The contracted pupils of his eyes stared at me in hate. I was hoping he would put up a fight, for my jumping nerves were dying to smash something and Raymond would have been a good start.

"Okay, Joe, this round is yours, only remember, what goes around, comes around, cop?" He edged out of the booth, pulling the girl with him.

"Yeah, I cop. But just so you don't make any mistakes when it comes around, the name is Guy, Guy Morgan, not Joe or Jim."

He nodded, dragging the doped-up girl into a back booth.

My selection began to play. The sultry voice of my favorite singer, lamented how gloomy Sundays were. I leaned and closed my eyes—

Sunday is gloomy, my hours are slumberless, dearest, the shadows I live with are numberless . . .

The scraping of crockery on the table caused me to open my eyes. Marion placed a plate with two ham sandwiches and a glass of milk before me.

"Here's the breakfast you overlooked this morning."

"Not overlooked, ignored," I said, biting into the sandwich.

"What's between you and that junkie Raymond?"

"Nothing."

"Huuuum, I bet, only I happened to see what took place over here. Clucky, you be careful of that one. He's mean as a snake and just as low. Him and his dope, ugh!"

"You sure as hell see a lot for a little girl. And for Christ's sake, stop calling me Clucky in public. Next thing you know people will be thinking I'm your pet chicken or something," I said indignantly.

"You are," she said, reaching out to pinch my cheek.

"Dammit, Marion, now stop it!"

"Okay! Okay! Okay!" she said, heading toward the back

of the store. "Don't go any place until I come back. I want to hear how you made out with your aunt." She went through the door that led to the upstairs apartment where she and her father lived, and returned a few minutes later carrying a pharmacy textbook and a notebook. Placing them down on the table, she flopped beside me.

"Wheeew!" she exclaimed breathlessly. "Climbing those stairs would kill a horse."

"Death has no sting, for in death I'm caressing you . . ." sang the sultry voice.

"How come you go for all those serious records. They're downright morbid, don't they make you blue?" Marion asked.

"Uh-huh, bluer than indigo. But at least I'm made to feel something. That jitterbug and bop noise don't frenzy me a bit." I drained the last of the milk and belched noisily. "Good stuff," I said pointing to the empty glass.

"Pig. So what did your Aunt Emma have to say about the money?"

"She said she was in a hurry to attend the A.B.S. charity dinner. A most worthy organization."

"Well, what in the world does A.B.S. stand for?"

"All Bull Shit," I supplied unsmilingly.

"Ah! Now, Guy, be serious. What did she say?"

I told her verbatim. When I had finished, the anger I had felt returned. I repeated my vulgar description of her.

"Now, Guy. You shouldn't speak like that. I'm sure she'll help you all she can. Oh, by the way, I phoned the hospital. Your mother is still sleeping."

"You're an angel," I said appreciatively. "And maybe you're right about my aunts. Maybe they'll come through."

After a moment's silence, I asked, "What time is it?"

"Twelve-thirty."

"You want to take in a flick?"

"Nope, I've got just loads of studying to do if I'm ever to be a good pharmacist. Besides, tonight's Sunday and this joint will be busy all day with the after-skating and movie crowd. I'd better stick around and help Dad."

"Well, I'm going to be dusting," I said, getting to my feet.

"By the way, you'd better take this." She extended a large manila envelope toward me.

I looked at her for a moment.

"Come on now, you promised."

I took the envelope, placed it in the inside pocket of my suit coat, and walked out into the June sun.

I walked south on Throop to 113th Street, turned west to Ada. Upon entering the tiny park, I saw Crow, Dipper and the rest of the gang lying on the grass near the ball diamond. I walked over to them.

"Hi, Guy! What's to it?" Crow asked, making room for me on the newspaper he was lying on.

"Ain't nothin' to it, little man. A baby can do it if ya put 'em up to it," I answered.

"A baby elephant, you mean," injected the stocky, light-complexioned Ding Jones.

"That makes you qualified to do it then, Ding."

"Uh-huh, I know and I intend to just as soon as that damn slow poke makes up."

The conversation had taken a twist which I was unable to follow. I looked at Crow and he smiled broadly.

"Momma! Would you look at this," exclaimed a tall kid named Sandy Ward. The boys began to crowd around him. I looked at Crow again.

"Ah, it ain't nothin'," he said reassuringly, "I just swiped some cards and some of dem ol' friggin' books outta my ol' man's dresser drawer. They're looking at 'em and gettin' horny as hell."

Looking around, I saw each of the boys held one of the books.

"Hey, dig this lame! Buddy!" exclaimed a kid named Earl. Running over to us, he dropped to his knees and shoved the book under our noses. The picture displayed a famous comic strip strongman making love to his skinny girl friend.

"I wonder what would happen if this was put in the Sunday paper by mistake?" Earl asked.

"Your Mom would get into a blue funk and have a cast iron baby," Ding replied, jumping to his feet and hurrying over to the thick hedged bushes where a boy named Harold had emerged. Harold lay down on the paper that Ding had vacated, clasped his hands behind his head and looked up at the clear blue sky with a sigh.

"Say, Guy, is it true that the bar is down on them apes from 119th Street?" Dipper asked.

"Yeah, that's what I came over to tell you guys. Next time you see any of the Gabriels over this way, slick their skimmers."

Crow jumped to his feet with a shout. Spitting on his hand, he began to throw punches at an imaginary foe.

"Ooooh, look! Baby! Baby! Dat's just what I've been dyin' for. Just you wait till I see one of them cats. Man, I'm gonna lam de loon like he's never been lammed before." He released a whistling right hand haymaker and dropped back down beside me, satisfied that he had KO'd his foe.

Ding came out of the bushes. Earl got up and scampered over to them and disappeared.

"Say, Deacon, wha'cha gonna do today?" Crow asked.

"Nothing, why?"

"Come and go skating with me, huh? Man, I know some real tough chicks at the rink.

"Yeah, and I know some real tough guys at that rink too. And, buddy, they don't like no outsiders putting the make on their broads."

"Amen!" Ding corroborated. "Why, Jim, the last time I was at that joint, I wasn't able to take off the skates until I was at 111th Street and the killing part is, I crawled all the way."

Everybody laughed.

Earl came out of the bushes and Dipper went in.

"Ah! But you ain't no gentleman, Ding," Crow said. "Ya got to use fi-ness, be diplomatic. Why, man I ain't never had no humbug with them guys down there. And every time I go skatin' I cop some choice bed action."

"Why, you little shrimp, you wouldn't know what to do with a lay if it was under your face and had instruction signs on it," Sandy accused.

Crow was on his feet like a flash, tears of anger were in his eyes, his small body trembled.

"Don't you call me no shrimp, you friggin' bastard. Don't you call me no shrimp, ever!"

"Hey, screw you, shrimp," Sandy said, getting to his feet.

Crow leaped for him. I stuck out my foot tripping him.

"Now look, you guys, there's to be no fighting among ourselves. That's a club rule and you all know it. So cool that action or suffer the penalty."

"Ah, hell, I didn't want to fight the little er - - - ru - - -, anyway," Sandy said sprawling onto the ground again to resume his study of the smut books.

"Come on, Crow, we've got some skating to do," I said. Instantly a smile split his impish face. "You gonna go with me?"

I nodded.

"Crazy, man! Let's leave these punks, they ain't into nothin' anyway. Pure lames, Guy, that's all. Pure de lames." We headed for the entrance. Looking over his shoulder, Crow yelled. "You lames hold them books close to ya chest, 'cause I've got to sneak 'em back."

"Yeah! Yeah!" they chorused.

"Man, if my loony old man knew I had boosted them books, he'd lam de hell out of me."

Dipper came out of the bushes and headed for the group.
Curious, I stepped over and parted the bushes. Millie was
lying couched upon a bed of grass. She looked at me through
mascara eyes. Thickly painted lips parted in a smile.

"You coming in?" she asked.

"Ha! For what, to drown?" I replied, letting the bushes
come together.

"You ride that train, Crow?" I asked as we left the
park.

"Naw! That ain't my go. But wait until you see this pepper
I'm meeting tonight. Hummmmmmmmmm!" he said, hugging
himself in closed-eyed ecstasy.

"Hot, huh?"

"Ooooh, baby!" he affirmed.

Arriving at 111th and Loomis, we waited for a bus in front
of a shabby restaurant appropriately called the Greasy Spoon.
A large black Chrysler cruised past us.

"Dig! That's Reverend Kelly. He's bootin' another new
car. Man, oh man, dat cat is really into somethin'." Crow followed the car with envious eyes.

"Hi, Crow, hello Deacon."

I looked up, Velma had walked out of the Greasy Spoon
and glided past us.

"Hi ya, Velma," Crow greeted.

"Hey, stallion," I said, remembering her pleasure at being
so called. The horsey comparison inspired the swaying hips
to a more sexy swing. Crow stared, pop-eyed.

"Buddy, she'll wring herself dry if she ain't careful," he
exclaimed admiringly. "A horse! A horse! My kingdom for
that horse! Right, Deacon?"

"Like hell and destruction are never filled," I quoted sol-
enmly, looking soberly into his shining eyes, "so the eyes of
man are never satisfied."

Rolling his eyes skyward, he breathed a fervent, "A-men,"
then said, "Preach on, Deacon."

"She walks nice," I said.

With his eyes still on Velma's grinding hips, Crow declared: "Walk, hell, that chick moves like she's been spilled."

"Pull in your tongue, Crow, here's the bus."

"Howl ye!" he replied.

Chapter 12

We got off the bus at 47th and South Parkway an hour later. Plunging through the hurrying throng of Sunday afternoon fun-seekers, we arrived at the skating rink. Teen-agers crowded around it, laughing and shouting wisecracks at each other.

"You cop de tickets, I'll be back in a jiffy," Crow said, darting into the crowd.

"Two," I requested, shoving a five-dollar bill through the cashier's window. Pocketing my change and tickets, I lounged against one of the doors and watched a girl shooting dice make seven the hard way. She wore a blue and white satin jacket. Across its back was lettered, "The 13 Kittens." Above that was the emblem of a cat pawing a ball of twine. Blowing on the dice, she cast them again with snapping fingers. The eyes of three boys and two other girls followed their roll intently.

"Seven again!" shouted one of the boys disgustedly. He wore a jacket of the same material and color as the girl. On the back was the emblem of a cat, below it was written, "The 13 Cats."

"I'm hot!" the girl shouted, rubbing the dice over her breast.

"Yeah, in a lot of ways," one of the boys affirmed, looking into the top of her thin low-necked blouse.

"Seven for me, baby!" pleaded the girl tossing the dice again.

"Well, for crapsake," howled one of the three boys, as seven came up.

100

"Come on, man, let's boot 'em up," Crow sauntered up.

Entering the crowded rink I handed the usher the tickets, clamped the rented skates on and rolled to the lavatory, where Crow pulled a pint bottle from his hip pocket, unscrewed the top and drank deeply. Wiping his lips, he extended the bottle to me.

"Ahhh! This is choice stuff. Three-fifty a pint. Go ahead, take a swig, it'll do ya good," he prompted.

I shook my head. "Knock yourself out, baby, I can't go that route."

"Ahhh!" he repeated, smacking his lips.

"Ahhh, hellie, come on! I didn't pay a buck-and-a-half just to watch you jockey a bottle in the craphouse," I said, skating toward the door.

"Ah, you just ain't got no sense of taste."

Gliding onto the rink, we skated a waltz together. After it ended, he bowed over my hand soberly.

"Excuse me for being frank, darling, but you skate like an ox, your hands are hard and your hips, ugh! They have muscles. This doesn't move me a bit, dig? So you'll just have to cop someone else to lean on, 'cause I'm dusting."

"Well, you can go straight to the pootie-war," I said in mock indignation.

"Well, thank you, I will. Which reminds me, you don't smell so good either." He glided away in pretended offense.

Stepping through the brass guard rail that encircled the larger of the three rinks, I sank into one of the chairs, propping my feet on the rail. The organ began rumbling a racy tune. The sign for backward skating flashed on the instruction board. Couples began to glide speedily past. Crow whirled by with a pretty, brown-skinned girl. They weaved through the other skaters with skillful movements. Skating was Crow's first passion and he did it expertly. Many times I had made the long trip to the rink just to sit and watch him perform.

After a half dozen numbers, Crow glided over and sat beside me.

"How's old daddy Crow doing?" he demanded.

"You're still the shack bully of the rink for my money. The girl, is she the hot momma you've been raving about?"

"Yeah! Yeah! That's her. Her name's Dot. Ain't she tough? A real looker, right?"

"Yeah, she's a real fox," I admitted.

"She skates like a champ. Watch this next call." He pointed to the instruction board.

It said, "For Women Only." The lights about the rink darkened. Small spotlights shone down on the figures of the skating girls. Anybody could pinpoint Dot, she was performing such difficult maneuvers. At the end of each one, the watching crowd cheered.

Crow was on his feet shouting new figures: "Do de swan twist, Dot. Speed around de world. Work, baby, work!"

After executing a dozen or so figures, Dot skated out of the circle of lights. The roving spotlight pinpointed another girl. At the sight of her, my heart began thundering like a trip hammer. She was the prettiest girl I had ever seen. With my eyes still on her, I shook Crow's shoulder. "Who is that?"

"Ah, some stuck-up broad who is always trying to steal Dot's thunder," he replied resentfully.

"But what's her name?" I asked hoarsely, an odd lump in my throat.

"Hey! What de hell's gotten into you, Guy?"

"Look man, all I wanted to know is who's the stallion. Is there anything wrong with that? Can't you get Dot to put in a fix for me with her?" I ended pleadingly.

"Hey, you have got it bad, ain't you?"

"Yeah, I guess I have. Can you help me?"

"Well, I'll see if Dot knows her. But I can't promise you nothin' 'cause this broad is real stuck-up. I mean she don't mess around with any of de studs here. She comes by herself and leaves the same way. A real icebox, you dig?"

"Yeah," I said, staring at the petite figure in the spotlight whose shapely bronze-colored legs' seemed to glow with warmth.

She completed another figure and stood tall and majestic, looking up into the spotlight as the crowd cheered.

"I'd better see what I can do for you quick, before you flip your lid," Crow said.

The lights went up. Crow skated hurriedly away. The girl had disappeared.

After a minute, Crow returned. Coming to a skidding stop, he grabbed my hand and snatched me from the seat.

"Come on! Come on! She just went into de can, I sent Dot in to talk to her. Her name is Kay Heath, she's eighteen and her father's in de racket, a minister of some sort, poor girl."

We skated to the men's room.

"Be cool, man, be cool," he cautioned, peering into the toilet stalls. Reaching the end one, he beckoned to me. I skated over to him, "Dig, I'm gonna let you in on something; some cats around here put me wise to. But don't you hip no one else to it, or get caught at it."

"Look man, I don't want to hear any mysteries. All I want is to meet this Kay, so can all this cloak and dagger stuff and let's go outside to wait for them."

Crow had stepped up on the toilet bowl and removed a screw from a small square piece of tile which was painted the same color as the wall. Easing it aside, he motioned me to climb up. Getting up on the bowl, I peeked in.

"Wha'cha see, wha'cha see?" Crow asked in an excited whisper.

"A row of queens sitting on thrones." I was looking into the women's lavatory.

"But what are they doin'?"

"How in hell would I know. They're just sittin' there."

Hearing Crow's name spoken from the other side, I shifted my gaze. Dot and Kay stood directly below the hole. Dot was peering intently at what obviously was a mirror, while applying lipstick to her mouth. Kay was looking in the same direction, combing her hair. She was saying: "Sure, I'll skate with your friend, but that's all, Dot. I don't go in for these roller rink romances, you know."

"Oh, but you'll like him, Kay, he's my steady's best friend and Crow is the swellest guy I know." They started toward the door.

"Jiggers!" Crow hissed, covering the hole. "Somebody has come in."

Three boys hurried into the booth next to where we were. One of the boys flopped on the bowl. His hands clutched his stomach.

"Oh, I'm sick!"

The other two—one short and dark, the other light-skinned and fat—squatted at his feet.

"Did'ja get the stuff, did'ja cop—huh-huh?" the skinny, sick kid asked.

"Cool it, Richard. Yeah, yeah, I got it, but I caught hell trying to get the stud to turn me on," the fat one said. He removed a bottle cap, eyedropper and a small square package from his pocket. "Gimme the spike," he asked, holding out his hand.

The short one got to his feet and began searching his pockets.

"Hurry up, goddammit."

The fat one shook some white powder from the package into the metal cap.

"I'm sick!" the boy on the toilet groaned.

"Here." The short one extended the hypodermic needle to the fat one.

He took it and inserted it in the end of the eyedropper. He

reached between the legs of the boy on the stool and drew water in it, expelling it into the cap, then struck a match and held it under the cap. After a second, he drew the contents of the cap back into the eyedropper.

"I'm first!" the skinny, sick one cried.

"The hell you are, Richard, I'm taking off first. I went and got the stuff, remember?" the fat one said angrily.

"But it was my damned money you used."

"Oh, for crapsake, shut up, Richard," the short, dark one requested.

"Ah, hell, leave him alone. The pusher wasn't gonna turn me on until I told him that Richard was bad sick and needed a shot."

"Okay, I guess he ought to be first," the short one said, handing Richard his belt.

Richard rolled up his shirt sleeve and tied the belt tightly around his upper arm. "Okay," he said.

The fat one plunged the needle expertly into the vein. The eyedropper filled with blood. Squeezing the bulb attached to the head of the eyedropper, he forced the fluid into Richard's vein, then withdrew the needle.

Richard leaped into the air, his body ramrod straight and teeth clenched. He jumped up and down in one spot like a human pogo stick gyrating slowly.

"Dig that cat, Purdom. That stuff is sure dyno," the light, fat one cried.

"Gimme the spike, Davis, and let me take off. Oh, baby, let me ride this white horse."

Snatching the makeshift hypodermic from Davis, Purdom stooped and began drawing some more of the cap's contents.

Richard suddenly slumped onto the stool again.

"What's the matter now, the spike plug up on ya?" Davis asked Purdom.

"Say, man, this stuff is bubbling and it's hot, feel it," Purdom said.

Davis took it. Squeezing a drop in his palm, he stuck his tongue to it. Instantly a look of horror spread over his face. Letting the eyedropper crash to the floor, he sprang to his feet. "Oh, my God, we've given Richard a hot shot! Jeezus, I'm getting out of here!" Davis lunged wildly through the door.

Purdom bent and felt beneath the front of Richard's shirt. Withdrawing it swiftly, he wiped it on his chest loathsomely.

"Why that dirty, rotten pusher! The murderin' bastard." He muttered backing from the stall and dashed out of the room.

I stood clutching the top of the partition, staring at the lifeless boy slumped on the stool. The body began to ease forward slowly, as if he was about to rise. It toppled to the floor, the head striking the tile hollowly.

"Man, oh, man! We'd better get out of here," Crow croaked, releasing the partition. He missed his footing. Grabbing me, we went crashing to the floor. Struggling with frantic hands, we untangled our interlocked skates that were wedged in the toilet bowl.

In getting to his feet, Crow's hand touched that of the dead boy's. "Jeezus," Crow muttered, spraying the front of my suit with vomit.

He skated out of the stall.

Grabbing the wheels of my skates, I snatched them loose from my shoes. Getting to my feet, I left the stall. Crow was being sick in one of the face bowls against the opposite wall. Stepping to one of them, I filled it with water. Using my hand-kerchief, I attempted to remove the stains of Crow's sickness. "Boy, just wait until de man finds that cat, ooh, Buddy!" Crow said in a frightened voice. "Guy, we'd better get out of here, de bull sessions those coppers hold in them stations are back-breaking. Come on man, let's move out!"

We raced through the door.

Outside, we nearly ran over Dot and Kay in our haste.

"Hey! What's the hurry, hot shots?" Dot called out.

"C'mon, we gotta get outta here fast!" Crow yelled, grabbing her by the arm.

"Look, it's going to get hot as hell in here in a few minutes," I said to Kay. "You'd better come with us." I reached for her arm.

Kay pulled away and said: "Now you start looking. I don't know what you're talking about, but I'm not going anywhere with you. I don't even know who—"

"All right, sophisticated lady," I said hotly, "keep that pretty nose of yours in the air. And when you cop a whiff of something burning, don't bother to look around. Just wet on yourself and sit down, 'cause it'll be that fine fanny of yours flaming."

I turned and ran away, leaving her with her mouth open and fire in her eyes.

Crow and Dot were waiting for me out on the sidewalk.

"C'mon man, hurry up," Crow yelled, jumping up and down with impatience.

"Where's Kay?" Dot asked.

"She's staying," I said. "Let's go."

As we walked swiftly to 47th Street, I pulled off my suit coat. The stain had soaked through to my skin and the stench was sickening. "Damn," I said.

Crow looked at me. "I'm sorry, Guy," he apologized, "but touchin' that cat shook me up. We'll go over to Dot's house and you can wash up."

We hailed a cab and rode the five blocks to Dot's house. As I got out of the cab, I handed the driver a ten-dollar bill. As he started counting the change back into my hand he asked casually: "Interested in buying some good horse?"

Remembering the bubbling fluid in the eyedropper that made that skinny kid a corpse back at the skating rink, I told him coldly: "No. Hell no. Not a horse, or mule or jackass either. Now on your way, hot shot."

"Say, buddy, I'm only trying to make a buck," he apologized.

I picked up a brick from the curb. "I said on your way, hot shot," I repeated menacingly.

The car roared away.

Crow was holding the door of Dot's house open for me. "What's happenin'?" he asked.

"There's more junk in this town than in China. And these rotten pushers—"

"Yeah, there's good bread in it, man," Crow said, "but cool that kind of talk around Dot's brother, he's a pusher too and may get de wrong idea, you dig?"

I walked with him silently to the top of the rickety stairs. Crow tapped on the door. Dot opened it and we went in. Reefer smoke was so thick inside you could cut it with a knife. Dot's brother, Jim, and another girl were sitting on a sofa in the living room, puffing away.

"Come on, Guy, you can wash up in here," Dot said, leading me to a tiny bathroom. She stepped into another room across the hall and took a shirt from a dresser drawer and handed it to me. "This ought to fit you," she said. "We'll be up in the front." She pulled the door shut and left.

Stripping to the waist, I washed hurriedly, then slipped into the sport shirt she had given me. Taking the envelope that Marion had given me earlier out of my coat pocket, I ripped it open and took out the neat stack of bills and counted them, three hundred bucks on the head. "Marion, you are an angel with shining wings," I said softly aloud.

I walked out of the bathroom toward the living room. Inside Jim and his girl friend were doing an exotic dance in the middle of the floor while over in a dark corner Crow was tearing at Dot's blouse as she whimpered and dug her fingernails into the back of his shirt. The reefer smell floated throughout the house.

Back at the roller rink, a skinny, pimply-faced kid lay dead on the cold concrete. Dead without ever having lived.

Suddenly I felt sick. I plunged from the apartment and down the stairs, out into the fresh night air. But it was too late. My eyes burned with the reefer smoke, and my stomach churned with the memory of that dead boy. I staggered between the buildings and began to vomit, as Crow had done.

Afterwards, I wiped the tears from my eyes and started to walk out when suddenly the harsh glare of a spotlight blinded me into immobility.

"Hey! You there! What are ya doing in there? Come out with your hands up."

I stumbled blindly out, my hands over my head. A gun was pressed at my side.

"Just keep 'em up, shine, just keep 'em up there if you want to stay healthy," cautioned the man behind me.

I stopped still on the sidewalk with the light still flaring in my eyes. The man ran his hand over my body. "Got any weapons, zig?" he demanded. "Carrying a gun or a knife?"

"What is this, a stick-up?" I asked in a voice trembling with fright.

The gun jabbed my ribs viciously. "Hey, coon, what are you trying to do, get smart?"

His hand touched the roll of bills in my pocket. "What's this?" he demanded as he reached inside to withdraw them. He leaned under the street light to examine them, and I saw a slow look of surprise creep across his pink face.

"Well, for Christ's sake, where did'ja get this? You'd better come over to the car. He gripped the back of my belt and shoved me toward the police car.

"All right, get in there," he commanded. "And don't try going out the other side, either, or I'll blow your black guts out."

I got in the car. He followed and slammed the door shut.

"Okay, Pat," he told the other officer behind the steering wheel. The car took off, turning West on 47th Street as the man next to me counted the bills.

The driver pulled the car to the curb at 47th and State and twisted about in the seat and asked of his partner: "What do we have here, Tony?"

"From the amount of money I took off 'im, I think he's outlaw people—a damned burglar."

"Look, mister," I protested, "I went between that building to—"

"Yeah, yeah, I know," the one called Tony cut in. You went between that building to take a leak. That's what all you catmen say, especially you spooks. If it ain't to take a leak, it's to take a crap. Jeezus! Why can't they say they were spittin' now and then?"

"How old are you, kid, and where do you live?" Tony's partner asked.

"I'm seventeen and I live in Morgan Park, 110th Street," I answered.

"Well, what the hell are you doing all the hell out here at this time of night?"

"I was coming from my girl friend's house," I lied, thinking of the dead boy at the rink.

"Where did ya get all the money?"

"From a friend of mine. She loaned it to me to pay a bill."

"She loaned it to you! Say, who the hell do ya think you're kiddin' with that bull?" Tony demanded. "I ought to belt ya one in the mouth!"

I cringed from the expected blow as he raised his hand threateningly.

"Look, punk, evidently you don't know who you're dealing with. I'm Tony Mancuso and I eat niggers for breakfast, ya understand? So let's have no more bull crap from now on."

"Where did ya get the money, boy?" Pat asked again.

"I got it from Marion Gale. Phone her if you—"

Tony's hand flashed out and struck me across the mouth, snapping my head back, then he chopped quickly with the edge of his hand across my throat. I gagged.

"Goddammit, Tony, take it easy," Pat yelled. "Wha'cha wanta do, kill him?" I struggled for breath.

"Jeezus, how I hate these black bastards," Tony snarled. "Yeah, I want to kill him. I'd like to kill every one of the crap-shootin', lyin', thievin', white woman-rapin' bastards."

"Look, did you really get this dough from this Marion babe, and you better tell the truth," Tony's partner said.

I nodded my head, still fighting for breath.

"Are you a pimp?"

I shook my head no.

"Do you work? You got a job?"

"Yes, sir. I work for Hank Johnson," I managed to say.

"Do you mean one-eyed Hank who runs the pool room at 111th Street?" Tony wanted to know.

"Yes, sir," I said.

"Yeah, well, you're a jump jobber then, 'cause that's Hank's main stock-in-trade. Three hundred bucks from a broad, boy! You black boys really start young." Tony turned to his partner. "Well, what do we do with him? Run him down to the bureau?"

"Naw, he's a good kid. Let him go."

Tony reached over and opened the car door. "All right, Sambo, make tracks," he ordered. "And when you see Hank, tell him that Tony from the robbery detail downtown said he will be out to see him sometime, and to have one of them hot-butt coon broads on the ready for me."

The two cops laughed. I didn't move.

"Hey, what's wrong, shine? I said that you could go, so go ahead and get before I run you in."

"But, what about my money?" I asked. "I need that money bad, mister. My mother is in the hospital and has to—"

"Oh, fer cryin' out loud. All you nookie bookies has got

111

dyin' mothers," Tony cut in. "Save that story for some rookie. I've been on the force too long. Now get your black butt out before I get mad and stomp your teeth in."

He shoved me from the car and slammed the door shut. As they pulled away, laughter trailed from the car.

"Did'ja hear that, Pat? His dyin' mammy—Oh, my bleedin' piles!"

I stood in the middle of the street, my hands going through my empty pockets. All the money I had in the world gone. And Mom in the hospital.

I looked up the street for a bus, feeling hopefully for a coin in my pocket. Not a quarter.

Across the street stood a shabby newspaper shack on the corner. I walked over to it and stole fifty cents off the counter while the old man behind stared at me. He was blind.

Rob not the poor because he is poor, neither oppress the afflicted at the gate . . . my father's voice said in the darkness.

"Frig you!" I muttered.

Chapter **13**

The June sun began its slow descent, leaving in its wake a
sweltering heat. Raising a bottle of pop to my lips, I drank a
grateful toast to its departure as I leaned against the frame
of the open door of the pool room, listening to the click of
billiard balls. Over the murmuring conversation of the Friday
evening crowd, I heard Crow reciting the tale of the monkey
who was a pool shark: "Away back in de coconut trees, lived
de pool-shootin'ess monkey de world evah seed. He walked in
de pool room one warm summer day, and looked 'round for a
sucker who'd give 'im a play—"

I fingered the roll of bills in my pocket—three tens and
four fives. Fifty bucks, all earned over the pool table, the
hard way; the same way Crow was putting the finishing
touches on a pretty good pool player who had a fair-sized
bankroll. The fact that he was quoting the tale of the monkey
meant that he was taking his inferior opponent to the killing
floor.

" 'Pop' monkey said, 'I'll play for money, peanuts or fun,
now what lame wants t' try de mastah one?' "

I thought of the measly one hundred dollar check my aunts,
Emma and Agnes, had sent me. With my fifty dollars, it was
a long way short of the necessary three thousand. For the
thousandth time I cursed those cops who had fleeced me of
Marion's three hundred dollars. I hadn't told her about it,
though I'd seen her every day. When I had tried, the words
just wouldn't come.

"De baboon reached up and copped him a cue, and say:

113

'Ya ugly bud-mout', ah b'lieve ah do. 'De monkey 'lucked' de eight on de bust, ran de one-to-de five, kicked de six in de co'nah an' de ten in de side—"

Each time Crow spoke a number, I knew he was sinking the balls he mentioned. There was a lull in the conversation which told plainly that the regulars were watching the suckers get taken, and the weeds were marking Crow down in their mental "Do not play for money" book.

I drained the bottle of pop and savored its momentary coolness, but my mind kept going back to the three thousand. I was betting the one hundred and fifty dollars on myself in the track and field meet. Hank was to give me even money on a four-event parlay, so by winning them all I'd collect twenty-four hundred dollars, leaving me six hundred short. Where would I get the rest from? Where? *Oh, God! Help me, just this once,* I silently prayed, *let me get the money, and let Mom get well—or, just let her get back like she was when I came home Saturday and I'll never ask you for anything again, so help me, please God!*

". . . Now de nex' was lined-up in a real tough shot, 'cause de cue was on de rail, an' de nine was on de spot—"

A low, black, special-built limousine eased up to the curb before me. The sight of it flashed a daring idea into my mind and set my heart to racing.

The sound of a cue stick pounding on the floor caused me to turn from the doorway; but my thoughts remained on my plan.

"Rack Man! Rack Man! Come and get dis black man!" Crow called triumphantly.

Setting the pop bottle on the front counter, I walked over to where the man Crow had fleeced was slamming his cue into the rack and muttering something about a clip joint.

"Hey! Take it easy on that stick, Pops," I yelled, thinking of the tedious task of re-tipping.

"Who ya talkin' to, me?" he asked belligerently.

Palming a ball in each hand, I answered, "You're the only one casting rod around, ain't 'cha, Moses?"

"But, goddammit, I've been sharked out of fifteen bucks! That guy cat-and-moused me, had me thinking he was just an ordinary player. Why, that little shrimp is a—"

Dropping one of the balls, I grabbed Crow as he lunged for the man yelling, "Le' me at 'im," and struggled against my hold on the back of his collar. "Le' me at de loon, dammit, leave me lam him."

He threw his stick. The sucker had already headed for the door when it landed and I let him get a good start before releasing Crow, who turned on me angrily: "Guy, you all de time holdin' me, why? By God, why?"

"Cool it, Crow, cool it. I've got something more important for you to do."

Looking towards the front, I watched the dapperly-dressed man get out of the limousine. He entered the pool room, seated himself on my shine stand, and began reading a newspaper.

"What's happenin'?" Crow whispered, catching my excitement.

"Listen," I told him, "I'm gonna try to put somebody in the trick bag, only I need time. I want you to run upstairs and make sure Hank doesn't come down for ten minutes, cop?"

Crow was looking alternately at me and then the newspaper reader on the stand.

"Say, momma, you ain't plannin' t' trick who ah'm thinkin' you is—is ya? 'Cause if you is, ah has to warn ya! Dat little dago's deadly!"

"Listen, Crow, I've got to get that money for Mom. You know that. And damn it, man, if I hadn't gone to the damned rink—"

"OK, OK. Ah didn't say ah wasn't gonna do it, ah'm jes' tellin' ya t' be careful, das all!"

He sauntered to the front end and entered the doorway that led upstairs.

Approaching the shoe stand, I spoke to my customer: "Hello, Mr. De Marco, hot isn't it?"

The newspaper lowered. Black eyes stared at me intently.

"Look, kid, I permit only politicians and coppers to call me mister. You running for mayor or are you from the bureau?"

I fumbled about in the polish drawer, silently cursing the tension which had made me forget to call him "Beano."

Antonio Benito De Marco was a regular weekly customer of mine. When I came to work a year-and-a-half ago, I had been informed in the same tone of voice and in the same words about not calling him "Mister." I had been careful and remembered, until a moment ago.

Slamming the drawer, I pretended vexation.

"Damn! I've run out of black polish. Excuse me a minute while I run across the street for some."

"Sure, go ahead," he replied behind the paper.

Dashing across the street, I entered the novelty shop and approached the counter displaying games.

"Hi, Guy! You see anything of that big little brother of mine?" asked the dark-complexioned girl behind the counter, taking off her horn-rimmed glasses and laying them beside the book she'd been reading. It was Crow's sister, Maxine.

"He's taking care of some business for me, Max," I answered, peering into the display case.

"Well, what can I do for you, Guy?"

"Give me some of that play money, some fast-drying glue and some black shoe polish, quick!"

Her eyes grew wide with surprise.

"Play money? Why, Guy Morgan, what do you—"

"Dammit, Maxine, don't be a broad all your life. Can the questions and get me the stuff—P. D. Q.!"

She reached into the display case and withdrew a stack of the "money," placed it before me and hurried off to collect the other items.

116

Pulling out my fifty-dollar roll, I yelled, "Bring me scissors, too!"

In a moment, I had everything I requested.

I cut the three tens and four fives in half.

"Guy! Have you gone completely nuts? Why—you're—"

"Shut up, please. Just do as I tell you, Max!"

Placing the half bills in a row, I lined up fourteen play bills beside them and applied glue to the end of one.

"Look," I directed Max, "stick these on like this," and pressed the edge of a half of a real bill against the glued phony.

She began doing as I asked.

My hands trembled as I thought not of what I was planning to do, but who I was going to do it to. Beano was the racketeering czar of the South Side. He had his fingers in every pie of vice and graft baked in this sin-hot City of Corruption. His power could reach out and hit hard.

"Get me a pair of dice, a rubber band and two of the biggest bills your dad's got in the cash register," I directed Max as she finished gluing the last two pieces.

"What? Now, Guy, you know I can't do that! Dad would—"

"Listen, Maxine, I've been ace-boon-coon with Crow since we were babies and I've saved him from many a crippling without asking questions," I cut in.

Turning to the cash register, she extracted two twenties and handed them to me. Her eyes were clouded with tears.

After carefully folding my phony bank roll to avoid detection, I placed a twenty on each side, slipped the rubber band around it and dropped it in my shirt pocket. Shoving the dice and polish in my hip pocket, I ran out of the store feeling like a heel.

"Sorry for making you wait Mr.—uh—Beano!"

"That's all right, kid, I've got plenty of time," he replied unconcernedly.

"How's business at the club?" I asked.

The second after the words were out, I realized they had been a mistake. Normally all I said to him was "Hi!" and "Bye," or now and then I answered some question he might ask.

He lowered the newspaper and stared at me intently. I bent my head over his shoe. *Another mistake,* I thought, *not looking him in the eye.*

"Business is grand," he answered, "why do you ask?"

"Oh, no reason, just thought I'd ask, that's all."

Beano's club, the Silver Slipper, was a sprawling roadside fun palace on the edge of the city, with luxurious rooms furnished to cater to every vice from perversion to pinochle; a huge black mahogany crescent bar and its ten expert bartenders; a menu that ran from flaming steak and cherries jubilee to hot dogs and apple pie; game rooms equipped for craps, poker, roulette and chuck-a-luck.

Above all this, on the third floor, there was a much talked of and supposedly fabulous suite occupied by Beano himself.

My hands began trembling again as I thought of the power of the little man I intended clipping, but the thought of Mom lying helpless in the big hospital had steadied them almost instantly.

I put the finishing gloss on the expensive shoes. Beano tossed his paper onto the chair next to him and looked down to admire the shine. As he did so, I carefully shifted my position so that he couldn't help seeing the phony roll in my shirt pocket. Snapping the rag with a flourish I pulled down his pant's cuffs and stepped back.

Ask for him! Ask for him! I begged silently.

He looked at his shoes and then at the upstairs entrance.

Ask for him!

"Where's Hank?"

Play it cool and unconcerned, I cautioned myself.

"He stepped out for a few minutes before you came in—said he'd be back in an hour."

Beano stepped down from the stand, pulled out his roll and peeled off a dollar and handed it to me.

"Well—guess I'll have to forgo our little play," he said turning.

Be cool! I warned my racing heart.

"He left his roll with me, just in case you came," I told him, as I put the top on the polish can.

He turned again, and faced me.

"You got Hank's roll? That's strange."

"Naw, it ain't. Hank says he never wins anyway, so—"

I shrugged and let it go at that.

"Well, if he don't mind your losing his money, I won't mind taking it."

He tossed his roll on the chair he'd just vacated. I pulled out my phony roll and placed it beside his.

"Okay," I said, "we'll use my dice."

As he peeled the cellophane from the dice I'd just bought, I remarked, "Your roll looks lighter than Hank's."

"That's the way we play it, kid, you know that. That's the kicker, I mean, not knowing. But for your information, there's about two hundred dead men in that roll."

He tossed the dice on the floor. My heart went wild at this switch on his and Hank's routine. I looked down and eleven black dots looked up.

"Well, you just won," I said helplessly.

"No—I was just tossing them to you. You know I never roll the dice."

"Oh, I forgot," I breathed, picking up the cubes. Then I prayed silently and tossed. They stopped on ten.

"Jesus Christ! Of all the luck!"

I tossed them three more times and then on the fourth roll a six and a four came up.

I reached for the two rolls and put them in my pocket.

He walked to the door, stopped just inside of it and turned. His normally swarthy face was pale, and his eyes glinted as he spoke to me.

"Say, kid, what did you say your name was?"

"Guy, Guy Morgan."

Fear was packing ice around my heart and putting pig iron in my stomach.

"Well, tell me, Guy—Guy Morgan, what have you got against gray hair?"

"Why—nothing. I mean, why do you ask?"

"Because if you ever try to shark me again, you won't live long enough to have any."

I didn't speak.

Reaching into his coat pocket, Beano took an object out and tossed it to me. I caught it.

"You can keep the money, kid, in a way you won it. But keep it as a present from me. You get that? As a present. Nobody beats Beano. Understand?"

He walked away and a few seconds later the big car shot silently away.

I closed my eyes and took a long slow drink of air. Opening them again, I placed the can of shoe polish that he had thrown me next to the one I'd bought when I went after the phony roll.

Chapter **14**

The fragrant smell of freshly-baked bread filled the kitchen as I closed the back door. The factory whistle at 120th and Halsted shrieked four o'clock. Marion shut the oven door of the range and went to the side board which held a partly-iced cake and a mixing bowl. Following her, I took the wooden spoon from the mixing bowl and licked the chocolate icing from it. It was delicious. I smiled and said to her:

"So what's the word, Pretty?"

"Work hard and save your money," she answered, applying a smooth coating of chocolate to the three-layer cake. She wore a tight-fitting brown skirt which revealed the slight imprint of her panties.

Catching the elastic between thumb and forefinger, I rhymed: "Work hard and save your money. Then spend it on some fine brown honey." Stretching the elastic, I let it go. Its snap against her thigh brought a squeal.

"Ooh, Clucky, you've got to stop doing that! Why, you've stretched all my panties in the legs. Not to mention the welts on my—well," she admonished, menacing me with the dripping icing knife.

"On your what?"

"Well, never *mind*. You just stop doing that."

"You know, Marion, you're an odd bit of fluff. I just realized that I've never heard you curse once, although you get so mad until you stamp your feet, like just then. Why don't you swear? All the other girls do."

"I do swear, yes, like a sailor. Only something always stops me from putting it into words. I guess you might call it shy-

121

ness; shy of offending a Being from Whom I know I will have to seek help. So rather than have to go to Him with that on my conscience, well, I confine the expressing of my frustration to stamping my feet. Some people count to ten."

"Gee! You're not only cute, you're smart, too. Why, wouldn't Father Murphy be surprised to hear me confess: 'Father, I stamped my feet fifty times this week.' "

We laughed.

"Seriously, Guy, you should go to Confession or at least attend Mass now and then. Why don't you go to church with me Sunday, tomorrow?"

I thought of the quiet little chapel of the Sacred Heart. I hadn't attended it since the accident which had made a wreck of my life and a cripple of Mom.

Stepping behind Marion, I embraced her about the waist and kissed the top of her head. Her scalp smelled clean; the clean, sensitive aroma of woman; the female volcano smoldering and alive with a consuming air you can feel.

"I can't go with you, Marion, I'd like to, but, well, I'd feel all guilty inside. The hate I feel for my father darn near kept me from praying for Mom. Yes, and for you. I've tried to make myself go to Confession, only I can't, for I know my hate would remain even while I was confessing. Yes, and afterwards, too. The odd part is, I don't dread the loss of heaven and the pains of hell any more. In fact, if anything happened to Mom, I think that I could easily forget both places."

I'd spoken more to myself than to her. She twisted around to face me. There was apprehension in the large brown eyes as they looked up at me widely.

"Guy, Guy, you don't know what you're saying. Why, you sound as though you—oh, you don't mean that, do you? You still believe in God, don't you, Clucky?" Her hands sprung up to clutch my shoulders. Her body was tense as she awaited my answer. I stared down at her, sorry for having divulged my thoughts.

"Clucky," she whispered, shaking my shoulder. "You do believe and love God, don't you?" Her voice held a plea.

"Yes, Marion, I believe and love Him," I answered, watching the concern vanish from her eyes.

She heaved a winded sigh and leaned back in my arms. "Whew! You had me worried there for a moment. You looked so—so, oh, you know. But everything's all right now, isn't it?" she peered anxiously at me.

"Everything is ninety-eight and two, one hundred per cent," I said, giving her an Eskimo kiss.

"Good," she exclaimed with a smile. "But Clucky, I want you to promise to have a talk with Father Murphy, because come next month you'll be eighteen and that's not very far from twenty-one you know."

"But what has seeing Father Murphy go to do with it? He's handing out permits to become twenty-one or something?"

"Now be serious, Clucky, you know that we can't marry with you feeling as you do about—well, you know."

"Lady, you sure are a good Catholic," I said, gathering her closer in my arms. "Okay, so I'll see your old basketball-bellied confessor. Now can I have a kiss?"

I bent to her lips; she placed a hand over my mouth.

"You ought to be ashamed to talk about Father like that," she said. "Basketball-belly—now isn't that a nice description to give a holy man. Why, he's—he's—aw, well, you know: pleasingly plump."

We laughed.

"As for my being a good Catholic, I'm not really, though I would like to be. Only every time you kiss me, I find it awfully hard to remember a few of the 'thou shalt nots.'"

"Say, are you trying to get out of popping me a kiss?" I asked in mock indignation.

"No, only you know what happened the last time we kissed," she pointed out.

"Okay! Oooh!" I said, remembering. "Shove all the blame

on Passion Puff Morgan, but remember, it takes two to tango."

I snapped the elastic in her panties again and ran from the room. Dashing into my bedroom, I slammed the door and leaned against it.

"Just wait till I get my hands on you," she shouted from the other side as she struggled to push the door open. I laughed. "You—you big—ooh! My cookies!" she ended in a wail. There was the sound of scampering feet.

Opening the door I caught the smell of burning pastry.

I went to the closet and took out the zipper bag. Rummaging about in a paste board box in the corner, I matched up a pair of track shoes from the dozen or so in it and dropped them into the bag. From the dresser drawer I withdrew a woolen sweat shirt, pants and a bath towel. Stuffing them into the bag, I went into the bathroom and picked up a bar of soap.

"Come on, slow poke," I yelled, coming into the kitchen.

Marion was closing the top of the bread basket. "I've got to get my uke," she said, hurrying past me into the living room. Returning with the instrument, she handed it to me.

"I ought to be mad at you for making me burn my cookies," she said as we went out the back door. "Dirty mind! Here, let me have the bag." There was sadness in her voice.

I handed her the bag and we walked through the vacant lot in silence. We were both thinking the same thing.

"Will you miss me, Guy?"

I took her small hand in mine. I couldn't speak what I felt. I squeezed her hand. We'd been together all of our lives, it seemed. We'd met at the Spencer School when I killed a snake which had frightened her away from her favorite lunching spot on the school lawn. That day we had vowed to marry each other when we were old enough. I was five, she was six. Every year thereafter we renewed the promise. This fall she was going away to college in Boston. A sudden feeling of foreboding smote me.

124

I stopped, she turned toward me.

"Marion, listen, don't go away. I've got the feeling that once we're separated, we'll lose each other. I can't explain what I mean, only, don't go, please, for my sake. Why, I don't know what I'll do without you, to look at and to talk to and to —to like," I ended lamely, completely at loss for words with which to express the desperation and fear I was feeling.

"Clucky, I don't want to go, you know that. Why, I'd much rather go to one of the colleges around here, but, well, you know Dad. And Clucky, he's been so nice to me, always giving me more than mere fatherly understanding and attention. I know that he was disappointed in my not being a boy, but after Mom died and all—then there's the business and although it's a little place, he's as proud of it as Walgreen is of his chains. I am, too, because it is the only one out here and being as though he's going to leave it to me, well, I wanted to be qualified to handle it."

"But why go to Boston? Why, my God, that's a million miles away."

"Oh, we've been over that, Guy, my uncle is a professor at the college and my aunt is house mother at the sorority house where I want to stay. I told you, Guy. My uncle can find me part-time work, maybe, and—"

"Muffet, let's get married right away. Today, if possible."

"Oh, Guy, that's out of the question. You're only seventeen—"

"For enough money, Hank could bribe me a license. Or we could go to some other state. After the race, I'll have the necessary money."

She dropped her eyes from mine to gaze at her loafers.

"No, Guy, we couldn't. I want to be married in the church. I've pictured it that way as long as I can remember. The stained glass, the organ music, the two of us kneeling at the altar. I—I can't, I just can't cast it aside," she pointed out dismally, "we both planned it that way, remember?"

125

"Yes, Marion, I remember," I said. "Come on or else I won't get any practice today."

We hurried to the school ground.

* * *

Stepping out of the shower, I padded across the tile floor of the field house locker room. The noise in the den the naked boys were making was deafening as they shouted about the past three hours of practice.

"Say, Sandy, you run like you got a ball and chain around both legs."

"Yeah, well I could pole vault higher than you today with a damn broom straw."

"Anybody got a cigarette?"

"Say man, don't you know smoking ain't no good for an athlete?"

"Who said that lame was an athlete. Why, a damn jumping bean could get farther than him. He's an ath-leak."

"So says you, but that ain't what Mr. Langley says. Just ask him who's the best broad jumper in the park. Just ask him, and buddy, the answer you'll get is old Bird."

"Yeah, you're in the best broad jumps in the park and if you don't stop jumping Millie Clay, you're gonna cop a gold medal for the most outstanding dose of claps ever caught. Haw! Haw! Haw! I guess that'll shut your trap."

"Hey, screw you!"

"You do and I'll nut ya! Haw, haw, haw!"

"Say, will you give me a smoke?"

"Hell no. If J. C. wanted you to smoke, he'd 'a put a pack up your pratt. Haw, haw, haw!"

I dressed hurriedly and walked out in the fresh night air, closing the door on the den. Marion detached herself from a group of girls and hurried over to me.

"Ready?" she asked, taking my bag.

"Yeah, where you want to go?" I took her uke.

126

"Let's buy some marshmallows and go over to the park," she suggested, taking my hand.

At 112th and Loomis we stopped in Brown's store for the marshmallows, two Cokes and the weekly Negro newspaper. Reaching the park, we went over to the fire that a group of kids had built at the edge of the ball diamond.

"Hey, Marion! Hey, Guy!" they greeted.

"Hi!" we chorused as we spread out paper.

"Marion, where have you been? We were beginning to think you'd gone highbrow on us," a girl said.

"No, I've got lots of studying to do," Marion said.

"Are you coming to the prom next week?" Crow's sister, Maxine asked.

Marion looked at me questioningly.

"Yes, we'll be there," I said.

"Oh, well!" the girl exclaimed, clapping her hands in glee. "We'll have a blowout for you, Marion, a sort of Fare-well-Old-Gal-Come-Back-Smarter-Than-Hell affair. What are you going to wear, Marion?"

"Oh, I've bought a simply beautiful dress . . ."

I let my mind drift away from the talk. I opened the bag of marshmallows and strung them on a wire someone had discarded. As I held it over the glowing coals, I thought about the four years Marion would be away. When she returned I'd be twenty-two. Four years was an awfully long time to be away from someone you loved. A lot of things could happen in four years. Yeah, and a lot of changes could take place. Time—what was it I'd once read about time and changes, something about the human mind being so constructed as to make the sharpest experience in life fade with the passing of time. I wondered if perhaps her father had not had this in mind when he broached his plan for sending her to Boston. I tried to remember whether Mr. Gale had ever resented me.

As if by some silent, instinctive signal I looked up and saw her approaching across the baseball diamond; hips swinging, black hair bobbing, heels stepping high. Luzon.

I watched her, gripped in the love-hate fascination I had felt for her ever since I saw her in the drug store shortly after the accident. As children we had known each other, played together and, before the auto crash, she had taught me the hand language of the deaf mute, learned because of her afflicted mother. But in the two years that I had been injured and recovered, she had changed drastically. She was no longer a little girl to play with, to tease, to enjoy talking to in a language that was all our own among friends. Now she was growing into womanhood, with curving hips and jutting breasts, an invitation on her lips but scorn in her eyes. Even the butter-colored texture of her mulatto skin antagonized me. Who was it she reminded me of, I wondered as she made her hip-swinging approach, who was it?

She weaved her way through the couples sprawling about the grass, then spotted me at the fire. I stared at her.

"You're burning your marshmallows, Guy," she said softly, but there was laughter in her voice.

"Thanks," I answered grimly. Of all the dopey things to do with her standing there.

"Want to fix me one?" she asked.

"Not particularly," I said, putting the wire down.

The sound of Marion singing *Sweet Leilani*, Mom's favorite song, caused me to turn from Luzon. I thought of Mom and how the doctor had not let me in to see her. I thought: *I'm a freak again, only this time I'm a horror to the sight of my own mother.* I shuddered with self-loathing. *Oh, God, sweet Jesus, make her well, please.*

I rolled over on my back, looking at the sky, and shuddered again. The twinkling stars laughed their merry indifference at me. Suddenly, my view of them was blotted out as Luzon's face hovered over mine. She had dropped to her knees beside me.

128

"Are you chilled?" she asked.

I stared mutely at her with unseeing eyes.

"You don't like me, do you, Guy?" she asked finally at my continued silence.

"Does it bother you?"

"Yes," she said. "I would like to know why."

I did not answer.

"Listen," she whispered hoarsely, "what right have you to treat me this way? Are you afraid to let yourself like me?" Her eyes bore into mine, the glow of the fire reflecting in them and giving them a strange glint.

Zola! my mind shouted. *Another Delilah on the prowl for a scalp.*

Luzon's voice still hissed in my ear. "You can't treat me this way. I won't stand for it, do you hear? What are you so proud of, your straining muscles and smelly sweat? You . . . You're vile and mean and nasty and for what reason?"

Her hot breath brushed my face. Opening my eyes, I stared into hers and spoke the most punishing words that I could think of: "Pure moorish blood flows through my veins, mongrel bitch, king's blood!" I whispered it with an angry pride I didn't truly feel.

She didn't move a muscle. Only a sharp intake of breath and a slight crimson tint sweeping over her pale skin signaled the insult she had felt. She laughed derisively.

Crow's voice cut through my inflamed mind: "Hey, Guy! Guy! Where in de hell are ya? Where's Guy, Max?"

"Here I am Crow," I said propping myself up on my elbows. He stood over me, jumping with excitement.

"Ooooh, baby! Baby! Baby! We got two of 'em. We caught 'em with de goods too, spying. Ooh, buddy!" He was beside himself with glee.

"Hey, what the hell are you talking about, caught who doing what? Cool the monkeyshines and tell me what's happening," I demanded.

"Here dey come," he said, pointing to six forms walking toward us.

"Who are they? Dammit, Crow, talk sense," I said, sitting up.

"Ding, Dipper, Earl and Harold, an' dey got Ray Miller and Treetop wit' 'em, caught 'em spyin'," Crow ran to meet the six approaching figures, everyone was quiet. Luzon, who knelt beside me, got to her feet. I stared at the two boys who stood before me. Their wrists were tied to each other with shoe-laces from their shoes.

"What's happening?" I asked the muscular Ding.

"We were helpin' Dipper restock the shelves in his old man's store when we dig these two punks pass by. Seein' Ray here's a jungle cat, we run out and put the snatch on him. He says he's on the legit, had to get a prescription filled at Gale's. Only, when we frisk him, he ain't got no prescription. But we did find this."

He handed a piece of paper to me, it bore the name of Sandy, Bird and myself and a few more guys who were at practice today. After each name there was inserted the sports event in which we were going to participate and the time we had made in practice.

"What are you going to say for yourself, hot shot?" I asked the dapper dope pusher.

"Look daddy, I'm not in on this duel that you cats got goin'. I was just tryin' to make a little bread on the side, so give me a play, huh?" The pusher was frightened, his habitual drawl was missing, and he scratched frantically at his nose.

"You was playing spy, hot shot, and when you play, you pay," I informed him, letting my dislike come into my voice.

"But look, man, I can explain, I was—"

I cut him off. "You've had it, hot shot." Turning to Harold, I said, "Hip him to the penalty of being caught spying in time of war."

130

There was a smile of satisfaction on Harold's lips as he said, "Fifteen lashes, the offender wearing covering of thin material." I nodded. "That's the rule, huh?" Harold nodded.

I stared at the pusher. Remembering his recent threat, the picture of a dead body sprawled on a tile floor flashed before my eyes.

"Uh-huh. Well, rules were made to be broken, right, hot shot? And for a long time you guys have been acting like you've got a priority on breaking them." I turned to where Marion sat clutching her uke.

"Marion, you and the rest of the girls clear out. We'll meet you by the swings when we're finished."

Getting up, she collected my bag and walked toward the park playground with June and Alice.

"Well, what's wrong with you, Max?" Maxine stood staring at the two bound boys, her eyes wide with fright.

"What are you going to do to them? You don't really intend to beat them, do you? That's—that's horrible," she stammered.

"Get her out of here!" I ordered.

Crow went over and took her by the arm. "Come on, Max, you gotta go, so don't give me no hard time."

"Don't have anything to do with that, Crow, please don't, it's bad and it's wrong," Maxine pleaded.

Crow pulled her off into the shadows and came hurrying back. "Okay," he said, pulling off his three-inch wide belt. Clutching it by the buckle he cut the air with it viciously.

"Separate 'em," I directed, pretending not to notice Luzon. She'd walked over to the gaudily-dressed Treetop.

Sandy noosed Treetop's neck from behind with his belt, and held the other end wrapped in his grasp.

"You try to take off, daddy, and you'll have one hell of a sore throat tomorrow," he warned.

"You don't have to worry about him running away," Luzon said, her eyes flashing around at us. "He's no coward, he can take anything you big bad bow-wows can put down, can't you Treetop?" She turned to demand of the multi-colored dandy. Treetop, it was apparent, was Luzon's latest heart throb. He tried to play the part which her words had created, but his darting eyes were full of fear.

"Yeah," he sneered, "I'll hang tough. Only you guys remember—What goes around, comes around." He nodded at me.

"Okay, Bogart, I'll remember," I assured. Turning to Ding, "Put that one on the cross, stripped," I directed, nodding at Ray. He began to whimper as they pulled him over and tied him spread-eagle to the heavy wire on the backstop of the ball diamond.

"You'd better gag him," Sandy advised.

Ray Miller hung naked to the waist.

Bird sauntered up to me. "Let me work this stoolin' hop head," he requested.

I nodded, turning to stretch out on my stomach. Resting my chin on my crossed wrists, I watched him hurry over to the water fountain and soak his belt. He trailed it in the dirt as he returned to the hanging boy. In a wide-legged stance he began to apply the wet, be-grimed belt to Ray's back.

"One! Two! Three! Four! Five! Six!" Harold continued.

I watched Treetop out of the corner of my eye.

"Nine! Ten! Eleven! Twelve!"

Treetop began to lick his lips.

"Fifteen! Sixteen! Seventeen! Eighteen!"

The rule on the article of war didn't apply to Miller.

"Twenty-one! Twenty-two! Twenty-three!"

Treetop was trembling like jelly. Luzon's encouraging hand on his arm didn't stop the shakes.

"Hold it!" I shouted to Bird, but he continued to lash the squirming Miller.

"Hold it, goddammit, Bird!" I shouted, raising to my elbows.

132

He still continued to flay.

"Grab that punk, Earl!" I shouted.

Earl snatched the belt out of Bird's hand with such force as to send him sprawling to the ground. He sat there with a dazed look on his face and an idiotic grin on his lips.

"Cut him loose, Ding," I commanded.

Ray ran as if a thousand demons pursued him as soon as his bonds were removed, animal whimpers trailing from him as he went.

Nodding to Sandy, I said, "All right, let's give Mr. Guts an opportunity to display his spunk to the palomino."

Fear made Treetop bold. "Listen chumps, I know my rights under the war article," he sneered. "You gave that cat a raw deal, he wasn't supposed to get but fifteen lashes and with a shirt on. You can't do me like that. You're dirty if you do, cause it ain't fair."

I waited for him to talk himself out. "Look, you stripe-assed ape," I said when he had finished, "who you telling what they can't do? You were caught spying in Gaylord territory and caught dead. Bang! Then you lied and said you had a legit reason to step over the bar. As for that dirty, stool pigeon pusher, the articles don't apply to him. You say I'm dirty? Good! I'm going to give you an opportunity to know just how muddy I am. We're going to make an example of you, for now and always." I turned to the others. "Put him in the cross, but leave his shirt on," I directed.

Sandy, Ding, Harold and Earl tied him quickly to the spot where Miller had hung.

"How many?" Crow asked.

"You wanta do it?" I asked.

He nodded.

"Okay, then, lay it on 'till I tell you to stop," I directed, looking into the coals of the fire which still glowed redly.

Crow adopted a wide-legged stance, and raised the belt

to strike. "Hold it!" I commanded, pulling a red hot wire from the fire. "Use this."

I heard the sharp intake of Luzon's breath and saw her pale. Treetop stared over his shoulder with wide-eyed fear as he strained at his bounds. His muffled cries were reduced to groans as Crow lashed him with the wire. The smell of burnt cloth and skin filled my nostrils. Every stroke of the wire made Treetop's body jerk distortedly. The two-toned shoes slid about in a frenzied dance, kicking up dust.

Who was it that I knew that admired and wore two-toned shoes? I wondered, watching the wild tap dance. *Someone I knew and hated; who was it?*

Was that him performing the crazy, pain-inspired dance?

Yes, that's him, and I have the power to stop the cause of that dance if I want to. But why stop it? Isn't that exactly what I've prayed for, those dancing shoes?

Two-toned shoes that could press an accelerator to the floor until the car flew at a speed of ninety miles an hour. Two-toned shoes that ran away when their presence was needed most; two-toned shoes that ran away beside the high-heel shoes of a prostitute. Two-toned shoes whose tread Mom listened to hear in worshipful silence. Two-toned shoes that had pressed the life from her legs.

But what goes around, comes around, Mr. Two-toned shoes. Why have you stopped? Tired? Or have your legs also lost life? No better for you, Mr. Two-toned shoes. I've always wanted to make you lifeless, old hated shoes, old lifeless shoes. Good! Good! Good! Mr. Two—"

"Hey, Guy, for crapsakes when can I stop? This guy is out colder than ice, man, he looks like he's dead," Crow said, peering at the slumped, unconscious Treetop.

"Good!" I said, involuntarily raising the thought I'd had.

"What?" Crow asked, not understanding me.

"Nothing," I evaded. "You tired?" I asked him.

134

"Hell, yeah, and a little sick at de stomach too, buddy, this wire has made a mess of his back," Crow said.

"Well, I guess that's enough then," I said, getting to my feet. Luzon stepped in front of me.

"What'll we do with him?" Sandy asked.

"Leave the bastard hanging there," Harold said.

"Don't worry about him," I said, staring into Luzon's green and angry shooting eyes. "Miss Luzon Switch here will take care of him."

I stepped past her. As I did she hissed, "Meet me in the tennis court at twelve o'clock, I dare you."

I continued walking in the direction Marion had taken. As I stepped out of the glare of the fieldhouse lights which flooded the ball diamond, Maxine detached herself from the shadows and blocked my path.

"You fagan!" she croaked, "you dirty, rotten, filthy fagan. You made my brother beat that helpless boy. I used to think that you were good, fair, and clean, that you were a good companion for my brother, but I was wrong and I hate you, you slimy, loathsome beast. Someday you're going to get yours, and I hope it's before you get my brother killed." She spat in my face, then wheeled and ran out of the park. I wiped away the spittle. Crow and the rest walked up.

"What's wrong?" Crow asked, staring into the direction I was gazing in.

"Nothing," I lied.

"Well, we'll see you tomorrow," they promised, heading toward the north-west park exit.

"Yeah, cool it," I said, looking back to the ball field. Luzon stood with her back to me. In her right hand she held Treetop's sport coat. She flung it to the ground; it burst into flame. She had thrown it into the fire.

I hurried into the playground, Marion was sitting in a swing, with uke and bag on her lap. At the sound of my footsteps she raised her head and peered into the darkness.

"Guy, that you?" she asked.

"Yeah, come on, intermission's over," I said. We walked from 112th and Ada to 111th and Throop in silence.

Reaching the side entrance of the drug store which led to the upstairs living quarters, I halted. "Well, what's eating you?" I demanded finally.

She pushed through the door and climbed the long flight of stairs. I followed, entering the apartment. I flopped into a big arm chair near the door and looked around the room. It was comfortably furnished, and its neatness bespoke of the constant care of a woman. I glanced at the grandfather's clock in one corner, it was fifteen minutes to twelve. What was it I intended to do at twelve o'clock? Marion had set my bag by the door when we'd come in. I knew that she was mad at me by the way her eyes avoided mine. Had she watched the beating of Ray and Treetop like Maxine? Shrugging inwardly, I asked:

"So why the silent treatment? If you're salty at me, hip me to the cause."

She swung her legs over the chair arm, her back to me, and replied, "I don't know if I'm salty at you or not, but I think I should be. June was watching what took place on the ball field. I told her not to, but she did anyway. Whatever you did to Ray and Treetop, made her vomit all over herself. I didn't look because something warned me that if I did, it wouldn't be the same between us afterwards. You've never had too many friends, Clucky, and now you're making the few you have sick of you, what has gotten into you? What are you knocking yourself out to prove?"

I tried to supply an answer and couldn't. The grandfather's clock began to chime. It's first stroke brought me to my feet. *Luzon's* challenge: *Twelve o'clock. I dare you."* I hurried to the door, feeling an unexplainable resentment.

"Where are you going?" Marion asked.

Opening the door, I said, "To make another broad sick."

136

The clock was still chiming as I slammed the door.

Taking the stairs three at a time, I dashed out of the entrance and sprinted for the park. As I raced down the dark street, the resentment in me mounted into a hot anger which increased with each stride I took and centered itself upon the girl I knew would be waiting in the park. *I may not know what's wrong with me, but I damn sure know what's wrong with her,* I told myself, increasing my speed and turning into the park. *If she thought I was going to supply her with an easy cure, then she'd better think again.*

I came to a panting halt a few feet inside of the tennis court. Wiping the sweat out of my eyes, I peered into its darkened corners. Delilah must have sheathed her shears and gone home after all, I decided, leaving the court.

"Over here."

I turned toward the sound of the voice. She was over near the fire. For a moment I stared at the lone figure sitting cross-legged in the glare of the floodlights. As I walked toward her, she got to her feet in one agile motion. *Hell has no fury like a woman scorned,* I thought, remembering the hot invitation Luzon's eyes had always held whenever and wherever we'd chanced to meet. Invitations which at first I had rejected. This continued rejection had brought a challenge into her look. I thought of the rage they had contained earlier tonight when she'd said that she wasn't going to stand for me to treat her shabbily. Yes, her eyes had always been upon me: Challenging eyes, daring eyes, defiant eyes, casting their taunt over the top of text books; flinging it across the school yard; telegraphing it across the dance floor; flashing it in the drug store, at the picnic grounds, at basement parties, from the edge of the swimming pool, in the dark and light.

I stopped a foot before her. She stood with her hands behind her. We stared at each other. Now her veiled lids cast slits of hot fury at me on a ball diamond in the park. The sight of her began to give reason to my earlier action. I'd let Treetop be beaten because I desired to make a liar out of her; because he'd tried to act the part she created. After that, the sight of the two-toned shoes had cast their spell.

My chest was heaving with the effort of my running. Perspiration plastered my T-shirt to my body. Her eyes lowered to its wetness, distaste pulled down the corners of her lips.

Taking a backward step, she sneered, "Straining muscles and smelly sweat."

I sprang forward as the wire she held behind her began to cut its glowing arch and grabbed the wrist of the striking hand. The wire bent searing my shoulders.

"You half-breed slut," I cursed, trying to grip her squirming waist.

She pistoned her knees at my groin. I twisted, catching the impact in my right thigh. Swinging the leg back, I kicked hers from beneath her. We fell sprawling to the ground. Dust clogged my nostrils, forcing me to breath from my mouth. She'd released the wire and was biting at my wrist. I threw some dirt in her face. Her fist struck me in the mouth. Blood mingled with the dust in my throat. I struggled to imprison the flaying fist, as it struck me about the head. The dust blinded me. We wrestled about silently, the pant of our labored breathing was the only sound to be heard. Her hand snaked to my ear trying to tear off the earring. Reaching up, I grabbed the clawing fingers, bending them back to the ground over her head. She squirmed, kicking wildly.

I pressed the full length of my body upon her, she tried to twist free, but my weight held her. The effort of her straining made her body tremble; mine absorbed the vibrations. My mouth found her lips in a brutal kiss. She strained with increasing fury to release herself. Pressing my mouth down harder, I crushed her lips between her clenched teeth and mine. The tension of her straining wrists in my grasps began to slowly slacken, until there was no resistance.

138

The anger I had felt at the beginning began to ebb with the first sign of surrender. In its stead arose the determination for her complete surrender. My mouth demanded this, as I released my hold on her wrist and ran my hand over her breasts and down the length of her body. Her lips relaxed and returned my kiss with an inflaming tardiness. She arched her back as I slipped my arm beneath her. I fumbled at the tight shorts as she made frantic little sounds in her throat. Her body trembled with aroused sexual passion, straining for satisfaction. I pressed.

"Oooooh!" she cried, clutching me tightly about the waist.

I tore free of her. Getting to my feet, I arranged my pants. She stared up at me through eyes veiled with aroused desire. I laughed at her and stepped two feet away.

"I will take vengeance and I will not meet you as a man, O virgin daughter of Zola," I sneered.

Tears welled up in her eyes and washed clean a side of her dust begrimed face. "I'll make you crawl for this," she vowed hoarsely.

Intentionally, I misinterpreted her meaning. "Don't flatter yourself, cherry," I mocked as I walked into the shadows.

For the second time I stopped and looked back at the ball diamond. Luzon was laying as I left her, as if basking in the glare of the flood lights, the dust our struggle had aroused, hung in a mist above her. The unbelievable discovery I had made caused me to laugh again. At the sound of it, she sat up and stared in my direction. I repeated the laugh, for it was funny: Who would have thought that Luzon of the many loves was a virgin?

Chapter **15**

"I caughtcha! I caughtcha! Now knuckle down and screw bone tight."

"The hell you did." Come on now Archibald, no fair cheating . . ."

The sound of the marble players' bickering was dragging me slowly into consciousness. Pulling the pillow over my head, I fought to stay in carefree dreamland.

"No changie, no changie," shrieked the kids.

"The hellie you say," came the heated reply.

"See there, see there, you busted my best toy, with that steel bolley of yours. Now ya got to buy me another one, cause you wasn't supposed to change!" wailed the voice.

"The hellie you say!"

I got up from the bed and staggered to the half-opened window, slammed it shut, reeled back to the bed and sprawled onto it. Placing the pillow between my knees, I prepared to return to sleep. The telephone rang. I groaned. Reaching for the other pillow, I placed it over my head. The jingle of the phone persisted. Flinging the pillow aside, I sat up on the edge of the bed. In a sleep drugged stupor I thought, "that damned ostrich action must work only in dirt." The phone began to really knock itself out.

"All right! All right!" I shouted, stumbling out of the room. Who in the hell could it be? I pondered. Muffet knew better than to call me this early on Sundays. The hospital. The possibility brought instant wakefulness as I snatched up the receiver.

"Hello!"

"Hello, Clucky," answered the voice of Aunt Emma. "What took you so long to answer?"

"I was asleep," wishing that she'd hang up so I could go back to sleep.

"Asleep! Why it's nearly nine o'clock."

"If you'd hang up, I'm sure I'd easily forget that," I muttered.

"What! What was that you're mumbling? I can't hear you."

"I said that I wasn't aware of that fact." I answered raising my voice.

"Well, you don't have to shout, I'm not deaf, you know. Did you receive Aunt Agnes' and my check? I was wondering, you didn't acknowledge it. Kids are so inconsiderate these days. That's what I was telling your Aunt Agnes, about kids being inconsiderate I mean, and by the way, she's well. Yes, as a matter of fact, so are all of us. How's Lonnie? Poor dear . . ." She was off, I held the crackling phone away from my ear. It continued to make rattling noises.

"You old chatterbox" I whispered, slapping at the sound coming from the receiver.

"Uncle Milton needs to spank your butt till it rings like a bell."

"Clucky, Clucky, hello, can you hear me?" she inquired.

Taking another swing at her voice, I put the receiver back to my ear. "Yes, I hear you."

"Oh! For a moment I thought you had gone back to bed, isn't that silly?"

I waited a moment, then agreed, "Yes, very."

"You know, Clucky, sometimes I think you're ill-mannered," she said, clearing her throat.

I remained silent.

"Well, anyway your Aunt Agnes and I will be expecting you."

"Expecting me? Expecting me where and when?"

"Why at the church today, silly. I thought you said that you could hear me?"

I thought the manner and tone in which she, Agnes and Mom spoke the word "silly" was the only thing that gave an indication to their kinship.

"Oh that," I said, faking remembrance. "And why am I to meet you at the church today?" I coached.

"To get the presents we have for you, of course. We would bring them by, but being business manager of the reception committee for the new pastor has my hands full and time filled. So you'll just have to come and get them. Besides, I want you to meet our new pastor. Rev. Heath is . . ."

"Rev. who?" I cut in, feeling a wild excitement.

"Now, don't shout, Clucky. Why I've told you two times now. Clucky, what's wrong with you? You aren't drunk, are you? You know, kids today are so wild."

I cut in with hurried reassurance. "No, no, I'm not drunk, not on what you think anyway.

"This Rev. Heath of yours, does he have a daughter?"

"Of course silly, I told you. Oh! Clucky you're hopeless," she said exasperatedly.

"I haven't time to talk to you anymore now, so we will see you at church, goodbye."

"Hey! wait a minute!" I yelled. The receiver gave a clicking sound. She had hung up. I dropped the receiver back into its cradle and went back to flop on my bed. Opening the window for fresh air as I went.

"Archibald, you're a cheater you're all the time changing the rule, ya don't play chase the fox that way and you know it."

"The hellie you say . . ."

The one-sided verbal controversy was continuing outside the window. I shifted my attention to the one-sided conversation I'd had with Aunt Emma. Rev. Heath's taking over the Greater Hope ministry, meant only two things to me. First,

142

that lady killer Kelly was taking off to greener pastures, and second and most important, I'd have an opportunity of seeing the sophisticated Kay again. I smiled at my description of the pretty Kay Heath. A feeling of disloyalty tugged at my heart. So what about you and Muffet? I asked myself. Why, hell, a guy can think about a pretty girl can't he? Besides Muffet will be one thousand miles away this fall. Then too, nothing or no one would change my feelings for her and Mom. The coupling of the two names made me realize how very similar my feelings for them were. Mom and Marion were alike in ways too. I began to make a mental comparison, they were the same height, weight and complexion. Muffet's hair was a bit longer than Mom's but of the same grade. Marion's feet might be a bit smaller, but not too much. Their hands were of the same doll size. A strange feeling started to crowd about in my stomach and curl into a loathsome ball. Their lips were the same, nose and eyes were also alike. I hesitated at the next comparison, then drove myself on. Their breasts were . . .

The furious jingle of the telephone startled me. I sprang out of the bed and stared at myself in the dresser mirror. Beads of perspiration stood out on my forehead, my hands were trembling.

"You vile thinking bastard," I cursed at the image in the glass and raised a fist to strike. The phone jingled again, I turned and went to answer it.

"Hello," I said dully into the receiver.

"How are you Guy?" It was Dr. Bruce.

Anxious concern for Mom pushed all other thoughts from my mind.

"What's wrong Dr. Bruce—Mother's all right, isn't she?" Apprehension made me grip the receiver tightly with both hands.

"Now take it easy son, everything's dandy, which is why I phoned you. Dr. Cherkow will be here tomorrow, and your mother regained consciousness last night. I didn't phone you because it happened rather late and I . . ."

I cut in excitedly. "When can I see her, Dr. Bruce? Can I see her today, please?"

"Now, son, I know how you feel, but well, let's wait a little longer, huh? We don't want to get her excited, you know."

"Okay, doctor," I agreed dejectedly.

"Ah, Guy, this Dr. Cherkow, ah, I hate to refer to it, but have you managed to obtain the money?"

"I thought of the two hundred dollars I'd sharked, or, rather, that Beano had given me.

"I'd added it to Aunt Emma and Agnes $100, which meant that I'd made a start. I hadn't any doubts about getting the money because I had to get it.

"Tell Dr. Cherkow that I'll have his money the last of July."

"All right, then, so I'll keep you informed on any further developments. Ah, how's your other little girl—what's her name, Marion?"

Was there anything other than cordial solicitude in his question, I thought?

"Just fine, thank you."

"Good, well, so long then." He hung up.

Dropping the receiver to its hook, I repeated his words: "how's your other little girl?" I'd walked into Mom's bedroom unconsciously. I looked around. It was the typical bedroom of a very fastidious woman. The furnishings were neatly arrayed, making objects readily accessible. Going to the closet, I opened the door and removed a pair of brown shoes from the pocket of the shoe bag hanging on the door. I looked inside them. They were size 5. I dropped them back into the pocket. Taking a dress from the row on the rack, I looked into the collar. It was a size 12. Replacing it, I shut the door. Going to the dresser, I opened two of its drawers, then a third. It held neat stacks of panties and brassieres. I noted their size

34. Closing the drawer, I re-entered the living room. What the hell did you do that for? I asked myself as I placed the record on the turntable. So maybe they do wear the same size clothes. What does that prove? I continued to question myself.

The husky female voice filled the room . . . *Them that's got shall get, thems that not shall lose . . .*

I sprawled upon the couch, and pursued my thoughts. I'd loved Mom even before I met Marion. I attempted to rationalize, then stopped, feeling that such logic was unbecoming of a child. "Hell," I cursed, shifting my position, "there's nothing complicated about my feeling for Mom and Marion. It merely follows as a matter of course. Mom, Muffet, Lonnie, Marion, as simple as B follows A, or M follows L. Now what the hell made me think of that?" I turned on my stomach. Is there anything wrong in a guy loving a girl that has the same looks and ways as his mother? I pondered. What about asking her to change her hair style—yes—and requesting her to wear blue more often? Blue was Mom's favorite color and the hair style was more similar to Mom's, but damn, that don't make me . . . No! No! I couldn't face my thoughts to go on.

"Ah, hell," I said getting up and going to the bathroom. Stepping into the tub, I turned on the shower. The shock of the water clarified my thoughts. What the hell. Didn't every guy want to love a girl just like his Mom? I recalled a song, how did it go—"I want a girl just like the girl that married dear old dad," I sang it loudly, without feeling. The "dear old dad" part struck a sour note. I tried to eliminate it, but couldn't, determined to forget the whole thing. I turned the cold water full blast. Stepping out of the tub, I rubbed myself with the towel until my skin burned, then ran for the bedroom . . .

Yes, the strong gets more, while the weak ones fade; empty pockets don't ever make the grade . . .

"Ah! chirp, lady, chirp." I encouraged the vocalist as I dressed. "As for money, these pockets are going to be chugged

145

come to the last of next month, and they'll get that way by my being strong," I informed the singer, while twisting a knot into the gray tie . . .

Money, you've got lots of friends . . .

"That's one thing I don't have to worry about, sexy," I continued to inform the vocalist." Muffet says, I'm making them sick. Yeah, well, I intend to make them even sicker." Now dressed, I went to the closet for my hat. Stepping back to the mirror, I placed it squarely upon my head, crimping the brim into the slight homburg roll and stepped back. Throwing a practice smile, I bow'd slightly and said, affecting an English accent, "My dear, deah Miss Heath, what a delightful pleasure to see you again." Laughing, I left the room. The lady was cooing. . .

Rich relations give, crusts of bread and such, you can help yourself, but don't take too much . . . In the front room, I clicked off the turntable, remembering the measly money my aunt had sent me, I erased the smile from my face. Looking down at the still record I admitted, "yeah lady you're right, but I'm going to return their crust to them and I'll never go begging again." These words returned my self-confidence. Whistling, I walked out of the house. By continuing straight down 110th Street to Loomis, I'd avoid having to pass the drug store and pool room. Some of the gang was sure to be in one or both of them; besides, I didn't want to run the risk of dampening the mood I was in. I felt a prick of guilt over intentionally ducking them, then shrugged it off. I was making them sick of me anyway, so Marion said. As I turned south on Loomis, the voice of a famed sports announcer declared:

"It's a beautiful day in Chicago."

I looked through the screen door of a house as I passed. A man of some 300 pounds sat leaning intently forward in the glare of T.V.; a quart of beer sat at his feet. I looked up at the clear blue sky.

"Yeah, it's a beautiful day in Chicago," I agreed, feeling

146

elated over Dr. Bruce's news of Mom, and the possibility of seeing Kay again. As I passed the Greasy Spoon, someone rapped on the window. It was Velma; I waved. She was a stallion who sure loved the feedbag. As I neared the church, the thunder of organ music vibrated the air . . .

A mighty fortress is our God, a bulwark never failing! . . . sang the well-rehearsed choir feelingly. Aunt Emma's big Cadillac was parked in the shade of the big cottonwood trees near the walk of the church entrance. Opening the car door, I got inside. Its interior reeked with perfume. I left the door open. I thought of Aunt Emma, disgustedly; buddy, what a broad. Poor old hen-hearted Uncle Milton, I sympathized . . . The choir broke into another song . . .

God be with you till we meet again! . . . I was wondering what presents my aunt had for me. Then noticing the small package sticking in the sun visor, I withdrew it. It was my present. Across its neat wrapping was written, "Happy Graduation and Birthday, from Aunt Emma and Agnes." They refused to accept the fact that I wasn't graduating with my class. Dropping the package in my pocket, I thought amusingly, "two birds with one stone." The large church door opened, releasing a horde of yelling kids of all sizes and colors. I stayed in the car, for my aunts went to church like a person who'd taken a laxative went to the can: they were the first ones in and the last ones out. I laughed out loud at the comparison.

"Wha'cha laughing at?" asked an urchin. I stared down at him. He was one of the marble players who'd awakened me this morning. The kid who'd taken my hill.

"I'm laughing at you, you smut doll."

"The hellie you say," declared Archibald.

I laughed again.

"Say, is you crazy, and is this your car?"

"Yeah," I said in answer to both questions.

"Will ya let me in?" he inquired in wide-eyed entreaty.

147

"Sure," I said, leaning over to open the other side of the door. "Come on around and hop in."

"Ooh boy!" he exclaimed, running around to the other side and climbing in. "Boy! Oh boy! Ain't she a be-aut!" he stated looking at the shiny instrument panel.

"Uh-huh," I agreed, enjoying his enthusiasm.

"Let me take it for a spin, okay?" he asked gripping the wheel.

"Sure! let's go, only take it easy on the tires," I cautioned.

"Okay, hold your hat—b-aaa outen, e-rk, a-aa outen," he sped off in pretense. Archibald was the youngest in a family of eight. His father had lost one arm beneath a train wheel, while stealing coal to sell in order to supplement his janitor's pay.

"Hey, man, look out for that truck!" I shouted, entering into his play.

"Jeezus!" he yelled, cutting the steering wheel sharply. Turning to me, he inquired in an awed whisper. "Say, didja see that doggone fool nearly sideswipe me?"

Bending over, I howled.

Archibald screamed with pain. I looked up. Aunt Emma held him by the back of his tattered shirt with one hand and slapped him viciously across the face with the other.

"Why, you filthy, nasty little pig. How dare you put your dirt and lice in my car. I'll teach you, you—" I sat dazed, uncomprehending. The kid's scream of terror made me leap from the seat and around the car.

"Lady, lady, I didn't mean to do you nothing," he told her. He was sobbing as I wrenched him from her grasp. He clutched me tightly about the neck, his tears ran around my collar. My own tears were blinding me.

"You heartless mean old bitch!" Anger choked me. "Filthy! Lousy! Dirty! Nasty! Pig! Why, this kid sparkles when compared with you."

Wiping the mist from my eyes and turning, I saw that a

148

crowd had gathered. On each face was a look of righteous indignation, except one.

Pushing through the circle they'd formed, I turned. "He's cleaner than all of you sanctimonious bastards with your Animal Benevolence Society!" I yelled.

I turned and ran down Loomis carrying the boy.

"Clucky! Clucky! You apologize this instant!" my aunt called behind me. I continued to run, turning east at 111th after passing the pool room. I slowed to a walk. The kid was sniffing and clutching.

"I didn't mean to do her nothing, mister; honest, if you hadn'a told me it was all right and stuff—"

"Shush, Arch, hush now; everything's going to be okay," I said, putting him down and stopping to wipe his face. "How about some ice cream and candy and just anything you want? Would you like that?"

He nodded his bald head and twisted a grubby fist in his eye. Entering the drug store, I headed for the first booth. He trailed behind me.

Marion stepped from the booth.

"Why, Clucky, what's this? Oooh, look, he's ruined your suit!!!" Archibald had wet his clothes and mine. Marion was trying to pull him from me. "Let go, Clucky, he's dirty!"

"Get your goddamned hands off him," I shouted. "So he's dirty. So he peed on me. So Goddamn what? The kid's scared to death. What do you expect? I didn't come in here to get you to say, 'Clucky, he's dirty.' All I want is some service. Do you understand. Service!"

Marion had stepped back from me, bewildered.

"But Clucky, I only—"

"Dammit, stop calling me Clucky!"

"Well, what service can I give you, Mr. Morgan?" she inquired chillily.

"Ice cream," I demanded, sitting the kid in the booth. "I want some ice cream, pop, candy, gum, and every other damn sweet junk that grown-ups make to distract kids from this son-of-a-bitchin' world.

My loud tone had attracted every eye in the store.

"What the hell are those lames gawking at? Especially you, Puff," I said to an immaculately dressed fellow about nineteen who stood leaning against the counter. His real name was George Marshall. A year ago he had been hailed as one of the most promising middleweights ever spawned from the filth of the South Side. The filth of his creation, however, had also worked his destruction. A fit of coughing now shattered the fixed cynical smile that habitually twisted his lips. Fumbling in his pocket, he withdrew a tissue, spit in it and tossed it to the floor. Puff had the bug and wanted to infect the whole world. Placing a large white handkerchief to his nose, he inhaled deeply. He was also a snowbird, all-around hustler and head dean of the pool room.

He spoke in an interrogative whisper. "Hey man, what you got there?"

"Is this new to you, this kid, you sparkling mass of active TB?" I asked, wiping some of the grime from Archibald's cheek and from the top of the table with my fingers. As he glided up, I held my fingers up to his face.

"Keep rantin', Deacon, and you'll be a preacher yet," he whispered, brushing my hand aside as he walked out.

"I'm my father in name only!" I shouted at his back. Turning to Marion: "Service! Let the party begin, yeah, we're going to have a party, hey Arch! A party in celebration of the virtue of dirt, year, the good virtue of the dirty! And baby, it's got to be good—damn good, because it grows more damn brats to the acre than any—"

"Don't shout, Clu—oh Guy. Don't be—"

"Shout! Well, I feel like screaming, but later for talk. Where is the gingerbread house and peppermint stick trees?" I asked, suddenly tired of talking. "Why you standing there? Want me to lose my cool?"

150

"You blew it already," she said icily. "Anything else?"

"Yeah, yeah, a lot more. But for now just bring me my bag, if it's not too much trouble."

"It's not," she said, walking away, her heels tapping angrily on the marble floor. Seconds later she placed my training bag beside me and returned to the soda fountain.

"We gonna have a party, mister?" Archibald asked me as he fidgeted in the seat. I'd thought it peculiar, Beano permitting only certain people to call him Mister; now I understand it.

"Yeah, we are going to have a party, but don't call me Mister. Call me Guy, okay?"

The boy nodded.

Marion returned with a tray lined with the sweets I had ordered and set it on the table.

"Boy, oh Boy! Is that for me?" Archibald exclaimed wonderingly.

"Yeah, dig in."

"He'll get sick," Marion reproved.

"The hellie ya say!" Archibald denied.

I laughed, relaxing and glad to see the boy returning to normal. The kid's hand flew from the gooey sweets to his mouth.

"Take it easy, Arch, all you can't eat you can take with you."

Archibald slowed down.

"How come ya were at the church—are ya a member?" I questioned.

"Naw, I ain't no member to no church," Archibald said. "I don't go in 'em cause they all the time laugh at me. I was waiting for a guy I play marbles with to come out. Say mister, I mean Guy, would'cha buy me a toy? I kind of owe it to somebody."

"Yeah, sure, Arch, I'll buy you one. Wait here till I come back."

Picking up my bag, I went back to the tiny lavatory. Locking the door, I stripped, took the neatly folded, freshly laundered sweat suit from the bag and slipped it on. Muffet had washed it, she didn't like dirt. Stuffing my suit into the bag, I returned to Arch who had polished off the ice cream.

"Hey, Guy, lookit, I've ate it all, lookit!" he pointed to his bulging stomach which his too short shirt exposed.

"Good Arch," I said, filling his pockets with the rest of the sweets. "Now what else do you want to do? How about a movie?"

He nodded. I paid Marion for his treat, and taking a dollar from the change, I gave it to him.

"Boy, oh boy!" he exclaimed, backing toward the door. "Thanks Mr., aw, Guy. Gee, thanks a lot." He disappeared out of the door at a run. Dropping the rest of the change in the bag, I headed for the door.

"Who is that boy, Guy?" Marion asked over the counter. I stopped.

"Oh, just a dirty little kid."

"Where are you going? Are you mad at me?"

"I'm going to get dirty; no, I'm not angry at you but at cleanness."

I went out and headed for the schoolground at a trot. I thought: *It's a beautiful day in Chicago.*

"The hellie ya say," I muttered, entering the schoolyard.

Changing my shoes swiftly, I began duckwalking around the large track field. After a few dozen more warm-up exercises, I broke into a run, alternately pacing and striding. Sweat was pouring down my body, and I thrilled to its musk as I leaped the last hurdle and with straining muscles broke the imaginary finish tape before Jesse Owens . . . when the jeering cheer jerked me back to reality.

"Wow! Some boy, Clucky!"

I wheeled toward the sound of the voice, an angry retort on my lips for the use of the hated nick name from an enemy.

152

Jackie stood up in the front seat of his father's convertible, clapping his hands and cheering mockingly. He looked like a Harlem sissy drumming up trade on a Saturday night I thought, regarding his loud colored sports clothes. Luzon and Kay sat in the front of the car with him. Reaching into my bag, I took out the towel and wound it about my neck, continuing my walking around the track.

"Oh! Clucky-wucky, don't you know that the good book speaks against working thy ass on Sunday?" he asked as I passed him.

I kept my face forward, ignoring him. How in the hell had he learned that name, I wondered, inwardly seething with rage. Marion?

Then I remembered Aunt Emma shouting to me as I ran from the church. Jackie had been in the crowd, naturally, for he and a few of the Gabriels were in the church choir.

"Dammit! I'll never hear the end of Clucky now," I cursed, flinging the towel over my bag. I broke into a trot. Who in hell had given me such a damn fool name, anyway? Mom, of course, and as long as she liked it, screw the friggin' loud mouth.

Changing the trot for a ground covering stride, I sped by him.

"Oooh! Girls! Girls! Dig the chest on Clucky-wucky; ain't he a big hunk of aw-aw-well, duck? Say, lame, I heard ya was betting a bunch on yourself? Who do you think you are, a technicolor Thorpe? Well, just let old Jetting Jackie hip you to something, my fine feathered friend. When I get through kicking gravel in your face, in the 220 and 440, they are going to cart you home to Mother Dear in a wheelbarrow. Yeah, then the whole damn family will be on wheels."

His words stopped me; I turned and walked to where I was abreast of the car, separated only by the high fence surrounding the field. The fury within me increased the pounding of my heart and heaving of my chest.

Gripping the fence, I said, "Bow-wow, that last remark erased whatever chance you may have had of winning. Jesus Christ couldn't stop me from winning now, not only over you, but every ass that squats in at the starting line. I'm in next month. I should kick your teeth in now, but there's more than a fence between us and you know it; that's why you're brave; that's the way it's always been with you chumps. You've never copped anything on your own spunk. It's always been 'that's Bishop Lindy's son,' 'give him this' or else you take advantage of a guy's belief in fair play, like you're doing now? Would you be where you are now, if it weren't for what happened up in Dr. Bruce's office? Hell, no! But that ain't gonna help you when the starter gun cracks next month. I hope you bring your peanut gallery here with you. Ha! you're going to be stripped to your spine, pretty boy, and baby, you're gonna jelly."

I'd spoken with the passion of hatred long suppressed. Staring at him, I began to laugh, knowing of how humiliating this would be to him. Bending swiftly to the glove compartment, he withdrew something—a gun. "I ought to hit you in the head, cunt," he snarled. The girls sat in shocked silence.

I matched his tone, feeling no fear. "If you do, pretty, you lose your last shield. Once you touch me, the vow is canceled, and as Treetop or Cherry over there may have told you, I don't play fair anymore. So shoot, goddamnit, I don't believe the powder in that particular gun will burn; if it does, you'll win the race."

For a moment we stared at each other. I turned and walked towards my bag. There was the screech of tires as the car accelerated into motion . . .

Chapter **16**

"Stride! Pace! Stride! Lift them knees up, lift 'em up!" the sharp commands of track instructor Joe Langley rang out.

Cursing aloud, I erected the hurdle I had knocked over.

"Keep 'em up, keep 'em up!" Langley ordered. "Dig them spikes in there!"

"I'd like to dig 'em in there! Right in your pratt, bow-wow," I muttered, walking off the track field.

As I neared the thirteen foot high giant slides, a jacket sailed out of the air and plopped on my shoulder. I removed a large towel from the pocket, wrapped it around my neck, then slipped the jacket on and zipped it up. I walked between the two steel bars descending from the slide until they pressed my shoulders, then I whistled. Marion slid down them from where she had perched while I had practiced. When her slight weight transferred from the bars to my shoulders, I started walking for the school ground exit.

"You quitting so soon?" she asked.

"Uh-huh."

"You were slow today and you knocked over a dozen hurdles. What's wrong, are you sick?"

"Uh-huh, sick of hearing old Langley's voice. He knocks me off pace with that damned funnel. I was slow intentionally. This ain't no ordinary race, you know."

"You're hiding your stuff, huh?" she asked.

"Yeah," I said, digging my spikes in and sprinting the twenty-five yards to the gate with her atop my shoulders. She screamed in mock terror.

"Swear that you love me, on your honor," I commanded, halting at the gate.

"I swear that I love you, on my honor—whatever it is," she said.

I lowered her to the ground and we walked to the old car her father had loaned me for the prom that night. I opened the door for Marion, then slipped off my track shoes and slid behind the wheel and put on my street shoes. Marion slid over close to me. I put my arms around her.

Our lips met and held in a kiss full of tender passion. Her body began to shake. I reached for her breast. My tongue begged entrance through her clenched teeth. The removal of her mouth left me licking my lips.

" My, but aren't you the hungry one. You're in training, remember?" she said, twisting free.

I reached for her and she dived into the rear seat.

"You touch me and I'll scream," she said dramatically.

I faked at her.

"Eeek!" she squeeked in a tiny whisper.

We laughed.

I put the car in motion, turning east on 111th Street. As we drew near Hank's pool room, she pointed to a parking place in front of it. "Pull up there," she said, "I'll walk over to the drug store."

I steered the car expertly into the space.

"You're a pretty good driver for somebody who doesn't like to drive," Marion remarked.

"Yeah, I guess it runs in the family," I said sarcastically, thinking of my father and the accident.

"Now, Clucky, let's not clutter up this night with hates and prejudices."

"You're right, Miss Muffet," I agreed. "Tonight will be our night of smiles. One we'll always remember with happiness, cool?"

"Crazy!" she said enthusiastically.

156

We kissed briefly.

"How's that for a start?" she asked, cocking her head.

I grabbed for her. She scooted out of the door and ran toward the drug store.

"Eight-thirty!" she shouted back.

Leaving the car, I entered the pool room. Hank was walking toward the upstairs entrance, counting his bankroll.

"Make sure you have enough of that stuff in stock the last of next month, house," I remarked, referring to my bet with him. He paused at the doorway.

"Don't worry, kid, I'll have it, but remember, you'll take down only what your hand calls for."

"That'll be a royal straight spade flush. Two thousand, six hundred bucks worth."

Nodding, he left.

Hank and I hadn't spoken over two words of a personal nature since he had slapped me around.

Crow sauntered from the back and climbed into a chair on the shine stand. He wore a broad smile.

"Hey, baby, what's shaking?" I greeted.

"Ain't nothing shakin', but de leaves on de trees and they wouldn't be shakin' if it wasn't for de breeze," he rhymed in bop lingo.

"Shine?"

"What de hell ya think I crawled way up here for? Besides we've been waitin' for a shine for de last seven hours," he exaggerated. I started to work on the shoes.

"Seven hours, hell, dad, these stomps ain't had a shine since they came off the steer."

Harold climbed in the next chair to Crow.

"What's to it?" I greeted.

"Nothing to the chicken but the bill, take that away and it's chicken still."

"Hey, why's everybody so damn gay this evening?" I asked, looking at them perplexed.

They exchanged glances, then looked at me, shaking their heads.

"Lame! You are a pure 'de lame who ain't into nothin'," Crow kidded.

They broke into lusty laughter.

"You clowns been eating feathers again," I said, bending to my work.

Earl swaggered from the back and sat in the third chair.

"How goes it, Earl?"

"Come see, come sigh."

"Ooh, for crapsakes, what's gotten into you cats?"

Taking a handkerchief from his pocket, Earl wiped the bluish chalk from his fingers with exaggerated fastidiousness. Raising his eyebrows he peered down his nose at me.

"Zigg, Zigg, mademoiselle, down to the mezzanine, oui?" he added.

I gaped at him.

They howled with laughter, holding their stomachs and pointing at me.

"Look at de lame, he don't even compre French," Crow howled.

"He ain't into nothin'," Harold panted.

I started on Earl's shoes. "What's this jazz you're spewing, dad?" I asked him.

"He asked if ya was taking your girl to the dance, I think," Dipper supplied. They broke into laughter again.

"Hey, screw you clowns," I said, putting the bootblack equipment away.

"Say, man, you should dig the tux I rented. Just like it was tailor-made for me," Harold informed the crowd.

"Say, Deacon, ya cop a tux?" Earl asked.

"What de hell do I look like, a penguin?" I quipped.

Their laughter rang out again.

"Bo-oy, you guys are mighty damned happy. Wha'cha been drinking, giggling gas?"

"It wasn't no juice, but baby, it's a gas. I'm three sheets in the wind," Earl said, jumping to the floor and cutting a step.

Bird and Sandy entered the front door carrying their bags. "Hey, weeds, what's going on?" Bird greeted.

"Nothin' going on but the rent, and it might as well stop, 'cause we ain't got a cent," Earl, Harold, Crow and Dipper chorused, breaking into laughter.

Sandy and Bird stared at me bewildered.

"I don't know what's wrong with them," I told the pair.

"Maybe we'd better call the bang wagon," Sand offered, sitting in the vacated chair.

"Fix 'em up, Deacon. Say, you should dig the corsage this trick bought Maxine, looks like a funeral wreath and cost eight bucks. Buddy! What a lame."

"It's my bread and my broad, you dig?" Sandy informed Bird.

The mentioning of the flowers reminded me that I had forgotten to get some for Marion. I finished Sandy's shoes quickly.

"Look, you gay birds, I'm closing for the day. What time does the florist close?"

"Four-thirty," Sandy supplied.

I looked at the clock, it was 3:45 P.M. Hurrying to the back of the pool room, I walked to where Shelley sat shuffling a deck of cards. She had consented to rack for me today.

"Hey, pretty, how's my man?" I greeted diplomatically.

Her slender hands dealt five cards to five imaginary players in lightning rapidity. I pointed to the hand nearest to me and looked at her questioningly.

"A pair of kings, an ace, eight and trey."

I turned the hand over. The named cards looked up at me. Shelley was a wizard with cards and other gamblers' devices.

"You're a star broad, Shelley. And I want to thank you for taking over for me and all. When I become president, I'll declare a holiday in honor of you everyday."

159

"Say, what's gotten into you Gaylords today, with all the grand gratitude. Trying to live up to the name? Crow just offered to take me to the prom for loaning him five bucks."

Remembering the flowers, I turned. "What kind of flowers do girls wear to formals, Shelley?"

"How in hell do I know?"

The gang was inspecting Ding's old man's Buick. His dad let him use it for the day.

"It's marked to do one hundred ten, but I bet the best she'll do is eighty-five," Bird stated.

"Eighty-five, hell, I can get one hundred out of this baby with ease. If you don't believe it, ask Sandy," Ding stated hotly.

"Hell, Sandy's mouth ain't no prayer book, nor do his butt fold like a bible," Bird stated with equal heat. Sandy and Bird disagreed on everything except their tight comradeship.

Ding is right, though," Sandy said.

"Ha! One hundred hell. I can out run that junk," Crow sneered.

"Yeah, I'll even betcha five bucks I can do it, usin' old man Gale's jalopy there."

Everybody hooted with laughter. Marion's dad's car was a '50 Ford. The scrappy little Ford had a fast pick up, but the old gray mare wasn't what she used to be.

"It ain't de car, anyhow, but whose drivin' that counts," Crow declared affecting the tone and look he reserved for setting up someone for the trick bag. I recalled Shelley's mentioning of his five dollar loan and smiled.

Everyone except Sandy joined in jeering at the truth of his statement. "Crow's right," Sandy corroborated. "It's just like a jockey and horse. The fastest horse running can't make a win if a lame rode it."

"Say, you calling me a lame on the Q.T.?" Ding inquired belligerently, " 'cause if you are, I'll kick your tail into your vest pocket."

160

"And that will be the day you'll start walking on your ankles," Sandy rejoined defiantly.

"Look here, Ding, I got a fin dat says I can out run you," Crow challenged. "With what?" Crow looked at me, then at the Ford.

"Aw, hell no, Crow, ain't nothin' shakin'," I said, anticipating his request. I got into the Ford.

"But Deacon, I'll take care."

I cut off his plea. "Hell no, Crow, Marion's old man loaned this car to me and nobody's going to drive it but me. Cop?"

"But, momma, I promised Dot I'd take her to de Slipper after de prom, and dat costs money, you know. So give me a play, huh? This clown can't wheel. I'll make an easy fin. Come on man, huh?"

"Who can't wheel? I'll wheel any lame out of this park," Ding boasted.

"Bull!" Crow scoffed.

"Wanta bet?" Ding said, producing a ten-dollar bill. "Oh, but I forgot, you ain't got no short to push," he sneered, sticking the bill into his shirt pocket. Crow snatched the bill out again. "It's a bet! Bet! Ya got a bet!" he shouted.

"How is it a bet?" Ding asked.

"Deacon! Deacon! I'll bet'cha Deacon can beat'cha in de Ford.

Ding glanced from the '50 Ford to the '56 Buick. "Cool!" he accepted. "Let Bird hold the stake. You wanta sweeten the bet a little more?"

"I'll cover the rest of your ten," Sandy said, handing Bird some bills.

"Say, Crow, don't be no gofer. That Buick's got ten years on . . ." I started to protest.

"Aw, hell no, ain't no backing out now. The bet's on," Ding said.

"But dammit, Ding, you can't . . ."

161

"The hell I can't," Ding cut off my protest. "What's wrong, Deacon, chicken?"

"Hell, no, I'm not betting anything."

"Well, head for the strip," he said, glancing impatiently at his watch. "I've got a date at eight."

"Oh, hell," I exclaimed, looking at the dashboard clock, it was 3:57 P.M. "I'll meet you at the strip as soon as I cop Marion a corsage."

Crow jumped in beside me, Sandy got in the back.

"Don't you lames freeze up on me, now," Ding shouted as we sped away.

It took less than two minutes to reach 103rd and Halsted Street. I halted the car before Higgin's Florists. Ol' man Higgins was closing up for the day. "Hey, hold it," I shouted, dashing up to bang on the glass door. "Hey! Ol' man, hold it, I want some flowers, a corsage."

The old man disappeared through a rear door.

"You old bastard!" I shouted, returning to the car. This was the second time he had pulled that crap on me. Hell my money spends. I thought. "Dammit, Crow, now what the hell is Marion going to think of me?"

"Aw, hell, don't worry about gettin' flowers, I'll get you all the flowers you want after the race," Sandy said.

"Where? The shops is closed."

"I said I would get you some flowers, didn't I, so stop worrying and head for the strip. I've got a date tonight, too, you know."

Making a U-turn, I drove south on Halsted to 111th and turned west.

The strip was a stretch of smooth highway extending from 115th to 135th and Ashland Avenue and Route 54. Its light traffic made it an ideal speed course. Sandy lit up what I thought to be a regular cigarette until I caught a whiff of the smoke. The cause of Crow, Earl and Harold's earlier gaiety was made clear. They had been smoking reefers.

162

"So that's what's making the joy ball bounce," I said.

Crow laughed. "Here, go for yourself," Sandy said, offering the tiny cigarette.

I was a stranger to the weed although I had been constantly around them and dope since I'd worked for Hank. I'd never been tempted to use them. "I'm in training," I refused.

"Training? Training, hell. Do you mean all those hurdles you knocked down today, or Langley's instructions you didn't take? Or do you mean that momma Marion would jump salty if she knew you was blowing weed?" Sandy asked. His application of the slang title of "momma" to Marion irritated me.

"I'm chest, not breast," I said. Snatching the reefer, I inhaled its harsh smoke. "And I'm not a robot who needs Langley's instructions on when to lift my feet up and down. But if you don't think I'm in shape, hit land, I'll rock your frame," I threatened.

"Say man, what's to you lately? You've been acting odd as hell," Sandy exclaimed.

"That does it!" I shouted, slamming on the brakes.

I got out of the car. "Hit land, punk and I'll jar your frame! Nobody's going to call me a queer and get away with it. I ain't no degenerate! I'm not odd, I'm chest, not breast. If you don't jar land, you're a mother-jumping coward. Jar land, chump! Jar land! Jar land!" I shouted.

Numbers flashed before my eyes, I subtracted them. I wanted to smash something, anything, Sandy preferably. He hadn't made a move to get out so I jerked the rear door open.

"You yellah, black boy?" I taunted. "I said jar land!"

"Okay, bow-wow, you asked for it," he said getting out. The ground began to tremble and shake as I measured him for a punch.

"Hey! Deacon! For crapsake, will you lames cut it out? Here comes a train!"

Startled, I looked about. I had stopped the car in the middle of the railroad crossing. A fast freight, a block away was bearing down on us. Sandy jumped into the car, with me right behind him. Crow gunned the car into motion.

Of all de damn places to start a fight," Crow said.

"Yeah," Sandy agreed, lighting another reefer. Inhaling on it deeply, he passed it to me. I took a drag. Remembering how the ground had begun to tremble at the exact time in which his foot had touched it made me laugh. They joined in.

"Jar de land! Jar de land! Crow mocked.

We were still laughing when Crow stopped beside the '56 Roadmaster parked at the corner of 115th Street. Crawling over the front seat, I reclaimed the steering wheel.

"What took ya guys so long? We had begun to think you'd chickened." Ding shouted, pulling the Buick abreast the Ford. Smoke bellowed from the car windows. A girl laughed.

"Hey, they've copped some broads on us!" Crow shouted, leaning out the window to peer into the other car.

"Not on me," I denied, drawing on the cigarette. The air in the car was warm and dense with smoke. I took off my jacket and heavy sweat shirt, wiping perspiration from my chest with the towel about my neck.

"Well, let's put the show on the road," Ding said, racing the Buick's motor. Luzon will give the count. We'll race to the Silver Slipper, cop?"

"Make it light on yourself," Crow told him.

"Light, hell, we'll be dancing and dining when you lames get there," Ding boasted.

Luzon laughed. My foot pressed the accelerator at her sound. So Cherry is over there, I mused, feeling a surge of impatience.

"Hey, toss me two joints, Crow," Harold yelled.

"Not unless you toss me a buck. I've popped all I'm going to for one day."

"On your mark," Luzon began to count.

164

"I'll have to run you wide open all the way, baby," I inwardly apologized to the Ford, racing its motor.

"Get set . . . Go!"

I released the clutch, the car leaped ahead of the Buick. Shifting into second, I held it there until I heard the Buick change into high.

"Tromp, baby, tromp! We've got 'em."

"Yeah, roll, Guy, roll 'em, we've got 'em."

"Boot 'em up, baby! Boot 'em up!"

Crow and Sandy were shouting wild encouragement while gazing intently at the close-following Buick. Their voices came from a long way off. I was lost in the straining motor of the small car and the road.

"He's gaining on ya, Guy, tromp it, put'cha foot in de tank."

"Jeezus, look at him come! Do something Ford. Guy, the son-of-a-bitch is on our tail. Double-clutch it! Double-clutch it!"

The impact of the Buick's bumper striking that of the Ford's, made Crow and the others howl with indignation.

"The clown's signifying that he's helping us along. Hey, Guy, do something. Why don't'cha double-clutch this damn thing?"

"Look, man, I can't, it'll snatch the rear end out," I said, angered by the humiliating bumps the Buick was delivering and the jeers coming from those in it.

At 120th, the Buick attempted to pass. I cut in front of it. It dropped back and tried to pass on the right. I swirled, blocking it.

"That's it, Guy, don't let 'em pass, block 'em. There he goes again," Crow yelled.

A large semi-trailer was bearing down from the south as the Buick attempted to pass. The Buick drew abreast of me.

"Hey, get the hell over and let me pass," Ding shouted. He eyed the coming truck, I kept the left wheels of the Ford glued to the white guide line. The Buick inched ahead, then dropped behind as the approaching truck shook the highway. The truck thundered past with its air horn blaring. "He's trying on de right now, watch it," Crow yelled. I cut the wheels, heading the Buick off. Bumpers clashed together as I braked the Ford on the gravel parking lot of the Silver Slipper.

"We won, oh, baby! Baby!" Crow yelled. Jumping from the car, he kissed the hood and ran to the Buick.

"Well, what do you know, we won," Sandy said, indifferently. He lit two reefers and passed one to me.

"Didn't you think we would?" I asked.

"Hell, no, I only bet you would because Bird said you wouldn't," he explained. "Whew, I'm three sheets in the wind. What about you?" he asked, choking the cigarette.

"Yeah, I'm like a fly on a spray," I told him.

Dipper, Ding, Harold, Earl and Bird ganged around the Ford.

"That wasn't de bet and you know it." Crow protested hotly.

"But you know damn well that Buick can out-run this junk," Ding said, kicking the Ford angrily.

Jerking open the door, I jumped out. "What the hell you mean it can? It didn't," I said, angered at the assault on the spunky old car.

"Yeah, but how did you go about doing it?" Ding inquired.

"You tell me how," I requested, spitting the cigarette out. Luzon stood with both hands in the back pocket of the tight-fitting blue jeans. A cigarette dangled from the corner of her mouth.

"You cheated," she said.

We stared at each other.

"You think that, Ding?" I asked him.

"Yeah, hell you blocked me, you . . ."

I cut him off. "Dig, man, the bet was that I could outwheel you. We picked 115th to here, as the distance to do it in. I beat you."

"You cheated," Luzon repeated, tossing the cigarette away.

"Yeah, Guy, you kept me from passing and . . ."

"Ding, you could have passed, but you chickened out at the sight of that trailer." My voice trembled with anger, which Luzon's presence and accusation was increasing.

"Ha! Listen to Mr. Guts pound his chest!" she sneered, walking over to Ding, she leaned against him. His arm encircled her small waist. "Why, Ding's got more heart than ten Mr. Guy Morgans," she taunted.

"De hell you preach," Crow denied. "Guy's right, he would have passed if he hadn't chickened back there. He was scared, which proves that it ain't de horse alone that wins but de . . ." Ding slapped Crow hard across the mouth and he sprawled flat on his back. I leaped to him.

"You can't call me yellow, ya little shrimp!" Ding shouted.

I helped Crow to his feet, then walked over to Ding.

"All right, iron man, here's where you get yours," I said reaching for him.

He stepped back, a knife flashed in his hand.

"Touch me and you'll bleed to death," he hissed. I stepped back.

"All right you guys, let's take the knife from Jack the Ripper, here," I commanded, looking at the rest of the gang. None of them moved except Crow. I grabbed him. "You guys know the laws on fighting among ourselves, now are you going to help me get that shank?"

Sandy cleared his throat. "What about our humbug at the railroad crossing," he said.

"I didn't touch you, mister," I informed him.

"Yeah, but you . . ."

I cut him off. "Okay, so you were lucky. Don't brag, just enjoy your fortune. Hold it close to your chest, dig? Next time you want to be as lucky, you won't be. As for the rest of you chicken-hearted chumps, if you don't help me get that knife, then I quit the gang."

167

"Why the sudden need for help, Mr. Bow-wow?" Luzon jeered.

"Keep out of this Miss Switch," I warned. "You started this, anyway!"

"Oh, Bow-wow," she mocked, stepping behind Ding. He stood with knife poised to strike.

"You're a coward, Ding. Chicken! Chicken! Chicken!" I taunted.

"I've got more heart than you!" His eyes were glittering slits of malice.

"Ha! Oh, yeah?" I sneered.

"Yeah."

"Look, Ding, you ain't into nothin' when it comes to heart and I'll prove it," Crow said. "I'll bet de double sawbuck that you'll freeze up in a game of chicken."

"Bet him," Luzon coached Ding.

"It's a bet," he accepted. "Luzon can hold the stakes. I'll go down to 120th, you start here. When I blink my lights three times, we take off, cop?" I nodded. "Okay, anybody going with me?" he asked, getting in the car. No one moved.

"Drop my money for the shine," I said. He tossed the coin out the window. The Buick backed out to the highway.

"See you, lame," Ding shouted.

"Yeah, in hell, if you don't chicken," I yelled back, picking up the quarter.

"All right, chumps, fork over my bread for the shine," I demanded of Sandy, and the rest of you forget you knew me, cop?" I got into the car. Luzon was in the front seat. "You're in the wrong car, Cherry," I told her. "Let her out, Crow."

"Oh, no, I'm in the right car, the safest anyway, chicken. But if you don't want witnesses . . ." She let her voice trail.

"Stay and be damned," I told her, leaving the parking lot in a shower of gravel.

168

On the highway, I halted the car, with the left wheels covering the white lane marker. In the far distance headlights blinked three times, I released the brakes and the clutch, tromping down on the gas. The car leaped forward, its tires screaming. I changed gears rapidly. The needle on the speedometer pointed to sixty-five, I held it here. Gluing my eyes upon the white lane marker, I made my mind a blank to the oncoming headlights. The white strip of light began to widen into a highway, a special road for the little Ford, my thoroughfare, smooth as a keyboard and wide as the dance floor.

Only it's not a dance floor, but a highway. Yeah and a special built too, for just me and the spunky little Ford. So what is that lame doing dancing on it?

"Hey! Weed, don't you know you are dancing on forbidden grounds? This highway leads to hell; it's got to, because Miss Switch here next to me don't believe I can take her there. She'll laugh like the devil if I weaken and pull off.

Ha! But I'm not going to pull off. No, Cherry, you and I are going to have a hot cherry Coke in hell tonight. And you are too, dancer, if you don't get off my highway with your whore.

Oh, so you're running, you're frightened? No? Well you should be, 'cause I recognize you now, gigolo! You and your loud-colored clothes and two-toned shoes. Yeah, I know you. It isn't snowing tonight, so I can see plainly. What's happened to the sneer on your lips? Ha! You afraid, you're running. Yah and you better, 'cause I'm going to run you down, do you hear? Run you and your sleek-hipped slut down; send you to hell. Fire! Fire! Fire! Kill you! You killed Mom's legs didn't you? Well, an eye for an eye said Moses, my man, or leg for leg. Run! Run! This is my round, Joe. Ha!

I laughed out loud, suddenly I felt weight on my right foot. Luzon's foot was pressing on mine. The needle jumped from sixty-five to eighty-five. Her green eyes stared at me defiantly. Her sensuous lips held a smile.

You don't have to sneer your dares at me, Cherry. I'm not going to ask you to remove your foot, 'cause you're helping me run down that dancing gigolo out there on my highway. Here, I'll help you. We'll both push down. How's that?

The needle jumped to ninety and quivered. Light flooded the car, thunder roared past, a tornado of wind struck the little Ford, shaking it from hood to trunk. Behind me came the screeching of tires and the crash of splintering glass.

"You did it, Guy! He chickened! He chickened!"

Crow's yells made me turn from the defiant stare of Luzon's eyes. I looked through the rear-view mirror, feeling disgusted. The Buick was on its side, Ding sat in the middle of the highway, pounding the pavement with his fist.

"Jeezus, his old man is gonna lam de hell out of him when he sees that car." Crow whispered.

Peering out of the rear window at the wrecked Buick, I pulled the car to a halt at the stop sign on a 115th. A car pulled next to me from where it had been parked on the northwest corner of Ashland. It was a sleek black Caddy. Beano was in the back seat. The man behind the wheel wore a stark black suit with hat to match. His shirt and tie were both white silk. Sliding to the window next to me, Beano asked, "What inspired that exhibition of madness you just treated me to? You still got something against gray hair, huh, kid?"

"Yeah, what's wrong with dying young and hep?" I replied, irritated at his tone.

"Look kid, if that guy hadn't turned off, you wouldn't have been hep."

"So what is it to you?" I sneered.

"Nothing, except I like you, but I thought you had brains as well as spunk. I'm an admirer of the superman if he's got some intelligence. You don't have to show the whole world that you've got guts by spilling them all over the highway. There's no profit in it, except the sorrow your mother will feel when they bring you home in a basket. If you were smart and tough, I might let you work for me. Then you could do something worthwhile. But you're too full of youth. I can't take that kind of chance. When you grow up, come around."

He turned to his torpedo. "All right, Toby, let's go," he commanded. Then to me: "Remember what I said, kid. Take it easy."

The big car roared away.

He's right, I thought, as I covered my body against the chill of the evening air. I began to shake. If Ding hadn't chickened, I'd now be a blob of blood and pieces of crushed bone. Then where would Mom be? Who'd take care of her? And Crow, what about him? I recalled the words Maxine had said to me in the park, before spitting in my face . . .

"I only hope it happens before you get my brother killed" . . .

Why am I doing these things? I asked myself, zipping up my jacket, *knocking myself out, as Marion put it*. I tried to construct an answer. My father had something to do with it; my love for Mom and Marion and . . .

"Why Guy, you're shaking. What's wrong, delayed action to the race? I guess the false courage the reefers gave you is wearing away. Ha!" Luzon mocked contemptuously.

I stared at the bills protruding from the low-necked, tight-fitting blouse, which revealed the oval swell of firm breasts. Their jauntiness angered me. Luzon was a part of the knock-out process too.

I grabbed for the bills; she twisted. My hand caught in the brassiere and blouse. She tried to bite, I snatched my hand back, material ripped and buttons popped against the dashboard. Smoothing the bills through my fingers, I stared at the naked golden breasts the broken brassiere and torn blouse had freed. They retained their jauntiness. She made no attempt to cover them.

"Bow-wow," she said sarcastically.

"Jesus Christ!" Crow exclaimed in wide-eyed admiration as he stared at her exposed torso.

She covered herself.

"So you like Cherry here, huh Crow? Okay Cherry, F.O.W.B." I commanded.

She frowned. "What?" she inquired.

"Screw, that's what. Or walk back," I said handing Crow the bills.

"Let me out, Crow," she said clutching the torn edge of her blouse. He let her out. "I'll make you—"

I cut her off. "Yeah, I know you're still flattering yourself. It's not worth it, or have you forgot that life's a bowl of cherries? Ha!"

Her retort was drowned in the roar of the motor, as I sped away.

I let Crow out at his house and raced for home. I began undressing at the door. When I reached the bathroom, I was naked.

Chapter 17

An hour later I quietly let myself into the apartment over the drug store. Marion's dad was downstairs. Tossing the top coat I'd carried over my shoulder onto the chair by the door, I went and sat at the piano, and played the wedding march. Marion emerged from the back, walking in time with the music, she stopped before me. Pirouetting, she asked: "Well, how do I look?" The white dress made her skin stand out like the black keys on the baby grand.

"You should be between two cookies," I said, pulling her onto my lap.

"Ha! That's cute," she said. I kissed her quickly and she squirmed free. "No, now, you'll muss me up, besides I've got a surprise for you," she said mysteriously.

"Do you mean that you can make yourself prettier?" I whispered in a conspiratorial tone.

"Just wait, you'll see," she said, leaving the room.

I turned to the keyboard, automatically playing *God Bless the Child*.

At the sound of tinkling glass I turned. She'd re-entered the room with a tray bearing two glasses and a small bottle of champagne. Placing it on the end table she smiled. "To launch our night of smiles," she said.

I walked over to her.

"Well, aren't you going to pour us a drink?" she inquired.

The champagne opened with a pop, and poured with a sizzle. I handed her a glass and said, "This is the first time I ever drank this stuff. Honey, you know, you're the most thoughtful person I know."

173

She smiled. "Let's drink to graduation tomorrow."

I thought of the event without enthusiasm, remembering the two years I'd lost because of the accident, and the fact that I would not be graduating with her. I had done school work in the hospital, but when it was all evaluated I didn't have enough credits. They had just let me know. "Yeah, to graduation. Thank you, father dear," I said raising the glass.

"No, Guy, don't drink in bitterness. This is our night of smiles, remember?"

"But I am smiling, honey, in fact I'm tickled to death, Ha! See."

"No, no, you're being sarcastic. Push everything from your mind tonight, except me of course, and dance and laugh and be merry, like we did when we were little kids. Please?" she entreated leaning against me.

"Okay, sweetheart, here's to graduation tomorrow, and your pretty face." Our glasses clinked together. I drank mine down at a gulp.

"No, no, you're supposed to sip champagne," she reproved. "You'll get drunk like that."

"Ha! Ha!" I laughed. "I already am."

"On what?"

"Why, on your intoxicating presence, of course," I said, refilling our glasses. We returned to the piano.

"I've got something else for you," she informed, unwrapping something in the large sheer handkerchief she held.

"What?"

"Stick out your right hand and close your eyes," she directed.

I opened my eyes. It was the gold wrist watch I'd made a great to-do over one day when we'd window-shopped on 63rd and Halsted.

"But, Muffet, I can't take this," I protested, admiring the watch, but remembering the exorbitant price on it in the window. "Why this cost—"

174

"Oh, but you must take it. I insist. Why, if you don't, I'll flush it down the drain. I know it's expensive, but I enjoyed saving for it, and you do like it, don't you?" she asked anxiously.

The tenderness I was feeling wouldn't let me talk. I pulled her into my arms and, despite her half-hearted protest, kissed her long and lovingly. Turning to the keyboard she began to play softly.

I refilled our glasses until the bottle was empty.

"How do you feel?" she asked looking up from her playing.

"As if I could reach up and rub some blue off the sky," I replied, kissing her cheek.

"You mean high?"

"No, happy. Happy over my good luck to have someone like you in love with me. I'm not worthy of it. I even forgot to get you some flowers," I confessed wretchedly.

"Now what do you think about me?"

In answer, she began to play and sing her favorite song: "I'll love you, dear, no matter what you are, a sinner or saint . . ."

I listened, enraptured at the sound of her voice and expertness of her playing. She'd taught me how to play, when we were seven and eight years old. There had always been Marion.

"A penny for your thoughts," she said finishing the last bar of the song. We faced each other, a wave of tenderness flooded my being as I stared at her brown elfin face.

"Marion, baby, if ever I do anything to hurt you, I hope I die on the instant," I fervently declared.

"Hush that kind of talk, Clucky, you won't. And even if you did, I would want you to live. Why you're my first and last love, remember?" She smiled, squeezing my hand.

"Sing that song for me," I requested, feeling a wild surge of sentimentality.

She sang: "I recall all the days of my childhood, and the bashful romance that we knew in my teens as I roamed through the wild woods, still my first and my last love was you . . ."

A shiver caressed my spine as I reflected on just how very like a wild wood, a dense jungle, were the streets below with their slinking shadows, vicious vice, and animal howls of drunken laughter; of the continuous wail of reed instruments, and rumble of jazz drums belching from the dim-lit bowels of the hutlike joy joints fringing their garbage gutters and permeating the musky air with an unnamed frenzy.

"Now the days of my youth are behind me and the years we have left may be few," I intoned.

Grabbing Marion's shoulders, I turned her face to me. We stared at each other in silence. "The years we have left may be few," I repeated, conscious for the first time of how very brief the span of a man's life was. The dull ticking of the grandfather's clock mocked the lateness of my realization.

"Muffet, Muffet, don't go this fall," I whispered. "Don't leave, four years is a big hunk out of life for anyone, especially two people in love. I can't rid myself of the feeling that if you do—"

"Yes, yes, tonight I feel it, too," she sighed. Leaning against my chest, she spoke softly against my shirt. "But probably it's just the mood we're in, the champagne, and all."

Silence held us for another moment. "Clucky," she called. I grunted in reply.

"Clucky, I—I haven't been quite truthful with you about my going away. I've wanted to tell you, only—well, you aren't a very easy person to talk to, you know. Anyway, well—Guy, Dad hasn't ever altogether approved of our relationship, but he couldn't very well forbid it in view of my shameful aggression. He is . . ."

"Phony," I supplied, standing up. "Like most people I

know," I continued hotly. "I knew it! I knew it! I knew it!" I shouted.

"Listen, Clucky, hush now, that's why I didn't want to tell you. Dad's merely doing what he thinks is best for me and—and you. It's not the way you think—nothing personal, really. Although, if you be honest with yourself, you have to admit that some of your actions would justify it being so."

"What do you mean?" I said loudly.

"I told you not to shout. I mean, Dad is a devout Catholic, and you haven't been to Mass in months. He knows your radical temperament. He—he feels that we aren't giving ourselves a chance to look beyond, you know—I mean—he only wants us to be sure that what we feel is real and lasting, so that once committed we'll never turn back, never regret. He thinks that four years away from each other will be a good test—give us a chance to meet new people and so . . ."

"People are the same all over the world! You mean give you a chance to meet some guy whose ol' man didn't run away with a yellah chippy, along with the church's poor box," I snarled. "One who doesn't shine shoes, rack balls, sell crooked dice and cards, girlie books, rubbers, and who's even thinking about adding weeds to the list in a shabby, run-down pool room . . ."

"No, now Guy, that's not it at all. He—"

"He-he-haw! You make him sound like a jackass god! He thinks, he feels. Well, so do I, but who cares? So he is a devout Catholic, well, I'm a devout wanter, and what I want a million Masses couldn't supply, so why go? As for giving ourselves a chance to look beyond, our future's aren't that distant or hard to figure out," I paused, thinking of my conversation with Hank, and the experience at Moreland Hospital.

"It's not like you think," she interposed. "It's actually all for the best."

"You want to go, I can tell that, it's just nine hundred ninety miles, Clucky," I mimicked.

"You've even got the exact mileage down pat, meaning that you've given it a lot of thought. You're eighteen, a woman by law, actually your father can't make you—"

"Oh, but Guy, I've never disobeyed Dad in my life. I'd—"

"So you'll have a long one," I sneered. "OK! but your ol' man ain't no great god Buddha to me. He's lived his life and loved his love, and I'm going to do the same. Don't expect me to sit at home . . ."

The sight of tears running down her cheek put an abrupt end to my anger. Taking her into my arms, I apologized: "Darling, I'm sorry, me and my damned temper. I really didn't mean what I was saying, but the thought of you up there with those rich high-brows bugs me. Plus you're so pretty and I'll be so lonely without you. In fact, I'm beginning to feel lonely already, and you are in my arms. Just think of how hellish it will be when you're away."

"I know, Guy, I feel that way too. Only believe me, I won't look at another boy while I'm away. And we'll write each other every day, and keep tab of all the lonely hours we're apart. Then when we're together again, we'll add them up and live them twice over with happiness. I don't mind the test, for as the song says, my first and last love is you."

Our lips met in a kiss when the chiming of the clock ended. I held her tightly, not wanting to let her go.

"Oh, it's nine o'clock, come on, Clucky, or we'll miss the dance," Marion said. I want to dance and dance until I drop from exhaustion."

"Let's stay here, honey, I'll run to the corner for more champagne and we can play the records—"

"No, now, I bought this dress especially for the prom and I want to show it. I also want to be seen with tall, dark, and handsome you. Oh! And just have the crowd around me."

She'd gathered her purse, gloves, and a sheer stole as she talked. At the door she asked, "How do I look?"

"Choice!"

"And my shape, how is it in this gown?"

"Humm, well you're small in the waist like a wasp; and broad in the uh, tail, like a horse."

This pleased her. She descended the stairs laughing.

I found a parking place in a dark alley, across the street from the school. Marion hopped out of the car and skipped on ahead of me, stopping now and then to perform a dance step.

"Oh! I just want to dance, and dance, and dance!" she exclaimed with arms uplifted, as though she could embrace the whole universe. "Come on, hurry, I'm dying to feel the crowd around me, and the press of your embrace."

Reaching the door, we wormed our way through the jostling bunch of kids. As I waited in line to check our coats, I surveyed the tightly-pressed crowd on the gym floor.

"So you want to feel the crowd around you, huh? Baby, if we step out on that floor, they're not only gonna be around, but on top, and under you. Buddy! I told you we should have stayed at home," I said disgustedly.

Mrs. Cunningham, my English teacher, approached us with a smile. "Why, Marion, how very darling you look. I'm sure that you won't have any difficulty in getting this filled," she greeted, handing Marion a small book.

"Thank you, Mrs. Cunningham," Marion replied, slipping the book on her wrist by the ribbon attached to it.

Mrs. Cunningham turned to me and said: "Why Guy, you actually look handsome in formal dress, real athletic. You'd better keep your eyes on him, Marion. Run along now and have fun."

Some few feet away I voiced the surprise which Mrs. Cunningham's compliments had caused me to feel: "Why that old battle ax, she is human after all." Mrs. Cunningham had been my most stern critic and severest censor.

"Hush, you idiot, she can hear you," Marion said reprovingly.

"I don't care, come this time tomorrow, I intend for us to be complete strangers. Her and her, 'you forgot to dot your I's, Mr. Morgan' 'Must you sit so sloppy, Mr. Morgan?' 'Please pull those baggy pants up,' God! She made me sick," I ended disgustedly.

"Why, Clucky, you old 'Dumb Duck.' So you finally shucked you way through another year."

I turned at the sound of Jackie's voice. He stared mockingly at me. By the dark glasses he wore and his dry lips, I knew that he'd been smoking weed. I didn't say anything, I only glared my dislike.

Turning to Marion, he said: "Hey pretty, how's about me and you showing these lames bugging at its best." His arms encircled her waist possessively.

"Look, chump, if there ever comes a time when I can't entertain my girl, I'll cop her a red rubber ball. Dig? Now stoke up and steam off," I advised him.

"Okay Clucky," he said, turning away. I grabbed for his arm. He spun, the knife in his hand arrested my movements.

"Just cool it, baby, cool it. You'll get yours soon enough," he said backing away.

The wildness within me mounted, I stepped toward him. Marion blocked me.

"No! Please Clucky, let it drop. Remember your promise? Forget it and let's dance," she said, stepping into my arms.

I was soon engrossed in the gracefulness of her movements and the warmth of her nearness as we danced. We danced well together and knew it. This fact was a source of pride to both of us for it meant that our constant patronage of the Viper, a South Side dance spot, had not been wasted. The combo playing was "Thunder Williams and His Jive Five,"

180

a group of young musicians from the neighborhood who were strictly progressive jazz enthusiasts. Upon completing two slow numbers, they jumped off on a racy, sweat-promoting tune. I led Marion off the floor. I wasn't for that action.

Though the gym was crowded, we had no difficulty in finding seats. Most of the teens in the park were jitterbugs. Marion handed me the little book Mrs. Cunningham had given her.

"What's this for?" I inquired, examining it curiously.

"That's my dance program, silly," she informed me in mock disgust.

"So what am I to do with it, play goat?" I asked flippantly.

She handed me a small pencil. "No, you're supposed to mark your John Henry in it and that way I'll know twenty years from now who I danced with tonight," she explained.

"I still don't get it," I lied, signing the book.

"Why, it's a memento, silly," she said, taking the book with a smile over my naiveté.

"Say, do you know, your use of the word 'silly' reminds me of someone else I know," I said, taking both her hands into mine and surveying her cute petiteness. "In fact, you're as pretty as a red apple, just like that person."

"Who?" she asked, leaning her pert face close to mine and smiling.

"Mom," I replied.

She leaned back; the smile disappeared.

"What's wrong?" I asked, noticing the sudden change.

"Nothing, only I'm, well I guess that I should feel greatly flattered by such a compliment because I know of how very much you love your mother and she is pretty. Only, well, I've many times felt that one of the main reasons why you like me is because I remind you of your mother, built small like her and all. I—I—I can't explain exactly, only, well, you know . . ." She ended haltingly.

I stared at her, remembering the thoughts I'd had of the

close similarity of her and Mom, of my comparing the sizes of their wearing apparel they were identical with the exception of one article: Mom wore a size 5 shoe and Marion wore a $4\frac{1}{2}$.

Suppressing the emotions which were angrily warring within me, I forced a smile and said, "I haven't read as many medical and psychology books as you. No, only enough to make me feel that your words have the earmark of a dig, a nasty dig. What are you trying to say, that I have some kind of mother fixation?"

"Oh now Guy, I didn't say that at all. Please forget the whole thing. Come on, let's dance."

I refused her suggestions and stood up. Looking down on her, I said, "Listen, baby, if loving Mom with all my heart is a fixation, then I confess that I'm fixed for life. Yeah, I'm funny that way. One fact I want you to know, though: I've never wanted to go to bed with her."

June and Alice, two of Marion's classmates, came up and began a profuse admiration of her gown. I left for the washroom.

The cry of "Fever in de fun house, spread whoah!" and the fervent snapping of coaching fingers greeted my entry. Crow stood crouched forward, his right hand clutching a bunch of bills, a half pint of whisky and a large white handkerchief. His left hand shook a pair of dice close to his ear.

"Come on baby, I need a half pint of booze," he informed the dice in a prayerful whisper.

The group of boys huddled around him were all weeds. Going over to Crow, I removed the pint from his hand, casually lifting the handkerchief along with it. Taking a long drink from the bottle, I handed it back, retaining the handkerchief to wipe my dry lips. The fiery liquid coursing through my body brought peace to my warring emotions, and removed the forced smile. Shouldering a place in the huddle group, I squatted, pulling out my twenty dollar bank roll.

"The whoah's in de fun house, spread for Crow." He made his point, and nudged the four dollars on the floor with the toe of his foot. "I'm letting de four ride. What lame wants to cover it?" he challenged with cockiness. The boys hesitated.

"You're covered, diamond Jim," I said snapping four bills and tossing them on those on the floor.

"Baby you've got more nerve than a toothache. That little cat is hot." The boy next to me informed with sympathetic eyes.

"Uh-huh," I grunted skeptically.

Crow tossed the dice, their roll stopped on ten.

"Big Ben, I've got it made then!" he shouted reclaiming the dice.

"He don't ten for a skin," I said to the boy with sympathizing eyes, dropping at his feet.

"Bet!" he accepted, covering my bill with one of his own.

Crow made ten on the next roll.

"I'm lettin' de eight ride like de four. You still on, mistah?" he asked, nodding at me.

"Why, hell yes," I said tossing eight dollars to the floor.

Crow shook the dice. "Ride me boy, I'm de hottest piece that hit this house in a long time, and de tricks are popping."

"Hold it then!" I shouted. "You wanta sweeten this a little, momma?"

"Would if I could, but I can't, dad. Everything I got is on de floor, but just hold it till next roll and you'll have de opportunity of fadin' me for de sixteen," Crow boasted.

I glanced hurriedly at the watch Marion had given me. It wasn't running. 'Got to cut in a second, anybody want to follow this lucky lame into bankruptcy?" I inquired waving the remaining eight dollars of my roll enticingly before them.

"Aw man, hold it to de next roll, I'll take you up," Crow pleaded.

"I'll take two of it," sympathetic eyes said.

"I'll take three," another one said.

When my eight was covered, I wiped my mouth again with Crow's handkerchief.

"Don't let me down, dice," Crow begged, tossing the cubes. They came up five. "Hot dog!" Crow exclaimed enthusiastically as he recovered the dice. "I never miss a five." He shook the dice. "Fever in de fun house-spread whoah!"

I caught the dice in mid-roll.

"Oh! What de hell ya wanta do that for? I gave 'em a good roll." Crow exclaimed indignantly.

Cupping the cubes in both hands I held them to my mouth, mumbling to them as I spit the misses out into my right hand and palmed the dice I had caught into the folds of the handkerchief in my left hand.

"Well, wha'cha gonna do with 'em, make rain? There's a church across de street if you wanta pray!" Crow said angrily.

I tossed the dice to him. "Look, mister, I got forty bucks invested in this toss and that gives me the right not only to catch these cubes but to blow your stuff away and put mine on. So just cool to hell down and toss," I spoke through clenched teeth simulating anger.

"All right Edward G." Crow sneered, tossing the dice. "Fever in de fun house, spread-whoah!" he shouted.

Seven dots faced upward when the cubes stopped their roll.

"Damn!" exploded the group in unison as I picked up the money. Crow went over and pocketed the dice.

"Going for twenty bucks," I said counting out the bills.

"Aw hell, that's too much," the boys said.

"What about you, Pops?" I asked Crow.

"I'm busted," he said dejectedly.

"I'll fade you fifty cents," sympathetic eyes offered.

"What do I look like, a slouch or something?" I replied, walking out the door counting the bills. Crow followed me. We divided the money in the hall.

"One day you're going to get both of our heads blowed off," I told him.

He smiled.

We polished the half pint off before entering the gym. The combo was still playing racy numbers. I went over to where I had left Marion. She wasn't there. I looked around the floor, my eyes found her instantly among the twirling, twisting, dancers. She was dancing with Jackie.

Anger blazed in me as I weaved my way through the dancing throng to them. Jackie's back was to me. Remembering the knife, I dipped my hand into the right pocket of his coat and withdrew it.

He spun around. "Hey, what the hell—"

"Look you son-of-a-bitch, I told you I would buy her a rubber ball if I couldn't entertain her," I snarled, my voice hoarse with suppressed anger. Couples had stopped dancing to watch us.

Jackie looked at the knife in my hand. "You've had it, mister, hoof, tail and head. All of it!" He whispered hotly.

"Ha!" I laughed dryly as he walked away.

Grabbing Marion by the wrist, I towed her hurriedly through the jostling crowd. At the edge of the dance floor, I turned on her angrily. "What the hell do you mean by dancing with that punk?" I demanded.

"Listen, Guy, I've known Jackie for as long as I've known you. I have no quarrel with him. Besides, I'll dance with whomever I please." I tore the little book from the ribbon about her wrist.

She had danced four times since my leaving and all with Jackie. I blacked out his name with the pencil attached to the book.

"Loyalty and faithfulness are my sisters. Incessant is my love of these twins," I informed her in a drunken burst of prose while inserting my name in the remaining blank spaces.

"This is our night of smiles, remember? If not, then look in this little book."

"Guy, I haven't any quarrel with Jackie."

"Well, I sure and the hell have," I asserted, leading her onto the dance floor. Her movements were half-hearted. The whisky had me reeling. I missed a few simple steps.

"Clucky, are you high?" she asked.

"Naw," I lied.

"Well, I am," she said with a laugh which vanquished my anger.

Kneeling, I took off my shoes. "It's these damn new shoes," I faltered, sticking one in each of my jacket pockets. We resumed the dance.

"Thunder Williams and his Jive Five are trying to make us love and hate progressive jazz in one night." I said, taking her into a fast spin which ended with the two of us sitting on the floor laughing.

Lurching to my feet, I extended my hand to help her. She grasped it and got halfway up when her slight weight pulled me off balance. I fell, sprawling on top of her. Our laughter increased. "Hey, you know, I believe I am twisted," I said.

We were oblivious of our surroundings until Mrs. Cunningham's voice cut through our laughter.

"What is the meaning of this?" she demanded. I looked up at her and about the room. Bishop Lindy and Reverend Heath were among those sitting in the space reserved for chaperones. Looks of distaste were on their faces.

"Marion, you ought to be ashamed of yourself, get up and fix your dress immediately." Mrs. Cunningham instructed disgustedly. Marion's gown had twisted above her knees. She pulled it down, hastily getting to her feet and running for the exit.

I got up staring into Mrs. Cunningham's angry eyes.

"Why are you so hot under the collar?" I asked. "It was our fannies that took the fall."

186

"What?" she asked as I staggered after Marion. All eyes followed me.

Outside, Marion handed me my coat. "Oh, Guy, I'm so ashamed."

"At what, laughter? Then I intend to make you doubly so before the night's over. Come on, we're going to the Silver Slipper."

We headed for the car. The alley where it was parked was pitch black. Suddenly there was a scurrying sound to my right and Marion stepped back with a little cry.

"It's just a rat," I said, then staggered from the impact of a blow over my right eye.

I struck out blindly, my fist connected with flesh. With my left hand I grabbed in the direction from which I'd struck and felt cloth. Gathering a handful of it I struck at it with my right, putting every inch of my five foot ten, one hundred fifty-nine pounds into the blows. The cloth began to whimper and struggle to tear free.

Marion was screaming.

Remembering the knife I had taken from Jackie, I reached for it. My hand struck the shoe. Strong hands twisted my arm behind me in a brutal hammerlock. For a moment there was nothing but Marion's screams. Then a voice from the darkness hissed: "You've had it punk, hoof, tail and head." It was Jackie.

I struggled furiously. The old hate of him boiled into a scalding desire to kill. My eyes had become used to the darkness. Some six boys surrounded me. I recognized Ray Miller, Bird, Treetop and Jackie. Jabbing my left elbow backwards, I felt it sink into the flesh of the person behind me. I repeated the jab, putting all of my strength into it. There followed a grunt, the grip on my arm slackened. I stamped at the foot which was next to mine. My heel connected with arch-breaking force. There was a cry of pain. Twisting free, I pivoted on my left foot, a sharp pain shot

187

through it. As I swung a right hand in the direction of the cry, my fist smacked against bone with an impact that jolted my shoulder.

"Oh, you bastard!" Ding cursed.

Tossing the shoe out of my pocket, I snatched out the knife. I whirled toward Jackie, pressing the tiny button which flicked the blade open with a click. I raised the knife to strike. The voice of Dr. Bruce, Nurse Ann and Mom cut through my enraged mind. *"You must never break this vow."*

Hands imprisoned my poised hand, wrenching with a viciousness that sent me to my knees and tore an involuntary cry from my lips. The knife fell from my hand. Warm moisture blinded my left eye.

"Goddammit Jackie, get it over with before somebody comes!" Ding instructed, jerking brutally on the hammerlock he'd reclaimed on my arm. Jackie took a step toward me.

"I'm your shield punk, your last shield!" I yelled as he launched a kick at me. It caught me in the stomach, cutting off my breath. His handkerchief-wrapped hand smashed against my lips, filling my mouth with blood. I strained at the grip on my arm. It held fast. In helpless rage, I spat the accumulated blood in my mouth upon Jackie. He kicked again, striking me in the neck. I sprawled to the ground, the hold on my arm loosened. Ray snatched the watch from my wrist. I tried to get up and a foot crushed my head into the harsh gravel and glass of the alley and trod a parade of pain over every part of my body. I curled into a ball. Marion's screams rang in my ear. I thought: *What the hell is she screaming about? It's me who's getting it.*

Unconsciousness descended on me. I welcomed it.

188

Chapter **18**

"On your mark!"

I crouched at the starting line of the track field.

"Get set!"

Digging the spikes in, I raised my body slightly. My muscles twitched in anticipation of the command. Marion was shouting from the shadows as she sat perched with a stopwatch in her hand atop the 13-foot giant slides.

"Go!"

The command and my obedience to it were as one action. I sprang forward, instantly adopting a ground-covering stride. I raced for the white-painted hurdles, leaping the first one with my old expertness. I took the second, the third, the fourth . . .

At the last hurdle, my right toe struck the barrier as I went over, sprawling me into the gravel of the track. The full weight of my body landed on the ball of my left foot. By the pain which shot up my leg, I knew I had strained some of the stitches which Dr. Bruce had sewn in it the night of the fight at the prom. Squeezing my ankle tightly while the pain subsided, I remembered the whirl of events that had taken place since the fight.

The angry, shouting voice of Hank had greeted my return to consciousness several hours later. Dr. Bruce had announced that I would be unable to participate in the upcoming track meet, and the news had sent Hank into an uncontrollable rage. He blamed me for starting the fight, or for at least not running away from it. He had ended by firing me from my job at the pool room because he stood to lose a bundle in bets.

When Marion had protested Hank's tirade, he had slapped her to the floor and stalked out. I laid blanketed with pain, too weak to move in her defense. But the sight of her lying on the floor had intensified my hate for Hank, and caused me to renew a hundredfold my vow for revenge upon him.

And, there was Crow, now awaiting trial in a juvenile detention home for fracturing Ding's head with a bottle after being attracted by Marion's screams during the fight. Somehow, Marion and Crow had managed to get me into the car and she sped away with me unconscious in the seat beside her. Crow, still fighting off the gang, had not managed to get away before the police arrived.

Neither had Ray Miller, who was arrested out of the crowd due to the swollen mass my fist had made of his face. When the cops questioned him, they found his pockets bulging with marijuana. He was at county jail, probably headed for a nice long rap. *No better for him,* I thought.

But Crow was something else. I remembered the dejected slouch of his shoulders and the look of misery in his eyes as he pleaded with me to get him out of the dreary confines of the detention home when I had gone to visit him.

"Go talk to my folks, Guy," he had pleaded. "I can't take too much more of this place. Baby, these people treat ya worse than a step-child." His voice had been hoarse with his effort to keep from crying. "Talk to Max first. She's always thought you were good people. She'll help ya make de old folks move, ya dig?"

I had nodded blankly, remembering the feel of Maxine's spit striking my face that night in the park, and what I had already heard her tell her folks about her brother being in jail. "He's getting too wild," she had said. "And Guy here is the cause of it."

I had slammed out of their house in disgust. I had to help

190

Crow by myself. Somehow I had to help him by myself . . .

"Guy, are you all right?" Marion's voice floated to me from her lofty perch as I knelt, still holding my injured leg.

"Yeah," I assured her, getting to my feet and limping in her direction.

"You've done enough for one night, don't you think? Let's call it quits," she said as I approached the slide.

"Okay," I said, putting on the jacket and taking the towel she tossed down.

She slid down to me and we walked to the car.

As we drove away, I rode in silence, thinking of Crow's plight. His mournful words came back to me.

"Dig, Guy, de old folks think this is a jelly; a mommy-spank-on-de-hand and make-ya-sit-in-de-corner deal. Yeah, it is like hell. Dig this." Then he had pulled up his pants leg and shown me that both knees were raw. "From kneeling down on de damn floor half de night because I talk after lights-out," he had explained. "Yeah, yeah, I know I shouldn't. But goddammit, this place scares me and I've gotta talk or do somethin', ya know, like whistlin' when you go through a graveyard."

Then he had told me of being locked in a special punishment cell called "The Blackstone" for seven days, receiving one meal a day and sleeping on the bare floor without covering, because he hadn't eaten all the beans on his supper plate. There had been a boy-loving escapee from the reformatory in that cell with him . . .

"A penny for your thoughts," Marion said, breaking into them.

"I was thinking of Crow," I answered.

"Well, what about him? You've done all you could. You talked to his family, so what is there left to do? A month isn't such a long time."

Placing a cigarette between her lips, she pushed in the dashboard lighter. That was another thing that had happened since the night of the fight: Marion had started smoking.

"Must you?" I asked, eyeing the cigarette.

"Must I what?" she inquired petulantly.

Taking the cigarette from her lips, I tossed it out of the window. "Must you smoke and must you be so cool about the plight of the guy who saved my damned neck?" I demanded.

"Look, Clucky," she said, "I smoke because I'm a free, black, eighteen-year-old woman and that smack in the mouth Hank gave me has done something to my nerves. As for being cool to Crow's situation, what else can I do?"

"How do you go about getting a guy out of the can without using dynamite?" I asked wistfully.

"If you knew someone with some political clout, I believe they call it; a precinct captain or something."

Another cigarette was in her mouth. Taking the lighter from the dashboard, I dropped it in my jacket pocket. "Turn west at 112th and Bishop, then go to Ashland and head south," I ordered her quickly.

"Where are we going?" she asked.

"To see the one guy I know who may be able to get Crow out," I answered.

"And who is that?" she inquired, thumping the unlit cigarette out the window.

"Beano."

"You won't get past the door in your present get-up," she scoffed.

Twenty minutes later she turned into the parking lot of the club. I got out. She moved to follow me.

"Uh, uh," I said, closing the door. "You sit here and watch my smoke." Her remark had boosted my determination to see Beano.

Limping to the door of the club, I pushed through and halted inside. The joint was packed with Saturday night merrymakers. Toby glided over to me from where he had stood leaning against the bar.

"You took the wrong turn, Sonny, the finish line is that way," Toby said, grabbing at my arm to turn me around. I sidestepped the hand.

"Look mister, I didn't come here to amuse you or these bottle junkies," I told him. "I want to see the bully of this shack and I'm not leaving 'til I do. Cop?"

"Oh, a smart punk huh?" he sneered. "So now you go out the hard way."

He reached for me. I kicked him in the stomach. He grunted from the shock of it and stopped dead in his track. Stepping in close, I launched a right hand to his jaw, the impact drove him backwards across the floor and slammed him against the bar. His knees buckled; he clutched the bar for support, shaking his head. Then, pushing himself away from the bar, he crouched. His right hand snaked beneath his immaculate dinner jacket, withdrawing a wicked snub-nosed .38. It pointed steadily at my stomach. I stood frozen.

I had started on the second Hail Mary when Beano's voice cut the stillness which had settled on the room.

"Put it away, Toby!" he commanded, walking between us. "What are you trying to do, give the place a bad reputation? Here, go fix me a drink." He handed Toby the empty glass. "While you're at it, wash your face, you look like a pig."

Then, turning to me he said: "I see you're still bucking death, kid." Placing an arm about my shoulder, he walked me to the bar.

The realization of the danger I had just escaped caused my fiery determination to free Crow to go frosty for a moment. My duel with Toby had been strictly a matter of unconscious reflexes, an everyday reaction, like breaking into a mad dash at the sound of a gunshot.

Beano leaned against the bar. Toby returned, handed him

193

the drink and walked silently away. He had cleaned his face of the blood I'd knocked from his nose. *But hell, he nearly blowed me away,* I thought, erasing the tiny prick of regret which the defeated slump of Toby's shoulders caused. I wondered who I owed my good fortune to, the Virgin or Beano.

Taking a sip from the glass, Beano nodded toward the disappearing back of Toby. "Toby's no slouch with his hands when he's sober. You're lucky he's had a couple."

"No, blessed," I contradicted, giving the Virgin the credit for my good fortune.

"Religious?" he asked with a surprised lift of his eyebrows.

"To an extent," I confessed.

He grunted. "So what do you want from me that God can't give? Another two hundred bucks?"

His sudden change to mockery made me hesitate in revealing the cause for my seeking him. Noting it, Beano said: "Come on Guy, it's obvious from your fancy foot and hand work of a moment ago, that you're in bad need of a favor. Okay, so you've come to the right place to see the right person. Doing favors is my racket. That's how I got on top. Now let's have it. What can I do for you?"

I told him.

He looked at me a moment in silence, his piercing black eyes were blank with thought. Turning from me to the bar, he commanded the phone from behind it with a snap and point of his finger. A bartender obeyed with cat-like swiftness. Beano dialed and waited.

"Pachecko? This is DeMarco. You got a kid out there at the home,—ah—" he raised a questioning eyebrow at me.

"Amos Byrd," I supplied.

"Amos Byrd. I want him to be in Sunday School tomorrow. What? The law! Don't mention the law to me. I want that kid in Sunday School tomorrow or else!"

He recradled the receiver and faced me. A look of satisfaction and the glint in his eyes matched the parade ground manner he'd just used on the phone in precise D.I. tone. "It is finished," he said, placing the tips of his fingers piously together, "without a knee bowing."

Mockery was again in his voice. Realizing what his words meant, I extended my hand in gratitude. Admiration made my heart race wildly. "Thanks, Mr. aw—Beano. Gee! thanks a lot," I said, pumping his soft, manicured hand warmly.

He accepted my enthusiasm with a nod.

"Thanks!" I repeated heading for the door.

"Say, Guy."

I turned at the sound of his voice.

"Where did you learn to move so fast and why?"

"From the street, and because of necessity," I replied without hesitation.

"That last moves the world."

I walked back to him, curious to know what he meant by his closing remark over the phone. "What is the 'or else' you spoke of?" I asked, pointing to the phone.

"It's another necessity, a power-giving necessity made so by burying Graves. Catch?"

I shook my head.

"Don't you read the newspapers?"

"Only the sport section now and then."

"Well, if you read all of it regularly you may get a hint now and then on what's happening in this town. Understand?"

I nodded that I did, but I didn't.

"Burying Graves. Ha! That's pretty good," he said with a laugh. Turning his back to me, he commanded another drink with a snap and a point of his finger.

Marion was asleep when I returned. I didn't awaken her until after I'd parked before my house. During the return drive I'd tried to figure out Beano's words regarding politics and connect them with the short bitter laugh and reference to burying Graves.

195

When I had pulled up before the house, I'd succeeded in concluding that Graves was the name of a person. I sat looking at Marion. *She does look like Mom,* I affirmed for the thousandth time since the prom.

I thought again of my return to consciousness. Remembering Hank's laughter when I asked him to off my bet or give me more odds because of my injuries. His refusal had spurred me to override Dr. Bruce's orders to stay off my feet. With Marion's eager assistance, I began putting myself into running shape again, starting with simple calisthenics done in bed and progressing gradually to practicing in the deserted school yard each night at ten o'clock. There was a grimness in the schedule we had adopted, and somewhere during those gruelling hours of training I had seen my love of Marion lose some of its fire, just as somewhere during those same hours she had adopted smoking. She'd been masseuse, crutch, trainer and doctor, helping me into Mom's wheel chair, to the tub, forcing me to take hot baths, pounding sore, bunched muscles and pulled ligaments back to order, charting my return to my old running standards with stop watch precision. She'd been a Blackburn, a Nightingale and a woman with the sweat of revenge on her brow. We had learned that Hank was making up on the money he expected to lose on me by betting heavy on Jackie, Sandy and a few more fast boys from the surrounding communities. If I won, he would lose a bundle. I refired my determination to do so by thinking of Mom and remembering the sight of him stepping over Marion's prostrate form.

Marion woke up.

"So what happened?" she asked, reaching for a cigarette.

Feeling good over the outcome of my talk with Beano and grateful for her help in my return to running shape, I covered her lips with mine in a long kiss as I removed the cigarette from her fingers and tossed it out the window.

"Well, now you're really hitting it in stride," she said.

196

"That's something you haven't thought to do in three weeks. How about trying it again? You know, sort of put me back into the feel of it."

I felt a pang of guilt for my neglect as I pressed my lips to hers again. I tried to recapture that old feeling, but couldn't. Leaning back and crossing my arms on my chest with a false air of satisfactory accomplishment, "How's that for size?" I asked, hoping my banter and look would make up for my lack of passionate action.

"If I were your sister, I would say it was just what I've been looking for. Only I'm not your sister. Of course, there's always tomorrow," she replied with surprising sarcasm.

"I'm sorry, Muffet."

"For what?" she asked in feigned surprise.

I couldn't tell her of how obsessed I'd become with the belief that my love for her was unnatural. So I remained silent.

"So what did Beano say or do, if anything?" she asked with a sigh, placing a cigarette between her lips. Taking out the lighter, I pushed it in the slot, then gave her a light. When I finished, she nodded her head meditatively and said: "He's a pretty big kick all right, he'd have to be in order to get a judge up at this time of night and talk to him in such a manner."

"Big kick, hell, that cat's a Bunyan in jackboots," I said fervently. So I told of the Italian's reference to burying Graves and newspapers. She told me of what she knew of the strange disappearance of a racketeering politician named Matt Graves. Her information was vague.

When she had finished, she looked at her watch with sleep-laden eyes. "It's 2:30," she said.

I thought of the watch she'd given me, and made a mental note to recover it from Raymond Miller even if it meant killing him.

Returning the lighter to its place, I got out. Marion moved

197

to follow. "No, you better cop you some nods," I said, then added, "that is unless you want to play house."

She started the motor. "No, you're in training. Now, don't forget to take a hot bath and make sure you rub down real good. Furthermore, please put on your pajamas," she directed with athletic coach proficiency.

I nodded.

"As for your 'play house' invitation, I've suddenly grown tired of the games." The cigarette between her lips glowed redly.

The dashboard clock indicated 9 A.M. just as Crow stepped through the large doors of the detention home. He stood on the top step for a moment, shielding his eyes against the glare of the warm July sun. Opening the car door, I blew the horn. He hurried over to the car and got in. We drove in silence down Roosevelt Road. As I turned south on California Avenue, he spoke.

"Hey, Baby?" he grunted.

"What's happening, momma?" I replied.

Sticking his nose out the window, he inhaled deeply of the morning air. It was heavily perfumed with the smells from the stockyards. "Humm-m-m, ah-h-h," he said, as if he were sniffing some heavenly fragrance. "All de happenings is love now that I'm in de free. By de way, how in de hell did you manage it?"

"Politics," I said, then told him of my experience of last night. When I'd finished, he looked at me with admiration and gratitude.

"So that's why they all but tossed me out of that joint. Beano, huh? And you lamed Toby? Buddy, you smacked a tiger," he said in an awed tone.

The red light caught us at 26th Street. I nodded to the County Jail. "There's the 'Graystone Hotel,' " I said.

He spat in the direction I indicated. "Yeah, that's where all de big leftfielders are."

The light changed. I put the car in motion. "The hell you preach," I denied, thinking of Beano's tone and manner in speaking to Judge Pachecko and his reaction. I pointed to the Criminal Court Building. "The leftfielders are probably in there. Them people in the Graystone are just a bunch of short-stops I bet."

"Well, no matter who's in there, if that house of many slammers is anything like de one you pulled me from, I feel sorry for dem," he sympathized fervently.

"Dig, Crow, I better hip you to the fact that your folks don't want you out."

"What do you mean, man?" he inquired with a frown.

I told him of my conversation with his family and of their decision to leave him in the house as a lesson. While I was at it, I told him of Maxine's dislike of me and the cause of it. When I ended, we were silent for a few blocks.

"Well, if that's de way de little ball bounces, then I ain't going home," he said bitterly.

"Well, I wouldn't go until after the day you were supposed to go to trial," I agreed. "After then everything should be cool."

He shook his head. "No baby, by them not coming to get me when I needed them to, they tore their tail with me. I ain't never going home, Guy, I ain't never going home."

The grimness of his voice made me regret having told him. "Aw hell! Crow, don't talk like that, you know how old folks are. They're probably making plans to get you out now. Before you jump frantic, why don't you just wait and see what they do next month? You can stay at my house until then, and I'll feel them out. Okay?"

"Look, baby, I appreciate de offer and everything ya done for me, but de old folks has had their last of me. Cop? As for staying at your crib, I couldn't, my old man would have de bulladeens on us in nothin' flat. I'm going to shack with Dot and Jim."

"Well, whatever you say, man."

At 51st and Halsted I parked before a small florist. Going in, I bought a mixed bouquet of flowers and returned to the car.

"Who are those for?" Crow inquired, smelling the flowers.

"Mom," I said, "being as I'm down this way, I'm going to try and visit her."

"Crazy, tell her I said hello and to get healthy as a corn cake quick. You can let me out at Indiana."

Before he got out of the car, I offered him 10 of the 20 dollars I had.

"Aw! hell no man, I can't take all of your bread, you did enough already," he protested.

I stuck the bills in his pocket. "Look, momma, we're ace-boon-coons, remember? So I helped get you out of the can, so you saved my noggin the night of the prom. You cop? Turn about is fair play, now get the hell out of the car."

"Okay, baby, I'll do that, and I'll be out Saturday to see you kick gravel in those lames' faces. Cool it now," he said, flashing his old smile and waving.

"Later, little man," I said driving off.

I arrived at the hospital minutes later. Taking the flowers, I ran up the steps, my heart surging wildly with tender yearning to see Mom. At the information desk I identified myself and asked permission to visit her.

The nurse referred to a chart, then told me that I'd have to phone Dr. Cherkov for permission.

Using the public phone, I called the doctor. After a few rings a cultured voice asked, "Yes?"

"Dr. Cherkov? This is Guy Morgan. I'm at the hospital and would like to visit my mother if you please."

He was silent for a moment, then said: "Yes, you may visit

her. Please remember, however, that she has a very weak heart. She is not to be excited. Do you understand? She is not to be excited."

I assured him that I understood perfectly.

"All right, I'll phone the desk to let you through. I am sorry that I have to be so strict, but your mother's case has been very difficult. I'm afraid that I must request that you phone me whenever you desire to visit her."

"I'll do just that, Dr. Cherkov, and you may expect your money next week," I told him in warm gratitude.

"All right, Mr. Morgan. Goodbye." He hung up.

I waited by the phone until I heard the phone at the desk ring; the nurse answered it. "All right, Doctor," she said into the receiver, then smiled at me, "You may visit Mrs. Morgan now."

I hurried to the elevator. Arriving at the third floor, I went to Mom's room. Soft organ music came from a radio on the other side of the door. I knocked on it softly. Mom's voice bid me enter, the sound of it intensified the tenderness I was feeling.

I entered, closed the door and walked over to her bed. She was sitting propped on the pillows. The small Bible I'd left her was in her hand.

Looking down at her, I said, "Hi, pretty, how's my heavenly flower?" She raised her arm. Instantly I was on my knees, her hand cupping my face.

"Clucky, Clucky, my baby, my son," she said softly, kissing my eyes, nose and mouth. "How have you been, Guy? Oh! I'm a bad mother for causing you all of this inconvenience. Why, I should be at home cooking you a nice dinner and here I am lounging around in all of this—" She waved her hand to include the room. I remained silent, enjoying the sound of her voice, her nearness, the touch of her fingers toying with my ear.

"You look peaked, Guy, you haven't been ill, have you?

201

Where are you taking your meals, at your aunt's?" she asked. "How was graduation? How's my—"

I interrupted her. "Whoa! You're speeding. One thing at a time," I said, standing up. I went over to the large window and placed a chair before it, facing out upon the park. Returning to the bed, I said, "Now if you'll promise me not to get excited and not to ask a dozen questions in one breath, I'll treat you to a peek of the park." She smiled and raised her arms, wrapping the sheet about her. I lifted her up and went and sat in the chair with her on my lap.

"Did you take Marion to the prom and did you have fun?" she continued to question.

"Hold it, you're doubling them up on me!" I admonished. "Yes, I went to the prom. We knocked ourselves out." I thought: *How true, how true.*

She was silent for a while. The portable radio continued to emit organ music, "Guy, who's paying for all of this, the doctor and all," she asked finally, not looking at me.

"Why, Aunt Agnes and Aunt Emma," I assured her. She sighed, laying her head on my chest. "I'm glad, I was so worried and that Dr. Cherkov wouldn't tell me anything nor would Dr. Bruce."

"Well, now you know, so please stop worrying." There was silence again. I was thinking of how she looked when she fell to the floor. "Mom! I'm sorry about—"

Her fingers covered my lips. "Hush, Guy, God works in mysterious ways."

I didn't attempt to deny this, or did I want to. It relieved me to unburden my feeling of guilt upon the all-forgiving shoulders of God.

"Why didn't you awaken me when you were out here last?" she asked in mild reproach.

"You were sleeping so well Mom, until I just couldn't."

"Oh, you're silly, that's all I do is sleep," she scoffed.

"Well, I think you've had enough open air for one morn-

202

ing sweetheart, so back to bed you go." I returned her to the bed.

After I'd satisfied all her questions, she handed me the Bible and I read to her.

After a while, the nurse entered with her lunch. "I'm sorry, but you'll have to go now," she said with a smile. Laying the Bible on the table, I took a flower from the bouquet I'd brought and placed it in Mom's hair. "Well, I've got to run," I said. "Oh, yes, Crow said to tell you to get healthy as a corn cake quick."

She smiled. "Tell Crow, I'll do that little thing."

I kissed her and I headed for the door.

"Clucky."

I returned to the bed. "Yes, Mom?" I asked.

She reached for my hand. "Happy birthday, son," she said, pressing a dark red rose in my hand.

"Thanks, Mom, this is the nicest gift I've ever received."

"I'm flattered, Clucky." She patted my hand. "It's belated, but given with all my love, and though it's small, it's a Godly creation. Now we mustn't keep the good nurse here waiting, so go with God and pray for me, hear?" I nodded. Closing the door, I began a mental Rosary.

Chapter 19

Parking the car before the drug store twenty minutes later, I remained sitting in it for a moment, to finish my fourth of them. Then I got out and entered the store. Stopping at the juke box, I made three selections and sat in the first booth. Marion was busy behind the fountain.

Hearing a burst of laughter, I glanced over my shoulder at the door. Jackie, Kay and Luzon were getting out of the Cadillac parked before it; Kay was laughing merrily. Facing around, I scooted into the corner of the booth so the juke box would block me from them, and pretended to be occupied in fitting the two straws I'd hastily snatched from their container. My hands trembled slightly as the laughter drew nearer. I intensified my concentrations on the straws, my ears not missing a tingle of Kay's chiming laughter.

They had passed the booth when Jackie exclaimed, "Damn! There ain't an empty booth in the joint."

"Here's one," Luzon said, stepping over to where I sat. "It's almost empty!" she laughed mockingly.

I looked up; Kay and Jackie turned. They walked over to the booth. Jackie stood between the two girls placing a possessive arm around their waists.

"Well, if it ain't the black liberator himself! How are you Clucky, old duck? I haven't seen you around much these past few weeks. I guess you've been resting from all that dancing you put down at the prom, huh? You really did get carried away, didn't 'cha? I mean, dancing all over the floor and alley," he said, breaking into insolent laughter. The two girls had removed themselves from his arms and sat across from me. Kay wore a frown of embarrassment; Luzon watched me through half-closed eyelids; Jackie looked down at me with a defiant sneer. Inwardly seething with rage at his words, I prepared to spring at him. But the sight of the rose in the lapel of Kay's smartly-fashioned white suit reminded me of the one in the left pocket of my shirt, beneath my suit coat. I made myself relax, remembering Mom's worry over the doctor and hospital bill and the fact that the meet was just six days away. No, I couldn't afford to run the risk of being injured again, not now.

"Now's not the time, your Reverence, but the wheel is turning. Your number will come up soon," I told him.

"That will be the day, lame," he sneered. Turning, he went to the fountain. My anger heightened. I crumbled the straws into a ball.

"... *Them that's got shall get, them that's not shall lose ...*" sang the vocalist on one of the three records I had selected.

"I'll bet that's your cut," said Luzon. She still looked at me through the veil of her long lashes.

I didn't comment on the statement.

Jackie returned to the booth, handing Cokes to the girls. He started to sit beside me. I put my foot on the seat, planting the one on the floor in a position to spring at the first move he should make.

He straightened, pretending not to see.

"Dig *my* two pretty palominos," he said. Then to the two girls he added: "Let's move out from this baby-bar and make it to one more suited to our mature tastes."

A sudden pang seized me at the thought of Kay leaving.

"And where is this place you speak of, around the horn?" Kay asked with an imperious lift of a long black eyebrow.

"It's just a hop, skip, and jump away. I'm sure you've heard of the widely celebrated Silver Slipper?"

Curiosity lighted her dark brown eyes.

"That suits me fine," Luzon said. She got up and surveyed

the crowded drug store contemptuously. "Come on, Kay, you'll like the Slipper," she said.

I took my foot off the seat and faced Kay, my eyes entreating her to refuse.

"Come on, Kay, I'll show you a time!" Jackie coaxed.

Luzon left the store. Kay started to slide from the booth. Her foot struck mine; the contact was electrifying. Bringing my feet together, I imprisoned her shoe between them. She stopped, looking at me with a frown. My eyes continued to entreat. We looked at each other for a long moment. I was oblivious to Jackie and to the chattering crowd of teens, completely submerged in the pool of her clear brown eyes. Their warmth sent shivers of delight up and down my spine. I knew that she was feeling something of the same for the frown left her face. Her even white teeth bit her full poutish top lip.

"Let's go, Kay!" Jackie commanded, vexed at her hesitation. She released her lip; it turned ruby red. A desire to kiss her filled my being.

"You and Luzon go ahead," she said, smiling demurely, "I have no desire to hop, skip or jump." Her eyes had not left mine.

"Now wait a minute, Kay! Your father told *me* to show you around. You can't—"

The look that Kay turned upon him halted his heated protest.

"It just so happens, Jack Lindy, that I'm not some object that my father just deposits with people. I'm free, black and eighteen. So let's drop it. You and Luzon have a nice time."

"Look, Kay," Jackie reached for her hand. "If you think you won't like the Slipper, we'll cut somewhere else. We—"

"Move out, Pretty Jackie," I cut him off.

He turned to me angrily. I palmed the salt and pepper shakers. "Boy, you really are a glutton for punishment, aren't you?" he asked sarcastically.

"Yeah, I'm funny that way."

206

He grunted. Turning to Kay, he declared: "I'm going to tell your father about this." I laughed at the childishness of the threat. He hurried from the store.

I kept laughing.

"Was it really funny?" she said.

Sobering, I said, "No, it isn't, really. Actually, I'm relieved and happy that you turned him down—and—well, you know—" I ended lamely.

She smiled. "No, I don't know."

"Well—I'm glad you didn't go."

Her short laugh was like a lovely song whose ending I regretted.

"I couldn't very well go without my shoes," she said.

I looked under the table; her foot was out of the black shoe which I held vised between my feet.

"Oh, I'm sorry." Bumping my head beneath the table, I held her shoe while she slipped her foot into it. Her legs were shapelier than any I'd ever seen. I regretted having to leave the vantage point under the table. In withdrawing, I raised my head too quickly. Its bump against the table was as loud as the impact was painful. I cursed with the hurt of it.

Marion was over at the fountain gaping at me with a frown.

"No wonder the days of chivalry are past," Kay said with a laugh which vanquished my pain. Marion still watched me. The voice of the vocalist on my third selection cut across Kay's laughter. We fell silent.

". . . *Sundays are gloomy, my hours are slumberless. Dearest, the shadows I live with are numberless . . .*"

Leaning back, I savored the sorrowful sounds, the accompaniment of the clarinet, piano, bass fiddle and drums to the vocalist's lament. The record ended.

"You really like that type of music," Kay said. "Why?"

"Because the world is a playground filled with merrily tinkling toys that seek to inspire me to mirth, but I dislike laughter, for it is a dangerous tool whose force attempts to make realists forget that sadness has a soul and morbidity a delight."

She frowned reflectively, shaking her head. "Might I have read that somewhere? Who is it by?"

"It's the thought of a fourteen-year-old kid as he lay in a hospital one Christmas. A kid with broken arms, legs, ribs—a kid who refused many gifts of doctors and nurses because he wanted to indulge himself in all the sorrow and pain he was feeling."

"But why didn't the kid want to take his mind off his pain?" she asked, still frowning.

"Because he knew that the one love of his life was sad. So he enjoyed his sorrow. Yes, and his pain, too, because she was in pain, too."

We were silent for a moment. She stared at me, shaking her head. "I'm afraid I'm confused," she confessed with a smile.

"I'm afraid he was, too, and maybe still is."

A racy tune blared from the juke box.

"Do you go for jitterbugging?" I asked, wanting to change the subject.

"Not particularly, but my father tells me that you really throw the girls around. I gathered from his description of you at the prom that you're a very accomplished Apache dancer."

She laughed. I joined in, remembering the spill Marion and I had taken at the prom. I glanced over at the fountain. Marion's back was to me. She was busy at the mixers. Our eyes met in the mirror; hers shot angry darts at me.

I turned back to Kay. She drained the Coke Jackie had brought her and asked: "Well! Where do we go from here?"

"That all depends on how far you wish to travel."

She glanced at her watch. "Well, it's 1:30 now and I promised I'd be home at 7:00, so let's not travel too far."

After a moment's hesitation, I said, "Then we have three choices: Go for a walk and see the unimpressive sights of the neighborhood; go to the record shop—which is actually a shack behind a tall white fence, but the owner, a guy named Slidell, keeps a good stock of platters; or, I could take you to Hank's Pool Room, but I wouldn't, even though you wanted me to. I only mention it to suggest the variety of activities the Park offers us. Of course, being as you are eighteen, we could go to one of the taverns around here for some fun. So, what will it be?"

Biting her top lip, she frowned as if confronted with a weighty decision. "Hmm, let's see. Walking? No, not in these heels. Pool room? No, not in this tight suit. Tavern? No! no! no! Preacher's daughter. So that leaves the record shop. Okay! let's go."

She got up and smoothed a few imaginary wrinkles at the hips of her suit and headed for the door. I went to the fountain and handed Marion the car keys.

Her eyes blazed. "I'll see you when you practice tonight. That is, if you still have time for such trivial matters." I'd never seen her so angry before.

"Look, Muffet—" I began.

"I don't want to hear it, Beau Brummell. Besides, your friend is waiting for you," she said bitingly.

I left the store.

"Which way?" Kay said.

I nodded to the west. We strolled slowly in that direction.

"Was that your girl friend back there?"

"No, my used-to-be," I said without guilt.

"She's cute."

I nodded.

"And very angry at you, if I'm not mistaken," she added smilingly.

I shrugged.

As we passed Hank's, a voice shouted: "Say, Tim, dig the stallion with Old Deacon!"

The shout was followed by the sound of many hurrying feet. Behind us, long wolf whistles shrilled.

"Hey! Miss Fine and Foxy! What's to it, pretty?"

"Prance, palomino, prance!"

"Wow! Dig the body action!"

"Man! That's ice cream and cake stuff!"

Grabbing Kay by the elbow, I hurried her the few remaining steps to the record shop. For the first time in my life I was ashamed of the pool room crowd's way of approving a well-built female, and the knowledge that this was my own way heightened my sense of shame.

Walking through the gate of the seven-foot high board fence which hid the record shop from the street, Kay halted to look at the clean white building.

"Look, Kay, I'm sorry about the guys back there," I said. "They were trying to be nice. They're good studs—"

Her laughter cut me off. "Oh, needn't apologize for that. I'd be worried if they hadn't whistled. Now, tell me, why does whoever owns this beautiful modern building hide it behind an ugly fence? It's completed, isn't it?"

I told her of how the short, rotund half-breed, whom we knew only as Slidell, had come to Morgan Park five years before with plans to build a center where teens could buy records, dance, skate, bowl, and have fun. He'd bought three lots on the main thoroughfare and had erected the first of three buildings of his planned center, which he had named Teenland Variety. Some months later, he gave a dance to announce the opening of his center. The party had just begun to be the best ever to be given when the bulls stepped in and ran everybody out. Slidell was given an injunction which forbid his doing further work on the center.

She looked at me perplexedly. "I don't get it. Who would be so mean and heartless as to prevent a man from doing something so constructive?"

"Why, the good Christian fathers over there," I said pointing to the church towers. "And the patron of that sanctum over there," I said, pointing to the large Greater Hope Church. "Zoning business, immorality, juvenile delinquency—some jazz like that."

"Now Guy, you don't mean to try and make me believe that the churches stopped Mr. Slidell," she scoffed prettily.

"No, I don't want to make you believe anything. I'm merely telling you the facts," I said. "You can believe what you like."

I'd spoken more shortly than I'd intended, feeling again the bitter disappointment all of us kids had felt then.

"But that—that's narrow," she exclaimed heatedly.

"Yeah, that's what we thought. In fact, some of us thought it was so narrow we went to the elders of the church. They laughed like hell, so we went out and raised a little hell."

"What do you mean—raised a little hell?"

"Oh, you know, the usual thing. Got juiced up on wine, tossed a few dozen rocks through the school house windows, also went in and burned a few books and desks; tossed a few more rocks through a few of the windows of the laughing elders' home, cut up a few of the tires on their cars, tore down a few grape arbors—things like that."

"But surely you all knew you'd gain nothing by that. Why, you were worse than they. Why did you do that?"

"For a few laughs," I said, walking toward the shack. I had grown weary of the subject.

"Why didn't he move his shop into that building?" she whispered as we entered the dilapidated shop.

"Because he's got pride, I guess. Look, how in the hell do I know or care? If it were my place, I'd tell 'em to move their churches off the main thoroughfare. If they didn't, I'd cop me some dynamite and blow them over to the side streets with the other twelve churches there are over there. I know what I'd do if the place was mine, but it's his," I said, pointing to

Slidell who emerged from the back of the shack, "so ask him."

I turned away angrily. As I shuffled through the records piled on the crude, makeshift counter, I heard her say:

"Mr. Slidell, why do you have your shop in this shack instead of that lovely building out there?"

There was no reply, as I knew there wouldn't be. We kids had hounded him with that question long ago.

He merely gave a funny smile and shrugged.

"Well, why don't you take the churches to court?"

"Me? No, no, young lady, never that," Slidell replied with an odd accent. "The people in the church, they know what is best for the kids, besides, I'm a Christian man. So it would not look right. No!"

Finding a new calypso record, I put it on the turntable. The volume was turned very low. I leaned over the turntable to catch every beat of the throbbing tom-toms. Kay came to stand by me as the rhythms of the drums took form. She leaned closer to the turntable, her side pressing against mine. The warmth of her body stole through the material of our clothes, causing my blood to run a merry race through my body. I prayed for the record to play endlessly on. In the past I'd always argued with Slidell over the loudness of the volume, but now I thanked him silently for the softness which brought Kay so close to me.

The record ended. Kay straightened with a sigh.

"I love that type of music, it does something to me," she said. "The bassy thump of those drums pulls at my insides," she said feelingly.

I nodded, setting the needle on the other side of the record. We leaned forward together again. Her love of the music began to take action. She closed her eyes and began to sway in time with its slow beat.

I looked up. Slidell sat perched on a high stool behind the counter, his chubby hands folded over his chubbier stomach.

His face was lit up with a benign smile. He looked like an impish Buddha as he watched Kay and me. He winked at me. I returned my attention to the record.

Kay was giving her shapely hips a good right turn when the record came to an abrupt end.

"Oh, but those drums kick me off!" she said, shaking her head as if to clear it of the spell the drums had cast. An idea flashed through my mind.

Looking at Slidell, I asked, "Dig, Buddha, is this the only new cut you have since I was in here last?"

He nodded.

I turned to Kay. Her large mouth seemed to pout more noticeably.

"Look, Kay," I said. "I told you there were only three things we could do. I forgot the fourth because I didn't want you to get any wrong ideas about my intentions, cop?"

She nodded.

I went on hurriedly: "You're strong for calypso. Choice, 'cause I am too. I've got the best collection of calypso cuts in the Park. Ask Slidell. Plus I got a choice congo drum. How about us doing this fourth thing and mopping on over to my crib?" I waited her reply with held breath.

She made the lip-biting gesture. After a moment, she said: "Okay, why not? Yes, let's do the fourth thing; only when we get there, don't you try to stretch this fourth into a fifth. Cop?"

Her lips laughed but not her eyes.

I nodded, feeling that her answer had thrown open heaven's door. I wanted to be alone with her. Taking the record off the turntable and slipping it into the paper covering, I handed Slidell fifty-five cents and started for the door.

"Hey! Wait a minute, I forgot one little something," he called, hurrying over to us.

He pasted a stick paper on the solid center of the record; on it was lettered "Teenland's Variety."

I looked at the fat man.

"Slidell," I said, "when you cop that dynamite, we kids asked you for way back—well, I'll personally put you in business by my lonesome. Dig?"

He shook his head and shrugged. "Do not talk like that, it is very foolish."

"Yeah, I know, but it is also very effective." I took Kay's hand and we left.

The memory of the wolf calls at the pool room caused me to halt at the gate of the white fence and suggest a short cut through the alley.

As we passed the rear of Hank's, Kay said, "I don't know whether to be flattered or insulted, you shielding me from the wolf calls. You know, you're a funny guy, Guy."

We laughed.

"Guy isn't a common name, is it? I wonder what inspired your mother to give it to you."

"My father named me. All the first-born males of his clan were named Guy. The name is a simplification of an African name by using the first three letters of it. The original was a jawbreaker to the plantation owner named Morgan, who bought one of my great-grandfathers in slavery. My father has got the story down pat. He cops a big bang from the purity of his Moorish blood. I've heard him tick off the family tree better than a preacher could read Genesis. He'd go on half a day, begetting and spewing names with twenty-five letters to them. Ha! Yeah, he was really good at that."

"Is he dead?"

I shook my head no. "But I wish—" I caught myself before I'd completed the sentence.

"You wish what?"

"Nothing, let's forget about it, huh?"

"Uh, uh, let's not, please. I'm fascinated, really," she said. Clutching my right arm with both hands, she squeezed it en-

214

thusiastically. "Tell me, why do you wear this earring?" she said, touching my right ear. "I've puzzled over it since I saw you that night at the rink."

"That's my father's doing also. He had Nurse Ann—she's the nurse who helped Dr. Bruce deliver me—put it in when I was—oh, just a few weeks old. It's a clan tradition for the first-born male. To my father, it symbolizes a warrior chief. He says Great Grandfather Somebody the 100th, who was the son of Great Great Grandfather 99th, a chief, was sent by Great Great Grandfather 99th to represent the clan in an invasion. Great Grandfather the 100th proved to be one hell of a stud with a spear and he copped many battle stars. That is, until they met their Waterloo at Granada. When things got too hot, he moved out and was captured trying to make it back to the fatherland and sold into slavery to this Morgan stud, whose last name I bear."

"That would have been a very romantic story, if you hadn't told it so sloppily," she reproved. "I bet your father could make it much more interesting. You know, names of battles, tales of exotic love affairs—"

"Yeah, I bet he could, too, especially that last. He got a big kick out of that 'I pure Moor' stuff. Me, it don't gas me at all. I'm an American."

"Well, why wear the earring?" she asked as I opened the door to my house.

Stepping inside, I said, "Because at first I was afraid to take it off, afraid of my father. Then I got to be afraid I'd forget my father; to me, this symbolizes the feeling I have for him."

"You must really love your father."

"I hate his bloody guts," I said vehemently.

She turned, suddenly, surprise widening her pretty eyes. "What?"

"I said I hate his bloody guts, every rope and strand of them. This earring reminds me never to forget that fact."

"Oh, I see. I mean, I didn't know. I'm truly sorry I reminded you of something unpleasant."

She sat on the couch. "You see, I'm so curious about things and I have such a childish love for tales until—well, sometimes it causes embarrassment. I am sorry, really."

I sat next to her. "Don't be, I'm not. I enjoy my hate because it's justified."

"But you can't—it's ugly and mean—"

"So are most things in life."

"No! That's not so," she said. "Everything in life is basically good, at least I'd like to think so. Sure, I've heard people say the opposite but to hate that way, the way I believe you hate your father—is—well—I mean, it seems kind of morbid—you can't—"

She stopped. She was staring at Mom's wheel chair. Looking at me, she asked, "Whose is that?"

"My mother's."

"Then you are the fourteen-year-old and your mother is the one you—?"

I nodded.

"I see," she said in a hushed voice, leaning back. Closing her eyes, she bit her lip. The gesture rekindled my desire for her. Twisting, I placed my knee on the couch, resting my hands on its arm and back. I pressed my lips to hers, her eyes flew open. We stared at each other. Her lips were unyielding.

I imprisoned her bottom lip between my teeth, passing my tongue back and forth over its fullness. Her gaze became blank and her long lashes descended slowly. Her glance through half-closed lids increased my desire. I pressed her lips, pushing her head into the softness of the couch.

She began shaking her head slowly, protesting with drawn-out moans arising from deep within her body to be muffled by the thick, silken curtain of passion in her throat. Still protesting, she returned my kisses. Her hands ascended my arms slowly, halting briefly as they went to clutch tightly, as if to pull herself from the pit of passion which was slowly engulfing us. The roll of her lips beneath mine had become an act of love in itself.

Her hands met behind my neck, pulling my mouth more tightly to hers. Her darting tongue slipped free from my teeth, and lured my tongue into a duel. I savored every moment of it all, fighting to delay the inevitable. Her hand fumbled at the front of my shirt.

I loosened my tie. My fingers grew impatient at the fastened shirt! I ripped it open in a shower of buttons. I tore off the undershirt.

Soft fingers played curiously over my chest. Unbuttoning her coat, I embraced her slender waist. My hand touched naked flesh; she stiffened. As I unloosened her brassiere, she tore her lips from mine.

"No! no! Oh please, Guy, please—I can't—you promised. Please—please help me—save me from myself," she pleaded as I kissed the tips of her breasts, her stomach.

I undressed her, covering her face with kisses. She sat, passive as a child being readied for bed, her only resistance tears and pleas.

"No, Guy—listen—I've promised myself not to until I—"

I kissed her, pressing her naked body prone upon the couch. Straightening, I stripped hurriedly, staring down upon the bronze curvaceousness of her. I moved toward the couch; she sprang to her feet and tried to get past me. I stepped before her, our bodies touched, my arms around her, our lips met. Moisture painted our chins as we sank to the floor.

"Guy, Guy, oh no, please, you mustn't, I promised myself —you promised. It's all that I have—that is all mine—to bring to love. You shouldn't. Could you love me? Do you love me? Will you love me?" she sobbed.

I covered her with kisses. "Yes, yes, anything I can I will do, I will, always," I said passionately.

"Swear it, say you swear it, please," she begged.

"I swear it by every color in the rainbow—by all the saints in the book—by the straw in the manger of the infant Jesus, I love you."

Her arms pulled me to her.

"Take me, then, I'm yours."

My body strained at her scream. I rode a star that streaked upward. The roar of the winds rushing mightily was in my ears. I ripped clouds, threw thunder and pounded on the sky. I strained at the doors of heaven; they flung open, sprawling me on the floor of paradise. I heard a song of ecstasy. The song began to fade, I strained to hold it, it faded into silence. With a sigh I rolled to the floor.

Chapter **20**

The feel of pain from the scratches Kay's nails had dug in my shoulders was pleasant. The sound of her quiet breathing and the tick of my old alarm clock were the only sounds in the room.

Closing my eyes, I remembered Crow calling Kay a real icebox the night at the rink. I smiled. *Crow ain't into nothing when it comes to classifying*, I concluded.

Lips pressed mine tenderly in a brief kiss. I opened my eyes. She hovered over me. Her hands straddled my body.

"Hey, pretty," I greeted.

"Hey, thief."

We laughed. Her breasts jogged above me like ripe fruit.

"What you must think of me, a preacher's daughter—"

"I think you're the most, to say the least," I interrupted, "and I hope you don't regret what we've done. When I asked you to come here, I didn't have any intentions of something like this happening, although I confess that I wanted you. Then you had to go and bite your lips in that funny little way of yours and well—hell! I had to kiss you."

"And stretch the fourth into the fifth."

I nodded.

"I don't regret it," she said. "I had promised myself that I'd go to the marriage bed a virgin, but what is there to assure me that I'll ever get married and not die an old maid?"

I let my eyes speak my reply as they traveled over the beautiful lines of her body.

"Do you really think I'm pretty?" she asked with a frown.

"As pretty as a speckled puppy," I affirmed.

"Do you love me?"

For a long moment I sought for words to convey my feelings for her at the rink. "I enjoy being with you—I don't mean just as we are now—if we'd decided to take a walk instead of coming here, I still would have enjoyed your nearness," I told her. "Hearing your laughter when you entered the store today made my heart sing and my hands shake. I've wanted to be with you since my first glimpse of you, and now that we're together, I hate the thought of us having to part. Is that love? I'll let you put it together and give it a name, because frankly, I don't know. I thought I did, with Marion, I mean, but something happened, I no longer feel the same way about her. I'd like to, because she's been wonderful to me as far back as I can remember. A few minutes ago I swore that I loved you. Then it was easy to give a name to my feeling, but now I don't know. But I do know that you do something to me, something that I enjoy."

"I'm still yours," she said, kissing my chest.

"And you still do something to me," I said, cupping her breast.

"What?"

"The same thing you said the drums do to you; pull at your insides, I think it was," I said, getting up.

Going to my bedroom, I withdrew the large drum beneath my bed and slipped off its leather covering. I took it back to her in the front room.

She jumped with a squeal of delight. "Oh, it's lovely. Here, let me play it."

She tapped the drum. It emitted a dull sound. "What's wrong with it?" she said.

I tightened the band which pulled the drumhead taut and showed her how to hold her hands to get the best sound.

We sat there, nude. I on the floor, she on the couch, while she knocked herself out with the drums for fifteen minutes.

"Do you know any calypso songs?" she asked, taking a breather.

"Sure."

"Do one for me."

"All right, but here, lay the drum down and straddle it, it's easier that way, plus you'll cop all the vibrations."

She laid the four-foot congo drum on the floor and straddled it.

"Now keep this beat," I said and demonstrated a rhythm. She thumped it out.

I closed my eyes and thought of her in the rink's spotlight. Then sang:

> *"Before you came, me eyes were blind*
> *Me heart was locked, me soul she sighed.*
> *You stepped in the light, you opened me eyes*
> *Me heart she flipped, me soul, she cried.*
> *Hey! Pretty girl, please be mine.*
> *You make me life a thing divine.*
> *If you go away, me fear me will die.*
> *Me lips will drink the tears I cry—"*

"More! she demanded impishly, shaking my head.

I rolled on my back and stared at the ceiling. Seeing the dust on it, I made a mental note to wash walls for Mom tomorrow.

Kay's face cut off my view. "Come on, sing some more," she demanded. "You made that up, didn't you?" Her brown eyes danced.

"Yes."

"About me?"

"Who else but you?"

"Well, I want you to add some more to it, make it longer," she entreated.

"But why? It tells all there is to know. That's the way ca-lypso is supposed to be, brief, and to the point."

She bit her lips. I reached for her. As I pressed her shoulders to the floor, she asked, "Guy, suppose I get a baby, a little chubby brown butterball of a baby? Guy, I don't want a baby, I don't, I don't . . . Oh! Yes I do, I want a baby, make me a baby, please, Guy, please."

I jetted through space . . .

"What time is it?" I asked as we tiptoed up the steps of the parsonage behind the Greater Hope Church.

"Nine-thirty," she whispered.

"Will your dad be salty with you?"

"I guess so," she said.

"Do you regret it?"

She shook her head. "You?"

In answer I pulled her into my arms and kissed her tenderly.

"I'm glad I told you about my dad and all," I said, "and I hope that won't make you think bad of me for—"

Her mouth on mine stopped me. She pressed against me tightly, returning my kiss measure for measure. We stood leaning against the door frame, I reached for her breasts.

The porch light flashed on, and at the same time, the door opened.

Key stepped back with a frightened gasp.

The six-foot figure of Reverend Heath stood framed in the doorway.

He wore a smoking jacket and house shoes. A Bible was in his hands.

"Pray tell me, what is the meaning of this," he demanded, "this wallowing in sinful body lust?"

"I'm sorry, Reverend Heath, I was just—"

"It isn't necessary to tell me anything, young man. I've got eyes," he cut in. "I saw it." He motioned Kay to go into the house. She went and stood behind him, her eyes over her shoulders flamed with tears.

"Look, Reverend Heath, I—"

"Now you listen to me closely, young man. My daughter has a respectable position to uphold in this community and I mean to see that she does just that, understand? So you stay away from her. I forbid her to ever speak to you and your kind. If ever I find you with her again, there will be trouble. Don't even come here again or I'll call the law on you."

I stood staring at the doorbell I'd leaned against when kissing Kay. *Of all the dumb luck, I thought.* Reverend Heath turned on Kay:

"He's no good, even his aunt says he's ungrateful. Why, isn't he the same boy you told me was at the rink that night? And you, my daughter, let a blackguard like that paw his hot hands over you. It's sickening me!"

"Dad," Kay's voice came, "listen, I—he—"

"Be still. You know what I'm striving to accomplish. Have you become insensible to my desires, my labor? Are you deliberately trying to drag me through the mud?"

"No, no, I know how it looks, Dad, but it wasn't—"

"I consented to your going out for fresh air and some clean fun with Bishop Lindy's son this afternoon and you return at 10:30 P.M. with that—that vulgarian—"

"He's—he's not like that—it's not even 10:00 and—"

"What has gotten into you, child? Have you completely lost your senses? Especially your sense of social taste. That boy—his own aunt said that his father was an adulterer, a vulgar preacher who profaned the doctrine. The boy himself has gone over to the Pope-worshippers and his mother is crippled because—"

Hearing the reference to Mom I spun around. Black hate blotted out the hurt I'd felt. Rage set up a roaring in my ears.

The edge of my left hand slashed upward in the same kind of judo punch the cop, Tony, had used on me. It struck Reverend Heath's throat, turning his loud tirade into a gurgle. I rabbit-punched a right to his neck. He fell with a loud thud. I raised my foot—

"No, Guy! Oh my God! What are you trying to do—kill my father?" Kay screamed.

I raised my eyes to her horror-struck face. She stood with one hand clutching her throat, the other covered her mouth with spanned fingers.

Turning from her, I left the house with Kay's cries ringing in my ears and her horrified face before my eyes.

"You really fouled up this time, pops. Yeah! You stuck your foot in it," I told myself aloud as I trotted towards Gale's Drug Store.

Chapter **21**

Entering the near-empty drug store, I walked past the three boys huddled around the juke box blowing imaginary saxophones to the racy record that played. Hazel Browning threw me a wide smile from behind the counter.

"Hi, Guy," she greeted, rinsing the suds from the glasses she was washing.

"Hi, pretty," I saluted.

I stopped before the first booth. My zipper bag sat on the floor beside it. A pack of cigarettes lay on the tabletop next to an ash tray littered with half-smoked cigarette butts. Marion sat with her head cradled in her arms atop the table. I flopped into the seat across from her. She lifted her head, her eyes were heavy with sleep. She glanced at her watch, reaching for the half empty pack of cigarettes. I beat her to them.

"Give me my cigarettes," she demanded, as I stuck them into my pocket.

"Look, Muffet, I don't want my girl to smoke."

"Am I your girl?" she asked.

I didn't answer.

"Am I your girl?" she repeated angrily.

"Forget it."

"Forget what? That I'm your girl or that I asked the question?"

Taking out the cigarettes, I lit one and placed it between her fingers. She raised it to her lips and inhaled deeply. Leaning back, she stared at me through half-closed eyes.

"I see that you're playing the part like a true champ," she said.

225

"What do you mean?" I inquired, puzzled at her remark.

Placing my feet on the seat, I leaned against the wall. The tiredness I felt pressed heavier on me.

"My reference is to the Beau Brummel kick you've suddenly developed," Marion was saying. "It seems to me that I recall you leaving here in a blue suit with that sophisticated society chick. Now it's brown. Why the change—to match her eyes?"

"Don't try to be catty, Muffet, it merely makes you purr and look like a pretty kitten," I replied with a yawn.

"Why the winded sigh?" she asked, smashing the half-smoked cigarette out.

"Too much walking. I took Kay on a sight-seeing tour of our illustrious community," I lied with another yawn.

Her eyes fixed themselves on mine for a long moment, then dropped to her watch.

"Well, it's 10:15. All the lovers should be gone from the school yard. We had better be going."

She started to get up.

"Let's ice that action for tonight, pretty. I'm tired and you need some sleep. Besides, I'll probably be in the slams Saturday."

Her eyes blazed angrily. The hand extracting the cigarette trembled.

"Now wait a minute, Clucky, don't give me a hard time. In case you let your attraction for Miss Heath make you forget the facts, I just want to remind you that you and I made a deal some weeks ago. We set a schedule which I devoted a lot of back-breaking hours to keep and we're going to keep it. Cop? I'm not going to let you rob me of my time, labor, and yes, money, too. I've got three hundred dollars invested in you, three hundred dollars I want back. So toss that tiredness talk and let's get going."

Shifting to a more comfortable position, I thought: Baby,

your three hundred bucks took wings with the smash I whipped on the good Reverend a few minutes ago.

"Well?" she demanded, puffing nervously on the cigarette.

I looked at her. The sting of the slap Hank had given her still hurt me.

She ground the cigarette beneath the heel of her oxford.

Her dad's right, I thought, *she needs to get away from me. I'm making her a nervous wreck, a hard case. She even adopts my street lingo.*

Despite my thoughts, my voice was harsh when I answered her. "You may look like Mom, but you're not. So stop giving me orders," I said, loading my pocket with toothpicks.

"I'm so happy that you've woke up to the fact that I'm not. And glad that I'm not dependent on you, as your mother is. You're so disappointing," she whispered bitterly.

Picking up the bag, she left the store. I followed, feeling a confusion of anger and disgust.

She had reached the pool room when a figure lurched from it and caught at her arm. I broke into a run; as I neared the swaying boy I lowered my shoulder. The impact of my body striking him, slammed him against the pool room wall. Pivoting on my left foot, I kicked him in the stomach with the right one and followed through with a left cross to the jaw. The boy sank to the sidewalk. It was Treetop.

Marion stood gaping. The pool room door was crowded with onlookers. Grabbing Marion's hands, I walked her away. After half a block she broke the silence.

"He was drunk," she said.

"I'm hip; so was I the night of the prom."

"For a fellow with a leg and arm that's been broken, you use them effectively in a dirty sort of way. If you're not careful, they're going to get you in trouble," she said slowly.

I inhaled the foul-smelling air off Lake Calumet.

"Dig, baby. Everything in this burg is dirty. If you don't

believe me, take a sniff, look around, and if you clamp your teeth down, they'll grind on grit. So I'm dirty? That's a compliment; it means I'm a part of the atmosphere. Maybe now I can make some headway, accomplish something. Sure, I kick, kick hard, rabbit-punch, too. I compliment my arms and legs that way, for heeding my pleas to mend when they were crippled. Dirty, ha!—Well, I guess some people are just meant to be like that, in spite of all they do to keep from it. Why, you saw where all of my All-American boy action got me—Hank and Brown. Oh, hell, what's the use, why talk about it? So I'm dirty and intend to stay that way," I ended disgustedly. A bitter taste was in my mouth. I spat, but the bitterness remained.

"Clucky, you don't know what you're saying. You're letting an unscrupulous person like Hank distract you from the fact that life is good—full of good people. This city may be dirty in appearance and all, but the people in it, the majority of the people, that is, are good clean Christians who—"

"Don't tell me any more about the good, clean Christians. I just kicked one of them in the guts a few minutes ago."

"You did what?"

"I rocked the good Reverend Heath's frame a few minutes ago. And he's probably put the bulladeens on me by now. That's why I didn't care to practice—what's the use, I'll be in jail Saturday." A feeling of hopelessness engulfed me as I thought of Mom, my promise to Dr. Cherkov and the household bills at home on the dresser.

"Oh, Clucky! you didn't? How could you?" Marion asked wretchedly.

"He called Mom a cripple and I got mad," I explained, hoping to remove the misery from her eyes.

"I always knew that temper of yours would get you into trouble. Don't you know that you can't go around hitting people for talking about you—especially preachers? You just can't."

"Ha! I bet you can't make Reverend Heath believe that," I mocked.

"Cut out the flip talk, Guy, we've got to do something for you. You've got to run in that meet Saturday. Too much depends on it."

We stopped at the school ground gate. Her forehead was wrinkled with thought.

"Isn't that your father's car over there?" I asked, pointing to the Ford parked in front of the Sacred Heart Chapel.

"Yes, they're holding a K of C meeting in the auditorium upstairs." She grabbed my arm. "I got it!" She exclaimed, jumping up and down.

"Got what?" I asked.

She began pulling me in the direction of the church.

"Father Murphy. He'll know what to do. He'll help us."

I halted, reluctant to commit myself.

"Oh now Clucky, come on. Don't be bull-headed. We need help and some advice. Besides, you promised me that you would talk to him the other week," she coaxed, "and Guy, think of what will happen to Mrs. Morgan if she found out you were in jail."

I thought of Dr. Cherkov's warning: *"Your mother is not to be excited."*

"Okay, Muffet, let's go rap to Old Basketball Belly."

I took her hand and we ran the half block to the church.

Father Murphy was coming out of his office just as we reached the second floor.

"Father, may we see you a minute?" Marion said.

"Why, I should say yes," he said.

Father Murphy was an ex-football player, who stood five-foot-nine and weighed two hundred and fifty pounds; he carried most of the weight in front. His blue eyes looked out at the world with benevolence. He was the favorite confessor of the kids.

Extending his hand, he said, "Well, well, what do we have

here? Welcome, stranger, even if it is 10:35 P.M. What are you two doing, sleepwalking?"

He burst into laughter, his stomach making with the Santa Claus action. Father Murphy was a wit, but, as Crow put it: "He ain't into nothin', Jim, he blows corn."

Still Marion flattered him by laughing.

"Well, what can I do for you young people?" he inquired as we entered the plain, sparsely-furnished office.

He sat down heavily in the chair behind the desk.

"Sit down, children, sit down," he directed with a wave of his hand.

"Of course, my office doesn't afford the modern comforts which one encounters in most offices nowadays. The parish is poor you know. But in the end, we manage to satisfy. Yes, we satisfy in the end. So you satisfy yours," he laughed.

Marion joined in. The good padre's attempt at humor was still corny to me.

Marion drew up a chair and satisfied her end. I remained standing.

"Oh, it must be a pretty serious matter. I see that Guy here has ants in his pants and can't sit down. So let's have it. What can God and Old Basketball Belly do to ease what ails you?"

I had been looking at the floor while he talked. His use of the description of "Basketball Belly" brought my head up with a jerk.

"Oh, I've known of the nickname you gave me for some time now, Guy."

My gaze on Marion accused her of stool-pigeoning. She shook her head in denial with an uplifted hand.

"Basketball Belly—for shame! Why couldn't it have been football—something I could take some pride in?"

I looked at him. His eyes were full of laughter. We all began laughing. After a moment, Father wiped his eyes. "Now, what do you youngsters want?"

Slowly, haltingly, I told him of what I'd done to Reverend

230

Heath, eliminating Kay and my earlier sex activities; of my fear that the minister had called the police, and of the importance of my running in the meet Saturday.

Father Murphy stared at his fingers as I talked. When I finished, he raised his sober eyes to mine. "This is a very serious matter, Guy, and must be acted upon immediately," he said. Reaching for the telephone on his desk, he dialed a number and after a moment spoke into the receiver: "Hello, this is Father Murphy from Sacred Heart Chapel. May I speak to Reverend Heath, please?" He looked up and motioned Marion and me from the room with a wave of his big hand.

Outside, Marion went over and sat on the top step. I joined her. After a moment of silence, she said in a hushed voice: "Guy, I'm going to confession tonight. I've just realized how full of sin my heart has become these past few weeks. I've permitted Hank's slap in the face to fill my heart with revenge. I helped you to recover from that beating, not because you were a person who needed help, but because through you I'd be able to gratify the meanness burning inside of me. Oh, Clucky, how bad I've let myself become. Yes, and common, too."

Withdrawing the cigarettes from her pockets, she flung them down the stairs. "Smoking like a common street hussy." She stood up, facing me, "Clucky, I love you, and because of that love for you I tried using you as a tool with which to acquire the sinful revenge I harbored in my heart. I know that power is the exclusive right of our Lord. I won't ever attempt its use again. I'm glad you're able to run in the meet, but not for the same reason I had when we first began your training. I'm glad you're able to run because I love you."

We kissed. As my arms pressed her to me tightly, my heart overflowed with sorrowful tenderness for I knew that she loved me and I felt I could never again love her.

Withdrawing her lips, she said: "I'll always love you, Guy,

always, no matter what." The fervency of her feeling reduced her words to a whisper. Thinking of Kay and my feeling for her, I said:

"Listen, Muffet, I know that you love me, but that's because I'm the only stud you've ever gone around with. Your father's right; you need to go away. Meet new people and all; then maybe you'll . . ."

"You think I'll change, don't you?"

I wanted to tell her that I wished she would change like I'd changed; that some guy would come along and capture her heart and soul, as Kay had captured mine. Instead, I said: "No, I don't think you'll change, but I hear there's a lot of handsome males up Boston way—guys with good family backgrounds who speak good English, you know, not using a whole lot of slang like I do, and real educated. I might as well tell you now, Muffet, I'm not going back to school this fall. I'm not a bookworm anyway, you know. I'd hoped to get by on athletics but that's out now." I paused, remembering Hank's description of the scout's little black books. "Then, too, I'd be almost twenty before I graduated, damn near ready for a rocking chair."

"Oh, no, Guy, no, don't talk like that. Twenty isn't old at all. And besides, what will your mother think? You know how badly she wants you to—"

I interrupted her, remembering the pile of household bills at home: "I'll make her understand, Muffet. Sure, she'll feel bad at first, but she'll get over it. Only, well, I didn't want to tell you before, but the bills have been pouring in of late. The furniture store wants their money or the furniture, and I can't have them repossessing Mom's stove and things. Why, she loves that house. The first thing she asked about today was how was her kitchen. Then there's a mortgage I didn't know about. And I want things, Muffet, things of my own and right now," I ended with a warm determination.

"I understand," she said, taking my hand, "but you'll not have to worry about those handsome guys with their Boston accents. Ever since we were tots you were my man, and that's the way it will always be. I'll never love or marry anyone but you."

A feeling of guilt smote me like a physical blow, rendering me speechless.

"Guy, let's both go to confession, please?" she whispered with imploring eyes. "Say you will. Do it for my sake. It will help you. Do come, please?"

Seeing the tears in her eyes, I nodded, desiring only to please her.

The office door opened. "You may come in now," Father Murphy said. We entered. Father was again sitting behind the desk. "I've just finished talking with Reverend Heath, who, I might add, impressed me as being a highly intelligent individual," he said. "As a result, I received from him the assurance that he'd contact the police and have the warrant for assault and battery, which he'd sworn out for you, dropped. In return, you are never to set foot in his home again, or see his daughter again."

Marion gave my hand a warm squeeze. "Oh! Thank you, Father! Thank you ever so much!" she said gratefully. The priest's eyes were staring steadily into mine. Their merry glint was gone. They were two blue pools of cool seriousness. The last words he'd spoken were echoing and re-echoing through my mind. They sent a chill through me. The price for the squashing of the warrant was too high, much more than I was willing to pay.

"Guy, aren't you going to thank Father?" Marion asked.

Father Murphy's eyes hadn't left mine. I looked at the zipper bag Marion had set in a chair nearby. *You've got some races to run, pops*, I told myself, remembering the promise to Dr. Cherkov and the mounting bills at home.

"Thanks, Father! I appreciate you saving me from the clink," I said, extending my hand across the desk to shake his. He grasped it firmly.

"I'm glad that I could be of service to you, my son. All that I do, I do through God and for God. I think that you were worth saving from the, uh, clink, as you call it. I only wish that there were more that we here at Sacred Heart could do to save our youngsters from your clink."

Turning to leave, I said: "Well, thanks again, Father. Be seeing you." Marion's hold on my hand halted me. She hadn't moved from the desk. Her eyes entreated. *Now what have I done*, I wondered with a reflective frown.

"When may I expect to see you, my son?" Father Murphy asked.

I turned from Marion, remembering my promise to make confession tonight.

Reaching in the drawer, Father Murphy withdrew his stole, then said: "My time is God's time, Guy." Turning to Marion, he asked, "Will you please excuse us, my child, and see to it I'm not disturbed."

Nodding, Marion left the room.

"Come now, Guy," Father Murphy directed, dragging his chair to the end of the desk. I knelt beside the chair.

"Bless me Father for I have sinned . . ."

A few minutes later Marion entered the office as I headed for the chapel.

Having dipped my fingers into the fountain, I made the sign of the cross as I knelt before the altar to do penance. Before beginning them, I closed my eyes to savor the deep hush which pervaded the room. This quietness had been the cause for deserting the religion of my parents; the quietness and Marion's insistence. Spreading my knees, I laid my arms upon the shiny communion rail, pillowing my head upon them. I settled myself snugly into the relaxing stillness. Silence spun a silken cocoon of comfort around me, wrapping each mem-

234

ber of my body in a delicate peace. Opening my mouth, I drank the quiet atmosphere rapturously. It wound a soothing course through every part of my being. I began my penance:

"Hail Mary, full of grace . . ." I whispered, shattering the stillness. Indifferently I'd confessed every wrong that I'd committed since my last confession, speaking them in a parrot-like recitation, without feeling the sense of guilt that had once made me stammer with shame at the offensiveness of the act. Nor did I now feel the mysterious buoyancy and sense of inner cleanliness which I used to feel after confessions as I muttered my penance.

"Our Father who art in heaven . . . " I gazed at the life-sized crucifix high upon the wall behind the altar, trying to figure out my lack of sorrow for the sins I'd confessed. Were they wrong? Was it wrong to fight when challenged?

Father Murphy's words flashed into my mind. "Render not evil for evil," he had said.

"*Don't be a fool. Self-preservation is the first law of nature,*" cut in the voices of the pool room philosophers, scoffingly . . .

"Forgive us our trespasses as we forgive those . . ." I muttered trying to forget the code of the streets. I should have given Treetop and Raymond Miller a pass, I thought. My not doing so was a sin.

"*When you play you pay,*" justified the philosophers. "*And pops, you paid in full the night of the prom. Yeah, hoof, tail and head . . .*"

"And lead us not into temptation . . ." My affair with Kay was sinful, Father had said.

"*Look, my man, you just may have intended to walk the plank with Kay then. And only a lame would buy a shoe without trying it on for size,*" consoled the philosophers . . .

"But deliver us from evil . . ." Was the taking of Kay's virginity really as evil as Father had said?

"*Man, when you feel froggish, hop. What's evil about cop-*"

235

ping a few cherries? If they're old enough to bleed, they're old enough to butcher," expounded the philosophers with a laugh.

Closing my ears to the laughter, I willed myself to feel sorry. "Oh my God, I'm heartily sorry for having offended thee . . ." I whispered, clenching my teeth with an effort to feel what I spoke . . .

"Oh, your God, your God? Why, black boy, your God was left over in the old country. Buddy, you are a weed, aint' cha? Open your eyes. Look at that figure on those sticks," demanded the voices of the pool room.

I obeyed.

What color is that stud hanging up there? Ha! He's white. That's because he's a white man's God. Why, Jim, if he was a white and black man's God, he'd look like a zebra, dig? Or if he was everybody's God, he'd be every color in the rainbow!

I wiped my hand across my forehead. It came away wet with sweat. I was shaking with the effort to close out the voice which spoke the words I'd heard daily while working in the pool room. I remembered Mom's request for my prayers. Staring at the statue of the Virgin I prayed:

"Hail Mary full of grace . . ."

"Hey, dig this weed, whispering to a white woman. Why, man, if you were down South, they'd hang you twice for that."

I strained to shut out the taunts, placing my hands over my ears and squeezing my eyes shut tightly.

"Oh, God, help me, Christ have mercy on me, Lord have mercy on me," I prayed fervently.

"The white man's got all the money; the coons got all the religion," the voices taunted as they faded away.

"Oh, my God, I'm heartily sorry! Oh, my God, I'm heartily sorry!" I repeated over and over like a broken record. I'd been unable to get past the first six words of the prayer.

A physical warmth began to overspread my being. Relaxing my taut muscles, the sweat on my forehead cooled, soothing my hot brow. I opened my eyes. Taking my hands from my ears, I stared at the image of the Virgin again.

"Pray for me, Guy," Mom's request returned. I prayed. As I did so the light above the altar reflected warmly. A peace began to settle over my body. As it did, the statue seemed to begin to fall. I sped up my whispering prayers, mingling them together. The statue halted its fall, leaning precariously. My lips and throat grew dry. I broke out in a desperate sweat. She would surely fall once I stopped praying. At the point of exhaustion, I turned to the large crucifix: "God, Father! Help your mother! Daddy! Help!" I shouted.

The image on the crucifix looked down on me through half-closed eyes. His lips smiled sardonically. His body was black.

Bowing my head upon the rail, with my hands clenched tightly to my ears, I cried, remembering a stormy night when I'd called a father to help another mother, who'd crawled swaying in the middle of the highway.

After a few minutes I got to my feet. Without looking back, I headed for the door.

Marion joined me at the door. She had sat in the back of the chapel all the while. Outside she said, "Come. I met Dad in the hall and got the car keys." As she started up the motor, she asked, "To the school ground?"

I shook my head. "I've got a headache." I rubbed my temple; pain throbbed behind my eyes.

As we drove, I thought of the few seconds of peace that I enjoyed before the statue of the Virgin had seemingly begun to fall. A longing to experience it again filled me. I promised myself I'd return to the chapel. If I did, maybe I could capture a larger portion of that peace.

"It didn't help, did it?" Marion said.

"Yes, a little."

"Maybe if you keep going back you'll capture it."

I nodded, feeling no surprise at her insight into my feelings. "I intend to—yes, everyday."

"Good!" she exclaimed with a smile. Taking one hand from the wheel, she squeezed mine as it lay on the seat.

We stopped in front of my house. Marion instinctively reached in her skirt pocket. Seeing the gesture, I withdrew the dashboard lighter. Then, we both laughed, remembering her discarding the cigarettes.

Replacing the lighter, I said: "I'm certainly glad that you're off that kick."

"I don't know what got into me in the first place," she replied. "Smoking, ugh! I'll never do it again. It's a weakness and I know I'm not that weak. In fact, just to prove to myself how stout I am, I'm going to give up sweets for awhile."

We got out of the car.

Inside the house, I went to the bathroom medicine cabinet for some aspirin to ease my headache. Marion called from the front room: "What did you say you and Kay did today?"

"Went for a walk," I replied, engrossed in my search.

"Guy, you bring the weakest stuff to the strongest people."

I found the aspirin and plopped two into my mouth, washing them down with water I drank from my cupped hands beneath the faucet.

"What?" I asked, puzzled at her remark.

The bang of the front door and the roar of the Ford motor answered me. I hurried into the front.

"Marion!"

My eyes caught the shining object laying on top of the congo drum. I picked it up. It was Kay's black garter belt.

Chapter **22**

The crash of cymbals and the staccato tap of snare drums awakened me. A bass drum thumped thunderous cadence as bugles blared the military march, *El Capitan.*

I glanced at the clock on the dresser: it was 1:00 P.M. Folding my hands beneath my head, I stared at the ceiling. *Well, baby, this it it. In another hour you'll be kicking gravel.* The thought caused my stomach to begin growling nervously.

My ears followed the sound of the band. Closing my eyes, I pictured the events which past experience told me were taking place in the street: the sidewalks along 111th Street were thronged. The sons of a Legion bugle corps, dressed in their red, white and blue were playing the snapping ground-covering march with a slowness which would permit the three young shapely majorettes to proceed at their head, to give their hips a good and complete right turn. Ahead of the majorettes was the color guard made up of the old vets from World War I. I recalled Crow's yearly description of the old vets' manner of march:

"Dig de loons, baby, they want people to think they won de war by themselves," he'd said with drunken indignation. He was always drunk on the opening of the week of this festivity, which was held annually in celebration of the tiny community of Morgan Park.

Behind the bugle corps came the multi-colored ribbon-decked floats, which bore shapely girls in bathing suits. After these girl-littered floats passed, Crow and I always lost interest in the parade. His concentration would return to his bottle

239

and mine would center upon the coming meet which would take place as soon as the marchers reached the school yard. After the meet, the night-time events began. The festival was always a source of delight to the teen-agers who could enjoy a solid week of pleasure before having to return to another fifty-one weeks of monotonous inactivity.

After the races, I usually found Crow and me a couple of girls to take to the slaughtering floor. Mom's handicap had made our basement an ideal place for this.

The thought of Mom increased the growling in my stomach. Kicking the sheet which covered me to the foot of the bed, I raised my legs and feet to view. "Everything depends on you," I informed them, flexing their muscles. "And baby, if you let me down, I'll reduce you to mincemeat." I threatened, bicycling them in mid-air. The movement stopped the nervous growl in my stomach.

After doing fifty sit-ups, I re-covered my naked body. While I caught my breath I thought of Kay. She'd phoned me Monday. I'd been washing the front room walls when the phone rang. The voice on the other end said: "Guy."

I'd recognized it instantly as being Kay's and waited for her to speak again. After a long silence, I began to talk. I apologized for my attack upon her father and told her that although I loved her dearly, I intended to respect his wishes. After I had finished there was a moment's silence followed by the click of the receiver being recradled. She'd spoken but one word.

Marion had entered an hour afterwards and found me lying on the couch pounding the congo drum which Kay's garter belt still adorned. She'd completely ignored the drum and looked disgustedly at the half-washed ceiling. Climbing the ladder she'd begun washing where I'd left off when the phone rang. Anger was in her movements as she strained on the tips of her toes. After having cleaned the area within her reach, she started down the ladder. Her movements made it see-saw.

240

Leaping from the couch, I'd caught her in my arms. She'd squirmed furiously to free herself as I attempted to kiss her. I'd almost succeeded in capturing her evasive lips when she slapped me. I'd ceased my pursuit instantly, dazed by the fact that she struck me. She jumped to her feet, her eyes blazed angrily: "I'm off sweets, remember, Sugar Daddy?" she informed. Pointing to the drum, she added, "If you must pat on something, pat on that; it seems to give you a thrill."

She had helped me clean the house each day thereafter. I'd sighed with relief when we'd completed the work, for she'd been a tyrant in issuing instructions on what was to be done. I'd many times during those five days been at the point of telling her to get the hell out. Only the desire not to further strain our already taut relationship kept me from it. After the slapping incident, we had spoken only a few words to each other, Marion treating me with frosty reserve. The fact that we had made it a practice to visit the chapel every night before training hadn't thawed her aloofness.

I turned my thoughts to those visits to the chapel. Each time I had the same experience as on Sunday night. The sensations came in a cycle; the doctrine of the street contradicting the Bible. After a hard struggle, the latter had prevailed. A moment of peace would descend upon me, then the statue of the Virgin would seemingly begin to fall. The first two nights I'd appealed to the figure on the Cross to save her; its dark, satanic face with veiled eyes had sneered its disdain to comply to my wish with sardonic lips. After that, whenever I'd reached that point in the cycle, I'd spring to my feet and steady the figurine myself, experiencing a wild exhilaration.

Turning onto my stomach, I said to my pillow: "I wonder if I'm crazy."

The sharp jingling of the phone interrupted my analysis. I hurried to it, thinking it was Kay. She hadn't missed a day in phoning me since Monday, although she spoke but one word:

241

my name. I'd never-the-less experienced the same feelings I'd felt the first night I'd seen her.

"Hello," I said into the phone.

"Hey, baby, what's to it?" Crow's voice inquired.

"Nothing that winning a few races can't cure," I answered. Then, "Where are you?"

"I'm at de drug store digging de booties of de beauties," he replied jubilantly.

I frowned, something was wrong.

"Your head bad?" I inquired.

"What?"

"I asked is your head bad? Are you drunk?" I explained.

"Oh hell naw, I'm waiting for you."

"You're not!" I shouted in surprised disbelief.

"Naw! Hold it, here comes another float."

There was a moment's silence.

"Jesus H. Christ! Guy, you shoulda' dug what just passed," Crow whispered reverently.

"What's that, man?"

"Luzon. Why, Jim, she's wearing a bathing suit that ain't got as much cloth to it as a G-string."

"So Cherry's cooling her can, huh?"

"Yeah, and if you'd seen it, you'd go some place and cool yourself into rigor mortis for not copping righteous on de gismo, when you had it on de slaughtering floor," he asserted fervently.

I had told him of my encounter with Luzon in the park.

"Say, you'd better hurry and get over to de school 'cause de last of de parade just passed. Uh, Marion just left out of de door, so I guess she's going over to your crib. By de way, what's to you and her, I mean de riff?"

Thinking of the phone call from Kay, I said hurriedly: "I'll hip you to the story after the race. I'm expecting an important phone call, so move out so it can come through, huh."

"Not until you promise to go skating with Dot, Dipper and

me. By de way, we're gonna' have a party to celebrate your winnin' . . ."

I cut him off impatiently: "Dig, Crow, you had better wait 'til I win first. Now, I'll go skating with you wherever that is. We'll really boot 'em up. I'll do anything you want after the races. I only ask one favor of you."

"What?"

"Get the hell off the phone!" I shouted, slamming the receiver down.

I turned to walk away. The phone rang. I snatched it up. "Hello."

"Guy?" It was Kay.

"Yes, pretty. I thought you'd never—"

She cut me off. "I've got to hurry. Lots of luck, Guy, I'll see you at the school ground. I won't be able to speak to you, but you must know that I'll be pulling for you. I've got to go now. I love you."

The phone clicked.

I stared at the receiver. Her fast flow of words had surprised me.

The front door opened.

I recradled the receiver and stepped into the bathroom. At the face bowl I brushed my teeth.

"Oh, the monkey swings his way up to the North Pole and cops a bad cold right up his boom, boom, boom, boom, boom, boom, boom, boom."

I was gargling my throat and the surprise at hearing Marion singing made me gag. There was a knock on the bathroom door.

"You all right, Clucky?" she inquired. Her voice was warm with concern.

"Yeah, yeah," I croaked between coughs, as I stepped under the shower. "Buddy, this promises to be a day full of surprises," I muttered, following Marion's songful description of the monkey and her tuba-emulation.

I let the water pelt me for ten minutes, then stepped from the shower. I dried, wrapped the towel around my waist, and went to the bedroom. Marion was examining herself before my dresser mirror, tugging lightly at the bowed end of the powder-blue gambler's tie she wore beneath the collar of a man's white shirt. She faced me with a broad and radiant smile.

"Hey, momma," she greeted. "How do I look?"

"You're sharp as Dick when Hattie died," I replied.

She turned back to the bed; I snapped the elastic in her panty-legs.

"Ouch!" she exclaimed, wheeling to face me angrily. "Let's freeze that action, momma, I'm the shack bully today," she said.

"Okay! Okay! But turn your head while momma slips into her bloomers," I said, reaching for the much-altered trunks she'd laid out on the bed.

She turned around.

"How does your foot feel?" she asked.

"It'll be okay, it's got to be," I replied, slipping into the trunks. They fitted snugly. I'd worn the trunks in every sports event I'd participated in. As I'd grown, Mom had altered them. She'd embroidered the word Alpha on the left leg and Omega on the right. This motto was on my bag also. The trunks were my only superstition.

Putting on my jacket, I said, "Okay, let's get cutting," and reached for the zipper bag.

"No, Guy, let me take it," she said, taking the bag from me.

I looked at her in surprise.

"Being as today is the last time you'll run and all, well, I've carried your bag in all the rest, and this is the very last time I'll have—" She stammered to a halt. Tears filmed her eyes.

"I'm back on sweets," she said suddenly.

Taking her into my arms, I kissed her, remembering as I

244

did so the great distance of years we'd traveled together in intimate companionship. But that was yesterday.

We left for the school ground. Crow, Dipper, Dot, Jim and Jet joined us as we passed the drug store. Crow kept up a round of chatter as we proceeded to the school. Dot was carrying a skate case, and Crow had a pair hanging by their shoe strings over his shoulder.

"So you been to see the old folks," I said, nodding at the skates.

"Naw, they ain't gonna' ever see me anymore. I copped my skates while they were watching the parade."

"Dig, Crow, how are you set for bread? I mean you cop a job yet?" I asked.

He pulled a roll of bills from his shirt pocket.

"I ain't had under fifty near my heart since you sprang me from de can. As for a job, I got de easiest yoke in the world. I'm swinging stuff for Jim," he said, nodding toward Jim.

"But isn't that kind of hot, momma?"

"Yeah, if you ain't hip to de game, but I've got a real cool system. Don't worry about me, I ain't taking no more falls," he boasted with a swagger which didn't ease my mind.

"Look, baby, why don't you go back home? I'm sure everything will be all right if you did. If it isn't, then come and shack with me. I just don't go for you being in Black Babylon by yourself." I remembered my encounter with the coppers Tony and Pat, as I talked.

"Forget it, Guy. I've told you I ain't goin' back to the crib and after today, I'm dusting this park. If it weren't for you bein' in de race, I wouldn't be here now. If what Marion's been telling me is true, then I think you need to dust this place, too, because when you win these races, Hank's gonna be one mad, broke fella."

I laughed, complimented by his blind confidence. "That's one thing I like about you, Crow! Once in a guy's corner, you stick," I said, slapping his back.

245

"Yeah, some monkeys just swing like that," he replied with a shrug.

We'd reached the school yard. The fence was lined with cheering people. Small kids darted about playing "I Got It." We'd wormed our way through them to the center of the field where boys and girls dressed in trunks and sweat suits were performing warm-up exercises. A womanish-walking man, wearing a white band on his arm which bore the word "Official" in black letters, minced over to us.

"Are all of you participants in this meet?" he asked in a high, piping voice.

"I am the only one," I said, taking my bag from Marion. I sat on the ground to put on my spikes.

"Well, you can stay, but the rest of you will have to return to the outer edge of the track. This inner circle is for the participants and coaches only," he said pompously.

"Says who?" I asked resentfully.

"Says me," he replied, bristling.

"Look, jackass, these are my friends, and I ain't letting no hen-chested clown order 'em to shove off."

"Listen, young man, don't you go getting smart-alecky with me. I'm one of the officials here," he said, pointing to the arm band, and waved a hand at the bunting hung on the stand before the field house. I glanced in that direction. The stand was crowded with the dignitaries of the Park. Bishop Lindy and Reverend Heath sat in the front.

"Now, either you obey the rules or I'll have you disqualified," he threatened. His high voice and arm-waving had attracted attention. People were staring at us, and laughing.

Angered at this and his threats of disqualification, I got to my feet, clutching my left spike shoe by the heel.

"You do, you little broad-voiced bastard, and I'll—" Crow caught my arm.

"Cool it, man, you've got a race to win, remember? It's all

right, we'll cut to de sidelines." The six of them headed for the sidelines. The official smiled smugly.

"Hold it, Muffet!" I called.

Marion came back. The official frowned. "She stays, she's my coach."

"Now, wait a minute, young man, I said—"

"I don't give a damn what you said, I say she stays. Now get the hell away from me before I smear you all over this yard!" I shouted, completely enraged.

The official swished away.

A loud-speaker crackled, "All senior participants report to the field house for sign-in."

"Damn!" I dropped to the ground, my hands trembling, my stomach growling and jumping. "I've wasted my warm-up period. Muffet, will you tape and gauze my left foot?"

After slipping the spikes on, we headed for the field house. The signing table was crowded with jostling boys. Reaching its edge, I found myself looking into Hank's one eye. He wore an official arm band.

"All right, sound off," he commanded. The sight of him increased the anger I was feeling. I continued to stare at him, letting my hate show in my eyes.

"I said sound off or move, I've got a race to get underway," he repeated.

"I hope you'll be just as eager to kicking in a couple of hours from now."

Removing a large cigar he'd clenched between his teeth, he pointed the chewed wet end at me. "Look, kid, if you could win, you wouldn't be here, understand? Now sound off." His confident air lashed my anger.

"Seventy-five-yard dash, 100, the 220, 440 and 440 hurdles," I said rapidly.

After checking off the first three events, Hank held his pen poised and looked at me with a frown, "What are you trying to do, impress someone?" he inquired.

I matched his tone. "No, break you."

"Ha! You can't."

Checking off the last two events I'd named, he shoved a numbered card to me. I took it and returned to where I'd left Marion. Handing her the card, I turned to let her pin it on the back of my trunks.

"Oh no!" she exclaimed.

I looked back at her. There was despair in her eyes.

"What's wrong?" I asked.

"This!" she said, holding up the card.

The number on it was "13."

"Pin it on, Dad! Satan and all his little imps couldn't stop me from winning these five races!"

"Five? But I thought it was to be only three. Your foot can't take it, Clucky. What happened?"

I told her of my encounter with Hank.

"Don't be foolish, you'll only cripple yourself. Stick to the three," she pleaded.

I shook my head. "Nothing doing, I'm going to upset a few applecarts. Besides, I need a warm-up."

The loud-speaker blared: "Contestants for the seventy-five yard dash, senior class, report to the starting line."

I removed the sweat suit hurriedly. Marion pinned the card to my trunks.

"This one's for you," I said, turning to her.

"Alpha!" she shouted.

"Omega!" I said, as I trotted to the starting line, feeling a wild elation.

Coach Langley assigned lanes and gave brief instructions on the starting rules. I stood in the lane assigned to me. My ears were deaf to his words as I stared at the finishing line tape.

"All right! On your mark!" The coach shouted, his eyes alternately glancing at his stop watch and the crouching boys.

Bracing my right foot against the starting board, I fixed my eyes to the tape.

"Get set!"

Elevating my body slightly, I raised my gaze from the tape to the sky behind it. *It's the same color blue as the Virgin's robe*, I thought.

At the report of the gun, I sprang forward, regulating the elevation of my body from its crouch, with the nearing of the tape before me. Just as my eyes stared at the sky at a neck straining point directly above my head, the tape broke against my chest.

The clamor of the crowd was drowned in the triumphant howl which screamed within me. I broke stride a few yards on the other side of the finishing line.

Marion flung my jacket to me, I slipped into it.

"Number 13, Guy Morgan, please report to the officials' stand!" requested the voice over the loud-speaker. I trotted to the stand, mounted its three stairs, and stood panting before the people sitting there. There was a movement to my left. I turned. Kay approached me, smiling radiantly. Her hands held a be-ribboned medal. She was within a foot of me when Reverend Heath stepped between us, his back to me. Taking the medal from her hand, he turned and laid it on the table before me.

"Your medal, Mr. Morgan," he said, with a nod. I stared at him a moment, then, snatching the medal, I turned to the stairs. Hank stood at their head; his teeth chewed the cigar nervously, his eyes glinted angrily.

"From rags to riches," I told him.

Disdaining the steps, I jumped over the railing of the stand to the ground and walked over to Marion. As I pinned the medal on her vest, I looked toward the stand. Kay was pinning ribbons on the trunks of the second and third place winners.

Reverend Heath shook their hands in congratulation. Tears

of rage blurred my sight for a moment, then passed. Turning to Marion, I said, "I won, didn't I, Miss Muffet."

She clutched my arm.

"You sure as hell did, Clucky, and beautifully," she said. I smiled at hearing her swear for the first time. "Yeah, I sure as hell did," I repeated, gazing at the stands. Jackie stood straddling its railing, one hand was on Kay's shoulder.

"How do you feel now?" Marion asked.

"Like a winning poison-tipped arrow," I replied, executing a half-dozen squats.

"All participants in 440 race report to the starting line!" Hank's voice requested over the loud-speaker.

"Oh, no!" Marion exclaimed. I looked over at the stand. Hank descended its steps, a broad smile was on his face.

"Why, that dirty one-eyed bastard," I whispered through clenched teeth.

"Guy, don't try it. Can't you see what he's doing. He intends to let you defeat yourself through your own bull-headedness," Marion said imploringly.

I slipped out of my jacket.

"I told you that nothing was going to stop me from winning, myself included. So stay here and pat your feet, momma's gonna' cop you some more medals and that big gold cup up here," I pointed to the gold cup which stood like a centerpiece on the table before the officials.

"Alpha!" she shouted.

"Omega!" I replied as I trotted for the starting line.

An hour later, we had repeated the motto three times as I'd headed for the starting line. After each race I'd trotted to the officials' stand to snatch up the first place medal pushed towards me on the table. After pinning the fourth of these to Marion's vest with fingers that trembled with fatigue, I dropped tiredly to the ground and pulled off my left shoe. It was full of blood. I covered it quickly with my sweat shirt.

Marion dropped to her knees, fumbled inside the bag and

250

withdrew a towel. I clutched my leg tightly with both hands, the pain I was feeling was nauseating. Clenching my teeth, I fought to hold it down but couldn't. Twisting, I retched on the ground. After a minute my stomach stopped heaving.

Marion placed a cube of sugar between my teeth. "I'll be right back," she said, hurrying away with the towel.

I sat clutching my ankle. Every muscle in my body seemed to twitch and jump uncontrollably. Sickness welled up in my throat again. I took another cube of sugar from the bag and placed it in my mouth. As the pain mounted in my foot, I began to regret my rashness at having run the other two races. Doubt as to my ability to run five times in succession began to assail me. Could I run and win this last race, the 100-yard dash, which Hank, in his attempts to tire me, had contrived to make last?

Jackie had finished first in the two mid-distance heats and seemed fresh. I looked toward the stand. Kay and Jackie stood on the ground before it. He held her by the hand as her father and his were engaged in smiling conversation.

I dropped my eyes to my covered foot. How in the hell could she knowingly let herself be used? I wondered, feeling hot jealousy over Jackie's holding her hand. Plopping another sugar cube in my mouth, I thought of the hours Kay and I spent enjoying the warmth and naked bliss of our bodies that Sunday. *Am I in love with her or is it merely the mood I'm in?*

My pounding heart was about to answer, when my inward concentrations were shattered by the removal of the sweat shirt from my foot. I looked up. The sight of Luzon made me smother the cry of pain which her rough removal of the sweat shirt had caused.

She stared at my bloody foot. "Why don't you stop acting like someone you're not—A thirty-five-cent novel strong man?"

The old feeling of being challenged, which the sight of her always inspired, sprang up within me.

"Just between you and me, I stopped being someone I'm not some weeks ago. To be more exact, the night of the basketball game. As for your thirty-five-cent novel strong man, if you dug the last four races, you'd have to confess that truth can surpass fiction. Now ain't you sorry that you can't cop a copy of me? And, you never will, half-breed. So, find some other stud to play Delilah with. You'll get nothing here, never," I said in hot determination, resentful and glad for her presence. My resentment stemmed from the fact that she was viewing me in what I felt was a weak moment, a time of doubt.

Luzon's piercing eyes appeared to read my thoughts. She looked at the vomit beside me.

"Give it up before you end up crippled. It's not shameful to give up when you stand to ruin yourself by running again today. You may never be able to run again," she said, with mingled concern and sarcasm.

As she talked, I struggled into the bloody shoe. I paused to let the pain subside; she knelt and tied the shoe. The gesture made me smile, despite the hurt I was feeling. Seeing this, she jerked the laces, I clenched my teeth against the pain.

We stood up.

"These people aren't impressed by you, you're merely going to wind up on those wheels Jackie told you about."

"All contestants in the 100-yard dash report to the starting line!" the voice on the loud-speaker requested.

"I'm glad you reminded me," I told Luzon. Her presence and words had removed all doubt. "I'm gonna' win if I have to crawl over that line. This is my last race, anyway, so I don't give a damn about the condition I'm in afterwards, just so long as I win." The thought of Mom flashed through my mind. "As for impressing these people, these jackals, yourself included, I'll leave that up to the phony—Pretty Jackie. There's only two people I'm running this race for. One of them ain't here, the most important one, and yet she thinks I'm the best athlete around."

252

"Guy! Guy! Hey, baby, dig!" Crow called.

"Yeah, man, what's happening?"

"How you feel, baby, you all right?"

I nodded.

"Well, get over to de starting line and make with de Crow action again, 'cause I've just caught me a trick. He! de loon, my whole bankroll is ridin' on this race, dig? My whole bankroll. So kick gravel, baby, we'll really boot 'em up tonight." He slapped me on the shoulder and ran back to the sideline. I started toward the starting line, the weight on my foot caused me to stagger with pain.

Luzon grabbed my arm; I jerked free of her.

"You've got your people mixed up, Cherry, I don't need your help. Oh, Yeah! That other person I want to impress. He just bet his last buck on me," I said, walking away.

Marion ran up with the wet towel. "I finally made it to the fountain. It was so crowded," she said breathlessly. "Here, sit down and let me clean that foot—"

I interrupted her, walking away: "Too late, dad. I've got to cut. Omega!"

"Alpha!" she shouted with simulated heartiness.

At the starting line, Coach Langley assigned lanes and gave instructions. My lane was next to Jackie's; a white boy from Roseland was on the other side of me. I knew him from former races; and although I'd always beaten him, it had only been by a step or two. I looked at Jackie without any concern. The dark circles under his eyes showed that he wasn't in as good condition as I had thought. The two heats had sapped him.

He turned to me. "Hey, Clucky-wucky old duck, you've been pretty lucky today. Wha'cha been doin', makin' black magic in the basement at night?" He laughed. A few of the boys joined in. I remained silent.

"Yeah, you're a lucky son of a—"

I stepped before him, hands clenched. "Go ahead, say it, son of a what?" I challenged.

253

"All right, fellows," the coach called.

"You stay away from Kay, that's all I got to say. She's my woman, cop," he said, squatting down. I wanted to kick him in the face.

"On your mark!"

I stepped to my lane and knelt. The position caused pain to shoot through my foot, my leg trembled as I fought to hold the position.

"Get set!"

I attempted to raise my body and wobbled with the effort. *Holy Mother of God, don't let me conk out now,* I thought, staring at the sky above the finishing line tape.

The crack of the gun rang in my ear.

The sky was blue like the Virgin's robe. I thought of the chapel's falling Virgin who no one could catch but me; the falling mother who I made fall. *Had I made her fall? No, he'd made her fall first, my father. If he hadn't, she could have walked over and taken the picture from my hand when I started to smash it . . .*

Pain leaped through me . . . The picture of Mom falling from the couch . . . I strained to catch her, raising my arm. Something brushed my chest lightly, like Kay's curious caresses . . . My body strained to reach Mom. I was thrown to the ground.

Dazed, I sat up. People were yelling wildly. I looked around. I was on the other side of the finishing line. Before me was a storm fence which surrounded the school. I'd run into it.

"Number 13, Guy Morgan, you will please come to the officials' stand!" requested the voice over the loud-speaker. I'd run the race unconscious of having done so.

Crow and Marion helped me to my feet. I slipped into the jacket Marion held.

"You all right, baby? you okay? huh? huh?" Crow asked.

I nodded, too tired to talk.

"Boy! Oh boy! what a race, you ran like crazy! You and de gray boy, neck and neck, until you put it in third. Then it was Guy all the way. Buddy!"

We'd reached the officials' stand. I limped up the steps. At the table I picked up the medal laying there. Reverend Heath stood up. Grasping one hand of the gold cup, he cleared his throat. The photographers about the stand lifted their cameras. I glanced at the long sheet of paper in the preacher's hand. My eyes caught words: ". . . Outstanding achievements . . . portraying the effects of good clean Christian living . . . symbolizing Negro youth at its best . . ."

"Ladies and Gentlemen!" At the sound of Reverend Heath's voice calling the cheering crowd to attention, I looked up. He paused to glance at his speech.

"Is the cup for me?" I said, nodding to the trophy.

He frowned at me in vexation. "Just a minute, young man, as soon as I complete the presentation—"

"Is that cup mine, did I win it?" I demanded.

"Why, certainly, you won it, but—"

Grabbing the handle of the cup, I tore it from his hand and limped down the steps.

Going over to Marion I dropped it at her feet. After pinning the medal on her vest, I picked up the cup and handed it to her. "Here's for being the best damned coach a guy ever had, Muffet," I said.

She clutched the cup to her tightly, staring at me through tears.

Turning to the stand, I looked at Reverend Heath. His hands were still raised as if holding the cup. A puzzled expression was on his face. Flash bulbs were popping.

I laughed, emptying myself of the tension, fear, pain and tiredness.

Crow pulled me toward the field house.

"Come on, man, let's forget these loons. We got a lot of partying to do tonight and these lames ain't into nothin'."

At the locker room door I paused. Hank came hurrying out of the field house office.

"I'll see you after the meet," I said meaningfully.

"Yeah, yeah, do that," he replied without stopping.

"All contestants for the 440 relays report to the finishing line," requested the loud-speaker as I closed the door to the locker room.

Crow had my clothes out of the bag.

"After you cop a shower, I'll fix that foot and give you a quick rubdown," he said, rubbing his hands together with enthusiastic satisfaction. "Buddy, what a race! Say, what made you run into de fence?"

I told him of how completely unconscious I had been.

He shook his head. Placing a reefer in his mouth, he lit up. "Well, conscious or un; you is de most hotfootingest steed I've ever seen," he complimented me, handing me the cigarette.

I inhaled deeply, then stripped.

Jackie walked out of a stall, halting when he saw me.

"You're the luckiest punk walking, Guy. If I hadn't—" he started.

"Yeah, yeah, I know, and if the little dog hadn't stopped to sniff the stumps, he'd have caught the rabbit. Shove off, pretty boy. Maybe you can make a little thunder now that I'm out of the meet. That is, if that gray boy from Roseland has grown tired of you sniffing his rear."

Crow and I laughed.

"So you won a few medals," Jackie said. "Good! Now you can go into the scrap iron business. When you do, remember to stay in the alleys. I happen to know that you've got eyes for Kay, but she's my woman, so stay away. I'd hate to blind you. Besides, you ain't her type. Dig what I mean?"

"So I'm not her type, huh? Why don't you ask her which type she prefers, mine or yours? Yeah, I understand you, I understand you so goddamned well until I intend to kick your

256

tail into your vest pocket the very first time you crawl across my path. Kay's your woman? Ugh! Don't make me puke. What makes a pampered punk like you think that he could possess a whole woman? God, how some cats swing! I know what's going down between your old man and hers, but you'll never actually possess her fully, pretty boy, because she loves me."

We glared our hate at each other.

"Remember, you're not her type and we aren't kids anymore," he said, and went out slamming the door.

"Well, for crapsake," Crow said. "What goes with this Kay deal? Does she really mean all that to you, man?"

Throwing the towel over my shoulder, I said, "Yes, and more. I think—my life maybe."

Chapter **23**

Seven hours later, I stood confidently watching the fifteen ball sluggishly make its way to the corner pocket of the pool table. I tapped the floor with the cue stick.

"Come and get him, House!" I yelled.

Shelley answered my call. She racked the balls expertly. Dipping into the pocket of her apron, she handed me six dollars. I chalked the tip of my cue and turned to the stranger I'd been playing One Pocket with for the past three hours.

"Name it, dad, I'm not choosey," I said.

He shook his head. "I'm hip you ain't, but I am," he sneered.

I had sharked him out of fifteen dollars.

"Look, weed, you asked me to play, remember," I said, taking his measurements. I concluded that although he was about thirty pounds heavier than I, a couple of whacks with the cue stick would put us on an even fighting basis.

"Yeah, but I didn't know that you was as good as you are," he replied with an offended tone.

"Well, now you do," I said, disgusted at hearing the age-old complaint.

Placing his cue in the rack, he walked out.

For a moment I stood watching the reaction of the cue ball to the English I had put on it with my stick. I'd come in six hours ago to wait for Hank. Marion, Crow, Dipper, Jim and Jet had gone on to my house. I'd promised to go skating with Crow and Dipper.

"What time is it, Shelley?" I asked.

258

Shelley had started dealing five-card stud to four imaginary players. She glanced at her watch without looking up or slacking the movement of her flashing hand.

"Ten-thirty," she said.

The pool room was empty. Everyone had crowded to the celebration.

The phone rang.

"Get that for me, will you, Guy?" Shelley requested.

I'd banked the cue ball into the corner pocket and went to the phone.

"Hank's Recreation," I said.

"Is Guy there?" Crow asked.

"Yeah, baby, wha'cha want?"

The pound of congo drums, loud laughter and jazz music came over the wire.

"Say, man, you ain't forgot our date, have you?" He asked.

"No, but I haven't seen Hank yet. Why don't you and Dipper go on without me. I can't skate with this foot anyway."

"Naw, we'll wait. De Ramblers don't start rambling 'til one o'clock anyway. Besides, I want you to compare my style with that of de other cats," he said.

"You people sound like you're doing some pretty good rambling now," I said of the sound I heard behind his voice.

"Yeah, Marion is giving a party for you," he said.

"Oh goody! I just love parties given for me, especially when I'm not there," I said.

He laughed. "Man, you knock me out," he complimented.

"Yeah, you throw a good punch too. But, later for now?"

"See ya later," he said, hanging up.

Shelley was standing by the upstairs entrance. She'd closed for the night.

"You can wait for Hank upstairs," she said, going up.

I picked up my bag from the shoeshine stand and followed her.

Upstairs, I dropped my bag near the record player. Searching through the stand near it, I collected my favorite record, placed it on the turntable, flicked a button and sprawled full length on the couch. The soft music filled the room.

Shelley now stood in the doorway, flicking the ends of a reefer with her fingernail. Lighting it, she flipped the light switch and came to sit at my feet. We listened to the music in the darkness, silently sharing the cigarette. The record began to repeat.

"I saw you run today," she said.

I grunted, enjoying the heady sensation the cigarette gave me.

"You've got a lot of heart, Guy." Her tone was mingled admiration and envy.

"Not heart, Shelley, but love."

"You still believe that love is like a song, don't you, all beautiful and soft?" She inquired mockingly.

I reflected on the effect which the thought and sight of Kay imparted to me.

"Uh-huh," I agreed. "Isn't that the way it's supposed to be?"

"That's the way it's supposed to be, only it isn't," she said.

We lapsed into silence.

"It's actually a scream, a mad, horrible scream," she said in a faraway voice.

I knew what she was thinking about. We had talked of it many times before when alone together. Shelley was a product of Chicago's South Side; a depression product, one of a family of six. Her parents and a sister and brother had died in a tenement fire when she was fourteen. She and her older brother, Bob, had struggled to raise their younger brother, Maurice, and sister, Aurelia. But the depression made their struggle impossible. Men and women had found little work to do; there was none for a seventeen-year-old boy and a fourteen-year-old girl.

260

Aurelia contracted tuberculosis six months after the fire, due to the unheated condition of the one-room basement flat which the bared overhead plumbing kept moldy with dampness.

On a cold December night, a month after Aurelia became ill, Shelley was leaving a run-down speakeasy, with a fifteen-cent trick when a trigger-happy cop halted her in the doorway; a cop who had won the nickname "Mr. Bullets" by emptying the hot lead of two shiny .38 Magnums into the shabbily-clothed backs and hungry guts of a dozen black teen-age boys. As his narrow shoulders jerked spasmodically and his hands made constant reaching motions for the guns hanging low on his hips, he said to Shelley: "I've just killed that goddamn jitterbug brother of yours. He was stealing coal."

A few nights later, "Mr. Bullets" had again stopped Shelley, this time to demand his cut of her hustling earnings. The ashes of her cremated brother, which she'd mingled with those of her family in the gold locket around her neck, seemed to still be warm from the furnace.

A year after that, Aurelia's ashes were added to Shelley's locket. Bob took to drinking and lost himself in the maws of Skid Row. Shelley was still hustling at the speakeasy when two handsome, sharply-dressed gamblers had blown into town. They entered the speakeasy and Shelley fell madly in love with the one wearing the white patch over his eye: Hank Johnson. From that night on they remained together. As Shelley took the gamblers on the game circuit, she learned their winning tricks. She caught on fast and in a short while the student was teaching the teachers. They began to hold games themselves and Shelley was their tout.

Then, Shelley became pregnant. Shelley was happy then, thinking that Hank would marry her now that she was carrying his child. But Hank was furious when he found out. Cursing and screaming, he kicked the unformed baby from her womb, charging her with trying to foster a trick baby off on him.

After a brief hospital confinement, she was back touting for the pair. Business boomed. Shelley was happy again. Hank had promised to marry her as soon as they'd picked up a steady trade. They had.

She became pregnant again. Hank's aborting foot went to work on her. During the hospital stay this time, the players fell off. Hank begged her on bended knees to forgive him and promised he would marry her.

About that time, Hank's partner skipped town with their bankroll, leaving their gambling operation a bust. So Shelley came out of the hospital and went to work again, her insides all jumbled up. Soon after that, she took in two half-starving streetwalkers, Ofelia and Velma, fed them, dressed them, and in a while she and Hank were back in business bigger than ever. They had added prostitution to their operation.

In two years, Shelley was pregnant and happy once more. This time, when she told Hank she was expecting and he raised his foot, she shot him in the leg. This time she had her baby—a monstrous, Mongoloid thing, the sight of which had sent Shelley into a screaming fit that only morphine could end.

An old midwife in Robbins now raised the child, who was my age, and Shelley went to see him a couple of times a year. She no longer screamed aloud at the sight of the stumbling, awkward hunk of slobbering human idiocy, whose head rolled grotesquely about its reddish neck. Shelley just screamed inside, and drowned those screams with whisky and reefers . . .

"Love is a cancer, Guy," Shelley was saying when my mind wandered back to the room over Hank's Recreation Room. "Whenever you believe that you're infected by it, cut it out from you quickly. It's crippling, Guy. It murders. Love's the cause of every wrong committed, every hate ever

262

felt. It's a feeling to be shunned, not embraced like the hypocrites would have you believe. Those great, big, broken-hearted 'I-love-you' people lie. Love is sorrow, pain, misery, disillusionment—all of the tortures of hell. Love is merely the top position in the sex act." She paused briefly, then added: "Love is a lie," as if her saying it would remove all contentions to the contrary.

The room now was silent, except for the record:

"*. . . Momma may have, Poppa may have, but God bless the child that's got his own . . .*"

"What do you think about a mother's love for her child, and vice versa?"

She got up, walked to the hall door and stopped. "It would be better for the mother and child if they could develop the same relationship that exists between the bitch and the pup," she said and went out.

I reached over and turned off the record player. Staring into the darkness, I wondered what terms Freud and his brain boys would apply to the way Shelley thought.

My concentration was broken by the sound of shattering glass. I sat up.

"Shelley?" I called.

Her low moan answered me. I ran down the hall. Glancing into the open door of each room as I went. A light showed beneath the closed door of the bathroom. I tried the door; it was locked. Pounding on it, I yelled: "Shelley! Shelley! You all right? Open the door."

She moaned again. Fear clutched at my heart. Grasping the knob, I rammed my shoulder against the door. The tiny lock shattered along with the full-length mirror built into the door.

Shelley was sprawled on the floor. The hypodermic needle sticking in her arm was slowly filling with blood, like a loathsome tick. I snatched it out and shattered it into the toilet bowl.

As I undressed her I thought: *From alcohol to reefers to junk. What about that, Mr. Freud, what kind of fixation is that?*

"A hell of a fix," I muttered, picking her up and sitting her down in the bathtub. Plugging the tub I turned on the cold water full blast. I looked at her as the water rose in the tub. She was as still as death. My eyes fell on the little golden locket around her neck.

I wondered what human ashes looked like. I reached for the locket. The feel of the cool, smooth metal caused me to withdraw my hand. Opening the locket would be like exhuming a corpse without permission. Six corpses.

She's a mobilized graveyard, I thought. *She carries the dead around her like the Ancient Mariner did the albatross.*

"Rub-a-dub-dub, one broad in a tub," I whispered. "Who put her there? I did."

The hell you did, my smoke-hazed mind said. *A fire? Nope. TB? Nope.* "Mr. Bullets?" *Nope. A water-head baby? Nope.*

I looked at the scar which extended from the darkness of Shelley's thigh to her navel.

The surgery was of the type Dr. Frankenstein might have performed on his monster. The dripping water seemed to give it a snakish animation.

Rub-a-dub-dub, a broad in a tub, I thought again. *Who put her there, Hank? Nope, wrong again, but you're getting warm. Try again.* I looked at the bloody inside of the toilet. *Junk?* Nope. I frowned with the effort of concentration, and surveyed her body. The sight of her breast solved the riddle. I turned off the cold water. Love had put Shelley in the tub. The lack of it!

Her body began to tremble. I turned on the hot water. Her eyes flickered opened. She moved to sit up. I pushed her back.

"Take it easy, Shelley. You can get out in a minute," I told her.

She lay shivering until the water got warmer.

"How long have you been taking junk, Shelley?"

She stared at me. The pupils of her eyes were contracted into pinpoints. "Three weeks," she said.

"After visiting the boy?"

She nodded sluggishly.

"What does Hank think about it? Does he know?"

"He knows all right, he knows everything, that boy. But he don't give a damn. He never has. Don't nobody give a damn but my two girls," she said groggily. "Nobody."

"That's not true, Shelley. I do."

I lifted her out of the tub and carried her to the bedroom. I put her in a chair and found a towel and fresh pair of pajamas in the dresser drawers. She sat with her chin on her chest as I dried and dressed her. Then I put her to bed.

"You've got a lot of heart, Guy," she drawled sleepily. "A lot of loving heart. I wish—I wish—" Her eyes closed in sleep.

I went into the front room to get my bag. As I turned to leave, the sound of hurried footsteps on the stairs halted me. A key was inserted in the front door lock. It opened and Hank walked in, carrying a brown paper bag in his hand. He hurried down the hall to the game room. After a moment I followed him, pausing in the doorway. Hank stood stopped before the opened door of an antiquated floor safe into which he was placing small snuff boxes he took from the paper bag. Completing the transfer, he threw the bag down and started to shut the door.

"Hold it, Hank," I said.

At the sound of my voice, he straightened with a jerk, and turned to me. His right hand snaked beneath his coat, then paused.

"Oh, it's you," he said, removing the hand. "How did you get in?"

I walked over to him. "Shelley let me in over seven hours ago."

"Yeah, well it's a quarter to twelve," he said. "You should have been in bed four hours ago," he said.

"Okay, Hank, cut out the comedy and fork over my two thousand, six hundred shumollions," I said, unzipping my bag.

I placed it on the sofa and arranged the spikes to make room for the money.

"Look, kid, it's late and I'm tired. Come back tomorrow, huh?"

Anger surged through me.

"Pay as you play, Hank, remember? So make with the payoff action."

"Yeah, you're right. Pay as you play."

Bending, he withdrew some bills from the safe and counted off three hundred and fifty dollars with paper-snapping rapidity. He placed the bills on top of the safe and stared at me, "Yeah, you're right, pay as you play. So cop and blow. I've seen enough of you for one day."

My right hand touched the heel of a track shoe at the sight of the money. I clenched the shoe and stared at him, not wanting to believe what I knew was true. Was he really welching on me? Fear clutched at my heart. I ran my eyes over his wide shoulders, remembering the rumors of the two men he'd killed, his brutality with Shelley, Velma and Ofelia.

The sight of a bulge beneath the left side of his coat increased my apprehension. I swallowed hard, trying to remove the lump in my throat.

"Oh, look, Hank, I ain't no bookworm and all that, but I know that there ain't no two thousand, six hundred slices of bread in that pile. I mean—so what do you mean—what do you mean?" I faltered to a halt. My dry lips and mouth made me speak in a thick jumble.

Hank stood rocking on his heels and toes, with his hands in his pockets as he gazed at the ceiling with pursed lips.

"You can only take down what your hand calls for," he said coldly.

"You mean you're welching on me?" I asked.

His rocking stopped. He looked at me, his one eye glinting maliciously. "I wasn't gonna use those words, kid, but being as you have, that's exactly what I mean. You think I'll let a punk like you make an ass out of Hank Johnson? Boy! You must think I was born yesterday. Ha! Lying around and faking that you're so hurt, so bad off. 'Gimme some more odds, Hank, because of my injuries. Off the bet, Hank, I may not be able to run!' you beg. And then you make with the strongarm action. Make a fool outta me! All right, all right, I'm offing the bet. Now you and that bantamweight piece of tail can—"

His flow of contemptuous words trailed off into a scream of agony as the spikes of my track shoe slammed into his good eye. I swung the shoe like a blackjack, lashing him as I remembered Shelley's hurt, a dark night on a snow-covered highway, Mom, and my father's advice that "God hates a brutish man."

Hank screamed again as the spikes bit into his flesh. He scrambled to get out of the way on flying feet, killing feet, feet that stomped out Shelley's babies.

Water-head baby, bloody-faced daddy . . . What goes around comes around, Joe.

I swung again and again with the track shoe. Hank reeled blindly to the other side of the room, bringing his gun-laden hand from beneath his coat. I struck at the hand twice with the track shoe, but missed.

Pivoting, I leaped out of the way as two shots thundered from the gun. Hot lead tore at my shirt, grazing my left forearm with fire.

"Where are you, you son-of-a-bitchin' bastard?" Hank screamed. "Say somethin', goddamn you! Did I get'cha?"

He rubbed his left hand over his face; blood oozed through

his fingers in tiny rivers of red. The shiny .38 snub-nosed revolver in his right hand menaced the room.

"Say somethin', goddamn you! I'm gonna kill you for this!" He shouted as he began to advance toward the safe, probing blindly with the toe of his shoe.

I reached into my bag and tossed out a bottle of alcohol into the far corner of the room. It struck the wall and clattered to the floor. Hank wheeled and fired two shots in that direction.

"Ha! Did I get'cha, ya son-of-a-bitch?" He shouted.

He fired two more shots wildly about the room, then the gun clicked emptily. I leaped for him.

"Kill me tonight, will you? Welch on me, will you? What does my hand call for now? This is called a good right cross. This is called a good left jab," I sobbed, as I sank punch after punch into his unconscious body. He sank slowly to the floor. I kicked him. "There! We Morgans have got some killing feet, too. There, you bastard!"

Sweat was pouring into my eyes. I reached down and dragged Hank from before the safe. Grabbing the bag, I dropped the gun into it and began to transfer the bills from the safe.

The stern voice of my father rang in my ears as I got to my feet and staggered around the room collecting the articles I'd thrown: *Thou shalt not steal.*

"I ain't stealing," I muttered, starting to grip the bag. "I'm only taking what I won, taking down what my hand calls for." There was over three thousand dollars in there, I guessed.

Thou shalt not steal! the voice persisted.

Kneeling before the safe I began replacing some of the bills into it.

. . . The strong ones get while the weak ones fade, scoffed the lady on the record. I paused.

Thou shalt not steal!

. . . Rich relations give crusts of bread and such . . .

you can help yourself! . . . Help yourself! Help yourself!
You promised! Help yourself! Take it all! All!

Thou shalt not—

The sound of a door slamming interrupted my thoughts.

"Velma is a stallion," the girl sang.

As I hurriedly withdrew the money from the safe and put
it in the bag, I knocked over two of the small snuff boxes
Hank had put in. They rolled about on the floor spilling their
contents: Horse, I realized. I stood up, my eyes fell on the
three hundred and fifty dollars on top of the safe. I stuffed it
into the bag too and hurried to the door on tiptoes.

The hall was clear. Velma was in her room.

Going to the back door, I opened it cautiously and tip-
toed out, easing it shut. Velma sounded as if she were approaching. "Velma is a stallion," the voice came, "a stallion,
a stallion—oh, riding her so much, sooo—Hank? Hank! Oh
God help! Help, somebody! Police! Police! Murder!"

I leaped down the remaining stairs. As I sped down the
alley, I wondered if I had actually killed him.

Thou shalt not kill! Thou shalt not steal! Thou shalt not!
my father's voice shouted in time with my running feet.

"I didn't mean to, I didn't—I didn't," I whispered.

Thou shall not commit sin! God punishes sin with fire!
Fire! Fire!

I stopped and turned, for a moment expecting to see him
behind me.

"Shut up, you son-of-a-bitch!" I expelled into the darkness.
"You shouldn't have gone away with Zola, either, but you
did. Now shut up. Mom's mine and I need this to fix up the
mess you made. Frig you and your 'thou shalt nots'. Let me
alone or I'll—"

Dropping the bag, I hooked and jabbed in the darkness:
"I'm not a kid anymore or a cripple, see? You saw Hank,
didn't you? So shut up and shove off before I—I—I—" The
object in my bag glinted in the moonlight and caught my

269

eyes. Stopping, I snatched it and crouched, menaced the darkness with the cold metal clenched tightly in my fist.

"Always a great one for the rule books, ain't you? We waited for you but you didn't come—now shove off and never call again or I swear, I'll—I'll—"

The empty gun click finished the sentence.

A rat scurried from a garbage can, its sudden movement giving life to the night and sweeping my mind clear.

I turned and ran from the alley in the direction of The Hill.

The Hill: my eternal refuge in time of trouble. I would bury the money in The Hill.

Chapter **24**

I stayed away from the pool room a couple of days because I knew that Shelley knew who had worked Hank over. The cops had been so happy to find him with so much dope on him that they didn't give a damn who had beat him up. A twinge of guilt hit me when I heard that he had lost the other eye as a result of the beating. But what goes around, comes around, big daddy, so you pulled down what your hand called for, I thought.

When I did stop in at the pool room to check my shine stand, Shelley greeted me as though nothing had happened. Maybe she was grateful to me in a way. After that I spent more time there. Shelley needed a man around to handle the heavy work, and I needed to be needed. I also did some driving for her. She paid me what Hank had paid me, but she got more work for it.

One afternoon she had me take her out to Robbins to see her monstrous idiot child. As usual when she left the rundown shack where the boy was kept by an old and kindly crone, she was a nervous wreck. We drove in silence for nearly ten minutes when she threw a ten dollar bill in my lap.

"At the next booze joint, Guy, get me a bottle. I can't wait to get back to the place and I'm too sick inside to go in anyplace." I parked and went into a roadside gin mill and came back with a fifth of bonded bourbon. That should ease her pain, I thought. After a moment of tearing frantically at the seal, she handed the bottle to me with trembling hands. I held it between my legs to open it, and then handed it to her. As she took the bottle from me her eyes looked like those of a wounded doe I had seen on TV. Their appeal twisted my heart with sympathy.

She drank the fiery liquid with the thirst of one who seeks quick and complete oblivion. The whisky trickled down the side of her mouth, staining her clothes. The sight of the normally composed Shelley in this state repelled me. I rolled down the window and, snatching the bottle from her, threw it smashing onto the highway. She stared at me for a moment in absolute disbelief, and then anger blazed.

"What in the hell do you think you're doing?" she cried. I didn't answer, only urged the car to a greater speed.

"Goddammit, Guy, answer me, what did you do that for?" she repeated, hysteria in her voice.

"Because I couldn't stand to see you slobbering in a bottle of juice, that's why. Not to mention the fact . . ." I kept my eyes averted.

"Not to mention the fact that I don't need some punk telling me what to do. If I disgust you Mr. High and Mighty Morgan, that's tough. Just look to your driving and don't look at me. I'm not ashamed of having turned fifteen-cent tricks, and don't you forget it."

"I won't forget it, Shelley," I said, my voice soft, "but maybe you should. Shelley, you don't want . . ."

"Want! Want! What do you know about my wants? What does anybody know or care?" she shouted hysterically as she fumbled in her purse.

The whisky she had drunk was beginning to take effect.

"Why," she looked up in surprise, "I don't have any more money."

"I've nearly four dollars left from your ten." I told her.

"Then baby, please stop and get me a pint of somethin', please," she implored.

"No," I said.

"What! You refuse me? And with my own money?" Her

272

hand gripped my arm, and I had to struggle to keep the steering wheel even.

"Shelley, I don't think you need any more booze. You didn't need that first bottle," I persuaded.

"Why you cheap ungrateful little . . ." Her teeth were clenched in cold fury.

My sympathy was running thin and I had an edge to my voice when I said, "Look, Shelley, my heart is as big as all outdoors where you're concerned. As for being little, I stand 5′ 11″ and weigh a good 175 pounds. Now, I tell you this, because if you don't take your fingernails out of my arm, I'm going to slap you into the state that the booze would put you in, for free."

She drew back into the corner of the front seat.

"That little speech just placed you in the ranks of the unemployed, Sonny."

I laughed. She turned to look out of the window and we drove the rest of the way in silence. When we reached the pool hall, she got out of the car and hurried to the private entrance.

"If you want your pay, flunky, you'll have to come up for it." After a moment I got out and followed her. The door at the top of the stairs was open and I walked in. Bills and coins showered about my head and against my face.

"Laugh at me, will you?" she shrieked wildly. "Tell me what I want and need will you, you insolent pup, you . . . you flunky! Pick it up, and get out!" Her body was trembling with the intensity of her anger. "Who needs you?" she spit.

I grabbed her wrist. Snatching her roughly around and pulling her against my chest, I embraced her tightly, kissed her briefly, then shoved her away from me. She reeled to the opposite side of the room where she clutched the door frame to keep from falling.

I knelt and began picking up the money that she had thrown on the floor.

"If I were a man, I'd . . ." she began.

"Stop pretending to be one," I injected.

"Kill you for that," she ended.

Shoving the money into my pocket, I stood erect. Sympathy began to erase the momentary anger I felt. I went over to her.

"You want to kill me for kissing you?" I peered intently into her face.

Her gaze fell, "No, I didn't mean that Guy. I'm . . ."

Embracing her tenderly, I pressed my mouth to hers in a brief kiss of apology which the command of her hungry lips quickly dispelled as her body clung to mine with an ancient hunger.

I freed my mouth. "May I?" I asked in a breathless whisper. Her closed eyes fluttered open and then closed.

The words of a sermon I'd heard my father preach when I was a child flashed across my mind with a sensual insistence . . . "Feed my sheep, feed my sheep . . . feed my lamb."

"I'm old enough to be your . . ." she murmured.

"Isn't old wine the sweetest?" I replied, nuzzling in her bosom. Her kiss of consent broke off further speech. We swayed, still embracing over to the bed. I turned from her to close the door. Velma stood there at the head of the stairs staring in shocked disbelief. I kicked the door shut in her face.

We undressed hurriedly. She came to me. Embracing her, I started to press her down on the bed.

"No, my way," she said, twisting around and pushing me back. I stared up at her, remembering her saying that love is the top position in the sex act. Her eyes challenged my biological position as the aggressor. I picked up the mental gauntlet. As my arms circled her body, I thought, *My kind of monk don't swing like that, Shelley.*

I pulled her face down to me as I pressed her lips firmly to mine, remembering as I did the snarling lips of Hank, spewing vile innuendos. I thought of his murderous kicks on her pregnant body. The kicks that had caused her to produce an insult to God's image.

Willing my fingertips into gentleness, I caressed every part of her boyish body. My hand touched the scar which disfigured her otherwise smooth stomach. She twisted and I thought of the cruel incision of the quack's knife. I kissed the erect nipples of her small, still firm breasts and felt her body shudder. I knew that her philosophy of love and sex was crumbling. She collapsed on my chest moaning in the mute language of desire which every lover understands.

Finally freeing myself from the clinging thighs and arms, I rolled onto my side. She sat up and laid her head on my chest.

"Guy, oh, Guy, Guy!" she whispered tenderly, as she drew invisible circles on my body with light, toying fingers. "You are wonderful."

Hours later, I lay staring into her sleeping face as she rested on my extended arm. Under the influence of passion, Shelley had displayed many facets of her usually one-sided personality, and I couldn't help but wonder if Shelley would still want women after me.

Chapter **25**

The crap game in the back of Hank's Pool Hall was going full blast. Jesse Motley stood with the dice in his hand, yelling: "A dollar-five I shoot."

The young rookie cop to his right, Sam Boston, tossed down a bill and a coin. "Shoot," he commanded.

Sam was a neighborhood kid who had made the police force. He and Jesse had always been good friends.

I turned from the game and walked back to my shine stand in the front. Grant Rucker, a thin, little dark boy who had been in Morgan Park just a few weeks from Mississippi, stood by the juke box.

"Lawdy, Lawdy, what a city," he said.

"What do you mean, weed?" I asked him.

"Ain't they got no blues in this here rockola?" he asked, pointing to the juke box.

"Just what you see, weed, just what you see."

"What's dis weed business?" he asked.

"A weed is a stranger, an outsider. It's slang," I explained. "It also sometimes refers to reefer, or pot."

"What's pot?"

"Pot—weed—gunion—mexico joints. You know, weed, reefers."

He looked at me, bewildered. "You mean dat is all those things? Lawdy, Lawdy, what a city."

I thought: *Lawdy, Lawdy, what a weed.*

"Say man," Grant asked, "why does you-all give one thing all them names?"

276

"It's a game, man," I explained. "It's a game we play when things get monotonous—blue, you know. Just like you weed corn. After a while, you chop the corn and leave the weeds. Sort of a change of pace, cop?"

He didn't. Shaking his head, he said: "Well, I don't see how you-all can get blue with all the fightin' and car-racin' and what-not that goes on 'round here."

"That's all part of it, Grant, being blue, I mean. You'll see. Just stick around."

Suddenly there was a commotion in the back. I jumped from the stand and started back to see what was happening. Jesse Motley met me in the doorway and steered me back to the stand. He was shaking with anger.

"What the hell—" I started.

"It's Sam, the son-of-a-bitch," Jesse interrupted. "He's fouled up the game—took the money."

Jesse limped about angrily on the cork leg he had as a souvenir of his wartime paratrooper days.

"Why?" I asked. "The game was on the up and up, wasn't it?"

"He did it because he lost, the chinchy son of a yellah-bellied, gutter-born bitch, and because he's a cop and be-cause—"

"And because the game was crooked," Sam said, coming out from the back room. He stepped behind the counter, pulled out a bottle of pop, opened it and walked back around and leaned against the counter. "Now what was you sayin', Jesse?" he asked evenly after taking a drink from the bottle.

The crowd from the crap game had now gathered in the front.

Jesse stared at Sam for a moment, then shrugged and climbed into a chair up on the shine stand. "What's the use?" he said sarcastically. "You're wearin' a gun and a star."

Sam drained the pop bottle and set it down. "That's right," he said. "I'm the law. But you're a citizen and this is a free country, so sing out." He spoke with dramatic coolness. "I'll listen, for old times' sake."

"You're the *law?*" Jesse laughed. "You're a glorified stool pigeon for Boss Charley. I've watched you ever since you've been in that monkey suit, watched you change from a buddy into the dirty black bastard that you are. And when I say black, I don't mean your face; I mean your filthy, stinkin' heart. Shall I go on?"

Sam's eyes were evil black dots. "Go ahead, chili pimp, you've got the floor," he said hoarsely.

"Yeah, I'm a pimp," Jesse said. "And it gripes me when I recall that it was money from some of those two and three dollar tricks my broads turned that helped pay off the alderman to get you on the force. Whore's money. And how have you paid it back? By arresting little free-laying Millie Clay and getting her sent up; by helping to shoot that kid Billy Williams from the top of a Cola bar because he was puttin' down the same kind of hustle you and I did when we were his age. What are you tryin' to do, get a rep for bein' a killer, one of a bunch of kill-crazy, coon cops who are exterminating their own race while the blond political bosses applaud them for lowering the nigger vote rate?"

Jesse paused and took out his handkerchief and wiped his face. There wasn't a sound in the whole pool hall.

"Give me a cigarette, baby," Jesse said, holding out his hand to Grant without looking at him. Grant complied with trembling hands.

"You wouldn't know about all that, though, would you?" Jesse said to Sam after lighting the cigarette. "Your knowledge extends to kicking kids in the butt for doing the only thing left for them to do around here, loaf. Yeah, that and cracking the hustles of your ex-buddies, and knocking over a penny-ante crap game you couldn't have gotten into in the first place if it hadn't been for the fact that you used to be a regular."

278

Jesse stopped and spat. It landed an inch away from the cop's feet.

Sam shoved away from the counter and walked over to the shine stand.

"Jesse," he said, "you're a lyin', drunk fool."

"Birds of a feather flock," Jesse said derisively, "you low son-of-a—"

Instantly Sam's long-barreled police special was out of the holster and slashing viciously across Jesse's cheek, cutting off his words and knocking him from the shine stand.

The cop backed into the phone booth, keeping the pistol trained upon the bleeding, unconscious Jesse. He lifted the receiver off the hook and began to dial. Shelley stepped over to the phone booth and said something quietly to the cop. He replaced the receiver and followed her out into the hallway. Shelley closed the door behind them.

Going over to Jesse, I removed the chair that had fallen on top of him. I re-stationed it on the platform and climbed onto it.

The spectators began filing away to other spots around the room.

"Dat sho'nuff was a dirty deal," Grant whispered.

I looked down at Jesse.

"It's all in the game, weed," I said. "He took down exactly what his hand called for."

Grant grabbed my arm. "They were buddies?" he whispered.

I looked into his eyes. The plea in them irritated me. I thought of the beating I had ordered for Treetop and how Ding had helped cripple me the night of the prom.

"Don't worry about it, weed," I said to Grant. "This is Frig Your Buddy Week."

Jesse was beginning to sit up from the floor, massaging his bleeding face.

"He's lucky," I told Grant, nodding to Jesse. "He's just got fifty-one more screwings to go until next year."

"What you mean?" Grant asked, frowning.

"Just stick around, weed, you'll find out," I said, brushing his hand from my arm.

"Lawdy, what a city," he said, as I opened the door. "What a mean, dirty, low-down city—"

Shelley sat on the upstairs steps smoking. The cop leaned against the wall. Seeing me, he straightened. I stared at him. The blue, silver and copper cop with the black on top. I thought of Tony Mancuso, the arch-deacon of the shake-down, a blue, silver and copper cop with white on top. Black, white, yellow or red, drape 'em in blue, stick a silver piece of tin on 'em and gird 'em with a belt of copper-coated bullets and you've got one of Christ's Only People, a c-o-p, a dirty son-of-a-bitch . . . It's the clothes that makes 'em . . . So say the pool room philosophers.

"What are you staring at?" The cop demanded.

I was tempted to say: a dirty son-of-a-bitch.

"Nothing," I said.

"What do you want, Guy?" Shelley asked, stamping out her cigarette on the stair.

"I was just leaving, Shelley, I've got to go get Mom from the hospital and I might not get back."

"Go on, don't worry about getting back, I'm glad your mother's well enough to come home." Her eyes begged me to get out, and quick.

"OK." I shot a disdainful glance at the cop who was obviously anxious to complete the pay-off. "See you tomorrow."

Closing the door to the hallway, I snatched my jacket from the stand and hurried out to my car. Mom was coming home.

Chapter **26**

The big, ancient touring sedan that I had bought with one hundred and fifty dollars of the money I had taken from Hank roared along the outer rim of Lake Michigan. I watched the giant waves roll against the breakers and explode in foamy, white patterns against the blackness of the night. Kay sat beside me, glancing now and then in my direction. We had been riding in silence since leaving my house, where she had met Mom for the first time.

Mom: I had hardly been able to wait when the doctors told me she could come home from the hospital. I was sure that everything would be as it had been before with us, only maybe she wouldn't mention my father so much because of the argument we'd had about him. But things weren't the same when she came home. Mom seemed to worship my father more than ever, taking out every photograph she could possibly find of him and placing them about the house. She seemed also to have gone into a shell, sitting quietly most of the time, not saying anything. I thought this might have been part of the after-effects of the stroke she suffered. Still, she livened up considerably when there were visitors in the house. She had been a real chatterbox earlier in the evening with Kay, even telling her all about the chicken I had been so fond of when I was a little kid, and how she had therefore nicknamed me "Clucky," a name I permitted only her and Marion to call me, and even then, not in public.

Marion: Where had the weeks gone? How long had it been since she boarded that train for Boston? We had argued about her leaving in mid-summer, but I think that deep-down inside we both had realized that it was for the best. What was the point in holding on to a love grown cold?

Marion had tried to heal the growing breach between us on the day of the track meet, but when I got home that night and told her what had happened with Hank—well, she just hadn't understood.

I jammed my foot down harder on the accelerator.

"Who are you chasing, Guy?" Kay asked, cutting through the silence.

"What?"

"Who are you chasing, driving so fast?"

"Oh, nobody—and everybody."

"What is it, Guy?" Kay persisted. "Something is bothering you."

Something bothering me—that was an understatement. But how could I start telling her when I wasn't too sure myself. All I knew was that I was straining against everything that seemed to be fencing me in. I felt as if I had to burst out of my world or go mad. I was eighteen years old, a man, and I was ready for life—a life other than that which I knew in Morgan Park. But how did you explain that to a girl?

I pulled up and parked a block from Kay's house.

"Is the gospel rider home?" I asked.

"No, not until 10:00. It's only 9:30 now," Kay answered, glancing at her watch.

I had kept my promise about not trying to see Kay. It had been easy: she had been managing to get out and see me.

"Is it your mother that's bothering you, Guy?" Kay asked, refusing to abandon her pursuit of my innermost thoughts.

"What makes you ask that?" I demanded.

"Oh, I don't know. She has had a rough time. First the accident, and then the stroke. And you seem to love her so. But I'm afraid she's a lonely woman."

"Now why should she be lonely?" I demanded. "She's got

me. She'll always have me. All she has to do is wiggle her little finger and I'm there to take care of her, to do anything she wants."

"Loneliness can't always be cured by a devoted son, Guy," Kay said, looking me straight in the eye.

"Mom's all right," I said too loudly. "I'm all she needs."

"You're jealous of her, aren't you, Guy?"

"Well for crap sakes what makes you say that? Sure, I love her and I take care of her—me, all by myself—and we don't need anybody else!" I fairly shouted it at Kay.

"I'm sorry, Guy. I just meant that—well, I can see how protective and all you are about her. I mean, well, you treat her wonderfully well."

I smiled, burying my face in the soft, clean-smelling mass of her hair.

"Guy, how come you never tell me that you love me? You make me do it all the time."

"I'm supposed to be laying off, remember, your old man's orders."

"Yes, I know. But that has nothing to do with your telling me that you love me."

"Haven't you heard that it's the important things in life that are left unsaid?" I dodged.

She toyed with my earring. "But—but you're so vague, Guy. Can't you say something to let me know that you're sincere, that—" she paused. "Guy, I've got to talk to you."

I placed my finger beneath her chin and raised her lips to mine.

"Do you love me, Guy?" she asked when our mouths parted.

I couldn't define my feelings for her, so I kissed her harder.

"No, no, no! What does that mean?" she demanded, pulling away.

"It means that actions speak louder than words," I told her. "Look, pretty, you're tops in my world. When I'm with you, I feel as if I could scrape the blue off the sky. Is that love? I still leave it up to you to name." I turned into 111th Street.

How could I tell her what I really felt when I didn't know for sure myself? Even then, I was hoping that she would get out of the car and go home.

"And what about your girl friend, Marion?" Kay demanded. "And Luzon. You know she's carrying a torch for you."

"Look, pretty," I said, allowing some of my impatience to creep into my voice, "you're worrying yourself for nothing. Marion was merely a cute little childhood ditty whose melody doesn't even linger. So enjoy the fact that you've got me to yourself, cop?" I stopped the car and parked.

I kissed her quickly and opened the door for her to get out. "Luzon?" she queried.

"Her torch is a blow torch, and I'm not about to get scorched," I grunted. I had to get back to the pool room and I was anxious for her to be on her way. "Guy?" She hesitated, then said, "Is it true what they say about you and Shelley?"

"What do they say?" I returned, without feeling.

"They say she's keeping you." She hurried on "Guy, she's old enough to be your mother."

I remained silent, thinking how alike women were, assuming that youth in all females ended around the twenty-fifth birthday. Shelley was nearly thirty-five.

"Let's talk about it another time, 'cause pretty, your time has run out." I placed my hand on the car door, in an effort to remind her, before she got wound up on Shelley.

"Why you, you arrogant—Oh, why did I let myself fall for you?—" she fumed, getting out of the car. "Sometimes you almost glow with conceit."

I shut the door behind her, as she ran for her house, and I headed the car for the pool room, and Shelley.

Kay, Marion, Shelley, did any of them really matter? And

what about Miss Switch? Miss Luzon of the Virgins. The bitch that never failed to remind me of Zola. Zola, the husband-father thief. Let her burn her torch! Let it burn, burn, burn! To hell with Luzon!"

The Saturday night shuckers and jivers and the pool room were in full swing when I got there. I stopped for a moment to watch a lively coon-can game between the ofay Dipper and a dark, elephantine man called Bloaty. Dipper was losing and Bloaty's signifying was getting on his nerves.

Dipper turned the six of hearts off the tattered deck. Then, spreading the four, five and six of the suit, he discarded the seven of clubs. Bloaty dropped the queen and jack of clubs atop the discarded seven and jumping to his feet, bellowed: "Out of his hand came Leapin' Dan! Boy, don't you know dat I'se de man put de coon in de can?"

"That's just one game, lame," Dipper yelled furiously. "Refit your rump to that stump and I'll coon your fat, funky butt if ya just don't jump!"

"Looka' here, boy," Bloaty said, settling down to play in earnest, "some coons can, and some coons can't. Some coons could learn, but you're one coon who cain't."

I turned and strolled away. Behind me, I heard Dipper yell: "Buck it, Mr. Bloaty-Butt. Count 'em, Mr. Bear. It may look crazy, but there's eleven cards there!"

In another corner, a dapper young man with long side-burns, thin moustache and a small goatee was holding forth on the art of living off the gay ladies of the evening: ". . . Say, man, I wouldn't work on a gospel train if it had only two stops: Hallelujah and Amen . . ." He was Ben Todd. He paused in his spiel to accept a bottle of wine passed to him by Puff Johnson, the now T.B.-wasted, philosophy-spouting, dope-sniffing, ex-fighter who once nearly won the light heavyweight championship. Ben raised the bottle to his lips.

Chapter 27

I walked on.

". . . So I opened the door, you dig? And this cute little brunette leaps into my arms, just a-pantin' . . ."

It was Bird talking to a group of the guys.

"Yeah, yeah. Go on, what happened next?" coaxed the pimply-faced Dale Poindexter, who had the tendencies of a sex moron.

"So I carried her over to the couch, man, and oh, Buddy, did she get frisky. Crawled all in my lap and began to lick me in the ears and all over the face, Frenchin' me, ya know."

"Yeah man, wow! Go on, go on, you lucky bastard," Dale urged.

"She really snuggles down and lays it on me, you dig? And me, I'm strokin' her soft hair and she's whinin' with delight—"

The boys around Bird were getting glassy-eyed, hanging on his every word.

"Yeah, then when she began to squirm and wiggle I says to myself, 'Bird, my man, this is it!' So I—"

"Yeah! Yeah! Yeah! What did'cha do, Bird?" Dale whispered hoarsely.

"I reached over and got the leash and put it around her neck," Bird said straight-facedly.

"You reached over and put the leash on her neck?" Dale howled.

"You're damn right. I didn't want the bitch to take a leak all over my new suit!" Bird exclaimed. "Say, what do you guys think I'm talkin' about?"

286

"A broad, what else?" Dale said angrily.

"Aw, hell naw. I was talkin' about my girl friend's French poodle," Bird said in mock indignation.

The gang swamped him in a flood of vile names.

I walked into the tiny washroom at the rear of the hall. A well-dressed boy washing his hands in the face bowl greeted me with a friendly smile.

"Hey, baby," he said.

"What's to it, pops," I returned.

He started drying his hands.

"Look, baby, I'm from Englewood," he said.

I looked at him. I had already recognized him as a weed.

"The name's Eugene; Eugene Towns."

I nodded.

"Dig, baby, like I know that I'm a weed out here, but I heard that there was some real choice stuff to be copped in this burg, and I made it out here to see if it's true."

I eyed him suspiciously. "So don't believe everything you hear, booby trap." The nickname was one we applied to the young plainclothes cops who came nosing around looking for suckers gullible enough to make a wrong play.

"I'm strictly a viper, myself, man," he said. "But, dig, here's the situation. The Vagabonds are throwing a little party tonight, and you know how that goes: one guy is elected to see to it that there's enough broads to play with, another stud furnishes the house, and another one cops the gay stuff. We need somethin' besides booze, and Englewood is kind of hot right now, cop?"

I studied him closely as he talked. "Who did you get your info from about this place?" I inquired.

"I just got up from doin' a ninety-day bit at the County, man, and a stud doin' time out there, Ray Miller, told me that things were cool here."

Still suspicious, I asked: "Who do you know out in the woods? Sportsmen, I mean."

"Well, there's Tank, a sprint man."

I had run against that guy in track. He was a good 220 man.

"Choski."

A mid-distance runner.

"Hoe Evans, a middleweight."

Hoe Evans was a tough man to tangle with. I had learned that first-hand before he went pro.

"And then there's—"

"That's enough, pops," I cut in, "I'm satisfied with the boys you named. Now dig; there's no stuff to be had out here. The bag was busted when the guy who used to run this joint got arrested a couple of weeks ago. The guy you met at the County was one of his pushers. Now, you got a short?"

He shook his head.

"Well, I've got one, and for a fee I'll connect you with some pot. But you'll have to trust me to transact the deal 'cause I'll be damned if I'm gonna' let my buddy take a bust, okay?"

He stared at me for a moment, then said, "Okay."

"Now then, how much weed do you want?"

"I got forty-five dollars," he answered, pulling the roll of bills from his pocket and handing it to me.

I counted rapidly. "Forty-five it is." Pocketing the roll, I added: "I'll take five for gas and oil and knowin' where to go, cool?"

"Cool," he said.

We left the bathroom.

Shelley was in the front of the pool room, leaning against a display case. I tossed the roll of bills to her.

"Hot," I said.

She nodded and went over to the cash register and rang up "No Sale." She counted the roll of bills into the register, and gave me a similar amount from it.

Eugene threw me an odd look, but I offered him no explanation. I wasn't about to be caught with marked money.

I drove to within a block of Dot's house, and told Eugene as I got out: "Sit tight. I'll be right back."

"Say, how do I know you ain't shaftin' me?" he protested nervously. "I mean, you got the bread and all and leavin' me here."

"Then you got yourself an automobile," I said with a grin. I didn't bother to give him the keys, though.

I trotted to the building where Crow was staying with Dot and took the rickety flight of stairs three at a time.

"Who de hell is it?" Crow's voice demanded from inside as I pounded on the door.

Dot opened up.

"Who is it, Dot?" Crow asked.

I was past her and half across the room before she could reply.

"It's Guy! Deacon, baby! Oh, momma!" he cried, leaping from the couch. "Dig de loon! Dig de loon!" he shouted to Dot as he danced around the room.

"Crow! Crow! Little man, how's tricks? Man, am I happy to see that monkey face of yours!"

We pounded each other wildly about the room.

"Hey, hey, you two!" Dot said sternly, "Cut out the Mau Mau action. Do you want people in this cracker box to think we're murdering somebody up here?"

"Damn what dey think! Me and my partner don't care, do we, Guy?"

"Hell, no, 'cause we can lick any ten guys, can't we, baby?"

In answer, Crow went into his familiar fighting stance, spitting on his palms and lashing out with two devastating punches at an imaginary foe. "See, I'm still in good shape," he declared.

I nodded, and looking at him choked me up for a minute.

It was hard for me to realize that we had not seen each other for so long—not since the day of the track meet, in fact. It was funny how much of a loner I had become.

"Tell me all de happenin's," Crow said, settling back on the couch.

I sat beside him and brought him up to date on Mom coming home from the hospital, Marion's leaving and my seeing Kay, and Beano helping me to line up a job for next summer at a kids' camp.

"Say, momma, why is Beano so interested in you?" Crow asked with a frown when I had finished.

"I'm not sure,"I said. "But he sure has helped me through a couple of spots. I guess he figures to use me one of these days, when I've learned the ropes."

"Yeah, ya gotta learn de ropes to make it in this world," Crow said reflectively.

I thought about our having quit school together. "Crow, baby," I said slowly, "maybe you shouldn't have cut out from school with me. After all, that was my problem and—"

"Forget it, man," Crow put in. "School don't get'cha ready for survival in Black Babylon. I don't need no book to tell me when to cop and when to blow. Mr. Need More will do that. Besides half de loons who graduated this year end up coming to me for advice and a fix anyway."

Crow fell silent for a minute, then went on: "Say man, did you ever get de feeling that you were growing up too fast?"

I took a good look at him, and realized he had grown up.

"I don't really know," I said.

"Well, if anybody should, you should," he said. " 'Cause a pretty big chunk of your time for being a kid was smashed out."

"Maybe I did grow up too fast," I said, "but then I always disliked being a kid. It's kinda hard to explain, but I've always wanted something in this world that I've never found. Maybe it's just plain security—a job that would pay me

290

enough money to do all the things for Mom that I'd like to do, take her traveling to places she's never been. Old fire-flinging Moses was the chosen one to travel in our family."

"Speaking of preachers," Crow said, "how are you and Kay's old man gettin' along?"

I told him. He grunted. Preachers weren't his favorite people either.

"Boy," he said, "when I think of de floors my momma scrubbed, de clothes she washed and de candy suckers I went without all because she had to help buy a long car for some con man with his collar turned backwards, screaming that God was lookin' into her pocketbook, I could cuss 'em from Amazin' Grace to floatin' opportunity. And some of them joes selling Holy Water, ha! Lake Michigan straight. And what about them well-used bed sheets some of 'em rip into strips and sell at five bucks a throw, yellin' 'This is de sheet Jesus was wrapped in and laid in de clay,' and wood said to have come from de Cross. I know one that even made his flock paper de walls of his church with dollar bills, while he yelled somethin' about it was better to give than to receive."

"Listen, later for all this," I said, not wanting to get started thinking about my father. "Look, little man, are you still pushin' stuff?"

Crow eyed me carefully. "Yeah," he said, "but not to you. You got too much to lose by messin' around."

"What do you mean, man?" I asked.

"Just what I said. Not to you, especially de stuff that's bein' sold now."

I frowned in puzzlement.

"Look, Guy," Crow went on, "de pot is doctored with formaldehyde."

"What?"

"Embalmin' fluid, de stuff they shoot in dead folks. De demand is so heavy and de supply is so slow, they're shovin' anything off: grass, drinkin' tea, sleepin' powder, sugar, soda, quinine and roots—anything. De junk is really j-u-n-k, dig? All they want is de dirty buck. So leave de weeds to de grasshopper."

He fell silent for a minute, then jumped to his feet and exploded: "God! You should see some of 'em, Guy. Some of 'em ain't nothin' but babies."

"Look, Crow," I said. "You can't be the conscience of this filthy, windy burg. Forget it. Damn how young they are. You shouldn't even have told me about the stuff being doctored. It goes against the rules of the game. Never pull a sucker's coat to the things he don't know. Now I came here for two cans of pot. I'm buyin' for a stud from Englewood, and I'll be damned if I'm going to smarten him to the dead man juice sprinkled on it and crumb this deal. So cop the grass for me."

Crow left the room, returning in a minute with the two cans, which he tossed to me. Then, flopping back on to the couch, he declared: "Everytime I swing some of this T.B.-maker or that heart-stopper, horse, that kid in the bathroom that night at de rink flashes before my eyes."

"Forget it, goddammit! That's the way the ball bounces. If they don't cop from you, they will from someone else."

"Yeah, yeah, that's what I keep tellin' myself," he said. "But I can't get used to seein' it. They crowd in here doubled-up, their guts tied in a painful knot that screams for a few grains of white dust. And Dot's brother, Jim, that big, muscle-bound, faggoty-assed bastard makes 'em roll around on de floor at his feet and howl like dogs before he'll toss 'em a fix. I'm gonna' kill him someday."

I turned to look at him. He was staring at the begrimed ceiling. He had spoken in a low voice filled with hatred.

"It seems like de whole South Side has gone fix-mad," he went on. "Why? Why is everybody wanderin' around on a hopped-up cloud?"

I clutched his knee tightly, feeling as if some dreadful hor-

292

ror had descended on him and I had to save him. "Baby, I don't know and I don't give a damn," I said. "You've got to get out of here, get away from this place. Why don't you go back home to your people, Crow?"

"I can't go back to that sanctified sty." he argued. "People! I ain't got no people. I lost 'em fightin' a booty bandit in a black cell, and when I copped de scars on my knees from kneeling on that cold, hard floor, waitin' for my people to come get me. They didn't, but you did, so you're my people, Guy."

"Okay, okay, if that's the way you want it. But get out of this hell-hole. There must be someplace to go where—"

"Go? Yeah, Guy, why not? I need to go some place besides up, up, up—rocketin' through space on a speedball fix for a few minutes."

I gripped his arm tightly; a hot sickness struck me with a cold dread.

"What the hell do you mean, Crow?" I croaked.

Inserting his fingers beneath the cuff of his shirt sleeve, he jerked. The material tore up to the elbow. I stared at the marks of the junkie. The burned-out vein looked like a loathsome serpent lying inert. Tears filled my eyes. Rage surged through me. Him of all people! Why? I flung the arm from me.

"My God, Crow, why didn't you wait? Buddy, how could you? Why?"

I sank back on the couch in despair.

He sat up. "Do you mean why is everybody doing it, or why am I?"

I couldn't say anything.

"Oh Dot, Dot, Baby, come here a minute, will you?" he called.

Dot came into the room and stood before us, her hands nervously twisting a handkerchief as she cast shy glances at me from beneath her lashes.

For the first time I noticed that she wore a maternity dress.

"Well, I'll be damned. I didn't notice when I came in— I didn't know. You're going to have a baby! And you look— you look—you look—" Then I noticed her face. I had started to rise. Crow pulled me down.

He got up and went over to her, embracing her and kissing her forehead, eyes, nose and chin. A world of love was in the look which he bestowed upon her emaciated face, and in the tenderness of his voice.

"Love me, Baby?" he whispered.

She nodded.

"Okay, pretty, you can go back to whatever you was doin'. I just wanted to show this lame I could hit the right spot."

Turning her around, he patted her on the behind.

Dot went out slowly, smiling a little over her shoulder.

Crow slumped listlessly to the sofa again.

"Why hell, man," I exclaimed, "that's no reason to cripple yourself with junk! So she's gonna have a—"

"She's gonna have one great big pain," Crow whispered harshly. "You saw her face. She's gonna have one big pain, and it's gonna be de last feeling she will know in life. Dot's got a tumor in her uterus, Guy. She'll be dead before de end of de year."

I stared at him unbelievingly.

He went on: "She thinks she's going to have a baby. De doc says it's best to leave it that way. At least she's happy. I love her madly, but I ain't God and I can't remove de growth. Nobody can. All I can do is pump her full of junk to keep down de pain, and if it's good enough for her it's good enough for me. So I get high and forget. Yeah, me and a few thousand other people."

We sat for a while in silence. Crow was shaking like a leaf. Looking at him caused my every heartbeat to become a sob of sorrow.

294

Slowly I got up from the sofa and headed out the door.

"Later, little man," I called back over my shoulder. "Stick with it."

I didn't hear him answer as I closed the door and walked down the stairs.

Chapter **28**

Summer's hot breath enveloped the August night as Dipper, Sandy, Bird, Harold, Earl and Crow of the old Gaylord bunch piled into my car. A few of them even wore the old club jackets. It was kind of like old times.

"To the city!" I shouted, starting up the motor.

"Well, hell, we can't go with a square head," Earl protested. "All right you clowns, dig down and let's see what kinda firewater we can raise."

"You in on this Deacon?" Crow asked.

I shook my head.

"Hey, there's a juice joint over there," Earl said. "Pull in, Guy, and let us cop righteous on the grog."

I pulled in.

Earl, Dipper and Bird got out and went in. Minutes later, Dipper and Bird hurried out carrying a case of wine between them.

"Open the door, goddammit, before that pig-eyed bastard spots us," Dipper said frantically.

They tossed the case into the laps of the boys in the back and jumped in.

"Jesus H. Christ!" Sandy shouted. "How in hell did you guys cop that? What are they runnin' in there, a rummage sale on grapes?"

"We just swiped the damn stuff while Earl kept the greasy pig busy. Jeezus! You should'a seen the dumbhead climbing around on the ladder looking for some Youassholia wine."

"For what?" Harold asked.

"You-ass-hole-ia," Dipper explained, breaking the name into its true syllables.

We howled.

Earl came sauntering out of the gin mill, his face full of wrathful indignation, while the owner of the store stood in the doorway, scratching his head. Earl got in the car and I rocketed away. Everyone was silent.

"What d'ya think of that, that assolia calls himself runnin' a gin mill and he ain't got no Youassholia wine in stock!" Earl said finally.

We roared.

Bottles were opened, and soon you could hear the gurgling of wine being poured down a half-dozen throats.

"God, how I hate de stuff," Crow said, smacking his lips.

"Say, man," Sandy shouted, "all we need now is some dim lights, a hot babe, soft music and a toothpick to really be into something." Then he leaned over the seat and said to me: "Say, Mr. Black Jeezus, will you kindly ease yo' little finger in yo' pocket and pull out a cute li'l ole chocolate gal with nipples on her tits as red as a plum and skin on her belly tight as a drum?"

"Yeah, and a behind shaped like the trunk of a Cadillac," Dipper added.

"And with lips as soft as medicated cotton," Earl supplied.

"With hair as soft as satin and as long as a horse's mane and a face like Cleopatra's," Harold put in.

"And a stroll that would freeze hell," Crow said.

"And with legs and thighs like the broad Solomon speaks of in the Bible."

"And a voice like The Lady," I said.

"What about the money?" somebody asked.

"Well, naturally she's gonna be rich as Blue Valley Butter."

"So now we've got the perfect broad. Who's first on the train?"

297

"I am!" Sandy shouted. "I'm the one who started buildin' her."

"Aw hell naw, Sandy, you horny bastard," Bird contested. "You're pullin' the caboose on this trip."

"The hell you preach, man," Sandy said. "Makin' this broad was my idea, so if anybody is goin' to cop righteous on the cherry action, it's gonna be me. Move back."

There was silence for a moment, then Sandy cried: "Aw, hell now."

"What's wrong man?" Earl asked. "Ain't you gonna cop?"

"How in the hell can I? You dirty rats forgot to hang a thing on her. Jesus H. Christ! And you're supposed to be my buddies!"

In a few minutes the gang began to sing loudly of enjoying themselves. It was later than they thought. Somehow, I got caught up in the gay yet melancholy mood. "Hey, you marks, pass me a bottle of that joy juice," I said.

Crow tore the seal from a bottle and handed it to me.

"Here's to us, Crow," I said, raising the bottle.

"To our lost youth, whatever that is," Crow said. "And to our loves, whoever they are; to heaven, whatever that is, and to hell, whose funky smell we now sniff!"

I began feeling drunk without having begun to drink.

"To sorrow, which is always, and the future which we now see about us," I cried, waving the bottle in a gesture which included the filthy streets and dilapidated buildings, the century of debris moving sluggishly into the gutter.

"De future which we see around us," Crow repeated, "and to de goddamned moment in which we recognize it."

"And for the wine which will enliven us and bring cheer, and make us forget we are what we are!" I cried.

We turned the bottles up. The sweet liquid flowing down my throat almost made me retch. When we lowered them, over half the contents in each was gone.

"Hey! Why don't we run another raid on them lames over in Englewood?" Dipper yelled from the back seat.

"The Vagabonds? Man, we barely got out of that last one alive," Bird said.

"You guys are always aching for a fight," I said.

"Hah, look who's talkin'," Dipper said. "If you hadn't been about to lay that lame's broad in the basement while we was all havin' a party, we wouldn't have had to fight our way out of th' house."

"She snapped the whip, I was just gonna make the trip," I said.

"And that's when all hell broke loose," Earl recalled.

"Yeah, but we really lammed de loons, didn't we?" Crow joined in.

"Uh-huh," Earl said, "and remember the one we found wandering off the reservation right after the fight? I bet he'll never forget us!"

Everybody laughed, remembering that after roughing him up a little, we had stripped the Vagabond club member of all his clothes, tied him up and left him buck naked on a door-step, then rang the bell and ran.

"Man, I can still hear the sirens and feel the cops breathin' down our neck that time," Bird said.

The tires on the old sedan screeched as I made a too-fast turn around a corner, remembering how we had to race to get away from the police after our brawl.

"Hey, pull over here a minute, Deacon," Crow said suddenly, "I wanna get some flowers for Dot."

I pulled up in front of Hollis' Florist. Crow got out, lurched over to the store with the closed sign on the door. I thought of the night Old Man Hollis had refused to open up to let me buy a birthday present for Mom.

Wrapping a handkerchief around his hand, Crow punched out a small pane in the door of the little florist shop, then reached in and opened the door from the inside. After a few minutes, he stumbled back to the car, carrying two colorfully decorated pots of flowers.

"Jeez, ain't they pretty, though," Dipper said, getting out of the car to examine the flower pots. "Any more in there?"

"Holy pink fart, what a dumb question!" Sandy said disgustedly. "What do you think greenhouses are made for?" Sandy got out of the car, too.

"Well, I guess I'll cop some, too," Dipper said.

I thought of Kay and decided that flowers were a pretty good idea. I got out of the car and ran into the shop. After a few moments, my eyes fell on a beautiful, long-stemmed yellow flower standing tall and majestic in the ray of moonlight. I extended my hand for the pot; it disappeared from my sight. Sandy had plucked it from its perch.

"Here's just the baby for my baby," he said, admiring the flower.

"The hell you preach, pops. I saw that one first," I told him, reaching for the plant.

"Aw, hell naw, Guy, first come, first served," he said, holding it out of my reach.

I stared at the flower. It seemed to glow with the same radiance as Kay's skin had the Sunday when she'd lain naked in my arms. I had to have it.

"Give me the bloody flower, pops," I said, stepping closer to Sandy.

He moved back. I grabbed for the plant and Sandy tried to ward me off. We grappled, falling to the soft ground of the greenhouse in the back of the shop. The perfume of many flowers filled my nostrils as we struggled among the hotbeds.

After a minute, Sandy yelled: "Now you've done it! You frantic bastard! You've ruined the damned thing!"

Panting and dizzy, I lay on top of him, staring at the crushed flower. I reached for it and he handed it to me.

300

I climbed to my feet, still looking at the crushed flower in my hands. Tears sprung to my eyes. I thought of the flower as it had stood a moment before, radiant, beautiful, whole.

"You ruined it," Sandy repeated, getting to his feet.

"Yeah, I ruined it," I said, dropping the broken plant, pot and all. I felt sick at the stomach.

"Hey, man, I've always wondered how a bull in a china shop felt, now I know," one of the gang hollered. "Waaahooo!" The shout was followed by the sound of splintering glass.

I stumbled blindly for the door, stopping outside to wipe the tears from my eyes.

"Hey, man," Crow called, "tell de lames to hurry up. I hear sirens."

I heard them, too. I turned back in the doorway and shouted over the crash of glass and pottery: "Hey! The bulladeens! Cop and blow!"

"Hey look! I'm a bull! A bull!"

"I wonder if this joint's got any money in it."

"Naw, I looked."

"Well, what the hell we doin' in here?"

"Bulladeens!" I shouted again as I grabbed two plants from near the door and ran out.

As the boys piled into the car, I turned and tossed one of the pots through the plate glass window of Hollis' Florist.

"Now what de hell was that for?" Crow asked.

"For old times' sake," I said simply.

Crow thought for a moment, then realized what I had been thinking. "Buddy, you got a long memory," he said.

I started up the motor.

"Hold it!" Bird shouted. "Sandy ain't here! Hold it!"

The sirens were getting louder and louder.

I turned and looked at the shop. Sandy came out, loaded down with flowers. Bird opened the door and pulled him in just as a squad car careened around the corner.

"Pull him in, for crapsake, pull him in!" I shouted, gunning the car forward.

The squad car shot past us, then came to a screeching halt. Three shots exploded the night as I turned north on Racine. Shifting gears rapidly, I held the accelerator down to the floor. The old car roared into high speed.

"Here they come, momma," Crow warned.

I looked into the rear view mirror. Headlights shone some four blocks back. I returned my concentration to the street ahead.

"Buddy, buddy!" Sandy said. "I sure wish I had a thirty-thirty rifle. I'd bang! Bang! And out would go the front tires."

"Yeah, everything would be over but the shooting—for you, not the police," Bird sneered.

"Hey, you scared of the police?" Sandy demanded.

I turned east after a few minutes and then, after a block or so, south into an alley, scattering rats, dogs, and cats, who had been feasting in happy comradeship. One huge gray rat stood in the middle of the alley, his teeth bared like a mad dog at bay, his eyes glinting defiantly. I cut the wheel a fraction and the car jarred slightly as it ran over him.

"De bastard screamed like a baby," Crow said.

"Maybe he is," I told him.

I turned east again and slowed down, confident that I'd lost the pursuing squad car.

"Do you believe in carnation?" Sandy asked.

"Oh, Connie's aunt! The word is reincarnation," Dipper said. "Jeezus! For a high school student, you're dumber than stupid!"

"Hey, screw you, Dip. Carnation or reincarnation, what's the difference? I asked him if he believed in it. Do you, Guy?"

"The flower once bloomed, forever dies," I said, remembering the plant in the florist shop.

"Oh, buddy, this ain't no time to be gettin' deep," Sandy

protested. "What a ball we had, huh? This is one day that didn't bore me stiff."

"Hey stop in front of de house, Deacon," Crow said to me as I neared Dot's house. "I got to go in with these flowers."

I stopped at the house and Crow got out and walked around to my side of the car.

"Well, momma, when will I see you again?" he asked.

"Why don't we take a trek to the rink next week?" I said.

"Crazy," he said.

I looked at him for a long moment. "Just remember to cool it," I said finally. "That way it won't be too hard to kick, cop?"

He nodded. "Later," he said.

"Later," I replied, as he walked away. I drove off.

"What ain't gonna be too hard to kick?" Earl asked.

"Your butt if you don't stop being so nosey," I said, stopping for the light at State Street. The newspaper stand on the corner there caught my eye. It was the same one I had taken the half-dollar from the night the cops Tony and Pat took me for the three hundred. I hopped out of the car, ran over and dropped four quarters on the counter in front of the blind man, then ran back to the car.

Day was breaking when I parked at 111th and Throop.

"So now what do we do?" Earl asked.

"So now we go home, go to bed, get up, go to the stick hall or Gale's Drug Store—" Bird said.

"Well, for the love of Pete," Sandy cried, cutting into the monotonous recitation. "Will you shut your trap? Ain't it enough to have to live in this—this dull dunghill, without havin' you give us a blow-by-blow description? Jeezus!"

"Damn! I forgot to cop the number!" Harold said suddenly.

"What number?" Earl asked.

"The number of the broad I took to the slaughter floor this afternoon."

"Say, you are the horniest cat I ever saw," Dipper said.

"So, you should talk," Harold said. "Besides, what else is there to do other than look for lays? Go to the stick hall or to—"

"Now there *you* go!" Sandy yelled, exasperated. "Christy, let me outta here before these marks run me crazy." Gathering up his looted plants, he stumbled out of the car and down the street, mumbling: "Go to the stick hall or Gale's—"

"Well, what the hell's the matter with him?" Harold asked in offended surprise. "I just said—"

"Yeah, yeah. We know what you said," Dipper cut him off. Then, holding an empty wine bottle up to his eye and examining all corners for a possibly missed drop, he muttered: "Damn! It's all gone." He tossed the bottle out of the window into the street. The crash made us all jump, although we had each followed his movements.

"Jeezus, Dip, will you stop breakin' things? It gets on my nerves. Besides it ain't constructive."

"Well, I'd better cut," Bird said, climbing out of the car. "Th' old folks are gonna want me to go to church. Damn!"

"Yeah, me too," Harold said. "If my old man finds out what time I come in tonight, he'll get so hot he'll roast his weenie."

"Guess we might as well cut," Dipper added.

Slowly, the gang unloaded from the car. Earl stood swaying in the street, his hands stuffed deep into his pockets, his shoulders slumped in drunken dejection. "Go? Go?" he asked bewilderedly.

I started easing the car away.

"Yeah, yeah," Earl said in a thick drawl. "Go to th' stick hall, go to th' drug store, go to a movie, go home. Hell! Let's go back to Englewood and start a fight!"

I drove home, got out, went in and stripped and took a shower. Then I set the alarm clock for 8:30, and crawled between the cool sheets, enjoying their smooth touch on my naked body.

The picture on the buffet in the dining room seemed to stare mockingly at me through the bedroom door.

"Go to the stick hall, go to Gale's, go to a movie, go home . . . Hell, let's go start a fight!"

The smoothness of the covering sheet became oppressive. I fought it.

Hurry time . . . Hurry time . . . Hurry time.

Chapter 29

The doorbell rang. "That must be Kay," Mom said, "she called again today. Guy, are you avoiding her? She's a lovely girl and seems so fond of you. Though, Agnes says her father doesn't think you're good for her. I don't much blame him. You spend too much time at that pool room for my liking. All hours of the day and night," she muttered as she wheeled her chair to the front door.

I was glad she didn't bother to wait for an answer. I was avoiding Kay, and if she was coming to the house, let her visit with Mom. I knew that would be her excuse, anyhow. Damn Kay and her damnation preachin' papa anyhow. Damn women, as a matter of fact, I thought Shelley had started acting like she owned me, head, tail and hoof! Hell, no broad could buy me with a couple of sport shirts and some slacks. I didn't like sports clothes anyhow, and Shelley knew it, but as soon as a chick thinks she's got an in, she starts making you over into the image of what she thinks you should be. Later for that off-beat jazz!

I still wasn't too sure that Shelley had put down the broads, although she swore they just worked there. I wondered if she was having her cake and cookies, too.

Damn! Damn! Damn! I pulled my drum from under the bed, and beat out some of my Damns on the taut drumhead. Love was a bitch. Did I love anybody, even Mom? Hell, I laughed out loud. Guy Morgan Jr., you don't know what love is!

I got up off the bed and went into the front room where Kay sat in earnest conversation with Mom.

"Oh, Clucky, I was just going to call you," Mom said, "but

306

seeing as how you're here, I don't have to." She wheeled around and headed for the kitchen. "I'm just going to fix Kay a cool drink and a piece of my pound cake."

With Mom out of the room, the silence seemed strained. Finally, I raised my head and looked at Kay. Since the night when I got caught with all the questions, I had stayed away from her.

She looked prettier than ever, there was a softness about her that I had not noticed before. A little absence ain't no bad deal, I thought. I struck the drum with a couple of desultory whacks, and then put it down on the floor. "Well, pretty, what you been into?" I asked.

"Guy, I've been trying to see you—Guy?"

"Well, you're seeing me now, so what's on your little . . ."

"Oh, Guy, who hurt you, and why do you have to hurt other people so?"

"Do I look hurt to you, pretty?" I was unable to keep the peevishness out of my voice.

"Maybe not," she said apologetically, coming over to sit on the couch beside me. I picked up the drum, and hammered my fist against its bald head. I stared at the ceiling as the sound seemingly left the pores of my body and faded into the walls of the room.

"Guy, do you remember the first afternoon, here on the couch?"

"Yeah."

She sighed, and hugged her elbows tightly, as if clinging to some rapture.

"So why the winded sighs and fond embraces?" I asked.

"You'll probably think I'm foolish," she said, "but when you struck that drum, I had the strangest sensation of being able to soar with the flight of sound. Isn't that funny?"

There was a tiny catch of self-consciousness in her laugh.

"Well, if you want to bust a gut, I'll gladly oblige," I said, posing a fist over the drum.

307

Her smile faded. "Well, seeing as how you won't let me be romantic, tell me what you've been up to since we were together last." Her hands were folded primly in her lap like a little girl at Sunday school.

"Well, teacher, I've kept myself physically fit, mentally awake, and morally straight," I replied sarcastically.

"Oh, Guy, please don't," she said, turning her face from me.

I said nothing.

"Guy, I've got to talk to you, please tell me what's wrong," she pleaded.

I went over to the record player and put on a side.

"Guy, what has happened to our love?" she whispered.

The record played: *"Gone with the wind, just like a leaf that has blown away . . ."*

I stared into space not daring to meet her eyes.

She got slowly to her feet.

"The message is very crude, Guy, but I got it."

With a sob, she ran to the front door, the full skirt she was wearing swirled about her knees.

I sat there like a stone man. Then suddenly, I lunged to the door, stumbling over the drum and feeling the delicate wood splinter beneath my weight.

Opening the door, I stared down the street for Kay.

"Kay . . . Kay," I whispered.

"Love burned brightly then became . . ." the record played on.

A breeze ran through my fingers as they grasped the emptiness. Turning and going back into the house, I stepped over the remains of the drum, and reached for my jacket and hat on the chair.

"Gone with the wind." The record came to an end. I shut the front door behind me, as I heard Mom call:

"Guy? Kay?"

I didn't answer.

Chapter **30**

I walked out into the mid-day sun and across the street to the novelty shop. Crow's sister, Maxine, was behind the counter.

"Well," she said frostily, "what ill-wind blew you in?"

"Hey, Max," I called, trying to feel cheerful about seeing Muffet again in a couple of hours. "I know you haven't any live flowers—unless you want to jump into a pot—but let me have some of those imitation ones you've got. They're soft and velvety and sorta pretty."

"What kind do you want?" she asked.

"I don't know, Max, any kind. They're for your buddy, Marion. You know she had to come home to mind the store on account of Mr. Gale's illness. I haven't had a chance to see her yet, but I talked to her on the phone." I took the money from my pants pocket to pay Maxine and reflected on the beautiful flower that had stood so majestically in the moonlight at the florist's shop. I thought briefly of Kay.

"Is that all?" Max had wrapped up the artificial flowers.

"You still angry with me about what happened in the park, Max?" I asked, looking at her sullen face.

"You underestimate my feelings about you, Guy Morgan," she answered coldly. "I hate you . . . you vicious, rotten . . . here take your cheap, phony flowers. They're just like you, cheap and phony."

"Well, to each his own," I said wearily. "I'm hated by many, which is all right with me, because I have quite a few hates myself. Hate is part of the atmosphere around here—hate and brutality. I see it every day; see it, hear it, smell it,

309

breathe it in with every breath, Max. It seeps into my pores. I guess it's all part of growing up, because I don't remember being bothered by it when I was little. You know, your brother asked me a couple of nights ago if I had the feeling I had grown up too fast. Maybe he—"

"Where did you see Crow?" Maxine interrupted quickly, reaching out to grip my arm. "Oh, Guy, please tell me where he is. We've been worried sick. I know we should have done something when he was in jail. But right then, it seemed the best place for him. Oh Guy, you've got to tell me where he is."

I thought for a moment, then I told her: "He's okay, Max. I can't tell you where he is, but I tell you what, I'll have him home for good before Thanksgiving. How will that be for having something to be thankful for?"

Maxine nodded wordlessly, and I could see tears mounting in her eyes.

I took my change and flowers and started toward the door. "Guy?"

I turned. "Yes, Max?"

"I love my brother, Guy. Thanks. I—I—"

"Forget it, Max. Crow's my best friend. I'd die for him."

Chapter **31**

The pale dusk of evening was settling over the early night sounds of Black Babylon as I cursed the lazy battery in the old sedan.

"Damn, little man, I guess she's dead. We're gonna have to hoof it to the Swanksters," I told Crow.

"Yeah, well let's don't forget de juice, huh, momma," he said, throwing his skates over his shoulder and slipping one of the two fifths of wine that I had bought into his hip pocket under his sweater.

I did the same thing with the second bottle, as we got out and started walking up the street. That dead battery was going to make my scheme a little tougher. As I had first planned it, it would be a fairly simple matter to get Crow loaded at the Swankster's Roller Rink and then, instead of driving him back to Dot's house, deliver him home to Maxine and the folks. He would never stay, of course, not with Dot in her condition, but at least he might be able to feel that he had ties beyond her, something to keep his life from seeming so miserably hopeless. It would help Max and the old folks for him to come back in time for the holidays. I'd work on him.

"How did you happen to get tickets to this place, Guy?" Crow wanted to know as we headed for the Swanksters. "I've never even heard of de joint."

"Where is it?" he continued, as we headed for the boundary line, the invisible but nonetheless real barrier that separated the Negro from the white community.

"It's new," I explained, ignoring his previous question.

"Just opened up a couple of months ago, I hear. Dipper got his hands on four tickets and gave me a couple. He had a date with a new broad so he went on ahead."

"That Dipper is one straight ofay," Crow said.

"Yeah," I said, thinking of the lone white boy we called friend.

"Man, it's hot walkin'," Crow said when we had gone about four blocks. He paused and took a long swig from his wine bottle.

Good, little man, I thought, glad to see him in a drinking mood, *you're doin' fine.*

We alternately walked and drank the rest of the way to the Swanksters, with me just taking small sips to encourage Crow. By the time we reached the lobby of the rink, Crow was feeling no pain.

As we approached the pimply-faced ticket-taker, he stared at us momentarily, then looked at our tickets before raising his blue eyes back to mine.

"Dig, man—I mean," he started apologetically, "like I hope you cats don't take offense. I mean, I just work here. But the fact is, man—I mean, I dig you cats the most and all that. Yeah, you may have seen me dancin' at the Vipers—"

I looked at Crow. He was staring at the white boy with open-mouthed wonder. A hush had settled over the crowded lobby, and a sense of shame engulfed me as I felt the play of many eyes upon us. I returned my gaze to the white boy. He was still talking:

"It's not me, baby, you dig? It's just—"

"Why all the gab, dad?" I interrupted, feeling a slow anger building up within me.

"Just this, man! I can't let you cats in, you dig?" he said.

I snatched the tickets. "Yeah, man, I dig you the most, and that's sayin' the least," I said with suppressed fury. "Come on, Crow, let's dust this democratic den of albinos."

"Ah, hell, Guy, why?" Crow protested. "De tickets was

312

bought on de square. This is a public place and I wanna skate, man."

Grabbing him by the elbow, I steered him back through the lobby, running a gauntlet of resentful stares.

As we started to cross the alley which led to the entrance of the rink's parking lot, a long blue auto pulled into it and stopped, blocking the sidewalk.

"Oh, honey, look at that funny-looking, runty little nigger!" the blonde girl inside the car exclaimed, pointing a red-painted finger at Crow. She wore more paint than a Japanese geisha girl.

I grabbed Crow as he lunged furiously at the car, yanking open the door. Hands grabbed the girl as she started to tumble out.

I fought to hold the struggling Crow.

"Lemme go, Guy," he yelled furiously. "Lemme lam de pig! No bloody slut's gonna call me no—no—no—"

"For crap's sake, cool it, Crow. We're off the reservation, man!" I shouted, shaking him.

Another car pulled up behind the first. Boys—six, seven, maybe eight—scrambled from it, hollering Rebel cries. The other three boys in the first car got out, too. They all formed a circle around Crow and me.

I released Crow. He stared around with drunken belligerence. The boy who'd been driving the first car swaggered to within a foot of Crow. A cigarette drooped from the corner of his mouth and his eyes were half-closed as he gazed insolently down at him.

"Say, spade, what was you intending to do to my broad? I know you didn't mean to put your black paws on her." The malice in his voice caused me to reach towards my belt.

"Whoa, shine," one of the fellows wearing a Rebel's jacket said, stepping up and snatching the belt from around my waist. "That action will only get you to the grave yard a little earlier."

313

His movement toward me left a fairly large hole in the formerly tight circle. As he turned, the girl cried out, "Slap that little black snot, don't talk to him."

I reached up and grabbed my hat, shouting, "Cop and blow, Crow!" Shouldering the boys aside and lunging through the open hole with Crow close on my heels, I ran. As we raced down the street, we could hear the girl screaming: "Get the nigger! Get the nigger, Jake, don't let him get away!"

"Ah hell, I came to skate, not to play in mud—"

After a couple of blocks of hard running I stopped for a breather, satisfied that there was no pursuit. I stepped into a doorway and called Crow as he came charging by. Sliding to a stop, he came back to where I was standing.

"Of all de damned dirty luck," he said finally.

"What do you mean?" I asked.

"We're black."

"Yeah," I said, passing him the wine bottle. "Well, drink up, Crow, and don't worry about it. Somebody had to be dark. *Look not upon me, because I am black, because the sun hath looked upon me: My mother's children were angry with me: . . .*" I quoted in angry disgust, then took a long drink of the sweet wine to clear the bitterness from my mouth.

"Yeah, they were angry, all right," he said, snatching the bottle from my hand to take a drink. "Come on, let's make it to the stick hall, there should be some tricks there by now. Buddy! If I ever meet that horse-faced ticket-taker at de Vipers, his head belongs to me," Crow said.

"Oh, he seems like people, Crow. The cat was only doing his duty."

"Yeah," he said, "but de good has got to die with de bad. His job! To hell with his job. De cat on de gate at de Vipers does his job, too, but he don't bar nobody. I don't understand."

"Well, neither do I, but life is a bitch. Here, have another drink."

As Crow reached for the bottle he hesitated, then shouted, "My skates! They're gone!"

I could feel the hurt and anguish in his tones. I knew the great attachment he had for the skates.

"Well, I told you to cop and blow, man, why didn't you hold on to the damn things?"

"Yeah, I know, but what am I gonna do," he asked wretchedly, "go to the cops?"

"For what?" I asked. "Your best bet is to chalk it up to experience."

"Yeah, but if I ever get my hands on one of those hunky bastards, I'm gonna—" He let the threat trail off ominously.

Tilting the bottle, he drank half of what was left. Noticing that he could hardly stand up, I took his arm and led him into a nearby hallway.

We sat on the steps, Crow with his head hanging between his legs and his narrow shoulders dropped in drunken dejection. He muttered, "My skates, damn." Then, in a surprisingly sober voice, "Guy, have you seen my family lately?"

The question and the loneliness in his voice were the last things I'd expected.

Hiding my surprise, I said, "Yeah, momma, I saw Maxine. I promised to get her a Thanksgiving present, in fact."

I nodded at the bottle. "Go ahead, man, knock yourself out."

"Hey, baby, I wonder how I'm gonna make it after Dot's gone? I mean, until summer when I go with you to this Phoenix place. You know, watching de person you love die is worse than dying yourself. In fact, I wish it was me."

"Aw, Crow, that's foolish."

"Naw, that's love."

"Love, hell—that's weakness."

"So all of a sudden you're a superman. What about you and your mama?"

"I've grown up. That's over."

Not wanting to pursue his line of conversation further, I grabbed him by the arm and got to my feet. "Come on, man, those tricks won't wait all night," I said.

As we crossed the railroad tracks, he said, "Guy, you know I'm trying to kick my habits. That's why I been drinking so much lately. I figure after Dot's gone I might go back. Back home, I mean."

Just then a car came speeding by. One of its satin-jacketed occupants shouted: "Hey black boy, here's one of your skates!"

The skate fell at our feet. Crow picked it up with tears in his eyes. The leather shoe was slashed to ribbons.

"Oh de bastards, I'll get even," he said, as we watched the receding tail lights. Screeching tires caused me to turn around quickly. The blue auto from the rink was coming up fast. Snatching the almost empty bottle from Crow's pocket, I threw it as it came even with me. The force shattered one of the car windows. Brakes locked, tires burned as the car skidded to a stop.

"Crow," I said, running for the car, surging with rage.

As I neared the car, heavily mascaraed eyes stared through the shattered window.

As I got within a few feet of it, the car pulled away with rapid acceleration.

I stood trembling as the tail lights disappeared into the night. Crow caught up with me and we continued to walk down the street. As we were getting ready to cross Bishop Street, the blue auto pulled up again.

A sense of danger gripped me. I made a desperate grab for Crow as he lunged toward the curb. His body slammed back against me, knocking me down. A thunderous sound was ringing in my ears. I tried to get up. Crow lay sprawled across my leg. I shoved his shoulder roughly.

"Hey, man, get the hell off my leg!"

316

Crow raised his head, a painful smile split his dark face: "I—I can't, momma, the dirty bastards shot me."

I sat up quickly, turning him over in my arms. His hands gripped his stomach, blood gushed from between his fingers, coloring his white turtle-neck sweater crimson.

I started to lift him.

"Hold it, momma," he croaked in pain. "Of all *the*—frigging luck. Tell Dot, Max, *the—the* old folks—I—I—"

His head slumped to my chest, I raised it. Blood trickled from the corner of his mouth.

"The dirty, foul-fighting bastards—*the—the*—momma, momma—*th—the*—Ha!" He laughed. "*The—the*—"

He sighed; his body shuddered and then was still.

I knew that he was dead.

Too horrified to speak or move, I sat and clutched him to me tightly.

Staring at the hole in his stomach which the fall of his lifeless hands had exposed, I realized he said "the" instead of "de" for the first time since I had known him. He wouldn't say "de" or "the" any more. Yeah, the "de" had been shot out of Crow. One "boom!" and the "de's" had begun to flow; a whole lifetime of "de's" flowing—going, going, gone. Dead! Killed!

Thou shalt not kill, son . . .

Never let a blow from a white man go . . .

I rocked back and forth with Crow's head in my lap as the voices rang in my brain.

Finally, there was a louder voice, saying: "All right, I said, turn him loose; we'll take care of him now."

I looked up in the direction of the voice. White hands extended toward me; I leaned away from their touch, clutching Crow's body close to me. I thought of my promise to Maxine. He'd be home way before the Thanksgiving holiday.

"Let go, boy, we'll take care of him," the voice repeated.

"Keep your hands off him!" I screamed, leaping to my feet as the white hands touched Crow.

Blue eyes opened wide with surprise. I jabbed my fists at them with all my might and felt my knuckles smack against flesh. The eyes disappeared.

White faces began to pop up around me. I lashed out at them again and again, trying to empty myself of all the frustration which I'd ever been made to feel. Hands tried to hold me. I bit at them.

The street lights reflected on a silver star. A woman screamed as I staggered from a blow to the back of my head. I reached out blindly for support and felt cloth.

"Guy, Guy, for God's sake! Stop it before they kill you!"

Another blow to the head knocked me to my knees. I felt myself sinking into oblivion.

"No, officer! He doesn't know what he's doing!" the woman's voice shouted again.

Was that Luzon?

"Luzon! Don't let Mom know!" I yelled as a third blow fell. Blackness covered me.

Chapter **32**

Clenching my teeth against the pain I sat up—on an oaken bench. Jail.

I remembered light reflected from a silver star, Luzon's shout, reaching white hands, blue eyes and an authoritative voice. Cops. Then nothing—until now, when I came to, fingering three lumps on the back of my head. Three lumps and a sticky half-dried gash. Lucky not to be in the County Hospital. Or the morgue. *That's the way the ball bounces when you fight the cops—Christ's Only People*, I told myself.

The dim, foul-smelling cell was packed with men. I saw several colors, a variety of shapes and sizes and various types of dress. Two alley-grimed cronies sat cross-legged, face to face; de-lousing each other Eskimo style. Their heated argument on petty politics made them seemingly oblivious to the kneeing and jostling they received from the half-dozen men frantically pacing the floor, puffing furiously on butts and making wild impatient gestures with their tobacco-stained hands as they talked loudly in nervous spasms.

Another group in one corner had a crap game going full tilt.

Near the game, three silk-shirted, reefer-high Mexican gandy dancers sprawled, strumming imaginary guitars and singing.

Two queens held court in the darkest corner.

I moved my cramped legs and kicked someone. I looked down into the sick gray face of a white teen-ager who had crawled halfway under the bench. One look and I knew: a kid with a gang of monkeys on his back—complete with slobbering mouth, twitching legs, clawing hands and sounds that only a real sick junkie makes.

Something about his staring eyes reminded me of Crow, and suddenly I was sick myself. I jumped up and bulled my way through to the filthy toilet bowl and retched and heaved and spit, until someone hollered: "Hey! For craps sake, Jack, watch your juice!"

I turned toward the voice. There was Puff on one knee with the dice in his open palm.

"What's to it," he said.

His hot tubercular breath brought the sickness welling up in my throat. "They're handing out free bug-cures at the County Hospital," I answered.

Turning away, my eyes met those of the sick junkie's and locked hypnotically.

"I saw the best minds of my generation destroyed by madness," Puff quoted in a sarcastic whisper. "Angel-headed hipsters dragging themselves through the Negro streets at dawn, looking for an angry fix." He ended the quote by spitting in the white teen's face.

I leaped at Puff and grabbed his lacy shirt front.

A gruff voice interrupted the general confusion: "Hey you there, space man—come here!"

Two burly plainclothesmen, one tall, the other short, stood in front of the cell. The latter crooked a commanding finger at the junkie. "Goddammit, Gabriel, you hear me talking to you. Cut the crap and come over here!"

The boy struggled to his feet, made wobbly steps toward the cops and sank to the floor, panting. After a moment, the short cop took a blackjack from his hip pocket and rapped the bars viciously.

"Come 'ere, you hop-brained bastard!"

The kid started to crawl slowly toward the cop. I took a step in his direction.

"When in Rome—you damn fool," hissed Puff.

320

I sat down.

Finally, the junkie and his monkey reached the front of the cell; then lay full length, clutching the bars, trying vainly to rise. The short cop squatted and held a cellophane bag in front of the kid's bleary, watering eyes. The kid froze at the sight of the dope.

"What d'ya say?—You give us your connect, we give you wings."

He moved the bag and the eyes followed.

"Come on, space man, we ain't got all day."

A tremor shook the boy and he uttered a nameless sound.

"Well, be quick about it. You're gettin' a break. Are you too stupid to know it?"

"To hell with him," said the tall cop. "Let's get out of here. Let him rot!"

The pair turned and started briskly away.

"Wait! I'll do it! Come back! It's Mike! Mike Rapoli! He's my connect."

The cops stopped. Giving a contemptuous laugh, the short one came back and opened the cell door.

With the bag of dope luring him on, the kid found strength to get to his feet. After a quick, apologetic look at the other prisoners, he lurched into the corridor after the detective, who strode rapidly to the adjoining office door. There the cop stopped, turned and saw the boy sagging against the wall. With a mock sympathetic look, a snap of his fingers, and a "Here, puppy" gesture, the short cop coaxed the sick boy into the office. The tall one locked the cell door and joined them.

"And that's the way the famed Chicago stool pigeon is made and maintained," Puff sneered.

"All right, Ladies and Genamuns, Smokey is here," announced a cigar-smoking, pudgy, soot-black Negro in white coveralls. He stood in front of the cell and went through his spiel to the inmates:

"Yassuh, I'se got everythin' a genamun and Miss genamun

in the slams could desire—'cept maybe de doah keys. But don't worry 'bout dat, no, siree—'cause I got a lawyer an' a bondsman who can take care of dat—Haw! Haw! Haw!" he shouted and laughed through thick, purple, Ubangi-like lips. His snow-white teeth were gold-capped.

"Hey Smokey, ya got any gum?"

"How much for cigarettes?"

"Got change for a ten, Jack?"

"How much is ya candy?"

The men stampeded to the bars and jockeyed for position to spend the bills they waved over their heads.

Smokey took his time.

"Candy twenty cents a bar."

"Gum twenty-five cents."

"Cigarettes fifty cents."

"Heah ya go, pops, seven dollars and fifty cents change from ten. Twenty-five cents on the dollar cost of changing. Next! Step right up, folkses—ol' Smokey'll change anything from a dirty shirt to a married woman's name. Haw! Haw!"

He harvested the field of green, made change, and dispensed items from his tin pail.

One of the old, lice-picked buddies broke out in rage: "Fifty cents for this," he shrieked, staring at a pack of cigarettes of an obscure brand.

He pushed his way back to the dice game. "Why, these bastards are thieves like us!" he complained bitterly.

"We should learn to be thieves like them," Puff rasped, climbing onto the bench where I stood gazing out the window.

It was raining. In silence, we viewed the drenched city. After a while I heard Puff's voice:

"Tame and ghastly coffins display their shame-faced grays and reds before the massive vividness of morning. From the base of these large coffins, men and women walk, like briskly serviced automata. Some repentant toy-maker has given them a cunning pretense of life."

322

"What's that?" I asked.

"Bodenheim. *North Clark St. Chgo,* by Maxwell Bodenheim."

We were silent again. Thunder rumbled and lightning slashed at the dark sky.

"What did they crack you for," Puff whispered.

I told him of the events of the night and asked what his beef was.

"I got snowed to the gills and sought a night's lodging at the Rosewood Y," he said bitterly, and with a string of vile curses, he went on: "What a goddamned town—to think that I once wanted to add to her laurels, to win for her, give her loving cups and plaques!"

He pointed a trembling finger at State Street: "Look down there. When I took the title from Jerry Fields, I rode down that street in the Mayor's limousine. Sidewalks were crowded and everyone was cheering. Miss Windy looked beautiful then, all hung with bunting and colored lights—looking like Christmas and Valentine's Day at the same time. Yeah, gorgeous, until I had to shag it home that night. Then, she looked like the Last Rose of Summer."

He paused. "State Street is a great street, south of 39th."

"Yeah," I agreed, drawing a mental outline of a woman from the sprawling lights and shadows of the city. "Yeah—State Street is a great street, after you get past 39th."

For a moment, the woman I'd hewed out materialized vividly. The glistening wetness of State Street was one shapely leg whose thigh was bright with the sparkling jewelry of gin mills, hash houses and pawn shops; and whose high, spiked heel speared the gaping red hole in Crow's stomach.

I shivered, and the scene dissolved.

"Hey, Puff! Out on bond!"

Puff leaped from the bench at the jailer's call. "Well, this is it. So long, Deacon!" he called as he started toward the door.

Fear seized me, and I grabbed his shoulder. "Christ, Puff —don't leave! This is the first time for me in one of these places. What should I do. Ya can't go, man!"

He pulled away. "Hey, what gives? Release the dry goods! So you're scared, huh? Now that's a hell of a switch from the iron guts and steel chest role you usually play. Go on, you're breaking my heart!"

"Look, Puff, I've got three hundred bucks stashed. Give two-fifty to Shelley to bail me out and fifty is yours."

He straightened up and stared at me unbelievingly.

"Where?"

"Promise you'll keep your end of the deal first."

He nodded.

The turnkey bawled his name again.

"C'mon, give. I ain't got all night."

I told him of the money I'd buried in the dirt hill as he hurried out.

"Don't forget!" I shouted.

His laugh made me shiver.

I returned to the window and in a few minutes saw Puff leaving the building. He paused to look up and wave, and then disappeared into the belly of the city.

I stared fixedly at the dark subway entrance.

"Guy Morgan! Guy Morgan! Goddammit, which one of you bums is Morgan?"

I climbed stiffly from the bench where I'd been since Puff's departure some hours before, and shuffled woodenly to the gate.

"You Morgan?" the turnkey snapped.

I nodded.

"Well, dammit, punk, jump when I call you. I ain't here to waste time paging ya!"

I followed him. At the end of the aisle, between the rows of cells, a giant stood at a desk.

324

"He's all yours, Lunt," said my escort.

The giant held out a pair of handcuffs.

"Stick out your mitts!" he commanded.

Fear gripped my heart and I wanted to lash out, to fight this added confinement.

"I've got experience, seventy pounds and a foot in height on you! Don't try it!"

He had read my thoughts.

I held out a hand and as the cool steel snapped on my wrist, a wave of complete helplessness engulfed me. Together we walked out into a hall lined with elevators and entered one of them. The operator slammed the door and we dropped.

The jolting halt of the elevator shook the sickness in my stomach into life. I stumbled blindly behind Lunt. We entered one of the fourth floor offices; and I stopped just inside the door to wipe the tears from my eyes. My glance fell on the man who sat in a chair propped on its hind legs against the far wall. He was cleaning his fingernails with a door key. As he looked up at my entrance, the keys fell from his hand and his mouth formed a hateful grin. The dammed-up nervous sickness I had been feeling broke through the lump of ice in my throat and spewed from my mouth.

"Cut it off, ya goddamned dingy bastard!" Tony Mancuso shouted as he grabbed my neck from behind and shook me with a grip like an iron noose. "Still your filthy guts, ya black son-of-a-bitch or I'll strangle ya!"

I fought the sickness into stillness, the strain causing me to wet my pants.

"Jeezus," grunted Lunt, "take him into the next room, he's made a pig pen outta the joint."

"A natural habit for a nigger," Tony snarled, as he shoved and flicked me into an adjoining office. "Park it, Sambo!" he commanded, kicking a chair in my general direction.

I sat down, trembling.

"Is this the black bully, Phil?" he asked the uniformed

cop who sat on a window sill applying an ice cube to his puffed and discolored left eye.

The young cop shot me a nervous glance, jerked a nod at Tony and Lunt, and the other two plainclothesmen, and stammered, "But—but look, Tony, the kid—he's upset—he was—"

Tony whirled around to me. "Okay, coon, what was you and that other bastard doing off the reservation?"

I didn't answer.

His stinging slap brought the instant taste of salt to my tongue.

"So you're gonna be tough, huh pardner?" he sneered, snapping my head from side to side with full-swinging slaps. "Good!"

Slap!

"Who threw that bottle at that kid's car, huh?"

Slap!

"You went up to that rink looking for a fight, didn't'cha? You pulled that girl from the car, didn't'cha?"

Slap! Slap!

"You wanted to rape her, didn't'cha? Feel her up, didn't-'cha?"

Slap! Slap! Slap!

"Well—didn't'cha?"

"No! No!" I screamed, struggling blindly to my feet. "That's a damn lie and you know it."

Tony shoved me back into the chair. "So you can talk, huh, coon?"

"Yeah, but you ain't got no right to punch on me, I didn't do nothin' to those people. It was them who killed Crow, not—"

Tony cut me off, "If somebody'd killed the little black bastard seventeen years ago he'd have been a better nigger today!"

326

I spit in his face; and rolled from the chair to the floor, kicking wildly to protect myself from what I knew was coming.

The first kick, landing on the side of my head, was almost merciful. For the next few minutes blows, kicks, and curses hit me from all sides. Then, through the pain and numbness I heard Tony's hysterical scream: "Let 'm up! Put 'm back on the chair! Gimme your stick, Phil, I'll kill the black bastard for that!"

I was slammed into the chair.

Snatching the nightstick from the uniformed cop, Tony wheeled on me to strike.

"Swing that stick, Mancuso, and you smash fifteen years of police work to hell and gone!" came from the doorway.

All eyes swung to the short, rotund man standing just inside the room. The circle of my tormentors broke and aimlessly moved aside at the little man's approach. He shoved past Tony and sat in the chair Lunt offered him. He looked at me squarely, his gray eyes narrowing slightly. After a few seconds his face relaxed and his voice came at me quietly: "Have a cigarette."

I shook my head.

"I'm Captain Gold and *I* run this damned department," he continued softly. "I want the lowdown on what happened at that rink tonight." He fingered my ripped jacket and T-shirt and threw a disgusted look at Tony.

"Aw, hell, Skipper, the black son-of-a—"

The clatter of Gold's chair as he sprang to his feet cut Tony short, and he was pinned to the wall by the captain's forefinger.

"Now you hear this, and listen closely. For the last time I'm going to tell you, Mancuso: I warned you for years about using your badge to carry on your stupid personal war against Negroes. This is the end of it! If I ever see you raise your hand without cause you're smashed! Understand? I'll throw you in the pen. I'll have you buried so deep they'll have to pump air to you!"

For a moment the tiny office was quieter than the night before Christmas. Then:

"Bravo! Bravo!" accompanied by handclaps. "Bravo, Goldy old boy," from two dapper men leaning casually against the wall just inside the room. With quick steps they crossed to the desk and perched upon its edge.

"God, Brooks, we should have brought a couple of newsbookies along with cameras. What drama! What flair! What—"

"What bullshit," Brooks cut in, removing a slip of paper from his breast pocket. "Besides, Binder, we are more humane than cops. We don't believe in dragging people from their warm bar stools into the filthy wet night."

Captain Gold had taken the seat behind the desk and with bored sarcasm he addressed the pair: "To what act of providence do I owe this visit from the city's most celebrated barristers? I'd hoped that all of the B and B boys' clients were enjoying the Florida sunshine and sipping mint juleps, or whatever it is that hoods drink."

"Milk," said Brooks sleepily.

Gold stared in mock surprise. "What? Milk—they drink milk? What d'ya know. Too much worry over whether the police captains they've positioned are kicking back properly, and—"

"Sh! Not so loud," whispered Binder.

"Cut the crap," continued Gold. "One day somebody with guts is going to get that big office in City Hall, somebody who'll clean up this burg, and—"

"And when they do," Brooks interrupted, "you'll be a process server and tough Tony there'll become a soda jerk or a bootblack and Binder and I will return to divorce setups

328

and elephants will start roosting in trees and the sun'll ask permission to set."

Binder took up where his partner had finished. "And the waters of the Most High will consign dear old Madame Windy back to the swamp and wild onions from which she sprang sans Hinky Dink, sans Capone, et al. But let's get down to business—do you happen to have a young man by the name of Guy Morgan wandering the illustrious halls of this monument to crime, Goldy?"

Brooks didn't miss the shift of the captain's eyes in my direction.

"Yes, I'm holding a youngster named Morgan; but you can't have him 'til I finish questioning him."

"Habeas corpus says to the contrary," Binder replied.

"Produce it, then."

"Ah, for Christ's sake, Goldy, don't be like that. It's raining and we've had a hard day in court."

"Produce!"

"Excuse me, may I?" Brooks said, reaching for the phone. He dialed quickly and after a moment, asked, "DeMarco. This is Brooks. We located the kid at the bureau but Goldy wants to act like a cop and make us get a writ and—Sure, he's right here."

He handed the phone to Gold who spoke into it firmly but gently: "Hello, Mr. De Marco. Yes—yes—of course. I didn't know you were interested. Will you see to it that he appears at the inquest? Good, good. Yes. Goodbye."

Gold slammed the receiver down and glanced around the room.

"Release him," he snapped to Tony.

Chapter **33**

Ten minutes later I stood outside on the sidewalk. The cold rain swept down State Street in blinding waves, but I made no attempt to find shelter. I needed a bath.

Across the street, a car horn honked insistently. I recognized it as a white Jaguar belonging to Beano De Marco. The honking stopped as the door was swung open.

I trotted across the street to the car. Luzon sat behind the wheel, looking lovely in an iridescent leather coat and beret. I got in wordlessly, trying to figure out why she and the two lawyers were there instead of Shelley and Puff.

Luzon steered the little sports car out into traffic.

"Where's Puff and Shelley?" I asked finally.

"I haven't the faintest idea, but I hope wherever they are, they have enough sense to keep dry," she said.

I wondered if Puff had taken that money from The Hill and not even seen Shelley, or if Luzon had been in such a hurry to play heroine that she beat them springing me from the clink.

"So you belong to Beano, too," I said sarcastically.

"What?"

"You belong to Beano, like the judge and the police and the lawyers and this car we're riding in—all Beano's."

"No man owns me, Guy Morgan, and don't you ever forget it! Luzon snapped.

"Oh no?" I said. "You just happen to tell him I got busted and he just happens to send two lawyers down to spring me and he just happens to let you have his car to joy-ride in, huh? What kind of fool do you think I am?"

330

"I could answer that, but it might take days. As for Beano, he's got eyes, sure, eyes and ideas. And I guess he figures if he treats me nice, one day I'll give in, just like he figures that if he does you enough favors, one day you'll be able to pay him back. Besides, what's wrong with a girl letting a man be nice, especially when he has so much to be nice with? What have you strong-arm guys around here with a sneer on your lips and a chip on your shoulder got to offer? All a girl will ever get from you, Guy Morgan, is a great big ache in her heart."

"If you got me out of the can to deliver a sermon, save your breath," I snapped, and the effort of growing angry at her remarks seemed to drain the last strength from me. I settled, exhausted, into the corner of the car and thought of Crow.

"As a dog returneth to his vomit, so a fool returneth to his folly," I muttered.

"Oh, feeling poetic?" Luzon asked quizzically.

"No, not poetic; repentant," I answered truthfully.

"Meaning?" she queried.

"That there is a way which seems right to a man, but the end thereof is death."

"I take it that you are blaming yourself for what happened," she said.

I was silent.

"Oh, Guy! You romantic fool!" she flared. "Don't dramatize death, it's already over-dramatized. And don't be so quick to accept the blame. You didn't cause Crow's death, nor did I, or even the boy who shot him. You just can't blame any one person, Guy."

"Does Mom know anything?" I asked her.

"No," Luzon answered. "I didn't know how long it would be before you could get out of jail so I went to see her, to make sure she was all right. I was surprised that she remembered me so well after all these years."

I looked at her apprehensively. I hadn't counted on Mom and Luzon ever getting together.

"You know," Luzon went on, "I thought you were a mass of straining muscles who spent his time pounding his chest for cheers. But not anymore. My long chat with your mother was most enlightening. Yes, I learned a lot about you today, and I don't know whether to laugh or cry."

"Oh stop it," I said, "you're breakin' my heart."

"You're confused. You're breaking your own," Luzon said.

"Meaning?"

"That all of your he-man action is just an outward expression of your inner frustration; that you're a baby, Guy, a big muscle-bound baby who's inwardly screaming for his mother's attention. I also know why—"

"You've said enough, Cherry, too much," I cut in. "Put the rest of it in your diary, or write a book."

Luzon pulled the car to a halt for a red light.

"I didn't say that to hurt you," she said. "No, you've been hurt enough. But Guy, you're going about salving your hurt in the wrong way. Both of us are—or were. I'm not anymore. I think I've found myself in the last couple days. And I did learn a lot about you when I saw your mother, seeing all those photos of your father all over the house, hearing your mother's constant references to him. And she told me about some of the times the two of you have had together, you dancing about the house with her in your arms."

The light changed. She started the car off again.

"I tried to help, Guy, I really did," she went on. "I realized what you really feel about your father, and I tried to get Mrs. Morgan to understand how your hate for him and unappreciated love for her are driving you to destroy yourself. Oh, Guy, don't you see—"

"I see that I'm a goddamned fool for sitting here and listening to you give a stupid psychoanalysis of a non-existent situation," I said hotly.

332

"Sorry," she said.

"Sure, you're sorry. We're all sorry. I'm sorry as hell about Crow."

I paused for a moment, and then muttered again half-aloud: "There is a way which seemeth right to a man, but the end thereof is death."

"Is that what you intend basing your self-condemnation for Crow's death on?" Luzon asked, raising her naturally arched eyebrows into twin peaks of exaggerated curiosity. "If so, like most of your concepts, it's stupid. All living action leads to death. Guy, it's the goal of every human action. Life is dying. Darling, the only thing of importance in between is our stumbling, savage, struggling will to live the dying hours happily. Actually living is merely a choice between two evils: dying trying to escape from the slap which marks birth and continues with increasing intensity throughout our existence until death, the grand-daddy of all pains, takes over—or dying minutely, conscious of dying. Indeed, there are many ways that seemeth right to a man and are right when some happiness is received before the all-dissolving, obscuring, un-answering blackness of death's inevitable eternity, the conclusion of all things, is reached. So why complicate a simple calculation by adding self-condemnation? You're no more responsible for Crow's death than I, or any of the countless nations of people, dating back to the time of the Cross, with their big and little hates, loves and prejudices. You can chart the progress of a man's life after he's dead and often the manner of his dying can indicate the progress of a nation. Crow's death reflects this. This is the disposition of a time. Who's to blame? You? Him? Let God and the Devil figure it out. We've got our hands full of dying."

"Well! That was some speech, Cherry," I said when she had finally finished. "I never knew you were such a philosopher."

"There are a lot of things you don't know about me because you never took the time to try to find out. You were so sure you knew it all," she said. Then she laughed and added: "But there's one thing I know about you."

"Oh yeah, what now?" I asked.

"It just so happens that I know you think you hate me, but actually you don't. You love me."

I bolted up in the seat. "Believe me, broad, the things that pop out of your face are funnier than—" I started.

"No greater kindness than this," she interrupted, "a man with sight who doesn't want to see."

Luzon fumbled a cigarette from her purse and pushed in the dashboard lighter. Then she repeated with a tone that indicated final confirmation to a long studied truth: "You love me."

I laughed, but the laughter lacked the scorn I desired.

"You laugh," Luzon said, "but your laugh cannot dispel the fact that you love me, Guy. Your hate is the lie you've adopted to escape from the truth. It's the only avenue that you believe you know thoroughly and feel complete master of. The reward of vengeance is mostly expressed by physical action."

"Jeezus! Here we go again!" I said.

Luzon seemed to ignore me as she went on:

"Put your mind to work, Sir Guts, rebel knight. Lower your weighty, highly-polished shield of hate an inch and peek over; still your whistling sound for revenge. You'll find, I fear, and so do you, that you fight phantoms. Are you sure that your hate for me isn't actually the jealousy of a very possessive man for that which he loves—me? Oh, God, Guy, when is this stupid round of hate going to end? Hate meeting hate because your father beat you when you were a little kid, or because he possesses something which you feel is rightfully all yours—your mother's love. Grow up. Guy, you never had it, not the kind you crave. It was never your mother's to give. She's never possessed it. I do."

"You've got more nerve than a toothache, Cherry," I snapped.

"Why? Because I tell you what you yourself know to be true but are too foolish, too childishly self-pitying to accept. Ha! I once thought that you had depth, but you're as shallow as spit, Guy—shallow."

"UH huh, and you're a deep trench of destruction. A whore like—"

"Like Zola?"

"What do you know of Zola?" I asked, unable to keep the shock of her having called the name from registering in my voice.

"Your mother has a lot of things pent up inside her for a long time, Guy. Today she finally had a chance to talk to another woman, a woman who loves one of the two people in the world that she loves, and who wanted to understand. She told me enough to give me a fair idea of why you want to dislike me, tried to love Marion and ended up hating everybody. I'll tell you all about it someday."

"Luzon—" I started threateningly.

"Let's not fight it, darling. It's bigger than both of us," she laughed.

I sank miserably back into the corner of the car and tried to compose my swirling, frightened thoughts. Crow had changed; I had changed, and now, Luzon? And was it too late for us, the way it had been too late for Crow?

Crow. A deep loneliness engulfed my mind in a black fog. Why had it happened, because Queen Bess was a greedy bitch who mercifully pardoned condemned murderers to become sailors and kill again. Or because the industrious North incited rebellion in order to snatch the gold crown from King Cotton? Or because Whitney invented the cotton gin too late, and the law of mathematics was flung into chaos when eight became the greater percentage of a hundred. Or was it because Nat Turner was dubbed murderer and a fugitive for

335

roaming the earth in search of his kidnapped soul? So Crow lay cold under the snow, wet under the rain, stamped into the cement, warm under the sun, mourned by the moon, covered by the sky. God over all? And John Brown's body lies a-mouldering in the clay . . .

"I've got to see Crow's family," I told Luzon, "but I need to change clothes. I can't go wet and dirty like this."

"I don't think you're in too good shape for seeing your mother, either," Luzon said. "You're about the same size as my father, close enough for some of his clothes to fit anyway. I'll take you home with me and see what I can find."

I heaved a weary sigh. I was wet and chilled and my body was aching from the pounding the cops had given me. I did not have the strength to fight even so ancient an enemy as Luzon.

She seemed to have been reading my mind as she looked at me and declared:

"You know, Guy, you react to love like a ten-year-old whose naive idea of a sophisticated manner to adopt with the woman he loves excludes tenderness and consideration and instead embraces stupid stunts and senseless exhibitions. It would be nice, for truth, if we were living in the days of old when there were holy grails to pursue and silver-laden clouds to fleece and balconies for me to toss red roses to you from. But this is the 20th Century, baby. All the dragons and giants have been slain. You're misdirecting needless energy in attempting to impress me with feats of arms and legs. Besides, you have no token, no silk ribbon of mine to wear next to your heart. But, still it's rather gratifying to see you make some kind of acknowledgment of my love. I've watched you perform for a long time and marvelled at your endurance. But it's really not necessary, you know, this muscle-straining and floods of sweat. All you've got to do is take me in your arms and kiss me. That would be the greatest!"

336

Luzon pulled the car to a halt, scattering the gravel of her driveway.

"You're very sure of yourself, tonight, aren't you?" I said.

She nodded and switched off the motor and moved closer to me.

"Well—well, I think you sound frustrated," I sputtered weakly, "—a candidate for a psycho's couch."

"I am," she whispered, almost in my ear, "but my need doesn't warrant such complex treatment, Guy. All I need is you."

I closed my eyes against the nearness of her and tried to send my mind racing away to another time and another place, but her lush wet mouth and hot flicking tongue lured me back to that moment and that place.

After a while she leaned back. "There, that wasn't so destructive, was it?"

The skyrockets going off in my brain kept me from answering.

"Come on inside," she said, sliding out of the car, "We'll see if we can find you some clothes."

Twenty minutes later, as I smoothed the tail of the dry white shirt into the smoothly tailored tan slacks Luzon had given me, I heard her call from the stairway in the next room: "Come, I've got something to show you."

I followed her up the stairs, stopping just inside the doorway of a large room. A filtered light came through a skylight, making the room as bright as day.

"My father's studio," she said proudly, casting a fond glance about the room. "I love it here."

I couldn't speak nor tear my eyes from the proud breast of the goddess statue in the center of the room. It cast off a soft radiance. Finally, I turned my stare from the statue to Luzon, then back to the statue.

"No, you're not seeing things. There's another one over

there, and there, and over here," Luzon said, pointing about the room and laughing with childish enthusiasm. "Come let me show you."

She took my hand and led me over to a large painting. "That's the fighting colonel, my father, Col. Frederick Evans," she explained.

I stared at the picture. The grim set of his lips in the tanned face bespoke a man of few words. His wide shoulders and tapering waist screamed virility. The belligerent set of the square, cleffed chin proclaimed him a fighter, and the penetrating black eyes and premature grayness of hair at his temples suggested a thinker to me.

Luzon led me quickly past a large screen to a wall full of trophies, cups, emblems and other awards. Her eyes sparkled happily as she explained: "My father was a man of many interests. He was a mountain climber, a bridge builder and one of the Army's top scientists; an intellectual giant with the physique of a Greek god. Why, up until the time he was retired from the Army he—"

An unearthly scream rose from behind the nearby screen, cutting Luzon in mid-sentence and causing me to jump and spin around. In an instant Luzon had knocked the screen aside, and I saw a yellow, old wreck of a man cringing before some unknown terror painted on the wall. The muscles of his seemingly once-powerful body jerked and twitched. His mouth drooled with idiocy, and his eyes were glazed.

Luzon gathered the frightened old man in her arms. "Now, now, Daddy, hush. Hush now, it's all right," she cooed, stroking his forehead. "Everything will be all right."

After a moment Luzon ran from the room, and I stood watching the trembling, moaning old man, until she returned. A moment after she came back, a handsome, dark woman entered the room silently, nodding to me as she hurried over to Luzon.

"My mother," Luzon said to me.

So this was the woman with whom Luzon had spoken in sign language, the hand-talk she had taught me in the years before adolescence, a language I still remembered.

Luzon bared her father's arm to the thrust of the hypodermic needle her mother held. The sedative worked almost immediately. Luzon and her mother lay the colonel on the couch, and her mother sat beside him, patting his hand.

Luzon replaced the screen, and together we walked to the statue in the center of the room.

"Yes, my father was also an artist and a sculptor," Luzon said in answer to my silent question. "He still is in his more lucid intervals. I'm his model."

Fingering the delicate contours of the marble replica of Luzon, I thought of the love which must have been in the touch of the artist. I ran my hand down the inner thighs of the statue. The contours seemed exact.

"His illness came from a fever he contracted years ago when he was stationed in the Philippines," Luzon said. "That's where I was born. When he brought my mother back to the states, he realized he was no longer a white man, but a nigger like my mother and me."

I looked at Luzon. A lot of questions were beginning to be answered.

Chapter **34**

"Shall I wait?" Luzon asked as she pulled the Jaguar to a halt in front of Crow's house.

"No, I'll go it alone from here," I said.

"When will I see you again?" she queried.

I shrugged and ran up the steps of the house.

The door opened moments after I pressed the bell. Maxine stood before me. She looked like a hag of hell who had dwelt in the thick crystal of a bottle of cheap wine for many a lost week end.

"Max?" I asked, almost not wanting to believe that the wasted vision I saw before me was really her.

"Guy," she whispered hoarsely and swayed into my arms, sobbing. I led her to the living room where the telephone was ringing furiously.

"Oh God! Those horrible people are driving me mad," she said, covering her ears with her hands and shaking her head.

I went to the phone and picked it up. It was a newspaper reporter on the other end.

"Yes, this is it," I said. "No, there wasn't any gang fight . . . Yes, it's true. He's dead. Now go wipe yourself!"

I slammed the phone down. Almost immediately it began ringing again. I tore the wire from the wall.

I looked to the couch for Maxine. She was gone. Sensing that she was behind me, I turned slowly and faced hysteria and a gun.

Maxine held the ancient revolver with both hands. "Where's Crow, Guy? You promised! You promised! You promised!" she screamed. "Thanksgiving, you said, you liar!"

340

I took a step toward her.

"No, no! Don't come near me!" she warned. "My brother is dead—and you—you're the cause of it. You filthy fagin! How I loathe you, you sick-minded, egotistical mass of black brutality! How could I have ever thought you were his friend? I'll pray every day of my life for God to damn you. It should have been you who was strangled by the umbilical cord, instead of your sister! It should be you in that wheel chair, with all of your sadistic savagery, instead of your mother! But now—now you can go to hell!"

I stood trembling, bathed in a sweat which became more profuse with the metallic clicking of the gun.

Maxine opened her eyes after the fourth click, and they held a peaceful repentance as she raised them from the gun to my wet face.

"Oh, my God!" she cried. "What have I done? I only wanted to—to—" She sank to the floor, sobbing softly as she hugged the revolver to her breast. She lay there, her torso convulsed in a twisting motion. "I only wanted my tiny Crow," she sobbed. "Tiny baby——of—'*Bye, Baby Bunting, Daddy's gone a-hunting . . .*'"

Choking back a cry, I ran from the house.

Outside, I paused, my body shaking with chills, my lips, cracked and dry. The wild muffled beat of a blues tune filtered through the thick draperies of the apartment next to the pool hall. It blended with the grayness and imparted a strange underlying primitiveness to the brooding night. I went into the pool room. I had a score to settle with Puff, and I prayed that it was only with him, and not with Shelley too.

Puff's back was to me as I paused just inside the game room door and watched him raise the large white handkerchief to his face. I wrenched his arm behind him in a vicious hammerlock that jerked him to his feet from the chair, spilling chips to the floor, and rushed him through the hall to the washroom. Kicking the door shut, I dumped him on the floor. As he

341

struggled to get his footing on the damp tile, I struck punch after punch into his bony body until he sagged like a gunny sack of old potatoes. Panting, I sat on the toilet seat to catch my breath. The pain in my stomach from the beating I had taken earlier was almost blinding. I clenched my teeth. Puff had struggled to a sitting position resting with his back against the grimy wall. His mouth was swelling where his lip had been split. We stared at each other.

"Look, Guy—baby—I—"

"Mother— . . . , shut up and fork over my three hundred bucks. Now. And if you ever pull anything like that on me again, it will be the fucking last time," I threatened.

He took a roll of bills from his coat pocket. They were damp and moldy. A cellophane package dropped to the floor. It was horse. I snatched it up before he could and flushed it down the toilet. His eyes held a plea that changed to hate as the toilet bowl flushed.

"You filthy hop-head. You were gonna leave me to rot in that pig-sty of a jail, weren't you, pretty baby? I ought to knock your friggin' block off, but you ain't worth it."

I took the money, jerked him to his knees by his necktie, and shoved him away from the door, so that I could get out into the hall.

I was glad that he had the money on him. I didn't want to have it out with Shelley. Not like that.

I was tired. I wanted to lay down and rest forever. I walked home slowly. I was so tired . . . tired of everything. Did any of it make any sense?

The instant I entered the front room at home I sensed a change. Taking a good look around, I realized that the photographs of my father were missing. I went quickly to each room except Mom's; each was the same—all the photos were gone.

I shook my head and walked over to the record player and

put a record on, then went into my room and flopped on the bed, staring at the photograph of Mom on my dresser.

"So at long last you've decided to let me be the cock of the walk, the shack bully, the man of the house, huh?" I said aloud. "Well, it's too late, too damn late, sweetheart. I don't want to be the main man anymore. I quit, cop? I quit. I'm sick of unseeing mommas and run-away daddys and head-whipping cops and hip-swinging broads and dope peddlers and flesh hucksters. I'm sick of this whole place."

"Where bored youth steal the knife of death and the gun of sorrow to destroy the monotony." I tried to recall where I had read or heard the description before but couldn't. I only knew that I had been introduced to it in a moment of pain. But then, didn't everything spring from pain? Quickly I tried to look back over my life for a happy experience, free from pain, and found none.

"Why?" I asked silently, *Why?* And then I gave a silent answer. *What difference does it make why.*

Slowly I climbed off the bed, reached under it, and pulled out my splintered drum. I began to thump as I chanted: *"No more wondering why . . . no more painful moments . . ."* The sound was flat.

Mom appeared in the doorway in her wheel chair.

"Guy," she said quietly, "you didn't come home last night. You've been gone for two whole days." She paused, waiting for an explanation.

I remembered the doctor's orders when they let her come home from the hospital: No excitement. Well, if I told her that Crow was dead and that it could have just as well been me, that would sure as hell excite her. And if I told her that I didn't care about being a second-class citizen in my own home anymore, maybe that would excite her, too. So I just looked at her, not knowing what to say.

Chapter **35**

Whistling, I slammed the bullet-proof door of Beano's custom-built Caddy and hurried up the steps to the Silver Slipper. Inside, I surveyed the Friday night crowd as I removed the nine bulging envelopes from my pockets and slid them to the bartender.

"What, again?" he asked with a raised eyebrow.

I nodded, reaching for the phone.

"Twenty grand?"

"Twenty-five," I said, holding out my hand for the five dollars he slammed in it.

"You missed by five G's."

Turning, he took the envelopes and went to the safe under the bar. After tossing them inside he returned with a tall glass of cherry Coke. "Say, Guy, how much do you think you've been tossing to me since you started working for the boss?"

"Guess, and if you come within three grand, I'll give you ten dollars; if you don't, give me ten," I snapped.

"Aw hell no! I always lose in that game."

"Not half as much as you'll lose if the boss ever hears you playing T-man guessing games," I said with a grin.

In the five weeks since Crow's death and my release from jail I had been working as a pick-up man for Beano. When Luzon told me that he wanted to see me, I figured that payoff time had come . . . Hell, what goes around, comes around and I couldn't forget that he had gotten Crow and me on the street. I'd gladly pay off for my buddy-boy and myself. Beano was straight. Working for him I was getting straight. I had money for Mom and the household bills, and I could tell Aunt Emma and Agnes to kiss my ass. Mom was worried about me, and constantly prayed over me, but I could stand that as long as it didn't interfere with the bread I was making.

I took a long sip of the sweet cherry Coke and walked over to the house phone; dialing, I waited a second for Beano's voice.

"Yes?"

"Guy. I've just completed the route with the same results as last week. Rose's refusal included."

There was a slight pause on the other end. Then . . . "I anticipated that. Did you deliver my message?"

"Yeah. And he said to tell you to . . ."

"I give less than a damn about his reply" . . . he hesitated, and then almost pleasantly said, "Oh Guy, I've a couple of visiting firemen here who have to make a little run. Stay at the bar so that you can take them for me when they come down. About ten minutes. See me when you get back."

Hanging up, I rolled the chilled glass of cherry Coke back and forth between my palms, and added my eyes to the others who watched Luzon as she entered the bar door.

"Hi, stranger, where've you been these days?" she purred.

"Working for your man, Miss Switch," I shot back, deliberately needling her.

"A man's a man," she flared, "and preferable to a snotty-nosed brat that doesn't know what he wants or needs." Her green eyes shot sparks in my direction.

"I've never believed in handling the boss' merchandise; besides I don't like used goods," I cracked, aware that I was in dangerous territory.

Her hand on my cheek was rapier-quick and had the sound of a pistol shot. "You black bastard; I hate you!" Turning, she ran up the stairs to Beano's private office and apartment. On the stairs coming down were Beano's out-of-town guests—hoods straight off TV.

345

I stepped to the door and held it open as they came out. Approaching the parking lot, they separated; one getting on the far side and the other behind the driver's seat. I slid under the wheel, little beads of perspiration covering my upper lip. *Was this for real? . . . God, I didn't want to be involved in a real hit, but I was damn sure they didn't have wash'n'wear suits in those specially designed suit cases they carried.*

"Where to, gentlemen?" I said, mustering as much cool as I could.

"Fifty-third and Michigan," the taller one said through unmoving lips. My heart skipped a beat, then raced on wildly as I accelerated the car and headed north on Ashland Avenue.

The tall boy was a back seat driver, and following his instructions, I parked the Caddy by the towering church at Michigan Avenue and 53rd Street, and let the motor idle.

Only a slight clank of metal indicated that some kind of equipment was being assembled in the back seat. I kept my eyes off the rear view mirror and stared straight ahead down toward State Street. The precise indifference with which the operation was taking place indicated to me that these boys were not rookies on their team.

"Hey, kid," the shorter hood spoke slowly, "how much do you know about this business?"

My eyes met his in the rear view mirror, and with forced casualness I replied, "I know that my mother's doctor and hospital bills are paid, the mortgage on our house has been caught up, I've got a suit on my back and some money in my pocket—What else is there to know?"

The door slammed shut behind them. I continued to murmur my knowledge of the business. My palms were wet and sticky on the steering wheel and I could smell the perspiration in my armpits. The two crossed Fifty-third Street and took up positions behind the billboard facing Michigan Avenue.

". . . and I don't have to wash latrines, and smell stinking filth . . . *and Rose is gonna be washed* . . . and I wear

346

shoes instead of shine them . . . *and Rose is gonna get washed* . . . and I don't have to prostitute myself to Shelley for some bread . . . *and Rose is gonna get washed* . . . and I can take care of Mom . . ." and five ear-shattering reports crashed through the night and I knew the "Independent" had been muscled in on.

"Airport," the tall hood said, as he followed his partner back into the car. Easing into drive, the big car slid away from the curb, and around the corner, before the windows on Michigan Avenue had been opened by curious residents to peer out at the scene by the billboard.

When I turned west on Garfield Blvd., the needle crept up to 55. "Cool it m'boy, we don't want to be stopped for speeding." The big car fell back to 35 and I hung on it until we rounded Cicero Avenue and into Midway airport.

As they got out at the Airline terminal, the short fellow reminded me to take care of myself; I seemed like a nice kid.

I sped away from the airport and wondered where in all the world I could hide. Back at the Silver Slipper, Mike the bartender greeted me with a cherry Coke and an inquisitive, "How's business?" I slammed the Coke back down the bar and into a woman's lap, choking to keep from saying . . . *Rose is washed.* Instead, I grumbled, "Can the comment, Mike. Gimme a jug with some alky in it will you?"

"Well, for crap's sake, what happened to turn you on all of a sudden?" he muttered as he set the bottle of bourbon and glass in front of me.

"Ask the lady I spilled the Coke on if she would like to have a drink on me, not with me," and I went over to the house phone to call Beano and report that Rose was washed.

I nearly died trying to figure the words I could use to say I was through, but I knew better than to let them come out. "I'm back," I said simply in reply to Beano's "Yes?"

"Stick around, kid. I'll see you later." His voice was noncommittal and unquestioning. The perspiration I had felt

347

earlier had now turned to chills. I gulped three shots of the straight booze before I felt warm blood in my veins again.

I was vaguely aware of the woman who had moved down the bar to the stool beside me. She was an almost transparent white. The soft mass of her hair was piled in a windblown fashion that blended with the smoke of the room. Her eyes searched me questioningly from beneath carefully arched brows. My eyes returned her direct gaze, moving from her face down her voluptuous form, and back to her face. I knew this woman, but who was she and where did I know her from?

"Thanks for the drink, Guy." Her smile was sadly amused.

She knew me, too, and then I caught the scent she wore and I was no longer in the Silver Slipper, but seated at a long banquet table in a church auditorium. As if in a dream, I saw the wide shoulders of my father as they were brushed by the provocative hipped siren . . . I saw his proud head bow submissively at their command, and I felt and smelt the excruciating pain and hot steel and burning flesh. Involuntarily, I jumped.

"Zola . . . Where is he?"

Her skin was like foam, I thought.

"You're hurting my arm, Guy!" Only then was I aware that I was touching her.

"Bitch, Hussy!" I snarled. "Where is my whoremongering father? How dare you come back to this town? I'll kill him!" and then I knew why she was alone in the Silver Slipper. My father was home with Mom. I flung the arm I had been clutching back to the bar and was running by the time I reached my car parked in the lot.

Chapter **36**

The lights were on in the front room as I slammed to a stop, ran up the steps and wrenched open the door. I was afraid of what I would see, and yet it would not be put off. My turmoil was blinding.

The first sight that caught my eye was my father. He was kneeling beside Mom's wheel chair, his head in her lap. I stood in open-mouthed wonder, my eyes traveling from him to the sickly smile of uncertainty that trembled on Mom's lips as she glanced nervously from me to him. My chest began to heave with the fury exploding beneath it, and I felt a warm damp trickle between the fingers of my fist. I knew that it was blood from my palm.

The years had changed him little, merely making him more distinguished-looking. His wavy, marcelled hair was gray at the temples, and he was a few pounds heavier around the middle. Other than that, there was no difference, and his every feature proclaimed him my father.

Tears trickled down his cheeks. "Guy, Clucky, son—my boy—how are you?" he finally stammered.

Extending his right hand, he stepped toward me.

I side-stepped quickly and got between him and the wheel chair.

Surprised, my father wheeled about with a suddenness that cleared his eyes of tears.

"Thank God—at last!" I said, measuring him for a right hand.

"Oh, Clucky, no! Not your father!" Mom screamed.

The bump of the wheel chair against my legs threw me off balance.

Dropping his chin behind his shoulder, my father blocked the punch and pinned my hands to my side with one arm, then slapped me across the mouth sharply.

"No, Guy, no!" Mom shouted. "That's your son—he's not a child anymore. Stop it!—" She struggled to wheel her chair between us.

Freeing my left hand, I hooked it hard into the soft haunch. My father went crashing backward through the still opened door and down the steps.

I leaped after him.

Springing to his feet, he tore off his coat.

"By the bloody rod of Solomon, boy, I'm going to beat some honor into your hide!" he shouted, rolling up his sleeves. Rain was falling in blinding sheets.

I ripped off my coat with a jerk.

"Oh God in heaven, don't let them fight. Clucky, that's your father. Guy, that's your son. Please, please don't! Don't do this to me! Don't kill me, Guy—Guy!" Mom's shout ended in a scream.

I lunged for my father. He smashed a right hand to my jaw that dropped me to my knees.

"Out of my way, you hot-headed fool—your mother has fallen!" he yelled, kicking me in the chest.

I sprawled backward in the mud, then leaped to my feet. The overturned wheel chair caught the light streaming from the doorway, outlining the grotesque angle in which Mom's legs were flung and silhouetting the rain spattering against the lone, doll-like house slipper on the porch.

My father tore at the imprisoning chair with frantic hands, sobbing.

"Lonnie, Lonnie, Sweetheart—Son—My God, what have we done?"

Snatching a stone from the flower bed I staggered over to

350

him as he raised up, holding Mom, and started up the steps. I leaped ahead of him.

He halted. His eyes stared long in mine, then dropped to the stone in my hand.

"You—you really hate me, son, don't you?"

"More than death."

Silently he handed Mom to me.

"Now get away from *my house* and stay away from *my mother*."

"But, son . . ."

Turning, I entered the house. A heavy tiredness pulled at my mind and mired my feet. I stared at Mom from a great height; she was as still as death.

I shuffled toward the telephone. The distance seemed miles away and I felt like I was standing in the past watching myself perform some act in the future. As the blackness descended over me, I clutched Mom to me tightly and sank to the floor slowly and fell backwards, pillowing her against my chest. "Stay away from my mother!" I screamed at the image of my father, hovering over me. "Stay away . . ."

I emerged from unconsciousness slowly at first. Then, missing Mom's weight from my chest, I sprang to my feet. I swayed, about to fall again until strong female arms caught me. A soft bosom cradled me.

Marion's voice called to me: "Guy, Guy, what happened? What did you do to her?"

"Mom! Mom!" I shouted.

"Your father and Dr. Bruce took her to the hospital. Oh, Guy!"

I stood, unable to move or think, cold fear freezing me.

"I happened to run into Dr. Bruce on his way over here. He said your father had called him. They rushed out so quickly with your mother that they didn't even bother about you. Your father said you must have been drunk."

"Liar! Liar!" I yelled. "I've got to get to her."

The phone rang. I snatched it up.

"Hello!"

"Guy Jr.? This is Dr. Bruce. Listen, son, your mother is in a bad way. You had better get over here. She's asking for you and—"

"Oh, God, don't let her die!" I pleaded.

"You'd better hurry up, son," Dr. Bruce said.

I hung up.

"The car's outside," Marion said.

I jumped behind the wheel and the roar of the motor was drowned in thunder as I raced into the storming night. As I swung the corner at the end of the block, I sideswiped a tree with the right front fender, sending glass clattering to the pavement. I slowed down only long enough to get the car back into control.

At 59th and State, I cursed as the light from the squad car flickered into my face as I halted at the intersection for the signal. I shoved the gear into second.

"Don't do it, baby, or it's your last gamble!" the young Negro cop shouted, leveling a gun at me through the window of the police car.

I flipped the gears into neutral and waited.

Getting out of the squad car, the cop walked over and ordered me out of the car.

"That's the right action, baby," he said, turning me around so that my back was to him. Then he frisked my pockets. "What, no gun? So what's happenin', Jack? What's back there that you don't want to catch up with you?"

"Look, man, I'm—" I started.

"Look, *officer*," the blue-clad jitterbug corrected.

"Look, officer, my mother is dying in—"

"Make it good, baby, because that busted headlight and record-breakin' speedway action you just put down rates you an automatic trip to the slammers, you dig? So you'd better—"

352

I twisted slightly and emptied my pocket of several bills.

"Look, mister—master—officer—blue-suited Jesus," I sobbed. "My mother *is* dying. If you want to write me a ticket, okay. If you want money, here it is, take it. It's all I've got. But whatever you want, *do it now!*"

A few moments later I left him standing in the rain, holding the handful of bills.

Dr. Bruce met me in the first floor lobby of the hospital. Without a word he led me through a doorway, down a long hall and into a small room.

Mom lay upon a table. I went to her and grasped her hand in mine.

"Oh, Mom, Mom! I'm sorry—I—"

I stopped with a shocking realization.

Her hand was still warm, the last symbol of the life that once had been hers.

For an eternal moment I stood beyond infinity and peered down into the impenetrable blackness of my future.

The movement of the nurse as she covered Mom returned me to the horrifying present. In a corner, my father stood with his back to me, his shoulders shuddering with the vibration of his sobbing.

I walked over to the window and looked out across the street at the flooded park whose trees were being lashed under the driving wind and pelting rain. Then I stared up at the angry black brow of the sky.

I felt a hand on my arm. "You missed her by ten minutes, son," Dr. Bruce said. "She's with God now. The good Lord giveth and the good Lord taketh away. Blessed be the name—"

"Shut up, you gray-headed old fool!" I snarled, brushing his hand from me. "What do you know about me missing her? Ten minutes? I've missed her all my life!"

A flash of lightning added a momentary brilliance to the sky. I turned back and faced the window squarely.

"Well, what are You so furious about?" I shouted to the sky. "You took what You wanted, so now what's Your beef? I should be the one knocking the branches off the trees, not You. I'm the loser, and because I hate to lose, you hate me, huh? *God hates a brutish man,* huh? All my life I've heard of Your hate. Now You hear mine: I hate You, God! Hate You! Hate You!"

My voice rose into a scream as I drove my fist through the glass of the window as lightning momentarily blinded me. Wheeling, I ran from the room and the horror-struck stare of the occupants . . .

I staggered into the darkened house and stood staring down at Marion on the sofa, where she lay cringing from the thunder and lightning. Seeing me, she sprang to her feet and flung her arms around my neck. Her body trembled as I lifted her into my arms.

"Oh, Clucky, Clucky—take me home, please. I'm frightened. Everything's so mean, so beastly. I—I wish we were kids again so we could—"

I crushed my mouth against hers in the grip of some insane passion that was part of the macabre night. Laying her gently on the couch, I freed her hair from the ribbon that held it, and caught a handful of it. I kissed her eyes, nose, ears and mouth with a hunger that refused to be denied.

"No, Clucky, no!" she protested, straining against the caresses of my hand.

I fumbled at the buttons of her blouse.

"No, Clucky, I'm not what you want—"

"You are—you are, Muffet. I need you—please, please," I whispered, freeing her breasts. I kissed them feverishly, then buried my face in their warmth.

"Guy, let me go! Stop it, Clucky! You're mad—sick—"

She squirmed from beneath me and scrambled to her feet.

I reached out blindly and caught at her hair, pulling her to the floor. For a brief moment, we struggled in silence.

354

"Guy—You don't want me like this—You don't want me!"
The warmth of her thighs set up a roaring in my ears and
flung me into a ship of desire that bounded over waves in a
wild sea of passion. After a moment of infinite bliss, a tremor
shook my body. I collapsed against her. The tide began to
ebb; the sea became stilled, the roaring ceased.

"Well, how do you feel now?" She said softly, clutching
the torn front of her blouse. "Now that you've had who you
thought was your mother?"

I stumbled toward the bathroom, the nausea spewing between my fingers.

Chapter 37

Following Mom's funeral, Muffet avoided me. Her reasons were good enough I figured. I guess if she hadn't been the kind of wonderful girl she was, she could have been real nasty. Instead she was just hurt. She had always been in my corner, though. I didn't have the guts to go to see her until I heard that she was taking her father back to Boston with her, and the store had been rented to some weed.

At the thought of Muffet leaving for good, a desperate longing seized me. She couldn't leave me. But I realized down deep, that she could. I guess, in a way, she had already left back in the summer when we said "goodbye" the first time.

I climbed the stairs to the little apartment above the drug store and for the first time my legs were leaden and seemed to drag up the short flight.

"Hi, Miss Muffet, how are you?" I greeted her as she opened the door.

"Guy, Clucky!" her voice was friendly, but, so polite. "How nice, won't you come in?" Suddenly concern clouded her face. "There's nothing wrong, is there?"

"No, no, Smallchange. I just wanted to see you. I heard you were leaving for the East for good," I temporized, not wanting her to know the real reason for my visit.

"Well, Guy, you know Dad hasn't been well. The store is too much for him to handle with me away, and after having been in Boston for awhile . . ." She looked at me intently ". . . Clucky, I just can't come back to Morgan Park. It's not that I don't miss my friends and . . . you, but Clucky, there's another world out there, that we don't know anything

356

about out here. I liked it, Clucky, and I'm going back. Dad agreed with me and we were lucky to be able to lease the store to a nice young man and his wife. They can take it. I can't, not any more." She sat back on the piano bench and closed her eyes.

"Muffet, I lied about there not being any thing wrong. There is, and with me."

There was a moment's silence.

"What is it, Guy?"

"You, Muffet. I need you. Need you badly." I gripped the arms of the upholstered chair and rushed on. "You've got to marry me, Muffet. I can get a job. Something that will pay good. I can support a wife. Cop? And I've . . ."

"Guy, we've been through all this before. I can't just—"

"Muffet, you've always said you loved me. What about that?"

"Guy, I do love you, and I probably always will, in a special sort of way, but honey, I'm growing up, and you're still fighting with windmills . . . I guess girls always grow up faster than boys, and know what they want sooner . . . Clucky, I'm leaving Morgan Park and all it stands for. The pool room, the vacant lots, the churches, the nasty kids hanging over the counter downstairs, and maybe, what I'm leaving for will turn out to be not much different. But I've got to try, Clucky. I've got to try."

Sensing defeat, I let the tension ease out of my body. Getting stiffly to my feet, I walked to the door. She put out her hand.

"Aren't you going to wish me luck, Clucky?"

"Yeah, sure . . . Crazy . . ."

I stumbled, blindly down the stairs, completely unaware of the tears coursing down my cheeks. *Yeah, Pops, what goes around, comes around. You've had it . . . hoof, tail and head.*

Chapter **38**

It was the first evening in April and rain had cleared the sky of clouds and left the city drenched and gleaming. The lights in the juice joints were like giant fireflies whose bright glimmering blinded the sight of the stars shining dimly through the web of the steel girders of the elevated. Twisting tracks twined about the mass of gray masonry of Dopeville, U.S.A., like a mammoth black python encircling an enormous tree. The intermittent roar of the train and the shrieking, hissing snort and growl of the traffic, coupled with the near-hysterical laughter and chatter of scurrying people, heightened the jungle atmosphere.

Recovering from a fit of coughing, I tossed the used tissue into the gutter; the blood speckling it blended instantly with the colorful surroundings. I looked around at the familiar scene: the hot tamale man who sold three, five and ten-dollar bags of heroin with every ten-cent hot tamale; the hot-eyed Lesbian who patrolled the elevated exits, spitting on prosperous-looking pedestrians and then, with profuse and tearful apologies, wiping away the stain—along with the luckless man's billfold; the dapper pimp sentinels of the area in glossy cars with glossier marcelled heads; the indifferent cop leaning against a mailbox, reading tomorrow's scratch sheet; the painted, fixed smiles of the sleek-hipped hussies who were loaded with booze or horse or reefers to disguise the perpetual longing in their eyes; the pretty man in women's clothing, casting come-hither looks at a goggling hillbilly who, hypnotized by the feminine charms, would follow trustingly into a dark hallway and the midnight vice of his strongarm lover;

358

the tearful mothers wandering about aimlessly with prayers on their lips in search of their prodigal children.

"Want to have some fun, baby?"

I looked up at the young but street-aged prostitute who had spoken. My stomach was a flaming pain. "Yeah," I grunted, "buy me a drink, mother."

"What? Listen, I don't pimp strangers—"

My sudden fit of coughing cut off her indignant retort. As I doubled over, hugging my stomach in both arms, she stepped to me and caught my elbows in her hands.

"Oh, daddy, you *are* sick," she said.

"Yeah," I wheezed, getting my breath back, "yeah."

"Ain't'cha got no place to go? No home or—"

"Look, mother, I don't need a home or a lecture but a drink," I whispered, still clutching my midsection.

Reaching into her bosom, the girl withdrew three one-dollar bills and shoved them into my hand.

"Buy somethin' to eat first," she pleaded, and then hurried away.

Pocketing the bills, I walked slowly the few doors to the Bohemian Basement, a quiet little sub-level club where I drank away the hours and coughed away my insides. Canvas mats, to absorb the dampness that trickled constantly into the basement, lined the mirrored wall. You could drink straight from the bottle in the basement, and conversation was whispered and seldom.

I ordered a bottle of wine and took a seat at a table across from the juke box. A saxophone's wail seemed to echo in the deep blue basement lighting and the shadows wavering about the walls. Throngs of eyes reflected a contagious despair from the mirrors. A dancing couple, making zombie movements, clutched together in a desperate fusion that bespoke a deep, unsatisfied hunger. Smoke, hovering two feet from the comic ceiling mural, was like a giant, unattached spider web whose density seemed to increase with every exhaled breath. Across the room, a chubby brown woman was lost in the shadows of her man's entwining arms. In the farthest corner, another thin, worn, charcoal woman sat with a glass of whisky before her. She was singing softly in a voice that contained the original pain and despair of constant denial of love, of hate and a million rejections, of hopeless futility and longing for death.

Gulping the sour wine, I tried to drown out both the present and the past, but when I swallowed and opened my eyes, I was still there. Nothing had changed.

I thought of the time since Mom's death; the lost days and nights, the sickness that had plagued me. After the visit to Marion, I managed to get a job at the steel mill, keeping a pledge to myself to keep away from Shelley and Beano. Within a month after I was hired there was an auto strike, causing a layoff in the plant. The last hired had been the first fired, particularly if they happened to be boots. After that, I had been too sick to hold the two brief jobs I had had. Unable to work, unable to sleep in the house where my mother's spirit still lived, still cursing my father, refusing the sanctimonious offers of help from my aunts, I had sought refuge in the Bohemian Basement. But even now it offered no further peace from the pain of memories or the ravages of fever.

I raised the bottle toward my lips again, but halted it in mid-air to study the shaking hand that held it. I felt a trickle of sweat from my hot forehead, and the pain in my chest warned me that the coughing would soon begin again.

I got to my feet and reeled over to the telephone booth and rifled through the directory for the listing. It took minutes for my inflamed eyes to find it: "Frederick Evans."

Luzon's voice answered.

"Hello, Cherry," I said, realizing for the first time how weak and hoarse my voice sounded.

"Hello—Guy?—Is that you, Guy?"

"Yeah, what's to it?" I said.

360

"Guy, where in heaven's name have you been? I've looked all over for you. I've been to your house and asked—"

Luzon's voice was lost in the roar of the coughing spasm that seized me. I shut my eyes against the pain wracking my insides and gripped the telephone receiver as tightly as I could.

"Guy! Guy, what's the matter?" Luzon's voice came back to me after a while.

"Look, Luzon—I—I'm in a joint called the Bohemian Basement—on 63rd Street. Luzon, I—I'm sick."

"I'll be there in ten minutes," she said. It sounded like she was crying.

I hung up the phone and staggered back to the table and sat down, collapsing my head upon my folded arms.

I stayed there, head down, until at last I felt Luzon's gentle tugging at my shoulder.

"Hello, Cherry," I mumbled, looking up at her.

Wordlessly she helped me outside to a small, black sedan.

"Where's the Jag?" I asked.

"I was playing for fun; Beano wanted to play for real. I told you I wouldn't go that route," she said.

"Bully for you," I said, patting her hand as she helped me into the car.

I slept all the way to her house.

The smell of bacon and eggs floating down the steps awakened me from a sound sleep on the sofa-bed in the basement den. I could hear Luzon singing gaily through the open kitchen door at the head of the stairs. I arose and went into the small downstairs bathroom to wash up.

When I came out, Luzon, with a parakeet perched on her shoulder, was placing a breakfast tray on the table near the sofa.

"Well, look who's all dressed up," she called to me.

"Don't you think it's about time?" I said, thinking of the

361

three weeks I had spent flat on my back on the sofa, three weeks in which Luzon had nursed me with hot food and medicines prescribed by a doctor she had called.

"I don't think you ought to overdo it all at once," she cautioned.

I've been sneaky about it," I admitted. "I've been walking around down here every afternoon for the last three days, getting the feel of being back on my feet again."

"And just who asked you to be so smart?" she asked, grinning.

"I didn't know you would get such a kick out of playing nurse," I answered.

"Well, I don't want to get philosophical again," she said, "but maybe it was the fulfillment of God's plan."

"Ah, come on, let's not cross our hearts and bow toward Mecca over it."

"Anyway you're here—and I've enjoyed every minute of it," she said.

"Even totin' dat pan and liftin' dat bag?" I asked, thinking of the humiliation of the enemas I had had to submit to.

"Even totin' that pan and liftin' dat bag," she laughed. "You see, I love you."

She walked into my arms and I kissed her. That had been a large part of her nursing—the kisses. As I pressed my mouth to hers, her lips held a lifetime of love; mine a lifetime of hunger.

Luzon pulled back breathlessly after a moment. "Mr. Morgan, I do believe your breakfast is getting cold," she said.

"Let it get colder," I suggested, reaching for her again.

"No," she said, stepping quickly away. "You're a sick man."

"I'm not *that* sick," I said, laughing.

I sat down on the sofa and began to eat from the tray while Luzon went back to the kitchen, singing with the parakeet chirping on her shoulder.

She came back when I had finished eating and sat beside me.

"How do you feel now?" she asked.

"Like a good walk and some fresh air is all I need to make everything okay," I said.

"You sure you won't disappear again?" she asked. "You know, the way you dropped from sight after—well, after your mother died and all. Then, some people were saying it was because Kay eloped with Jackie Lindy and it was really your baby and—"

I bolted from the sofa before she could finish.

"What?" I demanded.

"Well, you know that kind of gossip, Guy," Luzon said.

"Play that for me again real slow," I said. *"Kay is carrying a baby that's supposed to be mine and she's married to Jackie?"*

"Why, yes—didn't you know anything about—"

"Where's the phone?" I demanded sharply, cutting her off.

"There's one upstairs in the kitchen, but—"

I was up the steps before she could finish.

When I came back down I asked: "Can I borrow your car?"

"Guy, where are you going?" Luzon asked.

"Look, I asked you a simple question: Can I borrow your car?"

"Guy, don't go, don't go!" Luzon begged. "You're barely well. Everything is going fine now. Don't go looking for trouble, please, Guy, for my sake!"

"You don't understand, Luzon, I've got to go."

We walked up the stairs to the kitchen where Luzon picked up the car keys off the table and handed them to me.

"Will you come back to me?" she asked.

"You think I'm gonna run away with your automobile?"

"Will you come back to me?" she repeated.

I took the keys from her hand without answering and left the house.

Kay's bulging figure was barely recognizable to me as I pulled up to the corner three blocks from her house. I opened the door and she labored to get in.

"Guy, you know I shouldn't meet you like this," she said as we sped off.

"If we're going to talk about the things you shouldn't have done, I think we can start a lot further back than this," I told her. "Or is everything I've heard a lie?"

Kay didn't answer me. Instead, she suggested: "Drive out by the lake."

Ten minutes later I pulled the car over the low curb and onto the sand of the beach, then cut the motor.

"Well?" I inquired. "Why didn't you tell me you were pregnant?"

She turned to me, her eyes filled with what seemed to be an ancient hurt. "I tried—oh, how I tried. But you wouldn't let me, Guy. All the unanswered phone calls. You were too busy, too busy willing yourself to hate to recognize my attempts. And then, that night at your house when I asked you if you still loved me—"

"I was in a lousy mood that night, Kay," I said. "I didn't know anything then. If you had waited—"

"Waited? Guy, I waited until the disgrace of it all and my condition wouldn't allow me to wait another minute."

"So you turned to Jackie."

"Who else was there?"

"Did he know everything?"

"Yes. I—I never really thought he would go through with it. I knew how much you two hated each other. But he wanted to marry me. He didn't care on what terms. And now, the idea of the baby has gotten to be almost an obsession with him. It seems he can hardly wait."

"Well, he's going to have to wait. This is my child and it will never call Jackie Lindy 'Daddy' as long as I—"

"For God's sake, Guy, think of something besides your own

364

hate for once in your life!" Kay shouted at me. "It's going to be my baby too. Mine even more than yours, because I'm the one whose had to suffer the embarrassment of going to Jackie and the scalding curses of my father. I'm the one who will have to suffer to bring it into the world. Think of what I want for a change, and what I want is for this child to have a chance—a chance for something better than fighting and cursing and hating. Let me have some peace now, Guy, please—"

Kay collapsed in tears in the corner of the car. I started up the motor and headed back to Morgan Park.

When I let her out of the car, she looked at me with pleading eyes.

"Okay," I said, "okay, I'll try it your way—if I can."

The strain eased out of her face as she leaned against the side of the car and closed her eyes as if offering a silent prayer of thanks. Then she turned and walked away.

The old pressures, the old aches, seemed to be coming back.

Chapter **39**

The clock in the tower of Greater Hope Church showed 9:30, and I realized for the first time how long I had been walking the streets and alleys of the neighborhood that had been my home all my life. The last pale light of the sun was deserting the sky when I parked Luzon's car in front of her house and decided to come walking back. I had felt that somehow here, perhaps, I could find the answers to the puzzle of my life.

I hadn't. But at least I seemed now to realize that whatever the bitterness of the past, the weeks with Luzon had had a healing effect on more than just the sickness of my body; it had helped to heal the sickness of my mind, too. It wasn't going to be easy, but it was almost as if I had a chance for a fresh start.

I turned the corner and headed for Gale's Drug Store. It was the last of the old haunts to visit. But with Marion away it too was changed. I barely saw the two figures that stepped out of the alley just ahead of me. They were almost past when one of them said:

"WELL, what the hell! If it ain't old Guy Morgan Jr., himself, in the flesh."

It was Treetop.

"Well, for crap's sake, Mr. High and Mighty Musclebound," the other voice said. I recognized it as Ding's.

"Ain't seen you around in a long, long time, Big Man," Treetop said. "Hear tell you ain't had it so good."

"Well, he's around now," Ding said. "I saw him this afternoon makin' off in a car with Jackie's wife. You still lookin' for trouble, ain't'cha, Guy?"

"And you've still got a big mouth, Ding," I said evenly. "I thought when Crow busted that bottle over your head he taught you some manners."

"It's a good thing for that little son-of-a-bitch that the gray boys got him," Ding said hotly, "or I'd of killed him myself!"

"If you had, you wouldn't be here to talk about it now," I said, staring him coldly in the eyes.

"Still tough, ain't'cha Guy, baby?" Treetop said.

"Tough enough for you two bastards," I said menacingly.

"See ya around, Big Man," Ding sneered, starting to walk away.

Treetop followed him.

I turned and started walking again.

The knife landed between my shoulders with a force that almost brought me to my knees. Ding's hand was still on it as he slipped the other arm around my waist to hold me up as he spit in my ear:

"That's for your little dead black buddy! Yeah, and it's for wha'cha did to Treetop that time in the park! Yeah, and it's for messin' around with Jackie's wife! What goes around comes around!"

Ding turned me loose, and I heard the sound of their feet running down the pavement as I slumped to the sidewalk.

Slowly I pulled myself to my feet and looked about. The light from the parsonage behind the church shone like a beacon in a storm. Drunk with pain I staggered over to the open window and clutched the sill to keep from falling. Kay sat on the edge of the bed, brushing her hair. She was alone in the ground floor room.

"Kay! Kay!" I whispered over the pain.

She turned startled eyes to me. "Guy!" she cried, hurrying to close the bedroom door.

367

"Guy, oh no! You promised you wouldn't make trouble—you promised you—" she said as she came to the window.

"Help me in," I croaked.

"No, Guy, no! Jackie and my father are in the living room. They'll hear you. Go away, please—"

"I'm hurt, Kay, in the back," I said, pulling myself up on the window.

She reached down and felt my back. I heard her sharp intake of breath as she touched the knife handle. Then, catching me beneath the arms, she helped me through the window, the bulge of her belly pressing against my chest.

"Guy, what are you going to do?" she pleaded. "I can't let you be found here!"

"Pull it out, Kay. For Christ's sake, pull that damned thing out before I go crazy," I said.

I felt her tug at the blade and her involuntary cry as it came free. For a moment I reeled, then I reached out for Kay, clutching her to me as I steadied myself.

I looked up over Kay's shoulder at the sound of the bedroom door banging open, and stared into the startled faces of Jackie and Reverend Heath.

"So!" Reverend Heath roared, "This is how you reward Jackie's trust in you, and kindness to the bastard child of this whoremonger that you would bear! This is how you repay the love he has lavished upon you when this Godless swine befouled you with his lust! How vile can you be, rolling in your abominable filth beneath my roof!"

Suddenly I saw that Jackie had moved from the doorway to a nightstand, and now he stood with a blue-black revolver glistening in his hand.

"This time, Clucky," he hissed, "it's for keeps!"

"No, please," Kay cried, "You don't understand! Guy is—"

Kay stepped between Jackie and me as the thunderous

echoes slammed through the house. She took a step backward, then collapsed.

Jackie stood staring at her, horror-stricken, still clutching the gun tightly. I lunged for him, knocking it from his hand.

"Oh, my God! My God!" Reverend Heath screamed, running from the room. "HELP! Police! Police!"

Jackie slumped against the floor in a corner, his eyes still fixed on Kay, his mouth drooping open.

A gush of wind from the window slammed the bedroom door shut, cutting off Reverend Heath's mournful cries.

Slipping to my knees, I reached for the gun. Then I crawled back to Kay. I tried to lift her, but she protested:

"No, it hurts so. Just let me lie here next to you. We've had so little."

I stared down at her.

"Oh, Guy, our poor baby. Our poor little baby. I wanted it to have a chance, but it never even got to be born," she said tearfully.

"Don't think about it now," I said.

"You know," she said, and gave a short laugh, "you know, I've always been curious about—about things, even heaven. Now I'm afraid—only afraid."

She clutched me tightly. "Guy, close the window, please. There's a draft—"

I felt her go limp.

I thought the thunder was a part of the nightmare as the bedroom door splintered and Tony lunged in. The first bullet from his gun tore into my stomach with the force of a hot branding iron hammered by a pile driver. It knocked me free of Kay, setting me on my heels.

"In here! I've got 'im!" Tony shouted over his shoulder as I raised the gun in my hand.

His arms flung out wildly, sending his gun clattering to the floor. He took two wobbling steps toward me, then dropped to his knees. For a moment the hate in his eyes glowed brightly, then died as he sprawled, face forward, on the floor. The hole between his eyes spewed a small gusher of blood.

I staggered to my feet and looked down, puzzled at his immobility until the warmth of the gun I held conveyed to me the true meaning of what had happened.

I whirled to look for an escape. As I did so, there was another explosion in the room and I felt a slight tug at my side as a bullet passed through my shirt. Instinctively I whirled and ducked low as two more shots whistled past my head. There stood Tony Mancuso's partner, Pat Meuller, firing from the doorway. Backing away, I pulled the trigger twice, then leaped headlong through the open window.

The impact of my fall exploded Fourth of July colors before my eyes and ran a hot rod of pain into my brain. Clenching my teeth, I lurched to my feet and tried to run.

The Hill. If I could just make it to The Hill.

Thunder roared from behind me. I dropped to my knees as the lead tore into my shoulder and wrist. The gun slipped from my fingers as I began to crawl toward the shadows of the church. There I pulled myself upright and turned and rested with my back savoring the soothing coolness of the rough gray stone. I gazed at the parsonage as if from a great distance. A faraway siren added its hysteria to the insane night.

I saw Meuller's swaying outline silhouetted against the headlights as the squad car braked to a halt on screeching tires. Meuller was following the trail of my blood.

There was a loud clatter of voices, and then the searchlights began to sweep the churchyard. Panting, sweating, bleeding, my body a ball of fiery pain, I waited against the wall with my arms clutching the agony that devoured me as the lights came nearer. Then I saw Meuller coming slowly toward me. Blood streaked his shirt and he dragged one leg slowly behind him. His service revolver was clutched tightly in his hand.

The lights found and blinded me, just as the pain blotted out everything else from my brain. I closed my eyes and felt myself slipping slowly, slowly to the ground. With one last effort to hold on to consciousness, I made a desperate wish that what was happening now would turn out to be a nightmarish game of cops and robbers.

The voices came from very far away, reverberating through an echo chamber and into my brain.

"Hold it, Pat! He's on his face. Hey! Sid! Get that gun from Pat!"

"Christ! Oh, Christ, Chief! Sid, gimme back the gun! Lemme kill the dirty son-of-a-bitch! Jesus, let me—"

"Is Tony dead?"

"Right between the eyes. Blew his brains out. He must've killed the girl, too."

"Keep them people back on the sidewalk, Ray."

"Hey, Pete, get the stretcher in here quick. The old guy's had a stroke."

"Anybody find the gun? Get more light. Find that goddamn rod! You, Jake, Sid, turn him over. Let's see what he looks like."

"Is he dead?"

"Naw, naw, see the spit bubbles?"

"Let me finish the murdering black bastard, Chief, I—"

"Yeah, yeah, I know how you feel, Pat. But don't worry, he's gonna' get it."

"Christ, he's floodin' blood."

"Well, if ya got any sympathy, save it for Tony's son and widow. And get Pat outta here."

"Still a young kid—"

"He's a killer, a goddamned killer—"

"Hey, Chief! You're wanted inside."

"Pete, gimme ya gun, please!"

"Naw, Pat, you heard the Chief. Besides, even if he lives, he's gonna' burn."

"Did ja hear that nigger? Yah, gonna burn, killer, burn!" The faces hovered over me like a gray wall. Then I gazed beyond them, into the black sky.

Chapter **40**

In the courtroom, my eyes forsook the ivory visage of
Luzon for that of another—the white marble statue of Lady
Justice, who occupied a niche in the wall above the now-empty
jury box. Despite a thick accumulation of dusty debris on
the pan nearest the window, she held, with queenly finger tips,
a perfectly balanced scale. The cons in the Big House, the
petty hustlers across the street in the County Jail and House
of Correction, often cynically joked about the lady's "fixed
scales."

The judge had gone to his chambers while my jury retired
to deliberate the verdict. I glanced about the courtroom of
crowded spectators and thought: *Look not upon me, because
I am black, because the sun hath looked upon me: my mother's
children were angry with me; . . .* So I had pumped a pow-
der-hot slug into swarthy jowls, spilling the hating guts of one
of them.

And now I sit here, Lady Justice, I said silently to the ivory
statue, *You can't see me, but I sure can see you, you poor mis-
laid hunk of brick. You would have made a choice corner-
stone for a big, airy gym in Black Babylon. Y'know, old girl,
you're something of a looker despite your virtuous veil of
spider webs, that black smudge on your nose and your dusty
toga. Why don't they—whose mistress you are—they who love
you so ardently—give you a good cleaning? You'd really be
something. Why, then even those you didn't smile upon would
look up to you. I told you when we first met, that you looked
like the girls who parade before you daily, the honest whores
from 39th and 63rd Streets. Your cheeks and lips are rouged*

with dust, and your nose is powdered with the soot from a thousand winds. The difference is, the honest whores can be bought and are not ashamed to admit it.

My eyes left the ivory statue in disgust.

In the front row of spectators, a big, blond cop caught my attention with a furtive movement of his hand: Pat Meuller, out of the critical ward where I had blown him the night I killed his partner.

Under cover of his topcoat, Meuller pulled an imaginary electric switch with a sadistic slowness that matched his look of savage hatred. His deliberation and malice, I thought, were in direct contrast to my instinctive, unthinking action when I had cut down Tony Mancuso. Then, fear and self-preservation had pulled the trigger. Only after Tony lay dead and I stood over him with one of his slugs inside me did I feel any of the maliciousness the state's attorney had referred to so frequently in his dramatic speeches to the jury.

Now, sitting in the brothel boudoir of Lady Justice, with her hand maidens, attendants and procurers bustling about deciding my fate, I thought of Captain Ahab and Moby Dick. As the captain had concentrated his wrath upon the albino whale, so had my long pent-up hate against the vicious fates and circumstances affixed itself upon the already dead Tony. I had exhausted that hate by staring without remorse at his lifeless body, just as Meuller now, with a pull of the imaginary electric switch, emptied his hatred into me.

The cane I had been using since leaving the jail hospital slipped from the arm of my chair and clattered to the floor. As I bent to retrieve it, great flashes of pain shot through me. I straightened up, my brain screaming in agonized protest, and saw Meuller beaming his appreciation. I pointed the cane, pistol-wise, at his head and contracted my trigger finger.

The cane was snatched from me with a sudden jerk on my arm and I turned to find the hard eyes of my attorney, Jim Halloran, biting into me.

374

"What are you trying to do, Morgan, get us both lynched?" he demanded.

"What does it matter?" I said.

I looked—really looked—at the spectators for the first time since my trial had begun, and saw that all the faces wore indignation. All but Luzon's. "Hemp or electricity," I continued as her eyes embraced mine, "the results are the same."

"Oh, so you can talk," Halloran said in a low voice. "Then maybe you can also hear. If so, hear this: indifference in the face of death is a fool's reaction—"

"And tears are rank cowardice," I interrupted.

"Well, death is the exact verdict those drama critics are going to bring in," he prophesied bitterly.

I could understand his feelings. After all, he had the reputation of being an able lawyer who had risen fast in the office of the public defender, and was regarded as a formidable opponent by the prosecution. But my refusal to discuss my case with him had made effective defense impossible.

From the cluttered counsel table of the prosecution came smiles of satisfaction. Halloran raised his hand in acknowledgment and said softly: "That's all right, boys. The Oscar's yours for now, but it's going to take more than a wet hanky and bloodshot eyes to convince the old men on the state supreme court bench, and that's just where I'm taking this case. Not only that, but—"

The muffled buzzer from the jury room silenced him and set up a restless stirring among the spectators.

"Everybody rise, please!" the bailiff commanded.

The judge entered. I took the cane from Halloran and got to my feet.

"I'm not appealing," I whispered to him.

"What?" he exclaimed in angry astonishment. "Why? In God's name, why? We have a solid self-defense plea if you'd only—"

The judge rapped with his gavel and took his seat. The bailiff waved the jurors into the box. We sat.

Turning to face Luzon, I followed the swift, graceful motion of her fingers as she began to speak to me again in sign language.

"It is nearly over. Are you glad?"

"Yes," I answered.

"So am I," she wrote. *"Is there anything I can do?"*

"No. Too late. They wouldn't understand or believe anyhow . . ."

The judge's voice rumbled across our silent communication: "Ladies and gentlemen of the jury, have you reached a verdict?"

"You know what it is, don't you?" Luzon continued to write.

"Yes," I answered.

"Are you afraid?"

"Yes, but not of that."

"Of what, then?" she asked.

"Your not being there," I answered.

"Where?"

"You know."

"Yes," she said.

"Really?" I asked.

"Oh, Guy, Guy."

"No. But won't mind. We four together."

The jury foreman's voice rang across the courtroom: "We have, your honor."

"I love you, Guy," Luzon wrote, then added quickly: *"I'm frightened."*

"Me too," I answered.

"You don't look it," she wrote. *"Look like wounded hawk. Love you."*

"Think Mom there?" I asked her.

"Yes," she said.

"Crow? Kay?" I persisted.

376

"*All. Say you love me.*"

"*I love you.*"

The judge's voice rumbled out in the silence: "What say you then?"

"*Here comes the prelude to eternal kiss,*" Luzon wrote.

"*Hold you tonight?*"

"*Yes. Love you.*"

"*Why us? Why?*" Luzon pleaded.

"*Why anyone? The air, times, hate, fear, fate, death—*"

The jury foreman spoke, his voice falling upon the words like the knell of a giant bell: "We, the jury find the defendant, Guy Morgan Jr., guilty of murder in manner and form as charged in the indictment, and we fix his punishment at death—."

"*I've killed you,*" Luzon wrote swiftly.

"*No, no, no,*" I protested. "*Way the ball bounces.*"

"*You love me?*"

"*Sure.*"

"*I killed you and baby,*" she wrote. "*I should never have told you . . .*"

"*No, forget that. Past. Think of tomorrow.*"

"*Yes, tomorrow ours,*" she wrote. "*Can't we touch once?*"

"*No,*" I told her.

"*Tomorrow Always. I must go. Can't take any more. Bye, darling. Love you.*"

She stood in the courtroom which thundered with silence. Slowly, she wrote her two last words: "*Hang tough.*"

She hurried from the courtroom, the big oaken door closing slowly behind her with a silent finality. I thought: *And now I live; and now my life is done.*

More words—words which were only unintelligible sounds in my ear—were spoken in the courtroom and then I became aware of Halloran speaking to me as he walked back from the judge's bench and started stuffing papers into his brief-case.

377

"Morgan, I've just informed the court of your decision not to appeal; a decision I consider insane," he said. "If you had cooperated with me, I'm sure I could have at least saved your life, just as I'm confident now of winning your new trial if you'd consent to an appeal."

Lifting up his bulging briefcase, he looked at the seat Luzon had occupied and said sympathetically: "At least you'd be able to see your woman? How about it, Guy?"

I didn't answer.

"Think of the girl," he went on. "You can *live*. I'm sure that if the circumstances involved in this killing are brought out clearly—"

The judge's command to the two bailiffs interrupted Halloran. "Bring the prisoner to the bar," he said.

As the bailiffs came over and reached to assist me, I shrugged them off. "No appeal, Halloran," I muttered, looking into his beseeching face.

"But it's your legal right!" he almost shouted. "Why not, Morgan? Why not?"

I looked at him for a moment.

"Some monkeys just swing like that," I said finally. "Yeah, some monkeys just swing like that."

Halloran silently extended his hand as I started to shuffle past him. I ignored it.

"Aren't you going to shake?" he asked, a hurt expression in his eyes.

Pausing, I stared at the white hand and realized that I had clasped but one of that color in my lifetime. A feeling of having been cheated of something suddenly assailed me. Resentment at having a fragment of it offered to me now that my life was over pulled the corners of my mouth down in contemptuous disdain.

"I didn't put you in, Guy," Halloran said, "and I tried like hell to get you out." He reached past my wounded right arm and touched my left one. "Come on," he said, "don't be bitter."

"I'm not being bitter," I said, shouldering him aside. "I'm just preserving my sweetness."

Halloran turned his back to me.

I stood before the bench.

"Attorney Halloran has informed this court that you do not wish to appeal this jury's verdict, Mr. Morgan, is that true?" he asked.

Remembering Luzon's last plea, I gripped my cane against the increased pain of my wounds that movement caused and forced myself to a more erect stance.

The brief glint of curiosity in the judge's eyes turned to anger at my silence.

"Let the records show," he intoned, "that the court inquired as to the prisoner's intentions of availing himself of his right to appeal the verdict, and that the prisoner responded with silence to those questions propounded to him."

He paused to take a drink of water.

"Therefore," he continued, "the court will proceed with the pronouncing of sentence. I gather, Mr. Morgan, that you have no argument with the justice of the jury's verdict. If you wish to state any reason why this court should not pass sentence upon you, you may do so."

I thought, with bitterness, of the jury, and how all of the colored prospects had been systematically dismissed from the "twelve good and true." Halloran had bitterly denounced the prosecution's tactics in this, and had drawn only cynically raised eyebrows from the prosecution.

In a mechanical monotone, the judge began to pronounce sentence.

"And now, the defendant not saying further as to why the judgment of this court should not be pronounced against him . . ."

My head began to throb with the effort of trying to supply some answers to the many "whys" echoing through my mind. "Why?" Luzon had pleaded wretchedly during her visits at the jail.

"Why?" the cops in the darkened hospital ward had demanded in the middle of the night as they jabbed tobacco-stained thumbs at my re-opened and bleeding wounds.

"Why?" in the inflamed newspaper columns.

"Why? Why? Why?"

And now, with unconcealed morbidity, the judge had thrown me a final "Why?"

. . . as to why the judgment of this court should not be pronounced against him . . . "on the verdict heretofore entered and the finding of the court rendered to the indictment in this cause. Therefore it is decreed that you, Guy Morgan Jr., be taken from this bar . . ."

"Why?"

I turned from the judge to the window. My mind fogged in protest. The silent screaming inside me muffled the sound of the judge's voice. As I turned abruptly, a great flash of pain from my wounded guts wrenched my thoughts back to the courtroom.

". . . there to be put to death by having caused to pass through the body of Guy Morgan Jr. a current of sufficient intensity to cause death. And may God have mercy on your soul."

Meuller sprang to his feet. Pointing his finger at me, he shouted triumphantly: "You got it, Morgan! You're gonna burn, killer, burn!"

Chapter **41**

"Ya gonna burn, killer, burn! Do ya hear me? Ya gonna fry!"

Meuller's eyes were glassy with hate as he screamed at me across the courtroom.

"Order! Order in the court! Bailiff, remove that man!" the judge demanded.

Meuller was hustled from the room.

"Remove the prisoner from the bar," the judge continued with an impatient wave of his hand. "All right, call the next case."

"The People of the State of Illinois vs. . . . ."

The door leading to the large cell behind the judge's chambers closed upon the sonorous intonations of the court clerk. The breathing of the two bailiffs walking on either side of me was loud as they cast furtive glances at me from the corners of their eyes. The shortest of the two opened the bull pen with trembling hands.

"In here, killer."

I stepped into the black cell and tried to close my ears to the clang of the door by squeezing my eyes shut tightly. When I opened them, the bailiffs were gone.

I went over to the bench by the window and sat down. Wiping the sweat from my forehead, I gazed about the walls of the human cage. Every inch of it was covered. Crudely-drawn, erotic and obscene pictures, bearing such footnotes as: "How to lick the problem of old age sexual impotency," leered from every side. Interspersed between them were the names of old convicts, dead and forgotten except for barely

381

perceivable bloodstains upon some bullet-chipped sidewalk, or a tiny, limestone marker with name, dates of birth and death, and the brief epitaph that "Inmate 143384 has paid his debt to society" leaning in disarray at the head of a sunken, weed-covered grave beneath the eternal midnight shadow of some gray prison wall.

Scribbled also for crime's posterity were the immortal words of advice from men who had themselves learned too late:

"Gun, son, I will this fact to you (By my God and my life, I swear it's true): Never go heisting with a loaded rod. It'll be the death of you.—Killer Mike, 1945."

"The man with the gun must go, and the man with the crowbar must follow.—Gangster Fat from 47th St., 1949."

"He who enters these portals without money, give your soul to God and your ass to Warden Meatball.—Penitentiary Joe, 1952."

A two-foot section of one wall listed in alphabetical order some two hundred addresses and phone numbers of whore houses, and another section gave glowing instructions on the most gratifying positions to adopt when mating with the mythological, sexually-deformed Chinese girl; the hottest spot on a spic señorita; how to choke a nigger maid's pleasureable; how to tickle the sodomitic Greek's fancy.

The unlocking of the cell door interrupted my concentration.

"All right, killer-diller, let's go," the guard called.

Standing up, I took my last look at the city through the open window.

"Come on, boy, get a move on."

I turned and walked from the cell.

"I'll be glad when you're dead, you bastard you . . ." the short bailiff sang as he clicked on the cuffs. The other one was placing leg irons on my ankles. I bit my lip to keep from crying out in pain.

382

"Okay, killer-diller, let's head for the starting line of the last mile," the tall one said.

Laboriously I shuffled between them to the tiny elevator that was used to freight prisoners from the courtroom to the basement passage leading to the jail.

"What did he get, a hundred and ninety-nine?" the little old man operating the elevator inquired as we stepped off and he closed the gate behind us.

"Naw, naw. He's gonna burn."

"Christ a'mighty, how many they got on the row now? Fourteen, ain't it?"

"Naw, Pop, thirteen. That other cop killer bastard goes tonight. That is, if the governor don't go soft and commute."

"Who's that, Woodman?"

"Yeah."

"What about the nigger with the house brick? Ain't he going too?"

"Naw, his mouthpiece won him another stay an hour ago."

"Jeez, there goes another ten-spot. I bet Bud the smoke would go before Woodman. Christ!"

The elevator came to a bouncing stop. The door opened.

"Thirteen of 'em, huh? Christ a'mighty, if they fry 'em all, Edison'll have to buy more dynamos. Christ a'mighty."

"C'mon killer-diller."

The old man grabbed my arm. "Do you know God, boy?" he whispered, peering anxiously into my face.

"Better ask him if he knows how to isolate his asshole, Pops. C'mon, killer-diller."

"Haw, haw, haw! That's a good one. Haw, haw!"

I shrugged off the old man's hand and stepped from the car. The leg irons clanked loudly in the subterranean passage. Up ahead, a gate opened and two men stepped out, awaiting our approach.

"Knock off the noise, guys, there's Big John," one of the guards cautioned out of the side of his mouth.

We halted before the warden and his chief guard. The weight and awkwardness of the chains had me panting with pain and wet with sweat. The warden eyed the cuffs and chains, then wheeled on the four guards.

"My God! Are you really as frightened as all that?" he demanded, pointing to the chains, hooked to my cuffs, which one of the guards held on to. The men looked sheepishly at the warden.

"Get those irons off him," the warden commanded.

"But warden, he got the chair!" the guard protested.

"And he's got a couple of pounds of lead still floating around inside of him, too," the warden shot back. "I know what security says, and it doesn't mention anything about bestiality. Now get those irons off."

The irons were removed. The guards turned to go.

"We'll see 'ya again," one of them called to the warden.

"Yeah, when you have another white boy to burn brown, or a brown boy to burn black," the warden muttered. Then, turning to his chief guard he said: "Get his belt, tie and shoe laces, Mack, and let's go."

Chapter 42

". . . Now ah lies heah on Death Row . . . forgotten,
but t'night ah's gonna be th' star o' th' show . . . when dat
ol' hot chair'll be filled wit' life once mo' . . ."

I lit a fresh cigarette from the butt burning my fingers and
listened to the rich bass voice rumble its poetic death chant
as I looked out the barred windows of Death Row. A wisp of
cloud haloed the moon which had cut its dooming descent to
a point where it sat, humpty-dumpty like, atop the high, gray
wall.

"What time is it?" I asked the guard circling the cellblock.

"Nine-thirty," he said, pausing to look at the battered clock.
"How do you feel, Morgan?" His eyes were noticeably curious. "Look," he started again, apologetically, "I—I'm sorry
that you—"

I turned my back to him.

". . . Ah watched 'em las' week when dey burned Big
Son, who boasted of how cool he'd die. . . . But wit' tears in
his eyes he proved phony, when he kissed dis ol' world goodbye . . ."

I dragged deeply on my cigarette and thought of the chanter
in the steel room next to mine. Emanuel Williams was his
name, but the ghosts—as they realistically called themselves
in moments of braggadocio—on Death Row called him: "God
With Us." Up until that afternoon, an hour before they
brought me in, "God With Us" had been slated to go at a
minute past midnight along with Woodman. His fifteenth stay
of execution saved him.

". . . And dere was dat dago boy a year ago, ah's completely fo'gotten his name . . . but de way he screamed and pleaded fo' sho', Lawd, make a coward be ashamed . . .' "

An all-prevailing weariness gripped me as I turned to look at Emanuel sprawled on his bunk with his huge black calloused hands clasped behind the shaven spot on top of his head. Meuller's cry of a few short hours ago still shrilled in my ears, and I tried to shut it out by concentrating on the seemingly eternal conversation floating through Death Row.

"Hey! Goddamn you, 'God With Us,' cut out that godawful mourning. Christ, you get on my nerves. Cop Turk's law books, learn to read and write. You might make a chair cheating headline before it's over, who knows. But that moanin' crap—Jesus!"

"Just leave me alone, Cal Jackson. Just go about yo' own business. You die yo' way and ah'll die mine."

There was the sound of a toilet being flushed, then: "Ho, ho, ho! Down the crapper another generation goes."

"Jeezus, Jinks, don't'cha ever go dry? Don't'cha know that's a sin?"

"Sin? How? To push the button on my own seed before they push the button on me? Go'wan. At least I feed the fish."

"Jinks, you're an immoral bastard. Ain't'cha got no wife to—"

"Naw, naw. She got herself knocked up last year. Remember that last-minute stay I copped, the third one? Yeah, well, Big John brought down the divorce papers with it. Hey! Who's got a flick of Monroe?"

"What time is it, Turnkey?"

"Oh, damn you, Leroy. You've gone and done it again. I've lost it."

"What, Jinks?"

"My strength. Ya make me nervous with that death talk and my love bone goes down."

"Not with Monroe!"

"Haw, haw!"

"Hee, hee!"

"My wife says my son's beginning to ask her when I'm coming home from the hospital. Jeezus, I'd like to see the little bugger."

"What time is it, guard?"

"Say, Rich, who was that beautiful broad visiting you this morning?"

"My sister."

"How's about giving me a knockdown with her."

"Nothing doing, Jack-the-ripper."

"Ya son-of-a-bitch! I'll kill ya for that!"

"Yeah, you could kill a buck if it had on a skirt. You're funny that way."

"Jesus, Saviour of my soul, make dem let me go."

"Hey, officer, what time is it?"

"Why? Where ya going?"

"To your momma's house."

"Somebody gimme a cigarette for crap's sake!"

"Here, ya goddamn bum. Now shut up."

"Bum? Bum, hell! Man, when I was in the free world I had three Caddy's, five locomotives and a flock of whores!"

"Bullshit. You were as poor as Job's turkey, which was so weak with poverty he had to lean against a fence to gobble."

"Haw, haw, haw, haw!"

"Jesus, Saviour of my soul, make dem let me go."

"Hey, Morgan, you're now an official member of The Ol' Ghosts Who Walk. Dig this 'bout you in the paper today? Dig: Cop Killer Gets Chair. A jury of eleven men and one woman deliberated . . ."

"Killer? Killer? Who's a killer? The whole damned system is murderous. Now leave the kid alone. Hey, Screw! What time is it?"

"Man, I've had it. If I can duck this rap, I'll be knocking down the nearest church door 'cause crime don't pay, it just don't pay."

"What? Crime don't pay? What imbecile taught you to mouth an idiotic statement like that? Not anyone who has ever been behind bars in this jungle, I'll bet. Not my lawyer, whose fees would make Rockefeller a junkman, nor the judges nor the state's attorneys with their green kickbacks, fixes and lust for political distinction. Take crime from the city and they may as well give the place back to the Indians."

"Amen."

"What time is it, Bull?"

"Prejudice, prejudice! You're friggin' right, Plato, and you know it. Me, I ain't. I dig you cats the most. Why, hell, man, one of my best friends is—"

"Yeah, yeah, I know, Des. He's colored. All you marshmallows have one friend who's a gingersnap. But that's beside the point. I asked you to explain why it is that in every penal institution in the land niggers make up the majority population when we're the minority outside. Even here, we're ten out of thirteen."

"Politics in the courts, Des, tell him. Politics in the courts. The ancient, fatal results of capitalism. Somebody give me a cigarette."

"Write to Khrushchev, lame! And keep out of my conversation. Why is it that way, Plato, huh? I don't know why is it?"

"Genocide, Des, genocide."

"Hey, dig the letter Vic got. Some queer bastard wants t' give him one hundred fifty bucks for the clothes he wore to court. Buddy! Ya gonna sell 'em to him, Vic?"

"Damn right. I need it to get the coroner's minutes, without which I won't be needing the clothes. Say, we should start a rummage sale for queers."

"Yeah, a ghost fryer sale."

"I've got a pair of shorts."

"Y'all ought'n be spendin' yo' last days on earth in such vanities. Y'all should be preparin' to look on de Lawd's face. Get yo' souls right, fellahs. We need de Lawd's help and—"

388

"You need the Lord, Man. You and those who don't know that a thin veneer separates the barbaric from the civilized. That the Lord is just a tool ruthless politicians use to further murderous ambition. I know what I need, and that's five G's to hire some hip lawyers to suppress that damned confession that 'Christ's Only People' kicked out of me. Christ! You burn me up with your pray, pray talk."

"Yep, and hell's gonna burn you for yours."

"What time is it, Screw?"

"So there I was, see, three hours outta the joint, see. Been behind bars four years. I'm hot, hot for a broad, see. I'm fish-queening this broad in the car, see, when one of 'Christ's Only People' pops up and me with my head in the muff, see. Fifty bucks he wanted to nol-pros the action. You know, not to put me in, see. Fifty bucks I got that night, but when I paid it, he wants a hundred more 'cause he knew where I got it and how. Baby, I'm hooked, but good!"

"Say, anybody hear any more on Woodman?"

"Yeah, he didn't get no stay."

"You think he'll go, Jess?"

"He hit a copper, didn't he?"

"But he's nuts."

"He hit a copper, didn't he?"

"The paint gang was around today."

"So?"

"Hell, ya know when they start prettying up th' joint some-body's gonna burn. Hey, Cal! I wonder where ya go when ya light goes out?"

"Baby, as much juice as they put to you, you should shine eternally."

"Haw, haw, haw! Right, Preacher?"

"Ah don't want no part of y'alls tom foolery. Jesus said—"

"A lot of things that should have been left unsaid."

"Hey, Hack, what time is it?"

"I wonder if Tiger Mills kept his title. Anybody know?"

"I ain't heard nothin', but I bet'cha he didn't. Mills is a has-been."

"Oh yeah? Well, six packs says he makes it."

"Bet. What time is it, Skull?"

"Twelve o'clock."

"Jeezus! Woodman's gettin' it!"

The stillness suddenly settled deep and penetrated every nook and corner of the tier. In the silence, the unbuttoning of my shirt sounded like the crack of a breaking mast in the teeth of a gale.

I felt the stitches which the laboring in the irons had busted. Hooking my fingers into my wounds, I shut my eyes and clenched my teeth. *Hang tough*, Luzon had said. No appeal I had told my lawyer . . . there was no appeal from the sentence I was about to execute on myself. They had taken my belt, tie, shoelaces, but my deliverance lay in the wounds that the cops and Ding had placed in my body. Blood . . . the blood of the lamb . . . life's blood . . . without blood, no life. I had a right to choose my way to end it. Yeah, I hadn't any say-so in my birth, but I did in my death. "I am the Captain of my fate . . ."

"Stay with it, baby. Don't let it get you," the man in the next cell whispered at my involuntary cry as my fingers gouged deep into the wounds, seeking the life-bearing veins.

Someone giggled nervously.

"What's so funny, Jinks?"

"Nothing, nothing. Not a goddamn thing. I just can't stop the giggles. Hee, hee, hee, hee . . ."

The blood washed over my body, flooding me with a heavy lassitude. The light in the cell began to dim.

"Son . . . son . . ."

The voice was faint, as if from a great distance. I peered out from the blackness engulfing me. The clerical collar loomed ghostly.

"Son, son, I've come to . . . Oh Mother of God, what have you done?"

"Father, Oh, Father, forgive me."

The priest knelt beside the bars of the cell. The hand clutching his was covered with blood and nearly lifeless.

"In the name of the Father . . ." he began to intone for the second time since midnight.